CW01656539

Peter Lombard and His Students

Peter Lombard is best known for his groundbreaking theological work, the *Sentences*. But the exclusive focus on this work has tended to divert attention away from other aspects of his life and work. This book therefore takes a broadly biographical approach to Peter Lombard, examining him in relation to his environment and milieu.

The book is divided into two parts, corresponding to its title. The first details Peter's career. He came to Paris to study theology with the assistance of Bernard of Clairvaux and Uberto, bishop of Lucca, key players in the papal schism of the 1130s. After several years building a reputation in Paris, he gained entry to the canons of Notre Dame. This is seen against the background of wider changes in the church of Paris, while the canons themselves and their relationship with the cathedral school are outlined thoroughly. Part one finishes with Peter's greatest achievements, the composition of the *Sentences* and his rise in the church of Paris to archdeacon and finally bishop.

The second part, "The Master and His Students," opens with a comprehensive treatment of Peter's sermons, his most neglected and in some ways most revealing works. They were preached to an audience that included his students. The chapters on his students examine those who are known to have studied with him, as opposed to a loosely defined group of theologians who show his influence. This allows for a close focus on how a school operated in the twelfth century. While few of the students became full-time theologians, their training in Peter's school was of considerable value for their future careers, and it influenced their works. In the two decades following Peter's death, the students also increased awareness of their master's work and defended his reputation. This was particularly important during the controversy over his Christological teachings.

MEDIAEVAL LAW AND THEOLOGY 8

General Editors

Alexander Andrée
University of Toronto

John F. Boyle
University of St Thomas

Joseph Goering
University of Toronto

Giulio Silano
University of Toronto

STUDIES AND TEXTS 201

Peter Lombard and His Students

MATTHEW DOYLE

PONTIFICAL INSTITUTE OF MEDIAEVAL STUDIES

Acknowledgement

This book has been published with the help of a grant from the Federation for the Humanities and Social Sciences, through the Awards to Scholarly Publications Program, using funds provided by the Social Sciences and Humanities Research Council of Canada.

Library and Archives Canada Cataloguing in Publication

Doyle, Matthew, 1975–, author
Peter Lombard and his students / Matthew Doyle.

(Studies and texts ; 201)
(Mediaeval law and theology ; 8)
Includes bibliographical references and index.
Issued in print and electronic formats.
ISBN 978-0-88844-201-7 (hardback). – ISBN 978-1-77110-373-2 (pdf)

1. Peter Lombard, Bishop of Paris, approximately 1100–1160. 2. Theologians – France – Paris – Biography. 3. Catholic Church – Doctrines – History – To 1500. 4. Theology, Doctrinal – History – Middle Ages, 600–1500. I. Pontifical Institute of Mediaeval Studies, issuing body II. Title. III. Series: Studies and texts (Pontifical Institute of Mediaeval Studies) ; 201 IV. Series: Mediaeval law and theology ; 8

BX1749.P4D69 2016 230'.2092 C2016-900003-6 C2016-900004-4

© 2016
Pontifical Institute of Mediaeval Studies
59 Queen's Park Crescent East
Toronto, Ontario, Canada M5S 2C4
www.pims.ca

MANUFACTURED IN CANADA

In memory of my father

David Noel Doyle

Contents

Abbreviations

Brady, "Peter Manducator"	Ignatius C. Brady, "Peter Manducator and the Oral Teachings of Peter Lombard," *Antonianum* 41 (1966): 454–490.
Brady, Prolegomena	Ignatius C. Brady, Prolegomena to *Sententiae in IV libris distinctae,* ed. Ignatius C. Brady, 2 vols. (Rome: Editiones Collegii S. Bonaventurae ad Claras Aquas, 1971–1981), 1: 5*–169* and 2: 5*–100*.
Cartulaire, ed. de Lasteyrie	*Cartulaire général de Paris* 1, ed. Robert de Lasteyrie (Paris: Imprimerie nationale, 1887).
CCCM	Corpus Christianorum, Continuatio Mediaevalis (Turnhout: Brepols, 1971–).
Colish, *Peter Lombard*	Marcia L. Colish, *Peter Lombard,* 2 vols. (Leiden: E.J. Brill, 1994).
Gallia Christiana	Scévole de Sainte-Marthe and Louis de Sainte-Marthe, *Gallia Christiana in provincias ecclesiasticas distributa* (1715–1865), 2nd ed., ed. Paul Piolin, 16 vols. (Paris: Apud V. Palmé, 1865–1870).
MGH SS	Monumenta Germaniae Historica: Scriptores (Hanover: Hahn, 1826).
Mortet, "Maurice de Sully"	Victor Mortet, "Maurice de Sully, évêque de Paris (1160–1196): Étude sur l'administration épiscopale pendant la seconde moitié du XIIe siècle," *Mémoires de la Société de l'histoire de Paris et de l'Ile-de-France* 16 (1890): 105–317.

PL	Patrologiae cursus completus: Series Latina, ed. J.-P. Migne, 221 vols. (Paris: Migne, 1844–1864).
RHF	*Recueil des historiens des Gaules et de la France*, ed. Martin Bouquet, Michel J.J. Brial, Joseph Naudy, Pierre C.F. Danou, Joseph D. Guignaut, Léopold Delisle et al., 24 vols. (Paris, 1738–1904).
Rosemann, *Peter Lombard*	Philipp Rosemann, *Peter Lombard* (Oxford: Oxford University Press, 2004).
RTAM	*Recherches de théologie ancienne et médiévale*
Sententiae	Peter Lombard, *Sententiae in IV libris distinctae*, ed. Ignatius C. Brady, 2 vols. (Rome, Editiones Collegii S. Bonaventurae ad Claras Aquas, 1971–1981).
Smalley, *Becket Conflict*	Beryl Smalley, *The Becket Conflict and the Schools: A Study of Intellectuals in Politics* (Oxford: Blackwell, 1973).

Acknowledgements

I first read Peter Lombard in early 2000, while researching for my master's thesis. It was not the *Sentences* but two of his sermons, and there was something about them that intrigued me. I came back to them during my first year as a doctoral student in Toronto, and they remain a central part of this book. The idea to write about Peter and his students came to me in the summer of 2001, when I was back in Dublin and cycling down Dundrum Road, just before it crosses the Dodder River into Milltown. The idea to focus on Peter's career and to make the work genuinely biographical developed over time.

I owe thanks to a number of people. Brian Stock has been of great help in reading through the book and in discussing ideas and plans for it. It was a privilege to benefit from his knowledge of not only the twelfth century but also its intellectual heritage. He was always enthusiastic and encouraging about my work and provided illuminating comments. Isabelle Cochelin, Michael Herren, Seymour Phillips, and David Luscombe read early versions of some of the chapters and offered useful ideas and feedback. Joseph Goering did the same, and he was also involved in the latter stages. His affection for and understanding of the field was always evident. Drafts of the book as a whole were read by anonymous readers. They provided constructive suggestions for improvement and saved me from errors. In the summer of 2010, a time when a second pair of eyes was needed and appreciated, my father and Jackie Cowan read smaller portions of the text.

A work of this kind would not be possible without academic libraries, and I was fortunate to have access to the excellent resources of the University of Toronto libraries and the Pontifical Institute of Mediaeval Studies Library. My thanks are also due to the staff of these libraries, especially William Edwards, James K. Farge, and the late Caroline Suma. I would also like to thank Sandy Paul of the Wren Library, Trinity College, Cambridge, and Colin Harris, Department of Special Collections, Bodleian Library, Oxford, who allowed me to consult Herbert of Bosham's editions of Peter Lombard's commentaries in the summers of 2009 and 2010.

All translations from Latin are my own unless otherwise indicated. Translations from the Bible are based on the Douay-Rheims version, due to its proximity to the Latin Vulgate. I should also acknowledge that Hartwig Mayer helped me with the translation of some of the German scholarship on William of Tyre in 2004.

I think it is right to also mention my training at University College Dublin, in the department of history, and at the Centre for Medieval Studies in the University of Toronto.

I am very grateful to Joseph Goering and Fred Unwalla at PIMS for taking an interest in my work and guiding it through the process of publication. I would like to also thank Kimberly Booker for her conscientious work in copy editing the manuscript, and all the staff of PIMS publications for their efforts.

The support and encouragement of my family and friends has been immensely important. I have dedicated this book to the memory of my father, David Doyle, who died last year. He was always supportive, and I learned much from him about being a historian.

Introduction

Peter Lombard is inseparable from the book on which his fame rests, the *Sentences*. It was a groundbreaking book, and it became a standard work. For the next three centuries it was a required text in the universities of Europe. All the major theologians of the thirteenth and fourteenth centuries lectured on it and produced commentaries. It was a book that could not be ignored. The *Sentences* stood out for its coherence and manageability. That coherence lies both in the handling of authorities and in the overall structural conception. It was this approach to structure and authorities that helped to make the *Sentences* so influential, and it has pride of place among twelfth-century attempts to create a body of doctrine based on the reconciling of authorities.

Is there a Peter Lombard away from the *Sentences*? In one sense, no. It was a part of who he was. It summarizes almost twenty years of teaching theology. However, in another sense, Peter Lombard has much to offer the historian of the twelfth century, and not just the intellectual historian. The exclusive focus on the *Sentences* still diverts attention away from his other works, particularly his sermons, which are his most self-revealing pieces of writing. His career also demands attention. Beginning as an unknown in a village near Novara, he made his way to France and gained entry into the highest echelons of Parisian clerical society. Questions arise, such as how he did this, who assisted him, and what obstacles he had to face. Additionally, Peter was not a full-time scholar. As a member of the cathedral chapter of Notre Dame, he had significant responsibilities to the church of Paris.

It is also possible to examine Peter's school of theology in a number of areas. The names of several of his students are known, and their careers are well documented. Theology was an advanced subject, and students spent between six and ten years taking it. The relationship between a master and his students could therefore be very close, allowing ties of loyalty and obligation to develop. After his death, some of Peter's students worked to preserve their master's legacy and to protect his reputation. Also, the future activities of his students show how the school prepared them for their careers.

Peter Lombard's career, and his relationship with his students are the basic elements of what follows. As recently as the early 1990s, however, Peter Lombard was largely inaccessible to anyone besides specialists. There were certainly references in general works to the importance of the *Sentences*, but few opportunities to gain a further acquaintance, particularly in the English-speaking world. This was especially surprising given the popularity of the twelfth century as a field of study. Scholarship on twelfth-century intellectual life has followed a number of broad trends, such as the development of scholastic theology, the emergence of cathedral schools and universities, a preoccupation with literary humanism, the relationship of intellectuals with the church and/or the state, new developments in devotional writing, and literary biography. At one time, the twelfth century was viewed as a prelude to the achievements of the thirteenth. Generally, however, in the past century, there has been a recognition that something was new at this time. Words like renaissance, renewal, and reformation have been used to describe the century as a whole. Although these terms can still provoke a healthy debate, the achievements of the period are not in doubt. Intellectuals have often been seen in relation to a wider historical canvas, and it is a very user-friendly field.

Peter Lombard is still studied somewhat in isolation. Specialists have examined his theology, but he has never been portrayed in relation to the wider environment. Environment in Peter Lombard studies has always meant other practicing theologians. Even among specialists he has not received continuous attention. Sustained work on him has been concentrated in four periods: the 1880s and 1890s, the 1930s, the late 1950s and 1960s, and an ongoing period beginning in the mid-1990s. This inconsistency probably resulted not from changing fashions in scholarship but from the reception given to Peter Lombard in general works. That issue has been examined by Colish[1] and to a lesser extent by Philipp Rosemann.[2] They have traced a develop-

1 Colish, *Peter Lombard*, 3–10. A more detailed account of the reception of Peter Lombard's work is Ermenegildo Bertola, "Pietro Lombardo nella storiografia filosofica medioevale," *Pier Lombardo* 4 (1960): 95–113.

2 Rosemann, *Peter Lombard*, 4–6.

ment from a negative view in the early twentieth century to a more recent recognition of Peter's original approach.

Scholarly focus on Peter began in the late nineteenth century. Félix Protois produced an excellent monograph on him,[3] and a study of his thought also appeared in Germany.[4] Barthélemy Hauréau identified his sermons, which had been mistakenly attributed to Hildebert of Lavardin in the *Patrologia Latina.*[5] However, despite such admirable individual studies, Peter Lombard was dismissed in the key works of reference, which traced broad developments in either scholastic theology or in philosophy as a whole. Although there was an awareness of his popularity in the later Middle Ages, it was believed that his importance was minimal. The best example of this view is Martin Grabmann's *History of the Scholastic Method.*[6]

The publication at Louvain of a new journal, *Récherches de théologie ancienne et médiévale,* in 1928, stimulated new work on Peter Lombard. This journal experienced its golden age in the 1930s with regular contributions from Raymond Martin, Arthur Landgraf, and Odon Lottin. They brought to light all sorts of undiscovered and unedited material from the twelfth-century schools. They had a particular interest in the immediate tradition of the *Sentences,*[7] and they examined the early commentaries on the *Sentences* by Peter's disciples. These articles are still fundamental. Landgraf would ultimately produce a comprehensive work on early scholasticism.[8]

Also in the 1930s, a number of important articles by Joseph de Ghellinck appeared. He is best known for two books that take a broad view of twelfth-century theology. The first edition of his seminal work, *Le mouvement*

3 Félix Protois, *Pierre Lombard: Évêque de Paris dit le maître des Sentences: Son époque, sa vie, ses écrits, son influence* (Paris, 1881).

4 Johannes N. Espenberger, *Die Philosophie des Petrus Lombardus und ihre Stellung im zwölften Jahrhundert* (Münster, 1901).

5 Barthélemy Hauréau, "Notice sur les sermons attribués à Hildebert de Lavardin," *Notices et extraits des manuscrits de la Bibliothèque Nationale* 32 (1888): 107–166.

6 Martin Grabmann, *Die Geschichte der scholastischen Methode: Die scholastichen Methode im 12. und beginnenden 13. Jahrhundert* (Freiburg, 1911), 2: 369–407.

7 See, for example, Odon Lottin, "Le premier commentaire connu des *Sentences* de Pierre Lombard," *RTAM* 11 (1939): 64–71; Artur Landgraf, "Udo and Magister Martinus," ibid., 62–64.

8 Artur Landgraf, *Einführung in die Geschichte der theologischen Literatur der Früscholastik* (Regensburg, 1948).

théologique au XIIe siècle, came out in 1914, but it was in the 1930s and 1940s that he put his ideas into final shape with the second edition of that book,[9] and also with *L'essor de la littérature latine au XIIe siècle.*[10] De Ghellinck has been criticized for his somewhat negative view of the *Sentences.*[11] He did remark that the incredible popularity of the work in the Middle Ages was undeserved,[12] but it is important to recognize that he made substantial contributions to Peter Lombard studies. His account of the *Sentences* shows a full understanding of its achievements and an affinity (rare at the time) for its author. His two articles, "La carrière de Pierre Lombard: Quelques précisions chronologiques" and "La carrière de Pierre Lombard: Nouvelles précisions chronologiques," were also important.[13] They mark the first time that anyone had dealt with Peter's career outside of vague assumptions, and they laid the foundations for Brady's later work. Furthermore, de Ghellinck brought the later debates over Peter Lombard's Christology to life in *Le mouvement théologique.*[14]

In the 1950s, there was a new interest in Peter Lombard in Italy, stimulated by the eight-hundredth anniversary of the publication of the *Sentences,* in 1953.[15] A new journal, *Pier Lombardo,* was published in Novara, the birthplace of Peter Lombard.[16] The first issue, in 1957, is prefaced with letters from Pope Pius XII and Gilla Vincenzo Gremigni, bishop of Novara. Six issues were published between 1957 and 1962, and they include a variety of articles on the

9 Joseph de Ghellinck, *Le mouvement théologique au XIIe siècle,* 2nd ed. (Bruges, 1948).

10 Joseph de Ghellinck, *L'essor de la littérature latine au XIIe siècle,* 2 vols. (Brussels, 1946).

11 Colish, *Peter Lombard,* 9–10.

12 De Ghellinck, *Le mouvement théologique au XIIe siècle,* 2.

13 Joseph De Ghellinck, "La carrière de Pierre Lombard: Quelques précisions chronologiques," *Revue d'histoire ecclésiastique* 27 (1931): 792–830, and "La carrière de Pierre Lombard: Nouvelles précisions chronologiques" *Revue d'histoire ecclésiastique* 30 (1934): 95–100. De Ghellinck also played some role in the edition of the *Sentences* prepared by the Quarrachi Fathers during World War One. See Ignatius C. Brady, "The Three Editions of the *Liber Sententiarum* of Master Peter Lombard (1882–1977)," *Archivum Franciscanum Historicum* 70 (1977): 400–411.

14 De Ghellinck, *Le mouvement théologique,* 250–276.

15 1153 was the date usually given for the composition of the *Sentences* although Brady would later modify that to 1155/1157: Brady, Prolegomena 1: 122–129.

16 *Pier Lombardo: Rivista di teologia, filosofia e varia cultura,* 6 vols. (1957–1962).

philosophy and theology of the scholastic period. The most frequent contributor was Ermenegildo Bertola, and there is at least one article on Peter in each volume. The 1960 issue marked the anniversary of Peter's death and is devoted to studies of his work. *Pier Lombardo* seems to have resulted from the enthusiasm and support of Bishop Gremigni, who was an accomplished author himself.[17] His sermons on the gospels and epistles went through several editions,[18] and he also published a number of studies of saints.[19] He was also known as a strong-willed and authoritarian figure.[20] The journal was published in Novara, at the Seminario San Gaudenzio, but there were no more issues after 1963, when Gremigni died. Presumably, his successor did not see any need to allocate further funds to it. The volume *Miscellanea Lombardiana* was also occasioned by the anniversary of the *Sentences*.[21] Although it did not appear in print until 1957, it commemorated a month-long conference in Novara, held four years earlier. There was at least one presentation per day. This volume contains some very useful studies, particularly one by Damien Van den Eynde on dating Peter's works.[22] His article, along with those of de Ghellinck, meant that for the first time a chronology of Peter's life and works could be reconstructed. Some of the findings of Van den Eynde and de Ghellinck on chronology have since been challenged, but they laid important foundations. Finally, Philippe Delhaye produced a short but authoritative study of Lombard's thought in this period, *Pierre Lombard: Sa vie, son oeuvre, sa morale*.[23]

17 For Gremigni, see Alessandro Giordano, "La Chiesa Novarese dal primo dopoguerra al Vaticano II," in *Diocesi di Novara*, ed. Luciano Vaccaro and Dorino Tuniz (Varese, 2007), 369–383, and Vanessa Roghi, "Gremigni, Gilla Vincenzo," in *Dizionario Biografico Degli Italiani*, ed. Alberto Maria Ghisalberti (Rome, 1960–2015), 59: 310–312.

18 Gilla Vincenzo Gremigni, *In illo tempore ... : Vangeli delle domeniche e delle feste* 7th ed. (Rome, 1961) and *Lectio epistolae: Epistole delle domeniche* 3rd ed. (Rome, 1947). References to Gremigni's works have been obtained from the online catalogues of the Library of Congress and the Biblioteca Nazionale Centrale di Firenze.

19 Roghi, "Gremigni, Gilla Vincenzo," in *Dizionario Biografico Degli Italiani*, ed. Ghisalberti, 59: 312.

20 Giordano, "La Chiesa Novarese dal primo dopoguerra al Vaticano II," 369.

21 *Miscellanea Lombardiana* (Novara, 1957)

22 Damien Van den Eynde, "Essai chronologique sur l'oeuvre littéraire de Pierre Lombard," in *Miscellanea Lombardiana*, 45–63.

23 Philippe Delhaye, *Pierre Lombard: Sa vie, son oeuvre, sa morale* (Montreal, 1961).

In the same period, Ignatius Brady was preparing a new edition of the *Sentences,* to replace the Quarrachi edition of 1916.[24] His mandate included collecting material for an extended preface on Peter's life and works, and as he worked, he published his preliminary findings in articles. Two of the most important were "Peter Lombard: Canon of Notre Dame," which establishes for the first time that Peter was a member of the cathedral chapter, and "Peter Manducator and the Oral Teachings of Peter Lombard."[25] Many of these findings would reappear in the introduction to part one of his edition, which appeared in 1971.[26] This was the most complete account of Peter's life to date. Brady was able to establish matters that many had assumed could not be known, such as Peter's career in France, the offices he held, and the context and dates of his work. He also disproved a number of persistent legends. Brady's Prolegomena was thus a splendid addition to the literature on Peter Lombard's career. The relative inaccessibility of this work, however, explains why little attention was paid to Peter Lombard in the 1970s and 1980s.[27] It has remained unknown outside specialist circles. Brady published it in Latin, as a preface to a scholarly edition. It was never intended as a stand-alone volume and is by no means a staple of university libraries.

A new interest in Peter Lombard began in 1994 when Marcia Colish published her two-volume study, *Peter Lombard.* This is an indispensable resource for anyone wishing to know about Peter Lombard's theological positions. The book was designed as a comprehensive study of the *Sentences.* There is also excellent material on Peter Lombard's commentaries. Given the length

24 For the beginning of his involvement, see Brady, "The Three Editions of the *Liber Sententiarum,*" 400–411.

25 His findings on the students are not found in the Prolegomena, other than a brief mention in volume two, but in his excellent article, Brady, "Peter Manducator and the Oral Teachings of Peter Lombard," *Antonianum* 41 (1966): 454–490.

26 Brady, Prolegomena 1. The preface to volume two of the edition (Brady, Prolegomena 2) is also valuable. It addresses the question of whether Peter wrote any further works besides the accepted canon.

27 The only exceptions were the treatment of Peter's sermons in Jean Longère, *Oeuvres oratoires de maîtres parisiens au XIIe siècle* (Paris, 1975), and Jean Châtillon, "Latran III et l'enseignement christologique de Pierre Lombard," in *Le Troisième Concile de Latran (1179): Sa place dans l'histoire,* ed. Jean Longère (Paris, 1982): 75–90.

of this book, however, it is to be regretted that a chapter was not devoted to Peter's biography. Colish only included eight pages on this subject,[28] and this represented a step back from Brady. For much of the book, Colish's method is to survey the positions of Peter Lombard's predecessors and contemporaries on a given subject and to then demonstrate the clarity of his approach in the *Sentences*. This certainly helps to underline Peter's achievement. But Colish is so enthusiastic about Peter[29] that anyone who stands in the way is liable to face criticism. Peter's contemporaries, such as Robert of Melun, the Porretans, and Robert Pullen, are often disparaged, and it is difficult to gain a sense of their individual merits.

Interest in Peter Lombard has continued since Colish. There is much to praise in Philipp Rosemann's short monograph, *Peter Lombard*, published by Oxford University Press in the "Great Medieval Thinkers" series. His chapter on Peter's life is actually more detailed than the one in Colish and is substantially founded on Brady's Prolegomena. This forms the prelude to a concise and clear book-by-book discussion of the *Sentences*. Another milestone was the publication of an English translation of the *Sentences* by Giulio Silano.[30] This will undoubtedly stimulate further work on Peter Lombard, as will a French translation that has just completed publication at the time of writing.[31] A new collection of articles based on a colloquium in Spoleto has also recently appeared, which contains valuable studies of Peter's commentaries on the Psalms and Letters of Paul.[32] For the foreseeable future, it seems that the focus of Lombard scholarship will be the commentaries on his *Sentences*, a vast field that extends from the end of the twelfth century into the fifteenth.[33] Colish had drawn attention to the possibilities of this kind of work

28 Colish, *Peter Lombard*, 15–23.

29 See Rosemann's further comments on this subject, *Peter Lombard*, 6.

30 Peter Lombard, *The Sentences*, trans. Giulio Silano (Toronto, 2007–2010).

31 *Pierre Lombard: Les quatre livres des Sentences*, trans. Marc Ozilou (Paris, 2012–2015).

32 *Pietro Lombardo: Atti del XLIII Convegno storico internazionale* (Spoleto, 2007).

33 The standard catalogue of these commentaries is Friedrich Stegmüller, *Repertorium commentariorum in Sententias Petri Lombardi*, 2 vols (Würzburg, 1947). Recently the International Society for the Study of Medieval Philosophy has undertaken a major project to catalogue these commentaries. See William J. Courtenay, "SIEPM Project: Report on the Repertory of Commentaries on Peter Lombard's Sentences," *Bulletin de Philosophie Médiévale* 54 (2012): 55–57.

in her book.[34] Three volumes of studies on these commentaries have appeared, and Rosemann has also written a short introduction to the process, called *The Story of a Great Medieval Book*.[35]

Despite the valuable work of de Ghellinck, Van den Eynde, and Brady, a book that takes a broadly biographical approach to Peter Lombard has yet to appear. There are good reasons for this. There are no contemporary references to Peter longer than a few lines, and certainly nothing of a biographical nature. He left no letters, and very little is known of the first four decades of his life. Even his period as bishop of Paris does not yield much information. Since it lasted for less than a year, there are few documents and it is difficult to discern any kind of policy.

Another difficulty deterring a biographical treatment has been the nature of Peter Lombard's literary output. One reason why the twelfth century is such a popular field is that the authors' personalities are at the heart of the literature. Figures like John of Salisbury, St Bernard of Clairvaux, Abelard, and Gerald of Wales all wrote works in a variety of genres, and they put themselves into their writings. Later ages have responded gladly. Their works are read and translated. One can call them, without exaggeration, men of letters. Peter Lombard is very different. He wrote only theology. This was unusual. Even his students did not focus exclusively on theology.

This book aims to examine Peter Lombard in relation to his environment and milieu. It is especially focused on the people with whom he came into contact. By knowing them, we can come to know Peter. That milieu includes his patrons, colleagues, and students. It is divided into two parts, broadly corresponding to its title. The first details Peter's career, the second his relationship with his students.

It is important, first, to examine Peter's North Italian background. While his early years are an elusive period in his life, we can speak quite firmly about two areas: his education and his patrons. A surviving inventory of Peter's classical texts allows for a glimpse into his early education.

34 Colish, *Peter Lombard*, 1.

35 *Mediaeval commentaries on the Sentences of Peter Lombard: Current Research*, ed. Gillian R. Evans and Philipp Rosemann (Leiden, 2002–2015); Philipp Rosemann, *The Story of a Great Medieval Book: Peter Lombard's* Sentences (Peterborough, ON, 2007).

The assistance of Peter's first known patrons, Bernard, abbot of Clairvaux, and Uberto, bishop of Lucca, was vital to his career as a theologian. They were also key players in the papal schism of the 1130s. The focus then turns to Peter's early career in Paris, involving his study years and establishment of a school of theology. Soon after this, Peter became a canon of Notre Dame, and his entry is seen against the background of wider changes in the church of Paris in this period.

A discussion of Peter's colleagues, the canons of Notre Dame, follows. Few of them have received sustained attention, but often we can catch glimpses of their individual personalities. Peter is not a direct participant in this chapter, but any events that concerned the canons as a body also concerned him. The necessity of a theological training for a number of the positions in the cathedral chapter will also be clear. Part one concludes by covering the years of Peter's greatest achievements. The composition of the *Sentences* and the *Commentary on the Letters of Paul* is examined in tandem with his remarkable rise in the cathedral chapter and his participation in ecclesiastical politics. He rose among the canons to eventually become the bishop of Paris.

Peter is not absent from the second part of the book, *The Master and His Students*. His sermons are considered in detail here, because many of them were preached to his students. His commentaries on the Psalms and on the Letters of Paul are also addressed more in this part of the book because they were edited by Peter's student Herbert of Bosham. The students also recall Peter's teaching in the classroom. In discussing the students themselves, the value of a theological education for their future careers is one of the major themes. Another is the role of the students in defending and increasing awareness of Peter's works. Too often it has been assumed that Peter's works withstood the challenge of the 1160s and 1170s because of the ineptitude and weakness of the opposition. We must also take into account a sustained campaign by Peter Lombard's defenders. Without this campaign, the *Sentences* would not have held the exalted position that it enjoyed for the next few centuries.

PART ONE

Peter Lombard

CHAPTER ONE

Education and Early Patrons, 1100–1134

Peter Lombard's documented career both begins and ends with a papal schism. In September 1159, when Peter had been bishop of Paris for just two months, Pope Adrian IV died, and two competing candidates with powerful backers each emerged as possible successors. By the time of Peter's death, in July 1160, the Capetian king, Louis VII, and the French church, of which Peter was now part, had firmly decided in favour of one of the candidates, Alexander III. Thirty years earlier, Europe had undergone a similar upheaval, but without the imperial dimension. The rival claims of Innocent and Anacletus had divided ecclesiastical opinion in the 1130s. The struggle had lasted several years, and one indirect outcome of it was the emergence into history of an obscure scholar from near Novara, Peter Lombard.

Two key players in that earlier schism, Uberto, the bishop of Lucca, and Bernard, the Cistercian abbot of Clairvaux, helped to secure the acceptance of Innocent II as pope. They were also two of Peter's earliest patrons. At Uberto's request, Bernard recommended Peter Lombard to his closest friends in the intellectual community. Bernard's letter of recommendation is the earliest dated document to mention Peter by name. Yet Peter Lombard's place in this circle of well-connected people has scarcely been noticed at all.

Peter Lombard was apparently living in Lucca at the time of the schism, and he knew Uberto well enough for the bishop to give him a recommendation. To find out how this situation arose, some attempt must be made to piece together Peter's early life and career.[1] According to a note in a thirteenth-century manuscript, Peter was from Nomenonii. This village, now known as Lumellogno, is about four miles from Novara.[2] A twelfth-century manuscript of the *Sentences* refers to him as Peter of Novara.[3] No exact date is

1 Brady, Prolegomena 1: 10*–13*.
2 Ibid., 10*.
3 Ibid.

known for his birth, but it can be estimated as having been between 1095 and 1100. Bernard of Clairvaux, as we will see, described him as *vir venerabilis*, a "venerable man," in the mid-1130s.[4] He would have been at least thirty-five.

Peter's early years were lived in a region affected by division and conflict. In 1110, the German emperor, Henry V, led a large army into Northern Italy to reinforce his control there.[5] Political instability, related to the contest over investitures, had been a feature of the area for decades.[6] There were also divisions within Novara itself. The episcopal see was vacant, and some of the townspeople and clergy were refusing to accept the new bishop, Eppo, who was backed by Henry. When the town did not surrender after a siege, the emperor ordered that it be sacked and burned. The defensive walls were destroyed. This served partly as a warning to other cities, and Henry continued his march toward Rome.[7]

It is very probable that Peter was already attending grammar school in Novara at this time.[8] Even if he was not physically present during the sack, however, it would undoubtedly have left an impression on him. As a student at the cathedral school, Peter would also have been aware of the debates and divisions among the clergy, both before and after the sack. In the years after 1110, however, the various factions within Novara seem to have united to rebuild the city, and a period of sustained prosperity followed.[9]

Peter's family background was not illustrious. He had to rely on patronage for the first forty or so years of his life, as will be shown in this chapter and the next. Beyond that, nothing is known of his parents. However, when the *Sentences* became firmly established in the thirteenth century, the fame of the "master of

4 See the text of his letter below, 27–28.

5 For these events, see Giancarlo Andenna, "La Chiesa Novarese sotto l'Impero dei Sassoni e dei Salici," in *Diocesi di Novara*, ed. Luciano Vaccaro and Dorino Tuniz (Brescia, 2007), 83–110 at 102–103.

6 Ibid., 93–101. See also Giovanni Tabacco, "Northern and Central Italy in the Eleventh Century," in *The New Cambridge Medieval History*, ed. David Luscombe and Jonathan Riley-Smith (Cambridge, 1995–2005), 4.2: 72–93.

7 Andenna, "La Chiesa Novarese sotto l'Impero dei Sassoni e dei Salici," 102–103. For chronicle references to these events, see Gerold Meyer von Knonau, *Jahrbücher des deutschen Reiches unter Heinrich IV. und Heinrich V.* (Leipzig, 1890–1909, repr. Berlin, 1964–1965), 6: 131–132.

8 See the discussion of his schooling below, 16.

9 Andenna, "La Chiesa Novarese sotto l'Impero dei Sassoni e dei Salici," 103–105.

sentences" grew and stories were attached to Peter's name.[10] These stories all agree that his parents were poor. Other than that, there is no common ground among them. In one of the more appealing stories, his mother, who had worked as a washerwoman to support her son, made her way to Paris when he was bishop of that city. Peter failed to recognize her at first, but when he did, he embraced her warmly and proclaimed, "this is my mother, my poor mother, who bore me, suckled me, caressed me and brought me up."[11] This story can be ruled out, since it was told with greater frequency about Peter's successor, Maurice of Sully.[12]

When it comes to discussing Peter's education, we are on somewhat firmer ground. Primary education in twelfth-century Italy still closely followed the classical model. Children learned to recognize, write, and pronounce the alphabet and then every possible vowel–consonant combination. Finally, they learned to read and write short sentences or maxims. This process would take four to five years.[13] Although Peter would have grown up speaking the local vernacular language,[14] all of his education would have been in Latin. As Robert Black puts it, in his admirable study of the Italian medieval school curriculum, "Latin was regarded as an artificial, created, unchanging language, an *ars* suitable for teaching, whereas the vulgar languages were regarded as changeable, unstable ... learnt naturally but formally unteachable."[15] At the primary level, schoolmasters would certainly speak to their pupils in the vernacular, but when the students learned sentences, they were Latin sentences.[16]

10 Brady, Prolegomena 1: 10*–11*. See also Jacobus Aquensis, *Chronicon Imaginis Mundi*, in *Historiae patriae monumenta,* ed. Gustavo Avogadro (Turin, 1848), 5.3 (*Scriptores*): 1357–1626, at 1620; Antonio Massara, "La Leggenda di Pier Lombardo," in *Miscellanea Storica Novarese*, ed. Raffaele Terella (Novara, 1906), 117–120.

11 Brady, Prolegomena 1: 37*–40*.

12 Ibid.

13 For the system in the Roman republic and empire, see Stanley Bonner, *Education in Ancient Rome: From the Elder Cato to the Younger Pliny* (London, 1977), 165–176. For medieval Italy, see Robert Black, *Humanism and Education in Medieval and Renaissance Italy: Tradition and Innovation in Latin Schools from the Twelfth to the Fifteenth Century* (Cambridge, 2001), 37.

14 For documentary evidence of North Italian vernacular languages in the twelfth and thirteenth centuries, see Giacomo Devoto, *The Languages of Italy*, trans. V. Louise Katainen (Chicago, 1978), 195–200, 211–212.

15 Black, *Humanism and Education in Medieval and Renaissance Italy,* 42.

16 "Teaching alphabet sheets (*tabula/carta*), simple Latin prayers, and *Ianua* phonetically did not require active use of Latin, which was needed only at the later stages of the curriculum, when Latin syntax, composition and authors were studied." Ibid., 43.

Peter received his primary schooling either in the village or in one of its neighbours (such as Pagliate or Casalgiate), or he might have walked to Novara each day (a distance of four miles). He would have learned the alphabet and syllables from a sheet of parchment fixed to a wooden board. After this, the most common text to start with in Italy was the Psalter, the text of the Psalms.[17] Students would copy them into their wax tablets and commit them to memory.[18] Peter may also have learned to read the *Distichs* of Cato. This is an anonymous compilation of sayings, dating probably from the third century, to which the name of Cato has been attached.[19]

His education did not end when he completed primary school. At around the age of eleven, Peter would have started grammar school. Brady suggests that this was probably at the cathedral school in Novara.[20] This is a reasonable suggestion, since Peter's own parents would not have been able to meet the cost of having him educated privately. He must have received some form of support, based on already-observable intellectual gifts. Grammar schools were very important in the classical era. They combined a rigorous training in Latin grammar with the study of poetry. Poetry, particularly epic, was considered to be not only the high point of literary expression but also morally edifying.[21] Students usually attended from the age of eleven to sixteen. This system had not changed much in the intervening centuries, in that its broad ideas were still accepted.[22] In twelfth-century Europe, however, grammar schools held an additional importance. Although incoming students would be used to reciting and pronouncing Latin sentences, it was in grammar schools that they learned to really understand the language.[23]

Some clues to Peter's secondary education may be found in a twelfth-century manuscript, once held by the abbey of St Victor in Paris, which con-

17 Ibid., 37–42.
18 Ibid., 41–42.
19 Wayland J. Chase, *The Distichs of Cato: A Famous Medieval Textbook* (Madison, 1922), 1–2. For the possible use of this by Peter Lombard, see below, 21.
20 Brady, Prolegomena 1: 11*.
21 For this view in the classical era, see Bonner, *Education in Ancient Rome*, 212.
22 David Luscombe, "Thought and Learning," in *New Cambridge Medieval History*, ed. David Luscombe and Jonathan Riley-Smith (Cambridge, 1995–2005), 4.1: 470–471.
23 Lynn Thorndike, "Elementary and Secondary Education in the Middle Ages," *Speculum* 15 (1940): 400–408, at 403–404.

tains a list of some of "the books of master P. the bishop."[24] This bishop has been identified as Peter Lombard.[25] It is one of two different lists of Peter's books. The other describes all the volumes he used for teaching theology in Paris, and for this reason, it will be discussed in the next chapter. The first list, on the other hand, is largely a record of classical texts. Patricia Stirnemann has argued that Peter used some of these texts during his schooling in Italy and then brought them to France.[26] This book list is very significant because it is the only document that tells us anything concrete about Peter before the 1130s.

The books on this list are certainly consistent with those used in a program of studies that was quite standard in twelfth-century Italy. One of the names on the list is Priscian. This would have been Peter's basic text in grammar school, the *Institutiones grammaticae*, or "grammatical foundations," a standard work for learning Latin grammar in the twelfth century. Priscian's aim had been to help Greek speakers in sixth-century Constantinople learn Latin,[27] but the "erudite character" of the *Institutiones* made it unsuitable as a first text in grammar.[28] The study of Priscian was therefore usually preceded by two more manageable texts, the *Ars Minor* and *Ars Maior* by Donatus.[29]

Alongside Priscian's handbook, the book list presents a comprehensive selection of classical and late-antique authors, whom Peter must have known well. Peter's schooling was during a period when Latin authors "were being

24 Patricia Stirnemann, "Histoire tripartite: Un inventaire des livres de Pierre Lombard, un exemplaire de ses *Sentences* et le destinataire du Psautier de Copenhague," in *Du copiste au collectionneur: Mélanges d'histoire des textes et des bibliothèques en l'honneur d'André Vernet,* ed. Donatella Nebbiai-Dalla Guarda and Jean-François Genest (Turnhout, 1998), 301–318.

25 Ibid. The identification was first made by Constant Mews, who included the list in the preface to his edition of Abelard's *Theologia* because the manuscript in question, Paris, Bibliothèque de l'Arsenal, MS 265, also contains that work. Eligius M. Buytaert and Constant J. Mews, *Petri Abaelardi Opera Theologica III: Theologia "Summi Boni," Theologia "Scholarium"* (CCCM 13: 245).

26 Stirnemann, "Histoire tripartite: Un inventaire des livres de Pierre Lombard," 307.

27 For Priscian's purpose and the dimensions of his work, see Robert H. Robins, *The Byzantine Grammarians: Their Place in History* (Berlin, 1993), 187–190.

28 Black, *Humanism and Education in Medieval and Renaissance Italy,* 65: "Priscian's students tended to be sophisticated linguists, already thoroughly grounded in the Greek grammatical and rhetorical tradition."

29 Ibid.

read intensively in Italian schools," as Black has demonstrated.[30] In the twelfth century, the canon of authors was usually divided into *auctores minores* and *auctores maiores*.[31] The minor authors were texts more suitable for beginners, such as the aforementioned *Distichs* of Cato.[32] The list of Peter's books includes a number of standard texts by minor authors: the fables of Avianus, the third-century epic on the life of Christ by Juvencus, and the *Eclogue* of Theodulus, a tenth-century work.[33] The major authors were those presenting more of a challenge and requiring more explanation from the teacher. These are well represented in the book list, and the authors Black identifies as being the most popular in twelfth-century Italian schools[34] are all present in it: Lucan, Horace, Virgil, Juvenal, Ovid, and Statius.[35] Peter also apparently studied two texts used less often, the sixth-century elegies of Maximianus and, perhaps most intriguingly, *Pamphilus*, a comedy contemporary with his schooling.[36]

What techniques would Peter have learned from these texts? As in the Roman era, the teacher's explanations were highly philological. Rigorous attention was paid to historical, geographical, and mythological references.[37] The meaning of words in particular lines and the poetic metre were exhaustively covered. The teacher also introduced the texts through an introduction known as the *accessus*, which explained the subject matter, structure, and intention of the work.[38] Finally, teachers of grammar, in the upper years, sometimes subjected parts of the texts to a preliminary rhetorical analysis.[39]

30 Ibid., 185. His findings are based on an analysis of twelfth-century Florentine manuscripts of Latin poets, which contain glosses typical of the grammar school approach. See 185–191. Black provides a similar treatment of subsequent centuries.
31 Ibid., 73. The division was outlined by Conrad of Hirsau in his *Dialogus Super Auctores*.
32 Ibid. See also 275–277.
33 Stirnemann, "Histoire tripartite: Un inventaire des livres de Pierre Lombard," 302.
34 Black, *Humanism and Education in Medieval and Renaissance Italy*, 185–191.
35 Stirnemann, "Histoire tripartite: Un inventaire des livres de Pierre Lombard," 302.
36 Ibid. For the use of both as school texts, see Black, *Humanism and Education in Medieval and Renaissance Italy*, 199, although his evidence is from the thirteenth century. See the further discussion of the dating of *Pamphilus* in Stirnemann, "Histoire tripartite: Un inventaire des livres de Pierre Lombard," 306–307. She suggests that its appearance in the list backs up Peter Dronke's revised dating of *Pamphilus* to around 1100 (rather than 1150, as was formerly thought).
37 Black, *Humanism and Education in Medieval and Renaissance Italy*, 286–298; Bonner, *Education in Ancient Rome*, 227–240.
38 Black, *Humanism and Education in Medieval and Renaissance Italy*, 314–318.
39 Ibid., 308–309. This was also a practice that had its roots in antiquity. See Bonner, *Education in Ancient Rome*, 244–249.

In epic poetry, speeches could serve this purpose particularly well. A good example might be the speech of Aeneas to Dido in *Aeneid* 4, which, in explaining his reasons for leaving Carthage, follows the formal rules of rhetoric and recalls the Roman courts.[40] The ancient commentator Servius (himself a teacher of grammar) saw this clearly and described the speech as "a complete argument (*controversia*), in which he clears away the accusations, relieving himself of the charge of ingratitude[41] ... after removing the charge of ingratitude, he moves on to the reason (*causa*)."[42] All of this stayed with Peter Lombard. As a teacher of theology, he gave many courses expounding the books of the Bible. His exhaustive approach to parsing the text can be seen in his surviving commentaries on the Psalms and Letters of Paul. In these works he also uses the *accessus* to considerable effect. His *Commentary on the Psalms* gained rapid popularity, partly because it includes a separate *accessus* for each individual psalm.[43]

Grammar was an integral part of the arts curriculum. It formed part of the trivium, alongside rhetoric and dialectic, but all authorities recognized that it had to be studied first.[44] Peter's education in grammar probably took about six years. After that, he would have studied the rest of the trivium. This was possibly also at the cathedral school in Novara.[45] There is no question that Peter completed the arts course, since he would not have been able to proceed to the study of theology without it. His training in rhetoric set him apart. He had an ability to structure works in a coherent and logical fashion. This applies to the *Sentences* and especially to his sermons, both of which we will examine in later chapters. Regrettably, the list of Peter's books is less helpful for this period in his life. The standard works used for training in rhetoric in the twelfth century, Cicero's *De Inventione*, the anonymous *Rhetorica ad*

40 Virgil, *Aeneid* 4.331–361, ed. R. Deryck Williams (London, 1972–1973), 1: 84–85. See also Williams's commentary on 361–362.

41 "controversia est plena, in qua et purgat obiecta, removens a se crimen ingrati, et veniali utitur statu." Servius, *Commentary on Book Four of Virgil's Aeneid*, ed. and trans. Christopher McDonough, Richard E. Prior, and Mark Stansbury (Wauconda, 2004), 72–73.

42 "remoto ingrati crimine descendit ad causam." Servius, *Commentary on Book Four of Virgil's Aeneid*, ibid., 74–75.

43 See the discussion of the psalms commentary in chapters two and eight, below, 36–37 and 212–225. See also on this Colish, *Peter Lombard*, 187.

44 Luscombe, "Thought and Learning," 470.

45 Brady, Prolegomena 1: 11*.

Herennium, and book four of Augustine's *De Doctrina Christiana*, are not there. Also absent are the texts used for teaching dialectic.[46] This can be explained by the nature of the list. It is not a complete inventory of Peter's books, but rather a selection that was taken and (probably) returned by a canon of St Victor.[47]

Peter would have completed the arts course during his mid-twenties (c.1120–1125), and he does not seem to have continued his studies. Presumably, whatever patronage he had been receiving did not extend to advanced study in canon law or theology. Many scholars used to assume that he had studied in the law schools of Northern Italy, the environment that produced Gratian's *Decretum*. They pointed to his strong familiarity with canon law and to the copy of the *Decretum* that he owned.[48] However, Peter's lengthy studies in Rheims and Paris clearly indicate that he lacked a full theological training.[49] Also, in his letter of recommendation, Bernard described him only as a "venerable man," not as a master (*magister*).[50] Peter may have had some training in canon law, but had he spent a considerable period (of, say, six to ten years) studying advanced subjects, he would have been calling himself *magister*.

This is also relevant to his residence in Lucca. The belief that he was a student in a supposedly flourishing theological school of one Otto of Lucca is problematic. We will return to this later.[51] We do not know how he made his living until 1134, when Uberto recommended him to Bernard, or how he

46 For these works see, for example, Luscombe, "Thought and Learning," 471–472, Martin Camargo, "Rhetoric," in *The Seven Liberal Arts in the Middle Ages*, ed. David L. Wagner (Bloomington, 1983), 96–124, at 113, and Eleanor Stump, "Dialectic," in ibid., 125–146, at 128–135.

47 "Hec est summa librorum quod Gaufridus Moricii portavit de libris magistri P. Episcopi." Stirnemann, "Histoire tripartite: Un inventaire des livres de Pierre Lombard," 302.

48 Brady, Prolegomena 1: 11*–12*. See especially Joseph de Ghellinck, "La carrière de Pierre Lombard: Quelques précisions chronologiques," *Revue d'histoire ecclésiastique* 27 (1931): 792–830, at 792–795.

49 Brady, Prolegomena 1: 12*.

50 Bernard of Clairvaux, *Ep.* 410, *Sancti Bernardi opera*, ed. Jean Leclercq, Charles H. Talbot, and Henri Rochais (Rome, 1957–1977), 8: 391. Bernard always gave masters their proper title: see *Ep.* 205, ibid., 64; *Ep.* 13, *Ep.* 543, ibid., 7: 62, 510.

51 See below, 29–32, and, for this scenario, William of Lucca, *Commentum In tertiam ierarchiam Dionisii que est de divinis nominibus*, ed. Ferruccio Gastaldelli (Florence, 1983), xxi–xxviii.

came to the bishop's attention. He certainly was not prominent in Lucca.[52] He may have worked as a clerk in Uberto's household. Men trained in the arts were employed as notaries by bishops.[53] In the rhetoric course, they studied the art of letter writing (the *ars dictaminis*).[54] However, Uberto's notary was a man called Wido.[55] The book list may again help us to flesh out this period in Peter's life. An interesting feature of it is that two of the minor authors, Cato and Theodulus, are described as glossed.[56] Students in grammar school would often gloss their own texts, as Black has shown.[57] However, Cato's *Distichs* were learned by children who were still writing on wax tablets. Only their teacher would be using a glossed copy. This may indicate that Peter worked for several years as a *doctor puerorum*, a schoolteacher.

But whatever his reasons were, by the 1130s Peter Lombard had come to Lucca, roughly two-hundred miles south of his birthplace. It was a town with a high turnover of visitors from Northern Europe. For that reason, it was important in the diplomatic efforts aimed at resolving the papal schism. We should look more closely at this.

Things moved quickly in Rome when Pope Honorius died on the night of 13 February 1130. Two rival claimants to the papacy emerged, each claiming a legitimate election. One, Gregory Papareschi, took the name Innocent, while the other, Peter Pierleoni, called himself Anacletus.[58] As the months went by, clerics from all over Europe began to take sides, and the dispute escalated into a propaganda war. Uberto, bishop of Lucca, emerged as an early spokesman for the Innocentians. Norbert of Xanten, the founder of the Prae-

52 Raffaele Savigni, *Episcopato e società cittadina a Lucca da Anselmo II a Roberto* (Lucca, 1996), 399–613, contains an extensive appendix on the prosopography of Lucca. Among the twelfth-century cathedral clergy and eminent laypeople on 453–455 and 568, nobody named Peter fits the chronology.

53 For bishops and notaries in Italy see Robert Brentano, *Two Churches: England and Italy in the Thirteenth Century* (Princeton, 1968), 292–324. Twelfth-century examples are also examined.

54 On the *ars dictaminis*, see, for example, Camargo, "Rhetoric," 107–110.

55 *Memorie e documenti per servire all'istoria del Ducato di Lucca*, ed. Domenico Barsocchini and Domenico Bertini (Lucca, 1818–1844), 4.2: 169–172, 5.3: 683–884.

56 "glosas Catonis et Teodoli." Stirnemann, "Histoire tripartite: Un inventaire des livres de Pierre Lombard," 302.

57 Black, *Humanism and Education in Medieval and Renaissance Italy*, 275–277.

58 For a thorough account of the schism, see Mary Stroll, *The Jewish Pope: Ideology and Politics in the Papal Schism of 1130* (Leiden, 1987). See also Ian S. Robinson, *The Papacy, 1073–1198: Continuity and Innovation* (Cambridge, 1990), 69–76.

monstratensian canons and at this time bishop of Magdeburg, wrote to two contacts in the Italian church, Uberto and Walter of Ravenna, requesting information. Norbert's letters have not survived, but the replies have.[59] Uberto's letter is the most frequently quoted statement of the claims of Innocent, and its proximity to the date of the actual election makes it a vital source.[60] The letter only hints at the features of the later propaganda war. Uberto mentions Innocent's good character, but he can hardly be said to dwell on it. He also does not bring in Peter Pierleoni's Jewish ancestry as some would later do. In fact, the whole letter is remarkably concise. It is not an exercise in persuasion through emotive rhetoric. It is less than sixty lines. Significantly, Uberto underlined that he was acting in accordance with other churchmen from Northern Italy: "Embracing, approving and imitating the counsel and opinion of men who are religious, orthodox and catholic, from Tuscany, Lombardy and the Ultramontane, we disown in every way Peter Pierleoni, in this crime, as a schismatic, and as a heretic in every way because he defends his position. We hold, receive, and honour the Lord Innocent as the holy and supreme pontiff, and we attach ourselves to him."[61] Uberto was in the third year of his episcopate when he wrote the letter. He has often been mentioned in passing by historians, but he fails to receive sustained attention. Accounts of the schism do not have a place for his assistance to Peter Lombard. Similarly, his political importance has not been discussed by Peter's

59 *Pontificum Romanorum Vitae,* ed. Johann M. Watterich (Leipzig, 1826–1904), 2: 179–185. The letters can also be found in *Bibliotheca Rerum Germanicarum,* ed. Philipp Jaffé (Berlin, 1864–1873), 5: 423–427.

60 Stroll, *The Jewish Pope,* calls it the "best statement" of the Innocentian case and discusses it on 85–87. The contents of the letter are also discussed in Franz-Josef Schmale, *Studien zum Schisma des Jahres 1130* (Köln, 1961), 149–154, 299–302; Emil Mühlbacher, *Die streitige Papstwahl des jahres 1130* (Innsbruck, 1876), 31–36; Pier F. Palumbo, *Lo scisma del* MCXXX (Rome, 1942), 18–21; and Wilfried M Grauwen, *Norbertus: Aartsbisschop van Maagdenburg (1126–1134)* (Brussels, 1978), 394–399, 655. Mühlbacher and Schmale raise some questions about the authenticity of the letters to Norbert, but stop short of rejecting them.

61 "Nos autem sententiam et consilium religiosorum virorum catholicorum et orthodoxorum de Tuscia, de Longobardia, et de ultramontanis partibus amplexantes, approbantes et imitantes, Petrum Leonis in hoc facinore ut schismaticum et, quoniam suum schisma defendit, haereticum omnimodis abdicamus. Dominum vero Innocentium pro patre et summa pontifice tenemus, recipimus, veneramur et colimus." *Pontificum Romanorum Vitae,* ed. Watterich, 2: 181–182.

biographers. An eleven-page account of his episcopate was published in 1844 as part of a multi-volume work on the diocese of Lucca.[62] More recent work on the diocese of Lucca by Raffaele Savigni has helped to increase understanding of Uberto's role, while correcting some misconceptions.[63] As was standard practice in Lucca, Uberto had been chosen from the clergy of the cathedral of San Martino. He appears as a subdeacon there in 1125–1126 and became bishop in 1128.[64]

The bishops of Lucca were powerful figures in their local area.[65] According to Chris Wickham, the twelfth-century bishop of Lucca was "far and away the most substantial landowner in the Morianese,"[66] and he concludes that "the power of the bishop over his fideles in the Morianese was not so much as a ruler or lord, but rather as a rich neighbour and patron, in a traditional pattern of clientelism that goes back at least to the Carolingian period."[67] We should note the word "patron." This is exactly what Uberto was for Peter Lombard. Surviving administrative records from Uberto's episcopate also provide a sense of his considerable property.[68] Several relate to territorial acquisitions, some of them substantial,[69] and they may indicate that Uberto

62 Domenico Barsocchini, "Dissertazione IX: I Vescovi di Lucca, Saecolo XII: Uberto," in *Memorie e documenti per servire all'istoria del Ducato di Lucca* (Lucca, 1844), 5.1: 435–446.

63 Savigni, *Episcopato e società cittadina a Lucca da Anselmo II a Roberto*, 128–129, 403–404.

64 Ibid., 403. This revises the view of Barsocchini, "Uberto," 435, that bishop Uberto should be identified with an archpriest of that name ordained in 1099.

65 For the bishops of Lucca, see Savigni, *Episcopato e società cittadina a Lucca da Anselmo II a Roberto*; Chris Wickham, *Community and Clientele in Twelfth-Century Tuscany* (Oxford, 1988), 82–98; and Duane J. Osheim, *An Italian Lordship: The Bishopric of Lucca in the Late Middle Ages* (Berkeley, 1977).

66 Wickham, *Community and Clientele*, 82.

67 Ibid., 98.

68 Four documents from Uberto's episcopate were edited in *Memorie e documenti per servire all'istoria del Ducato di Lucca*, 4.2: 169–172 and 5.2: 683–684. A further seven acquisitions by bishop Uberto are listed in Osheim, *An Italian Lordship*, 135–136. The archepiscopal archive of Lucca, or *archivio arcivescovile*, is particularly rich for the period 685–1000, and much of this was printed in the *Memorie e Documenti* volumes. Most twelfth-century material remains in manuscript. See Wickham, *Community and Clientele*, 243–244.

69 See the transactions with John, prior of the monastery of St Thomas in the neighbouring territory of Pistoia, *Memorie e Documenti per servire all'istoria del Ducato di Lucca*, 4.2: 169, and with Count Guido Malaparte, ibid., 5:3, 683–684.

continued the trend of his predecessor, Benedetto (1118–1128), whose episcopate "saw a sharp increase in gifts to the bishop, notably by aristocrats."[70]

The bishops of Lucca were also well placed to know about events beyond their immediate sphere of influence. Lucca was an important economic centre, partly because it stood on the road known as the *Via Francigena*.[71] Duane Osheim, in his study of the medieval Luccan bishopric, has described the impact this had on the town: "Lucca was a main station on the *Via Francigena*, the most important medieval highway between France and Rome. This road connected Lucca not only to Northern Europe, but also to its strongest economic and political ally, Genoa. The international traveller, almost without exception, had to cross the Luccan diocese and stay in one of the Luccan hospitals."[72] Bishop Uberto was therefore in a position that would allow him to be a vital link between the supporters of Innocent II.

Before the schism, Uberto had become acquainted with Norbert of Xanten, the recipient of his letter. Norbert had visited Lucca twice: in 1110–1111 and 1125–1126.[73] Norbert and Uberto formed part of a growing network of church figures who supported Innocent. This was very much a coalition of different groups, interests, and individuals. Within Rome itself, the rivalry between two prominent noble families, the Frangipani and the Pierleoni, had helped to ignite the schism.[74] Anacletus was himself a member of the Pierleoni family. The Frangipani family supported Innocent. The North Italian church, as Uberto's letter makes clear, strongly supported Innocent.[75] The

70 Wickham, *Community and Clientele*, 90. He comments that Benedetto was responsible "for re-establishing a certain political centrality to his office ... he had close political links with the commune, for city consuls appeared at his court as early as 1119."

71 Ibid., 12.

72 Osheim, *An Italian Lordship*, 6–7.

73 Grauwen, *Norbertus*, 398–399. Barsocchini, "Uberto," 441–442, speculated that Uberto had been part of the delegation that accompanied Pope Gelasius II on his French journey of 1118, and had met Norbert at Cluny, where Gelasius died. But if Norbert was there, neither Uberto nor anyone else from Lucca is mentioned in Pandulphus's *Life of Gelasius*. See *Vita Gelasii* (PL 163: 473–484, at 483). Gelasius had gone to France via Pisa and Genoa.

74 Robinson, *The Papacy*, 6–7. They had both emerged as power brokers in the late–eleventh century, supplanting the much older Roman families, the Crescentii and the Tusculani.

75 See the text of the letter above, 22. For a discussion of the strength of Innocent's support in Northern and Southern Italy, see Stroll, *The Jewish Pope*, 102–110, and Robinson, *The Papacy*, 71.

schism moved beyond Italy, however, as both sides looked for support in Germany and Northern France. Uberto's letter to Norbert was part of this process, as were other contacts.[76] It was precisely at this point that the dispute began to develop into a propaganda war.[77] Some mid–twentieth century historians saw the two groups of supporters in the schism – the Innocentians and the Anacletans – as rival parties within the church, still divided over the Concordat of Worms.[78] However, the evidence for this view has been discredited, and it is now seen as too much of an oversimplification.[79]

At the same time, the schism was not simply "a coalescence into groups based upon immediate circumstances."[80] The coalition supporting Innocent was made up of different groups and individuals who already had ties of obligation to one another (whether within the North Italian or French church, or as members of the Roman nobility, or as associates of the papal chancellor). The Northern European group in particular can be described as a "friendship network,"[81] so called because their letters are marked by the language of friendship.[82] Julian Haseldine's observation on the role of such networks in the later Becket conflict is also of relevance here: "These were not characters thrown together by their support for Becket; rather, their mutual obligations as friends led them into varying degrees of involvement in the affair."[83] In the same way, many of Innocent's supporters would never have met him, but they

76 As mentioned already, Walter of Ravenna also wrote to Norbert, while a letter from the papal chancellor Haimeric to a number of contacts in France can be found in Timothy A. Reuter, "Zur Anerkennung Papst Innocenz II: Eine neue Quelle," *Deutsches Archiv für Erforschung des Mittelalters* 39 (1983): 395–416.

77 Stroll, *The Jewish Pope*, 156–178, comprehensively covers this aspect of the schism.

78 See the overview of the historiography of the schism in ibid., 1–9. These readings of the schism are particularly associated with Hans Klewitz and F.J. Schmale.

79 Ibid., 9, 103–105. Robinson, *The Papacy*, 71.

80 The quotation is Stroll's paraphrase of Maleczek's arguments in *The Jewish Pope*, 9.

81 For the prominence of these networks in the schism, see Colin Morris, *The Discovery of the Individual: 1050–1200* (New York, 1972, repr. Toronto, 1987), 104; Stroll, *The Jewish Pope*, 9.

82 For friendship networks see *Friendship in Medieval Europe*, ed. Julian Haseldine (Stroud, 1999); Morris, *The Discovery of the Individual*, 97–107; Julian Haseldine, "Friendship and Rivalry: The Role of Amicitia in Twelfth-Century Monastic Relations," *Journal of Ecclesiastical History* 44 (1993): 390–414.

83 Julian Haseldine, "Thomas Becket: Martyr, Saint—and Friend?" in *Belief and Culture in the Middle Ages: Studies Presented to Henry Mayr-Harting*, ed. Richard Gameson and Henrietta Leyser (Oxford, 2001), 305–317, at 316.

took up his cause through shared mutual friends. As the schism continued, this coalition broadened, and further ties developed. Uberto of Lucca and Bernard of Clairvaux were two such figures who came into contact because of the schism.

Bernard of Clairvaux was in Italy on three occasions in the 1130s.[84] On his first visit, from February to June 1133, he stopped at Pisa to meet Innocent II. They then went on to Rome. On his second visit, between May and November 1135, he made stops at Genoa and Milan and attended the council of Pisa.[85] Uberto was also at the council. There is no record of Bernard actually visiting Lucca, but he would have at least passed through, given its position on the *Via Francigena.* To reach Pisa, it was necessary to leave the *Via Francigena* at Lucca and take another road.[86] Uberto was therefore probably involved in the first visit when Bernard met Innocent at Pisa. As a powerful local figure, and a high ranking ecclesiastic with a large estate, Uberto could well have extended hospitality to Bernard. As the spokesman for the North Italian Innocentians, he would certainly have updated him on the situation.

Now Bernard's *amicus,*[87] Uberto recommended Peter Lombard to him. Bernard responded by supporting Peter's studies at the cathedral school of Rheims. Then, when Peter went to Paris, Bernard ensured he would receive material assistance at the abbey of St Victor. This we know from Bernard's letter 410, the first documented reference to Peter Lombard:

> Brother Bernard, abbot of Clairvaux, offers his greeting and his prayers to his reverend fathers, his lords, and his dearest friends, G[ilduin] the venerable abbot, by God's grace, of Saint Victor of Paris, and his whole holy community. I need to ask much of you, because much has been asked of me. I cannot be sparing of my friends, because they are not sparing of me.

84 For the dates of Bernard's visits to Italy, see Elphège Vacandard, *Vie de Saint Bernard,* 3rd ed. (Paris, 1902), 1: 327–342, 364–389, 2:1–25.

85 Ibid. See also de Ghellinck, "La carrière de Pierre Lombard: Quelques précisions chronologiques," 802–804, and Damien Van den Eynde, "Essai chronologique sur l'œuvre littéraire de Pierre Lombard," in *Miscellanea Lombardiana* (Novara, 1957), 45–63, at 52–53.

86 For maps that show the *Via Francigena,* see Wickham, *Community and Clientele,* x–xiv.

87 See the text of the letter below.

> The lord bishop of Lucca [Uberto], my father and friend, has commended to me the venerable man P[eter] Lombard, asking that I support him materially through my friends during the short period that he is in France for the purpose of study. I did this for as long as he was at Rheims. Now that he is going to be spending time in Paris, I commend him to your care, because I know I can count on you for more. I ask only that you provide him with food for a short period, which will be until the feast of the nativity of the blessed Virgin Mary. Goodbye.[88]

This support proved crucial for the advancement of Peter's career. It was not unusual for Bernard to recognize intellectual gifts in others and to encourage or assist them, especially if they were recommended by his friends.[89] Bernard, having such abilities himself, gravitated toward like minds. At the time of the schism, he had not yet commenced the work that would really make his intellectual reputation, the *Sermons on the Song of Songs*, but he had written several short devotional treatises, the satirical *Apology*, and a theological work on baptism. Bernard was becoming the literary spokesman for the Cistercians, but this was an isolated path for him to take since, at that time, literary activity was not a feature of the order. It is therefore not surprising that he had intellectual contacts elsewhere. There was the Benedictine William of St Thierry and the regular canon Oger, and he had a long-standing association with the school of St Victor on the outskirts of Paris.[90] He also had links with the cathedral school of Rheims. He had recommended Alberic, who was the

88 "Reverendis patribus et dominis, et amicis carissimis, G. Dei gratia venerabili abbati Sancti Victoris Parisiensis, et universo conventui sancto, frater Bernardus Clarae Vallis vocatus abbatis, salutem et nostras qualescumque orationes. Necesse habemus multa requirere, quia multa requiruntur a nobis: nec amicis possumus parcere, quia ab aliis amicis non parcitur. Dominus Lucensis episcopus, pater et amicus noster, commendavit mihi virum venerabilem P. Lombardum, rogans ut ei parvo tempore, quo moraretur in Francia causa studii, per amicos nostros victui necessaria providerem; quod effeci, quandiu Remis moratus est. Nunc commorantem Parisius vestrae dilectioni commendo, quia de vobis amplius praesumo, rogans ut placeat vobis providere et in cibo per breve tempus, quod facturus est hic usque ad nativitatem beatae Virginis Mariae. Vale." *Ep.* 410, *Sancti Bernardi opera*, ed. Leclercq, Talbot, and Rochais, 8: 391.

89 Matthew Doyle, *Bernard of Clairvaux and the Schools: The Formation of an Intellectual Milieu in the First Half of the Twelfth Century* (Spoleto, 2005), 15–40.

90 Ibid., 47–83.

most famous master at that school, for a bishopric.[91] At this stage, however, Bernard does not appear to have had any contacts with the Parisian cathedral schools, which differed in atmosphere and approach from St Victor.[92] Peter's choice of Rheims and St Victor as places to study suggests that Bernard had recommended them to him and had also told him about the masters who were teaching there. He was certainly a powerful patron to have. Bernard was coming into his own in the 1130s as a man of influence. In the 1120s he had been involved in church politics in France, but it was the papal schism that really turned him into an international figure.

Bernard clearly envisaged that Peter would be staying at St Victor for less than a year. The feast of the the nativity of the Virgin Mary was on 8 September.[93] Recent authorities agree that the letter dates not from 1139, as was once supposed,[94] but from either 1134 or 1136.[95] Those dates leave us with two possible scenarios based on what we know of Bernard's movements at the time. The first is that, in 1133, Peter would have accompanied Bernard to France in the summer or made the journey himself a little later. At some point in the first half of 1134, he went to St Victor. That would place the letter in

91 *Ep.* 13, *Sancti Bernardi opera,* ed. Leclercq, Talbot, and Rochais, 7: 62. Bernard recommended him for the diocese of Châlons.

92 Doyle, *Bernard of Clairvaux and the Schools,* 14–16.

93 Frederick G. Holweck, "The Nativity of the Blessed Virgin Mary, Feast of," in *The Catholic Encyclopedia: An International Work of Reference on the Constitution, Doctrine, Discipline, and History of the Catholic Church,* ed. Charles G. Herbermann (New York, 1907–1914), 10: 712–713.

94 Vacandard, *Vie de Saint Bernard,* 2: 115; de Ghellinck, "La carrière de Pierre Lombard: Quelques précisions chronologiques," 802–804. This date is not consistent with what we know of Peter's career in France. By 1144 he had been a master for some time and was being described as the "famous theologian Lombard" (see chapter two, 40). He would hardly have gained such a reputation if he had arrived in 1139 without being a master.

95 Brady, Prolegomena 1: 8*, and *Sancti Bernardi opera,* ed. Leclercq, Talbot, and Rochais, 8: 391, preferred 1134 or 1136. Piero Zerbi, "I rapporti di S. Bernardo di Chiaravalle con i vescovi e le diocesi d'Italia" in *Vescovi e diocesi in Italia nel medioevo (Sec. IX–XIII)* (Padua, 1961), 219–313, at 305, and Van den Eynde, "Essai chronologique," 52–53, had viewed 1134 as the most probable date, although that was partly because of Van den Eynde's view (which is now in doubt) that Peter's commentaries had been finished by 1142. Gastaldelli, in William of Lucca, *Commentum in tertiam ierarchiam Dionisii que est de divinis nominibus,* xxx–xxxi, viewed 1136 as the safest date because of the certainty that Uberto and Bernard met at the council of Pisa. He restated his point in the commentary that was published in his Italian edition of Bernard's letters and in Winkler's German edition.

1134. The second scenario is that Peter accompanied Bernard to France in November 1135 and began his studies at Rheims. However, upon discovering that Alberic was soon to depart the school for a bishopric, he instead went to Paris in January or February 1136.[96] While the latter scenario does at least offer a reason for Peter's departure from Rheims, the earlier date would allow ample time for him to study theology and gain the title of *magister*.

Uberto of Lucca and Bernard of Clairvaux were the kind of powerful figures whose help Peter would need if he were to move outside of Italy. It was a significant achievement that he managed to interest them in his plans. Sometimes, however, a third figure is brought up in this context, either as a direct patron or as a kind of go-between with the bishop. This is Otto of Lucca, who was bishop from 1138 until 1146.[97] He was not Uberto's immediate successor, since a bishop Guido was in office for a very brief period in between.[98] Before Bernard's letter had been firmly dated in Uberto's episcopate, Otto was sometimes named as the bishop who recommended Peter.[99] This has been occasionally repeated, even in very recent works.[100] There has been an unwillingness to let go of Otto and this is because of a very appealing scenario.

Otto has sometimes been named as the author of the *Summa Sententiarum* ("the Sum of Sentences"), an important work that comprehensively

96 Van den Eynde, "Essai chronologique," 52–53; Brady, Prolegomena 1: 8*–9*.

97 For Otto as bishop, see Domenico Barsocchini, "Dissertazione IX: I Vescovi di Lucca, Saeculo XII: Otto," in *Memorie e documenti per servire all'istoria del Ducato di Lucca*, 5.1: 452–462; Osheim, *An Italian Lordship*, 136–137; and Savigni, *Episcopato e società cittadina a Lucca da Anselmo II a Roberto*, 404.

98 Savigni, *Episcopato e società cittadina a Lucca da Anselmo II a Roberto*, 404. Although no contemporary documents bear Guido's name, a list of Luccan bishops made in 1168 refers to him. His episcopate lasted less than a year between late 1136 and 1137.

99 De Ghellinck, "La carrière de Pierre Lombard: Quelques précisions chronologiques," 794–795.

100 For David Luscombe, *The School of Peter Abelard: The Influence of Abelard's Thought in the Early Scholastic Period* (Cambridge, 1969), 261 n2, it was either one or the other. Richard W. Southern, *Scholastic Humanism and the Unification of Europe II: The Heroic Age* (Oxford, 2001), 138–140, in favouring Otto, cited de Ghellinck and Luscombe. Giulio Silano, "Introduction," in Peter Lombard, *The Sentences* 1 (Toronto, 2007–2010), x, dated the letter incorrectly at 1138–1140. Although he mentioned that Brady and Colish favoured the earlier date, he preferred Otto: "Southern's view that Odo is the more plausible seems elegant."

presents theological material by topic.[101] This was something a number of masters in Paris were doing from the late 1120s, including Hugh of St Victor, Robert of Melun, and others. Peter Lombard himself would make his name with this kind of work, and the *Summa Sententiarum* considerably influenced his own *Sentences.*[102] There has not been widespread agreement on who wrote the *Summa Sententiarum*. It was once assigned to Hugh of St Victor, but it has usually been described as anonymous.[103] The possibility that Otto of Lucca is the author was first raised in the 1920s and 1930s, although this view lost favour after the mid-1930s.[104] Ferruccio Gastaldelli returned to the question in the 1980s.[105] He found five manuscripts of the work where a master Otto is listed as the author. In three of these, master Otto is also the bishop of Lucca.[106] These grounds are quite good but not completely definitive. Gastaldelli does not appear to have evaluated and dated all the manuscripts of the work. Such a task, of course, would only take place as part of preparing a new critical edition of the *Summa*, something that would be very welcome.

Gastaldelli acknowledged that Uberto was the bishop mentioned by Bernard,[107] but he viewed Otto as the driving force. He imagined Otto as a cathedral master in Lucca who introduced Peter Lombard to the bishop, leading to the recommendation from Bernard.[108] Looked at this way, Uberto

101 A good overview of the *Summa* can be found in Luscombe, *The School of Peter Abelard*, 199–213.

102 Brady, Prolegomena 1: 106*, 119*.

103 For an overview of the authorship debate prior to Gastaldelli, see Luscombe, *The School of Peter Abelard*, 198. Luscombe refers to the possibility that it was the work of more than one author and believed that many questions relating to the work could not be solved without a new critical edition.

104 See, especially, Heinrich Weisweiler, "La *Summa Sententiarum*: Source de Pierre Lombard," *RTAM* 6 (1934): 143–183.

105 Ferruccio Gastaldelli, "La *Summa Sententiarum* di Ottone di Lucca: Conclusione di un dibattito secolare," *Salesianum* 42 (1980): 537–546. He also addresses the issue in his introduction to William of Lucca, *Commentum In Tertiam Ierarchiam Dionisii*, xxvii–xl.

106 Gastaldelli, "La *Summa Sententiarum* di Ottone di Lucca: Conclusione di un dibattito secolare," 540–541.

107 Ibid., 543.

108 "Questo vescovo Ottone di Lucca è l'autore della celebre *Summa Sententiarum*, frutto delle sue lezioni di teologia quando, prima dell'episcopato, era *magister*, nella scuola della cattedrale di Lucca. Ed è per seguire le sue lezioni che Pietro Lombardo si recò a Lucca prima di andare a Parigi munito delle raccomandazioni di Bernardo, sollecitato a sua volta dal vescovo Uberto, al quale il maestro Ottone l'aveva pre-

becomes only a go-between: the man in high office who facilitates such meetings of minds, without having much actual interest in what they do. Gastaldelli also speculated that Peter had come to Lucca to hear Otto's lectures.[109]

There are problems with this. The Otto who became bishop is quite an obscure figure. A number of documents throw light on his episcopate but not on his career leading up to it.[110] The *Summa Sententiarum* is usually seen as a Parisian work, in that its author was influenced by developments there, particularly by Hugh of St Victor's *On the Sacraments*.[111] It was also read in Paris in the 1140s. This would mean that the author (or authors) studied in France in the 1120s and 1130s, probably at St Victor. Already, in the late 1120s, Hugh was teaching an early version of the initial chapters of book one of *On the Sacraments*.[112] According to Patrice Sicard, the first book was completed after 1131, while the second book was begun in 1135.[113] Gastaldelli considered

---

sentato come meritevole di completare la formazione teologica presso le celebri scuole parigine." Ferruccio Gastaldelli, "Le tre ultime lettere dell'epistolario di San Bernardo," *Analecta Cisterciensa*, 50 (1994): 251–292, at 277. See also ibid., 280: "È infatti l'azione combinata di Ottone e di Bernardo con la mediazione della lettera di Uberto che conduce Pietro alle scuole di Parigi e gli apre la via al magisterio e all'episcopato."

109 Gastaldelli, "La *Summa Sententiarum* di Ottone di Lucca: Conclusione di un dibattito secolare," 543.

110 Savigni, *Episcopato e società cittadina a Lucca da Anselmo II a Roberto*, 404, remarks that his family background is not known and that he cannot be located within the cathedral chapter. He believes that Otto had probably only recently joined the cathedral clergy. Osheim, *An Italian Lordship*, 130, comments that "nothing is known of his origins," while Barsocchini, "Otto," 452–462, concentrates on the events of his episcopate.

111 Luscombe, *The School of Peter Abelard*, 198–200, 212. For the complex relationship between Hugh of St Victor's *De Sacramentis*, and the *Summa*, see also Odon Lottin, "A propos des sources de la *Summa Sententiarum*," *RTAM* 25 (1958): 42–58, and Roger Baron, "Note sur l'énigmatique *Summa Sententiarum*," Ibid., 26–42.

112 The report of Hugh's teaching by his student Lawrence of Westminster, known as the *Sententiae de Divinitate* has been edited by Ambrosio M. Piazzoni, "Ugo di San Vittore, 'auctor' delle *Sententiae de Divinitate*," *Studi Medievali* 23 (1982): 861–955. A translation appears in *Trinity and Creation: A Selection of the Works of Hugh, Richard and Adam of St Victor*, ed. Boyd T. Coolman and Dale M. Coulter (Turnhout, 2010), 103–178. The work presents an early version of the first three sections of *De Sacramentis*, book one.

113 Patrice Sicard, *Diagrammes médiévaux et exégèse visuelle: Le "Libellus de formatione arche" de Hugues de Saint- Victor* (Turnhout, 1993), 119–138. See especially the table on 138. The earlier *Sententiae de Divinitate* dates from 1127.

that the *Summa* had been completed by 1138 if not earlier.[114] It is possible that the Otto who became bishop in 1138 had returned from Paris to take up the post. However, he would hardly have been able to come back to Lucca, start a school, and teach Peter Lombard before 1135 (the last year Peter could have been in Italy).[115]

One more piece of evidence has been used for the "Otto thesis." This is a later letter to a bishop of Lucca by Bernard of Clairvaux, congratulating him on his elevation.[116] The recipient was either Bishop Otto or Bishop Gregory (1146–1164). Bernard added at the end that the bearer of the letter would explain its real purpose: "The son we have in common (*communis filius*) will deliver the remainder in person, more plainly and more fully."[117] Gastaldelli has identified the *communis filius* as Peter Lombard, the son of his patrons, Bernard and Otto.[118] This is a very problematic supposition. It seems bizarre to suggest that Peter Lombard, who was making his name as a theology master in Paris in the 1140s, would be working as a letter bearer for Bernard of Clairvaux.

All this is not to say that the author of the *Summa* was not Otto. The *Summa* substantially influenced Peter, but he would have encountered it in Paris anyway, during his study years at St Victor. If there was a master Otto from Lucca who had gone to Paris to study theology, then Peter could cer-

114 Gastaldelli, "La *Summa Sententiarum* di Ottone di Lucca: Conclusione di un dibattito secolare," 546. For him, 1138 was the *terminus ad quem* since the work must have been finished in 1138, during the first months of his episcopate.

115 As we have seen, he may have left as early as late 1133.

116 This was not contained in the Leclercq–Rochais edition of the letters, but it is in the Italian and German editions that Gastaldelli contributed to. It is also printed and discussed in Ferruccio Gastaldelli, "Le tre ultime lettere dell'epistolario di San Bernardo," *Analecta Cisterciensia* 50 (1994): 251–292, at 272–274. De Ghellinck also discusses it in "La carrière de Pierre Lombard: Quelques précisions chronologiques," 800–804.

117 "Reliqua vobis communis filius ille plenius et planius viva voce referet." Bernard of Clairvaux, *Ep.* 551, in Gastaldelli, "Le tre ultime lettere dell'epistolario di San Bernardo," 272–274.

118 Ibid., 280: "Resta da spiegare l'importante dettaglio dell'ultima parte dove Bernardo dice di affidare a un *communis filius* alcune cose che non ritiene prudente affidare alla lettera. Questo comune figlio, di Ottone e di Bernardo, puo essere individuato solo in Pietro Lombardo, prima discepolo dell'uno, poi protetto dall'altro. È infatti l'azione combinata di Ottone e di Bernardo con la mediazione della lettera di Uberto che conduce Pietro alle scuole di Parigi e gli apre la via al magisterio e all'episcopato."

tainly have heard of him. But it is wrong to see Otto as a patron or teacher of Peter Lombard. The evidence is not there, and the chronology simply does not work.

Peter Lombard had managed to gain considerable and meaningful support for his plan to study in France. At a time when – as far as we know – he had not circulated any written works, he attracted the attention of a group of people whose influence was considerable. Bernard of Clairvaux, Uberto of Lucca, and others achieved the acceptance of Innocent II, who at one time had fled Rome, as pope. These men were his patrons. Why should they take an interest in Peter? Throughout this chapter, he has perhaps appeared as a passive figure, borne along by men of influence. But he must have had impressive qualities for them to become interested in him, and, in turn, Peter must have been aware of what they could do for him. He may have had a good sense of how to make use of connections. Bernard brought him to France to study for a short time, *parvus tempus*. Had Peter always intended to stay longer? Studying theology seems to have been his main ambition, and this was not something that could be done in a short time. He had relied on patronage from a very young age, and he probably had a certain amount of confidence, or at least hope, that this would continue in France. His later career suggests that being a well-known teacher and author of theological works appealed to him. This did not guarantee a secure position, but, as we will see, both Peter and his students were firm in their belief that being a theologian brought its own rewards. It meant joining an elite group and doing something that few others could. Peter probably could not have imagined, however, when he set out for France with his small library of classical works, that he would end his life as the bishop of Paris.

CHAPTER TWO

Growing Reputation, 1134–1145

Peter's move to France changed his life. His activities there had three broad focuses. First he spent several years as a theology student. This was preliminary to the second activity, that of setting up his own theology school and writing. Concurrently with being a theology master, Peter also had a distinguished career in the church of Paris. He gained entry to the canons of Notre Dame and rose to be archdeacon and finally bishop of the city.

Peter arrived in France in 1133 or 1135, probably in the returning entourage of Bernard of Clairvaux. The journey would have taken several weeks, providing Peter with the opportunity to know Bernard, or, at least, to gain a sense of him. The intellectual interests of the two men were certainly not opposed. Bernard was aware of what was happening in theology. He had connections with the masters at the school of St Victor.[1] This had begun with his friendship with William of Champeaux, who had set up the school.[2] More recently, in 1127, Master Hugh, the leading light of the school, had consulted Bernard when preparing *On the Sacraments*,[3] a theological work that deeply influenced Peter's *Sentences*. Also, a new thoroughness was emerging in

1 Matthew Doyle, *Bernard of Clairvaux and the Schools: The Formation of an Intellectual Milieu in the First Half of the Twelfth Century*, Studi 11 (Spoleto, 2005), 47–81.

2 Ibid., 48–64. For their friendship, see William of Saint Thierry, *Vita Prima Sancti Bernardi* (PL 185: 223–367, at 245–246) and Bernard of Claivaux, *Ep.* 3, *Sancti Bernardi opera*, ed. Jean Leclercq, Charles H. Talbot, and Henri Rochais (Rome, 1957–1977), 7: 23.

3 Doyle, *Bernard of Clairvaux and the Schools*, 70–73. Bernard's response is his letter, *Ep.* 77, *Sancti Bernardi opera*, ed. Leclercq, Talbot and Rochais, 7: 184–200. See also, Hugh Feiss, "Bernardus Scholasticus: The Correspondence of Bernard of Clairvaux and Hugh of Saint Victor on Baptism," in *Bernardus Magister*, ed. John R. Sommerfeldt (Cîteaux, 1992), 360–377. For Bernard's influence on Hugh's work see Jean Châtillon, "L'influence de S. Bernard sur la pensée scolastique au XIIe et au XIIIe siècle," in *Saint Bernard théologien* (Rome, 1953), repr. *D'Isidore de Séville à Saint Thomas d'Aquin* (London, 1985), 268–288, at 276–277.

Bernard's literary personality at this time. On returning to Clairvaux from his second Italian journey, in 1136, he began his great project, the *Sermons on the Song of Songs*. While each of the eighty-six sermons is self-contained, they also form a developing, structured series. A thorough, organizational sense also marks Peter's works. On their journey, Peter would also have noticed the political side of the abbot's connections as they received the hospitality of his friends and as diplomatic activity regarding the schism continued. The man of prayer, devotion, and contemplation would also have impressed Peter.

There is no question that Peter read Bernard's works at some point. The final item on the list of Peter's books is simply called *Bernardinus*, and this was probably some kind of anthology.[4] It may have been a selection of early treatises and sermons that Bernard gave to him. Peter could also have had it made later on. There is a clear Bernardine influence on parts of the *Sentences* and on the sermons, as we will see in the following chapters.

The cathedral school of Rheims was Peter's destination.[5] It was a thriving, healthy, and vibrant intellectual centre. A number of masters taught the arts, and there were also two notable theologians, Alberic of Rheims and Lotulph the Lombard. Lotulph was also from Novara, so Peter may have known of his reputation for some time.[6] Alberic was well known as a master, and there are a number of testimonies to his popularity.[7] Bernard of Clairvaux also knew him. He had recommended him ten years before for the bishopric of Châlons, held at one time by William of Champeaux.[8]

4 Patricia Stirnemann, "Histoire tripartite: Un inventaire des livres de Pierre Lombard, un exemplaire de ses *Sentences* et le destinataire du Psautier de Copenhague," in *Du copiste au collectionneur: Mélanges d'histoire des textes et des bibliothèques en l'honneur d'André Vernet*, ed. Donatella Nebbiai-Dalla Guarda and Jean-François Genest (Turnhout, 1998), 301–318, at 307, points out that "Bernardinus" is usually used of a thirteenth-century anthology of his works compiled by William of Tournai.

5 For the school, see John R. Williams, "The Cathedral School of Reims in the Time of Master Alberic, 1118–1136," *Traditio* 20 (1964): 93–114.

6 Brady, Prolegomena 1: 13*–15*.

7 Williams, "The Cathedral School of Reims," 93–114. These included verses by Hugh of Orléans, discussed in Stephen C. Ferruolo, *The Origins of the University: The Schools of Paris and their Critics, 1100–1215* (Stanford, 1985), 106–107. Referring to the school, Hugh wrote that "Alberic raised her supreme/ graced her with a diadem." Ibid.

8 Bernard of Clairvaux, *Ep.* 13, *Sancti Bernardi opera*, ed. Leclercq, Talbot, and Rochais, 7: 62.

Alberic and Lotulph had studied under Anselm of Laon in the early years of the century,[9] and their theological instruction would have depended closely on his. Peter Lombard later told his student Herbert of Bosham that when he compiled his *Commentary on the Psalms,* his intention was to make Anselm of Laon's glosses clearer in his own mind. He found Anselm's glosses on the Psalms to be too brief.[10] Herbert did not say where Peter started this work, but it is thought to have been at Rheims, where Alberic and Lotulph used Anselm's glosses in their classroom.[11]

It is difficult to discuss the commentary as a work dating from a particular period in Peter's life.[12] What he told Herbert suggests that it originated as a student exercise. Later, a year before he became bishop of Paris, his students asked him to lecture on it, and he began to revise it. He had not completed these revisions when he became bishop.[13] It is also difficult to assess it as an original work. It relies very heavily on the *Commentary on the Psalms* by Gilbert of Poitiers (which itself expands on Anselm of Laon's gloss).[14] The preface is virtually identical, and Peter follows Gilbert in grouping the Psalms into categories and in providing a separate introduction (*accessus*) for each individual psalm.[15]

Although Peter may have started working on the commentary at Rheims, he certainly did not finish it there.[16] Manuscripts of Gilbert's gloss were being

9 Peter Abelard, *Historia calamitatum,* ed. Jacques Monfrin (Paris, 1959), 68–69, 83.

10 "Nam cum hec opera scriberet, nequaquam, sicut ipsomet referente didici, ipsi venit in mentem, quod in scolis publicis legerentur; solum ob id facta, ut antiquioris glossatoris, magistri videlicet Anselmi Laudunensis, brevitatem elucidarent obscuram." Herbert of Bosham, *Praefatio,* in *History of the Vulgate in England from Alcuin to Roger Bacon,* ed. Hans H. Glunz (Cambridge, 1933), 342–346 at 343. See also chapter eight, below, 212–216.

11 Brady, Prolegomena 1: 14*–15*.

12 For the work, see Colish, *Peter Lombard,* 170–188; Brady, Prolegomena 1: 50*–70*; Damien Van den Eynde, "Essai chronologique sur l'oeuvre littéraire de Pierre Lombard," in *Miscellanea Lombardiana* (Novara, 1957), 46–52.

13 Herbert of Bosham, *Praefatio,* ed. Glunz, 343.

14 For Gilbert's gloss, see Theresa Gross-Diaz, *The Psalms Commentary of Gilbert of Poitiers: From 'Lectio Divina' to the Lecture Room* (Leiden, 1996).

15 "Much of Peter's prologue, his comments on the titles, the abbreviated accessus he supplies for each psalm, and his categorization of psalm groups are all influenced by, and often taken verbatim from, Gilbert's psalms commentary." Ibid., 148. See also the summary of Gilbert's prologue on 79–96.

16 Brady, Prolegomena 1: 14*–15*, 53*–55*, comments on the difficulty of assigning sections of the work to specific dates and places.

used in Paris from the 1140s, so it was probably there that Peter incorporated that material.[17] The list of Peter's books contains several "little notebooks compiled on the psalms," which may represent Peter's working notes for the commentary.[18] At this stage the date cannot be narrowed down any further, although that may change, since research is ongoing.[19] We will be examining aspects of this work in more detail in chapter eight in our discussion of Herbert of Bosham. At that time, in the mid-1170s, Peter's commentary had become very popular and had actually supplanted its model. There was also an accepted text. So it is best approached, from that period, as an example of how Peter's students were elaborating on their master's work and making it accessible.

Peter left the Rheims theological school after less than a year. This may have been due to the imminent departure of Master Alberic, who would become archbishop of Bourges in 1136. Peter needed another master to study with if he was to become a theologian. This is where Bernard's letter takes up the story. He asked Gilduin, the abbot of St Victor, to provide meals for Peter "until the feast of the nativity of the blessed Virgin Mary."[20] Bernard had a good reputation at St Victor, not just with the masters at the school but with the community as a whole. In August 1133, soon after Bernard's return from his first visit to Italy, Thomas, the prior of St Victor, was murdered. Stephen of Senlis, the bishop of Paris, had been with Thomas when the two were attacked, and he sought refuge afterwards at Clairvaux. Bernard worked hard to see that the murderers were brought to justice. This is not the place to go

17 See the discussion of the date of Gilbert's gloss in Gross-Diaz, *The Psalms Commentary of Gilbert of Poitiers*, 27–34. Gross-Diaz argues (at 35) that the work was first completed "in its essentials at Laon, prior to Anselm's death in 1117," but there was "a time lag between its conception and its appearance in public."

18 "Quaternulos de sententiis et alios super psalmos compilatos." Stirnemann, "Histoire tripartite: Un inventaire des livres de Pierre Lombard," 302.

19 Patrizia Stoppacci, "Le *Glossae Continuae in Psalmos* di Pietro Lombardo: *Status quaestionis*, studi pregressi e prospettive di ricerca," in *Pietro Lombardo: Atti del XLIII Convegno storico internazionale* (Spoleto, 2007), 289–331, is a recent example. She argues on 329–330 that copies of a version of the commentary appeared in Italy in the early 1150s. Continuing research on the *Glossa Ordinaria* and its relationship to the glosses of Gilbert and Peter is also relevant.

20 Bernard of Clairvaux, *Ep.* 410, *Sancti Bernardi opera*, ed. Leclercq, Talbot, and Rochais, 8: 391.

into the details of these events.[21] The important point is that, from late 1133, Bernard's good relations with St Victor were solidified. He knew he could expect a favour from them.

Peter was supposed to stay in Paris for less than a year, and depart on 8 September (the feast of the nativity of the blessed Virgin Mary). He ended up staying much longer. It seems probable that he studied under Hugh of St Victor and found in him the kind of master he was looking for. We know that Hugh took on external students. One of them, Lawrence of Westminster, even became his official notetaker.[22] It was thus possible to study under him without being a novice of the Victorine order.[23] This does not mean that large groups of students poured out of the old gate of St Victor to hear Hugh lecture. Student numbers in the advanced discipline of theology were small.[24] External theology students would presumably require some kind of letter of introduction, like the one Peter had.

The influence of Hugh's *On the Sacraments* on Peter's *Sentences* is considerable.[25] Hugh was one of the pioneers of a kind of theological instruction that went beyond commentary on set biblical texts and sought instead to provide a coherent body of doctrine.[26] Despite the title, Hugh's work was not

21 For the matter in detail, see Fourrier Bonnard, *Histoire de l'abbaye royale et de l'ordre des chanoines réguliers de St. Victor de Paris* (Paris, 1904–1908), 2: 32–37, and Lindy Grant, *Abbot Suger of St. Denis: Church and State in Early Twelfth Century France* (London, 1998), 132–133.

22 For Lawrence, see F.E. Croydon, "Abbot Lawrence of Westminster and Hugh of St. Victor," *Medieval and Renaissance Studies* 2 (1950): 169–171; Richard W. Southern, *Scholastic Humanism and the Unification of Europe* I: *Foundations* (Oxford, 1995), 170–171; and Doyle, *Bernard of Clairvaux and the Schools*, 77–81. Lawrence's *reportatio* of Hugh's teaching, known as the *Sententiae de Divinitate*, has been edited by Ambrosio M. Piazzoni, "Ugo di San Vittore, 'auctor' delle *Sententiae de Divinitate*," *Studi Medievali* 23 (1982): 861–955. A translation appears in *Trinity and Creation: A Selection of the Works of Hugh, Richard and Adam of St Victor*, ed. Boyd T. Coolman and Dale M. Coulter (Turnhout, 2010), 103–178.

23 Colish, *Peter Lombard*, 18–19, also refers to the example of Clarenbald of Arras.

24 See chapter five, below, 118–119.

25 Brady, Prolegomena 1: 16*; Colish, *Peter Lombard*, 18.

26 For Hugh, see Paul Rorem, *Hugh of Saint Victor* (Oxford, 2009); Franklin T. Harkins, *Reading and the Work of Restoration: History and Scripture in the Theology of Hugh of St Victor* (Toronto, 2009); Dominique Poirel, *Hugues de Saint-*Victor (Paris, 1998); Patrice Sicard, *Hugues de Saint-Victor et son école* (Turnhout, 1991); David Luscombe, *The School of Peter Abelard: The Influence of Abelard's Thought in the Early Scholastic Period* (Cambridge, 1969), 185–197; and Colish, *Peter Lombard*, 57–63.

restricted to a discussion of the sacraments of the church. The guiding principle of the work is that the sacraments offer a remedy to fallen humanity and point the way to salvation.[27] Hugh uses the sacraments as a backbone for a work that discusses topics from creation to the end of the world. Peter was thoroughly conversant with Hugh's opinions, without following them completely.[28] But Hugh seems also to have given him an idea of how to structure theological works in an innovative fashion. Hugh's work is in two books, which deal with what he calls "the work of foundation" and "the work of restoration."[29] Book one examines topics such as the creation, the fall of man, the natural law, and the written law. Book two begins with the coming of Christ, and then describes the church and the sacraments, finishing with the end of the world. This is a structure based around the Bible, but it is also chronological. The technique of using chronology as a secure foundation for a theological work also characterizes Peter Lombard's *Sentences,* as we will see in chapter four.

Hugh was also a Victorine canon living under a rule, whose works are marked by the experience of the contemplative life.[30] This side of St Victor would also have been witnessed by Peter. According to Bernard's letter, Peter was to take his meals there. Meals at St Victor followed a carefully set out etiquette. Hugh provided a detailed description of how the Victorine novices should behave at mealtimes in one of his works, *On the Formation of Novices*[31]:

> At table the custody of discipline is twofold. For there a man ought to keep discipline in his appearance and in his food. And discipline in appearance is divided in three ways: the discipline of keeping silent, the discipline of seeing, and the discipline of containing oneself. ... There is also a threefold observance of discipline applying to food: the observance applies to what is taken, how much is taken, and in what way it is taken. A man observes discipline in the food he takes, so that he does not seek anything too precious or delicate, so that he does not require anything too

27 Rorem, *Hugh of Saint Victor,* 80–81.

28 Rosemann, *Peter Lombard,* 56; Colish, *Peter Lombard,* 18.

29 "Primum est opus conditionis. Secundum est opus restaurationis." Hugh of St Victor, *De Sacramentis Christiane fidei,* ed. Rainer Berndt (Münster, 2008), 31.

30 For example, *De arca Noe* (PL 176: 617–704) and *De modo orandi* (PL 176: 977–988).

31 Hugh of St Victor, *De institutione novitiorum* (PL 176: 948–951).

> rare and unaccustomed, and so that he does not desire anything too closely or carefully prepared. For the first denotes luxury, the second curiosity, and the third superstition.[32]

This period in Peter's life is obscure. Apart from the meals, which Gilduin provided "for a short time," we do not know where he lived or what he lived on. Student accommodation was not lacking in Paris. He probably continued to receive some assistance from Master Hugh and Gilduin. He may also have supported himself through some form of teaching. The list of Peter's books might suggest this, since it shows that he had with him in Paris the texts necessary for elementary and grammar-school instruction.

How many years would Peter have spent studying with Hugh? As we have seen in chapter one, he was not using the title of master when he left Italy. It was by no means easy to become a theology master. It required years of apprenticeship.[33] By the time of the thirteenth-century university statutes, five years studying theology (after studying the arts) was the minimum requirement for teaching it.[34] In the twelfth century, when there were no regulations of that nature, it was probably longer. John of Salisbury studied theology for six years but did not call himself a master or a theologian.[35] Neither did William of Tyre, who studied with Peter Lombard for six years and with Maurice of Sully for one more.[36] Peter Lombard had certainly become one by 1144, when he is described as the "renowned theologian Lombard" in the *Metamorphosis Goliae* fragment.[37]

32 "In mensa est duplex custodia disciplinae. Ibi enim debet homo servare disciplinam in habitu suo, et disciplinam in cibo suo. Disciplinam in habitu, tribus modis, in disciplina tacendi, in disciplina videndi, in disciplina continendi sese. ... Sequitur etiam triplex observatio disciplinae in cibo, observatio in eo quid sumat, observatio in eo quantum sumat, observatio in eo quomodo sumat. Observatio in eo quid sumat, id est ut neque nimis pretiosa et delicata expetat, nec nimis rara et insolita requirat, nec nimis laute et accurate praeparata concupiscat. In primo enim luxus arguitur, in secundo curiositas, in tertio superstitio notatur." Ibid., 949–950.

33 See also chapter five, below, 116–117.

34 Ferruolo, *The Origins of the University*, 306.

35 Ibid., 134.

36 William of Tyre, *Chronicon* 19.12, ed. Robert B.C. Huygens, Hans Eberhard Mayer, and Gerhard Rösch (CCCM 63: 880).

37 Brady, Prolegomena 1: 17*. For these verses, see also Nikolaus M Häring, "Chartres and Paris Revisited," in *Essays in Honour of Anton Charles Pegis*, ed. J. Reginald O'Donnell (Toronto, 1974), 268–329, at 323–324.

Hugh of St Victor died in 1141. It seems reasonable to suggest that Peter started teaching around this time or a little before. To do this, it would have been necessary for him to obtain a licence to teach from Algrin, the chancellor of Notre Dame.[38] Peter's timing happened to be opportune. As well as Hugh, two other prominent masters of theology had departed the scene after dominating it for so long. Abelard had died at Cluny after his condemnation at the council of Sens, and Gilbert became bishop of Poitiers in 1142. Other practising theologians had only recently begun to teach, such as Odo of Soissons and Simon of Poissy, both of whom we will hear more of. From 1142 to 1144, the English theologian Robert Pullen was teaching in Paris. His surviving work, also called the *Sentences*, shows considerable ability, and he could have rivalled Peter Lombard had he stayed in Paris and revised it, but he was made a cardinal in 1144.[39] Robert of Melun was teaching in Paris from the late 1130s, and he wrote his own *Sentences* in the 1150s.[40] Only Adam of the Petit Pont was a senior figure with a group of disciples, the *parvipotani*, but although one theological work is credited to him, he was better known for teaching the arts.[41] All in all, it was a good time for a new theologian to make his mark.

Setting up a school involved attracting students. With the departures of the three giants, Hugh, Abelard, and Gilbert, there were certainly students looking for masters. When Hugh died, some of his students would not have finished their studies. Those who had been externs like Peter could have come to study with him. It was also possible to gain a reputation through public

38 On Algrin, see chapter three, below, 54–56. For the chancellor's role in the granting of teaching licences, see chapter seven, 169.

39 For Robert, see Francis Courtney, *Cardinal Robert Pullen: An English Theologian of the Twelfth Century* (Rome, 1954). For some of the strengths of his *Sentences*, see Smalley, *Becket Conflict*, 39–50. For weaknesses, see Colish, *Peter Lombard*, 70–71.

40 Constant J. Mews, "Between the Schools of Abelard and Saint-Victor in the Mid-Twelfth Century: The Witness of Robert of Melun," in *L'école de Saint-Victor de Paris: Influence et rayonnement du Moyen Âge à l'époque moderne*, ed. Dominique Poirel (Turnhout, 2010), 121–138, at 122–124. For Robert, see also Mary L. Rampolla, "Melun, Robert de," in *Oxford Dictionary of National Biography*, ed. Henry C.G. Matthew and Brian Harrison (Oxford, 2004), 37: 763–764; Colish, *Peter Lombard*, 72–73.

41 For Adam, see Häring, "Chartres and Paris Revisited," 321–322; Raymond Klibansky, "Adam of Balsham," in *Oxford Dictionary of National Biography*, 3: 615–616; and Lorenzo Minio-Paluello, "The *Ars Disserendi* of Adam of Balsham, *Parvipotanus*," *Mediaeval and Renaissance Studies* 3 (1954): 116–169.

debates, known as disputations, between Paris masters. It does seem that Peter gained quite a reputation through word of mouth, since, as we have seen, he was being described as the "renowned theologian Lombard" as early as 1144.[42]

Thanks to Brady, we are fairly sure of what Peter taught in a given year from about 1154,[43] but the 1140s are less certain. A second inventory of his books may help us in this regard. After Peter's death, his theological library was donated to the chapter of Notre Dame. This included, along with his copies of the *Sentences* and Gratian's *Decretum*, glossed books of the entire New Testament and many of the books of the Old Testament.[44] There may be some overlap with the other book list, since that also included the four gospels, the book of the Apocalypse, Ezechiel, and the Pentateuch. In that list, however, they are not described as glossed.[45] It is unfortunate that the glossed books donated to Notre Dame have not survived.[46]

These books unquestionably formed the basis of Peter's teaching. There has been some debate over whether any of them constitute works in the same sense as the commentaries on the Psalms and on the Letters of Paul.[47] There are numerous references in the works of other masters to Peter's positions on biblical texts besides these.[48] The references of Peter Comestor (who studied with Peter) and his school are particularly important. Comestor himself mentions that Peter Lombard taught the Gospel of Luke. Comestor's student Peter the Chanter refers to Peter Lombard's position on a passage in Luke. He had not read this position but had heard it from Comestor.[49] Comestor also

42 Brady, Prolegomena 1: 17*. For these verses, see also Häring, "Chartres and Paris Revisited," 323–324.
43 See chapter four, below, 97, 99, 107.
44 Brady, Prolegomena 1: 19*–20*; Rosemann, *Peter Lombard*, 39–40. The Old Testament books are "the psalter, the five books of Moses [i.e., the Pentateuch: Genesis, Exodus, Leviticus, Numbers, Deuteronomy], the four major prophets [Isaiah, Jeremiah, Ezechiel, Daniel], the twelve minor prophets [Osee, Joel, Amos, Abdias, Jonas, Micheas, Nahum, Habacuc, Sophonias, Aggeus, Zacharias, Malachias], the Canticles, Job, Esther, Tobias, Judith, Wisdom, Ecclesiasticus."
45 Stirnemann, "Histoire tripartite: Un inventaire des livres de Pierre Lombard," 302.
46 Brady, Prolegomena 2: 22*–23*, speculated that the canons may have sold them to pay debts.
47 Colish, *Peter Lombard*, 28–29; Brady, Prolegomena 2: 19*–52*.
48 Brady, Prolegomena 2: 19*–52*.
49 Beryl Smalley, "Some Gospel Commentaries of the Early Twelfth Century," *RTAM* 45 (1978): 147–180, at 153–157; Brady, Prolegomena 2: 20*–21*.

indicated that Peter taught the twelve minor prophets.[50] Brady has assembled further evidence to show that Peter glossed the books of Exodus and Isaiah.[51] The references in Comestor and his school date from a time when Peter's oral teachings were still being reported and were still current in the schools. However, no complete – or even fragmentary – work has survived.[52]

As a teacher of theology, Peter spent much of his time expounding the sacred text, the Bible. His basic classroom materials would be his glossed books. It is one thing to own a copy of a work for teaching purposes, with comments added either in the margins or above the text (glosses). It is quite another to prepare a commentary for a larger readership and have it copied. In the late twelfth century, however, this distinction became blurred, since works credited to some masters were, in fact, notes taken by their students, or *reportationes.*[53] But in the 1140s and 1150s, "the technique of reporting lectures was still in its infancy,"[54] so this did not happen in Peter Lombard's case. There was a continuing tradition in the later Middle Ages that he had glossed most of the Bible, and this led to many spurious attributions. None of these have been accepted as genuine.[55] The same applies to fragments of glosses that have been tentatively attributed to Peter in the past, including a gloss on Isaiah[56] and a different preface to his *Commentary on the Letters of Paul.*[57]

50 Brady, Prolegomena 2: 43*.

51 Although no fragments survive of the gloss on Exodus, Brady has carefully used evidence from Peter's sermons and the *Sentences* to show that he taught the books of Isaiah and Exodus: Prolegomena 2: 35*–38*.

52 The question of whether any further glosses may survive has been revisited by Mark J. Clark in *The Making of the* Historia scholastica, *1150–1200* (Toronto, 2015), 3–4, 55, 257, and in "The Biblical *Gloss,* the Search for the Lombard's Glossed Bible, and the School of Paris," *Mediaeval Studies* 76 (2014): 57–113. This appears to be an exciting new development in Peter Lombard studies.

53 Beryl Smalley, *The Study of the Bible in the Middle Ages,* 3rd ed. (Oxford, 1983), 203–206; Brady, "Peter Manducator," 488.

54 Smalley, "Some Gospel Commentaries of the Early Twelfth Century," 157.

55 Most of these are prefaces, or *accessi,* and are discussed in Brady, Prolegomena 2: 22*–28*.

56 Fragments of a gloss on Isaiah appeared in Beryl Smalley and Georges Lacombe, "The Lombard's Commentary on Isaias and Other Fragments," *New Scholasticism* 5 (1931): 123–162. Brady rejected this attribution in Prolegomena 1: 115*–117*, and Smalley herself agreed in "Some Gospel Commentaries of the Early Twelfth Century," 157. Brady did believe that there was enough evidence from Peter's other works to show that he had glossed Isaiah (see note 51, above).

57 Jean Leclercq, "Les deux rédactions du prologue de Pierre Lombard sur les épîtres

What did Peter's theology courses consist of? If students remained in his school for between six and eight years, then a complete course in the Bible would seem to be plausible. This probably would have commenced with an introduction to studying the scriptures. Something very like that occurs in one of Peter's sermons, in a lengthy and valuable section. Peter was discussing the significance of a text from Samuel: "you shall come to the oak of Thabor, and there you shall meet three men going up to God to Bethel, one carrying three kids, and another three loaves of bread, and another carrying a bottle of wine."[58] Peter took the opportunity of explaining the three loaves of bread to include this extended section on how the scriptures should be studied:

> Bread should be understood as spiritual nourishment, in other words, the erudition of sacred scripture. But note, the text does not say "bread" but three loaves of bread ... for the prevarication of our first parents brought such misery to us that we are not strong enough to take in the truth of the divine mysteries, except in shadows and enigmas, and not without meditation of the yoked mind and application of the spirit. Therefore the three loaves of bread are the three ways of understanding the holy page. The threefold bread is therefore the threefold understanding: tropological (i.e., moral or historical), mystical (i.e., allegorical), and anagogical. The moral sense arranges good character, removing evil things and fostering good things. The allegorical sense makes the eyes of the mind keener so that they may be strong enough to penetrate the hidden mysteries. The anagogical sense pours the mind out beyond itself so that, in a voice of exultation and confession, on the appointed day, it may be seized from the dense thickets as far as the house of God itself.[59]

---

de S. Paul," in *Miscellanea Lombardiana,* 109–112, at 111. Although Leclercq accepted this as genuine, given what has been said about the lack of *reportationes* while Peter was teaching, it is very unlikely. Brady, Prolegomena 1: 74*, believed that it was a fragment of a later gloss dependent on Peter Lombard's.

58 1 Samuel 10:3

59 "In paene refectio spiritualis intelligitur, scilicet sacrae paginae eruditio. Non tamen dicit panes, sed tres tortas panis ... Primordialis enim praevaricatio ac parentalis hanc nobis ingessit miseriam ut veritatem mysteriorum Dei non misi in umbra et in enigmate, nec sine mentis jugi meditatione animique applicatione, capere valeamus. Tres igitur tortae panis tres sunt modi divinam paginam intelligendi. Triplex igitur panis triplex est intellectus: tropologicus, scilicet moralis vel historicus; mysticus,

Peter then moved on to a discussion of the historical, moral, and mystical senses and how they reflect different stages of spiritual progress: "The historical is suitable for those beginning, the moral for those setting out, and the mystical for those going forward."[60]

Peter's courses on the Bible in the 1140s also helped to shape the *Sentences.* Although he wrote it in the mid-1150s, and presented it in his classroom at the same time, some of it had originated in earlier teaching. The sections dealing with the incarnation, in book three, revolve around two key scriptural texts: Romans 1:3, "he was made," and John 1:1, "the word was made flesh." Peter would have discussed these texts in detail in the 1140s. Also, the exposition of Romans 1:3 in the *Sentences* derives from the first version of Peter's *Commentary on the Letters of Paul,* which dates from the late 1140s.[61]

One could take this further. Creation is the subject of book two of the *Sentences.* Distinctions twelve to twenty-four dwell on questions related to the six days of creation and the fall of man. Genesis 1–3 is the starting point and structural framework for these sections.[62] The remainder of book two, which discusses sin, grace, and free will, relates back to the subject of the first fall on numerous occasions. It is therefore safe to assume that Peter first addressed many of the questions in book two during his course on Genesis in the 1140s.

There were other questions in the *Sentences* that Peter would already have dealt with in the classroom. In book one, when explaining the Trinity, he examines the scriptural authority for the three persons.[63] He would certainly have discussed these passages in the context of the Trinity in the classroom. He did the same in his sermons whenever he encountered passages with trini-

---

id est allegoricus, et anagogeticus. Moralis mores componit, exhauriens malos et confovens bonos; allegoricus mentis acuit oculos ut mysteriorum abdita penetrare valeant; anagogeticus mentem super se effundit ut in voce exultationis et confessionis, constituo die, e condensis usque ad domum Dei rapiatur." *Sermo de Trinitate et de pascha partim,* in "Notice sur les sermons attribués à Hildebert de Lavardin," ed. Barthélemy Hauréau, *Notices et extraits des manuscrits de la Bibliothèque nationale* 32 (1888): 107–166, at 122.

60 "Historicus incipientibus, moralis proficientibus, mysticus perficientibus congruit." Ibid. The discussion of this is on 122–123.

61 Brady, Prolegomena 1: 86*–88*. See the further discussion in chapter four, 93–94.

62 *Sententiae* 2, dist. 12–24, ed. Brady 1: 384–450.

63 Ibid., 1, dist. 2, ch. 4–5, ed. Brady, 1: 63–68.

tarian potential.[64] But the structure of the *Sentences* allowed him to bring together these observations in a more coherent framework. The first book of the *Sentences* does not depend on any one book of the Bible for its structure.

Did Peter's students learn anything besides the course on the Bible in the 1140s? We will see in part two that few of his documented students became theology teachers themselves. Some attained high office in the church.[65] Others became advisers to senior church figures. Peter would certainly have prepared them well for the interpretation of the Bible, but, given their future careers, one would imagine a complete course in theology would also have to include the sacraments. It is therefore plausible to suggest that, in the 1140s, Peter gave a course in some of the material addressed in book four of the *Sentences*. That would be consistent with his training under Hugh of St Victor, who presented theological material by topic in his classroom as far back as the 1120s.[66]

The beginning of Peter Lombard's teaching career coincided with the departure from the schools of several older masters, as we have seen. This changing of the guard in theology was characteristic of the 1140s in Paris. Similar changes were happening in other spheres, with new men taking the place of those who had dominated the century thus far. Part of the reason for this was simply a generational shift. Also, the succession of Louis VII in 1137 had brought about changes. Some, like former royal chancellor Stephen de Garlande, found themselves out of favour.[67] The king flexed his muscles by refusing the results of a number of episcopal elections and by preventing others from taking place. He also took on his powerful neighbour, Theobald, count of Champagne. Theobald had granted refuge to the archbishop of Bourges,

64 See chapter six, below, 157–158.

65 Giulio Silano, "Introduction," in Peter Lombard, *The Sentences* 2 (Toronto, 2007–2010), vii, has also explained this well.

66 According to Patrice Sicard, Hugh's *Sententiae de Divinitate*, the report of his lectures by Lawrence of Westminster, dates from 1127: *Diagrammes médiévaux et exégèse visuelle: Le Libellus de formatione arche de Hugues de Saint- Victor* (Turnhout, 1993), 138. On the relationship between this work and parts of the *De Sacramentis*, see *Trinity and Creation*, ed. Coolman and Coulter, 105, and Rorem, *Hugh of St Victor*, 59–62.

67 For the subject of old and new men among the king's advisers, see Grant, *Abbot Suger of St. Denis*, 142–145; Eric Bournazel, *Le gouvernement capétien au XIIe siècle, 1108–1180* (Paris, 1975), 18–25; and Jim Bradbury, *The Capetians: Kings of France, 987–1328* (London, 2007), 163–164.

Peter de la Châtre, whose election Louis would not recognize. This became the pretext for war. As the year 1143 drew to a close, Louis was excommunicated and waging a war with Champagne.[68]

The church of Paris also saw changes in this period. These require some consideration, since they provide the background to Peter Lombard's entry into the canons of Notre Dame. He had achieved this by 1145.[69] Notre Dame, the cathedral of Paris, was administered by the canons. They were the clerical elite of the city. They also assisted the bishop in administering the diocese of Paris as a whole. They elected the bishop of Paris, although the king could veto that choice until 1145.[70] Even after that, no bishop would be appointed if the king objected to him. As we will see in the next chapter, the canons were usually members of elite families, often the same families who held royal offices. They held substantial property, and some combined their canonries with positions elsewhere. This makes Peter's entry into their number all the more interesting. He was one of the exceptions.

Predictably, for a body with that kind of influence, there was also infighting. Divisions came to a head in 1108 when one of the archdeacons, William of Champeaux, resigned and founded a religious community at St Victor. His rivalry with one of the other archdeacons, Stephen de Garlande, played a significant role in his decision to depart.[71] There were more upheavals when Stephen of Senlis became bishop, in 1123, and attempted to curb the power of the canons.[72] He objected to their property holdings and also to Stephen de Garlande, partly because the two were members of rival families.[73] The quarrel between bishop and chapter was resolved in 1127, thanks to the arbi-

68 For these events, see Marcel Pacaut, *Louis VII et son royaume* (Paris, 1964), 39–46; Theodore Evergates, "Louis VII and the Counts of Champagne," in *The Second Crusade and the Cistercians*, ed. Michael Gervers (New York, 1992), 109–117; and Grant, *Abbot Suger of St. Denis*, 144–152. For the crisis over episcopal election, see Marcel Pacaut, *Louis VII et les élections épiscopales dans le royaume de France* (Paris, 1957), 93–103.

69 Ignatius C. Brady, "Peter Lombard: Canon of Notre Dame," *RTAM* 32 (1965): 277–295, at 288.

70 Pacaut, *Louis VII et les élections épiscopales*, 100.

71 Robert Henri Bautier, "Paris au temps d'Abélard," in *Abélard en son temps*, ed. Jean Jolivet (Paris, 1981), 21–77, at 53–55.

72 Bautier, "Paris au temps d'Abélard," 65–69; Grant, *Abbot Suger of St. Denis*, 124–125.

73 Bournazel, *Le gouvernement capétien au XIIe Siécle*, 31, 40.

tration of Suger of St Denis and Gilduin of St Victor. The canons were able to keep their property, but the bishop was given control of the cathedral school.[74]

The relationship between the chapter and the cathedral school, by the time of Peter Lombard, is difficult to define. For the beginning of the twelfth century, it is much easier. At that time, some of the canons were also masters and their students lived in the cloister of the cathedral.[75] This was why William of Champeaux had set up a community at St Victor, rather than simply retiring to an existing religious house. When he left, he brought his students with him, and he needed to find somewhere for them to live. After 1127, the students of Notre Dame no longer lived in the cloisters, and the canons were also no longer allowed to let out their houses to them.[76] The schools were placed under the direction of the cathedral chancellor, appointed by the bishop, who granted masters their licence to teach. The chancellor usually came from the ranks of the canons and had to be a master himself. The office of chancellor thus allowed the church of Paris to retain some control over the growing numbers of masters and students, which the old system could no longer accommodate.[77]

After Stephen of Senlis died, on 6 June 1142, there was a period when the see of Paris was vacant.[78] Louis VII apparently forbade the canons to elect a successor. Bernard of Clairvaux described the situation in a letter: "Episcopal elections are forbidden; and whenever the clergy dare to hold one, their chosen candidate is prevented from fulfilling the duties of his office. The church of Paris is sorrowful because she is deprived of her pastor, and no one

74 Bautier, "Paris au temps d'Abélard," 67; *Cartulaire de l'église Notre-Dame de Paris*, ed. Benjamin Guérard (Paris, 1850), 1: 338–339.

75 Astrik L. Gabriel, "The Cathedral Schools of Notre-Dame and the Beginning of the University of Paris," in *Garlandia: Studies in the History of the Medieval University*, ed. Astrik L. Gabriel (Notre Dame, 1969), 39–64, at 41–42.

76 Ibid., 42.

77 The chancellor subsumed the earlier office of *magister scolarum*, which one of the canons, Galo, held: Bautier, "Paris au temps d'Abélard," 66–67. For the chancellor, see Ferruolo, *The Origins of the University*, 189–192, and (for the later development of the office) Gaines Post, "Alexander III, the *Licentia docendi* and the Rise of the Universities," in *Anniversary Essays in Mediaeval History by Students of Charles Homer Haskins*, ed. Charles H. Taylor and John L. LaMonte (Boston, 1929), 255–277. See also chapter four, below, on Peter Comestor's chancellorship, 169.

78 Pacaut, *Louis VII et les élections épiscopales*, 99–100.

dares to utter so much as a whisper about finding another."[79] Bernard was against the king's interference in episcopal elections, and he was also a close ally of Count Theobald of Champagne. Another problem, however, was that the canons themselves were divided on the issue of an election. Their archbishop (Paris did not become an archbishopric until 1622), Hugh of Sens, wrote to them, first sympathizing with them on the death of their bishop, but then warning them to stay away from discord: "I am much troubled about you, because frequently, at such times, envy can creep in, and through envy, discord, and through discord, division, and through division, the breakdown of unity, and then, the face of opposition, the tongues of dissonance, the loss of possessions, and the laughter and mockery that come with rivalry and envy. But allow God to turn this from you, my brothers. Let the fullness of the Holy Spirit descend upon you, let him unite your spirits, let him remove all divisions."[80]

The eventual appointment in 1144 of Theobald, the prior of the Cluniac house of St Martin des Champs, also indicates that the canons were fiercely divided. Unable to agree on one of their own number, they chose an outsider as a compromise candidate.[81] There is very little literature on Theobald. In comparison with Stephen of Senlis, his was a moderate episcopate. It was also not noted for the kind of radical programs that characterized Maurice of Sully's tenure. On 12 March 1144, Louis's excommunication was lifted, and the various episcopal disputes were resolved, following negotiations with the new pope, Celestine, a figure more amenable to compromise than Innocent II had been.[82]

79 Bernard of Clairvaux, *Ep.* 224, *Sancti Bernardi opera,* ed. Leclercq, Talbot and Rochais, 7: 91, trans. by Bruno Scott James in *The Letters of St Bernard of Clairvaux* (London, 1953), 369. Bernard also complains about the situation in Paris in *Ep.* 221 and 222.

80 "Circa vos enim non mediocriter sollicitus existo, quia frequenter in talibus subrepit invidia, per invidiam discordia, per discordiam divisio, per divisionem unitatis confusio. Tunc adversae facies, tunc dissonae linguae, thesaurorum diminutio, et invidiarum et aemulorum cachinnus et irrisio. Deus hoc avertat a vobis fratres; Spiritus sancti plenitudo descendat super vos, spiritusque vestros uniat, divisiones removeat." Hugh of Toucy, archbishop of Sens, *Epistola ad canonicos Parisiensis ecclesiae, RHF* 15: 711. Hugh of Toucy had only recently been elected himself, in 1142, replacing Henry Sanglier. See Pacaut, *Louis VII et les élections épiscopales,* 48, 140.

81 Brady, "Peter Lombard: Canon of Notre Dame," 280. Pacaut, *Louis VII et les élections épiscopales,* 151. His first document as bishop, from 1144, is *Cartulaire général de Paris,* ed. de Lasteyrie (Paris, 1887), no. 313, 292–293.

82 Grant, *Abbot Suger of St. Denis,* 152.

The settlement package probably included both the election of Theobald and the agreement of Louis to relinquish his veto over the election of the bishop of Paris. He did this in the following year. The elder statesmen Suger of St Denis, Joscelin of Soissons, and Bernard of Clairvaux had been central to the negotiations. Later that year, in October, amid much ceremony, a peace treaty between Count Theobald and Louis was signed, and a close alliance developed.[83]

Peter Lombard became a canon at around the same time. Brady has successfully identified a *Magister Petrus*, who appears among the canons of Notre Dame from 1145 to 1159, with Peter Lombard. He rises from being a cleric in minor orders in 1145 to archdeacon in the mid-1150s. He is replaced as archdeacon at the time when Peter Lombard becomes bishop of Paris.[84] Like Bishop Theobald, he was an outsider coming into a tight circle. This may suggest that, after the years of infighting, there was a recognition among some that new men, without ties to the old divisions, should be brought in. Peter could have gained his canonry through Bernard of Clairvaux, whose position, after the settlements of 1144, was stronger than ever. Bernard certainly had some influence at Paris. In 1142 he had helped Robert Pullen to set himself up as a theology master at Notre Dame.[85] Robert is found witnessing a document along with some canons in 1144, the year he was appointed cardinal.[86] There is no indication that he was also a canon,[87] although it should not be entirely ruled out. Gilduin, abbot of St Victor, a senior figure in the diocese of Paris,[88] could also have spoken up for Peter Lombard.

83 Ibid.

84 Brady, "Peter Lombard: Canon of Notre Dame," 278–288. He is also (ibid., 288) distinguished from the other Peter in the canons, Peter de Monciaco. Documents which list the names of the canons of Paris in this period can be found principally in *Cartulaire*, ed. de Lasteyrie, 280–361, which has the advantage of chronological order, and *Cartulaire de l'église Notre-Dame de Paris*, ed. Guérard. For 1160 on, it is also important to consult *Archives de l'Hôtel-Dieu de Paris*, ed. Léon Brièle (Paris, 1894), and Mortet, "Maurice de Sully," 285–314. Documents where a full quorum of canons signed are usually prefaced by phraseology like "the names of the canons of Paris are here included."

85 Bernard of Clairvaux, *Ep.* 205, *Sancti Bernardi opera*, ed. Leclercq, Talbot, and Rochais, 8: 64.

86 *Cartulaire*, ed. de Lasteyrie, no. 313, pp. 292–293.

87 Brady, "Peter Lombard: Canon of Notre Dame," 290.

88 For Gilduin's influence, see Rolf Grosse, "Entre cour et cloître: Saint-Victor et les Capétiens au XIIe siècle," in *L'école de Saint-Victor de Paris: Influence et rayonnement du Moyen Âge à l'époque moderne*, ed. Dominique Poirel, 79–100, at 91–94, and Bonnard, *Histoire de l'abbaye royale et de l'ordre des chanoines réguliers de St. Victor de Paris*, 1: 19–20.

There were a number of masters at Notre Dame who would have known Peter's reputation and might have favoured his entry. They included Ivo of Chartres, Master Bernard, and Master Walter.[89] Interestingly, Peter's entry coincided with a significant rise in the number of masters in the chapter. In 1142, there were four: Ivo, Bernard, Walter, and Albert.[90] By 1147, the number had risen to seven.[91] Albert had died, while Ivo, Bernard, and Walter had been joined by Peter Lombard, Odo of Soissons, Simon of Poissy, and Hugh of Champfleury. What is more, three of the four new men – Peter, Simon, and Odo – taught theology.[92] These changes in the chapter reflect the growth of Paris as a scholastic centre and may also show that Peter's entry was part of a wider policy of promoting theologians. Although all the clerics in the cathedral required an education, positions like chancellor, archdeacon, and lector would be significantly enhanced if held by men from the theology schools.[93]

This does not mean there was a takeover by the *magistri*. There were plenty of masters teaching in Paris who did not become canons of the cathedral, like Manerius the rhetorician, Peter Helias, or Robert of Melun. Teaching theology did not guarantee a clerical position. Also, the majority of the canons were not masters. At this high point, the masters numbered about one-third of the canons.

Whether masters or not, they were now all Peter's colleagues. He had arrived in France dependent on patronage ten years before. In the interim, he had set up a school and gained a reputation as a brilliant theology master. Now, in his mid-forties, after two decades of eking out a living through patronage and teaching, he had a position of security. He was a canon of Notre Dame Cathedral. His greatest achievements, however, still lay ahead.

89 On Ivo and Bernard, see chapter three, below, 73–75. Little is known of Master Walter, who appears from 1142: Häring, "Chartres and Paris Revisited," 327. He is *Magister Galterus* in *Cartulaire*, ed. de Lasteyrie, no. 291, pp. 280–281, and continues to appear as a master and priest (distinct from the Walter who is chaplain to the bishop from 1160–1176) until at least 1180.

90 *Cartulaire*, ed. de Lasteyrie, no. 291, pp. 280–281.

91 Ibid., no. 319, p. 296, no. 327, p. 302. If we can identify a subdeacon Maurice with Maurice of Sully, and a *puer* called Hilduin with Hilduin of St Denis, then we can say that two more canons of this period would later become theology teachers. Hilduin is a *puer* in ibid., no. 319, p. 296. Maurice appears in a document fully edited by Brady, "Peter Lombard: Canon of Notre Dame," 285, no. 10.

92 For more on Simon, Odo, and Hugh, see chapter three, below.

93 See the discussion of these positions in chapter three and four, below.

CHAPTER THREE

Peter's Colleagues: The Canons of Notre Dame, 1145–1160

The canons of Notre Dame were Peter's colleagues for fifteen years. They were part of his social environment, and he saw them on a daily basis. Some of them were masters of theology as he was, while others taught the arts. But the majority (roughly two-thirds) were not masters at all. This should not remove them from our attention. It would be a mistake to refer only to fellow masters in discussing Peter's milieu. The canons of Notre Dame performed various, specified roles within the cathedral and within the diocese. Any matters that concerned the canons as a body also concerned Peter. It is important to take a closer look at them.

The main function of the canons was to conduct the religious services of the cathedral.[1] The different offices they held also involved managing different aspects of cathedral business. The canons had a wider administrative role within the diocese where they assisted the bishop.[2] The cathedral chapter comprised at least eighteen canons at any one time. In the documents where they appear as witnesses, there is always a dean, a chancellor, a precantor, and three archdeacons.[3] The same people hold these positions until they are

1 Jean Gaudemet, "Les institutions ecclésiastiques en France du milieu du XIIe siècle au début du XIVe siècle," in *Histoire des institutions Françaises au moyen âge III: Institutions ecclésiastiques*, ed. Robert Fawtier and Ferdinand Lot (Paris, 1962), 143–335, at 190.

2 Gaudemet, "Les institutions ecclésiastiques en France du milieu du XIIe siècle au début du XIVe siècle," 191.

3 *Cartulaire*, ed. de Lasteyrie, 280–361. Complete lists of names occur in documents relating to Notre Dame itself. Selected names, particularly of the archdeacons, will sometimes occur in other documents. For the main collections, see chapter two, above, note 84. The account of the cathedral dignitaries in Robert Gane and Claudine Billot, *Le chapitre de Notre-Dame de Paris au XIVe siècle: Étude sociale d'un groupe canonial* (Saint-Etienne, 1999), 29–41, is also worth reading, despite its later focus. The same is true of a recent article on the canons in the mid–thirteenth century, Pascal Montaubin, "Les chanoines de Notre-Dame de Paris à la mort de l'évêque Guillaume d'Auvergne (1249)," in *Notre-Dame de Paris 1163–2013*, ed. Cédric Giraud (Turnhout, 2013), 195–216.

replaced. The documents show some variation and overlap when it comes to the other offices.[4] There will usually be three priests (one of whom doubles as succentor), three deacons, three subdeacons, and three clerics in minor orders known as *pueri.*[5] There could be more, however. In one document, the priests, deacons, subdeacons, and *pueri* number four each.[6] In another, five deacons sign, and four subdeacons.[7] So there could be as many as twenty-two canons at a given time.[8] It is worth remembering that canons could often be absent from Paris due to commitments elsewhere (some held canonries in other churches) or illness.

When Peter joined the canons in 1145 as a *puer*, there were still some veterans of former disputes around. Stephen de Garlande, well into his eighties, was still archdeacon, a post which, remarkably, he had held since 1097.[9] He was also still dean of the abbey of St Geneviève, the house of secular canons and school that he had set up with Abelard.[10] His power was not what it had been during the reign of Louis VI, when he had been royal chancellor and seneschal (head of the king's armies).[11] He must have been a towering fig-

4 For example, the deacons from 1145 to 1147 are Simon of Poissy, Peter de Monciaco, Goslin, and Herluin. In 1145, Simon, Herluin, and Goslin sign: *Cartulaire,* ed. de Lasteyrie, no. 319, p. 296. In 1146 and 1147, Peter, Herluin, and Goslin sign: ibid., no. 298, p. 301, no. 321, p. 325. In 1152, Peter, Simon, and Herluin all sign, together with two other deacons: *Cartulaire de l'église Notre-Dame de Paris,* ed. Benjamin Guérard (Paris, 1850), 1: no. 22, pp. 388–389.

5 For the meaning of *puer* as a cleric in minor orders, see Charles du Fresne du Cange, *Glossarium mediae et infimae Latinitatis,* ed. Léopold Favre (Niort, 1883–1887), 6: 558b, and the discussion in chapter four, below, 82–83. The roles of subdeacon, deacon, and archdeacon will also be examined in more detail in chapter four because Peter Lombard held those positions himself.

6 *Cartulaire,* ed. de Lasteyrie, no. 325, p. 301.

7 *Cartulaire de l'église Notre-Dame de Paris,* ed. Guérard, 1: no. 22, p. 388–389.

8 For the numbers, see also Robert Henri Bautier, "Paris au temps d'Abélard," in *Abélard en son temps,* ed. Jean Jolivet (Paris, 1981), 21–77, at 30, who points out that, between them, they owned at most fifty houses. Craig M. Wright, *Music and Ceremony at Notre Dame of Paris, 500–1500* (Cambridge, 1989), 18–19, refers to 51 canons, but it is not clear what period he means.

9 His presence as archdeacon can be traced through *Cartulaire,* ed. de Lasteyrie, no. 119, p. 144 until no. 327, p. 302.

10 Bautier, "Paris au temps d'Abélard," 63.

11 Ibid., 68–69. Stephen became seneschal, head of the king's armies, when his brothers who had held the post died. This caused Bernard of Clairvaux to describe him as a "monster." After Stephen's death, the power of the Garlande family was in evidence at the ecclesiastical level through his nephew, Manassès, who was bishop of

ure around Notre Dame. By 1147 he had died, as had two other veterans, the subdeacons Andrew and Anselm, who had been canons since 1119.[12] This meant that most of the canons in Peter Lombard's time were new men.

Algrin d'Étampes, the chancellor, was the most senior canon for much of Peter Lombard's time in the chapter.[13] He had first signed a document as chancellor in 1124.[14] We noted in the previous chapter that supervision of the schools had been added to the chancellor's duties in 1127.[15] Algrin was also in charge of preparing and sealing the acts of the cathedral and its dependant churches.[16] He was the only person with access to the cathedral's seal.[17] The documents of the cathedral always state that they were written in the chancellor's hand.[18] He would have had a notarial staff to help him in these duties. He was also the cathedral librarian and saw to the conservation of its books.[19] Given these responsibilities, it is not surprising that all the twelfth-century chancellors after Algrin were noted masters: Odo of Soissons, Peter

---

Orléans from 1146. No members of the family were in the chapter of Paris, however. See François-Alexandre Aubert de La Chesnaye-Desbois, *Dictionnaire de la noblesse* (Paris, 1770–1786), 7: 102–103.

12 Andrew and Anselm were *pueri* in 1117, *Cartulaire*, ed. de Lasteyrie, no. 182, p. 203–204. They make their last appearance, as subdeacons, in 1146, ibid., no. 321, p. 298.

13 For Algrin, see Gunnar Teske, *Die Briefsammlungen des 12. Jahrhunderts in St. Viktor, Paris: Entstehung, Überlieferung und Bedeutung für die Geschichte der Abtei* (Bonn, 1993), 182–185; Achille Luchaire, *Remarques sur la succession des grands officiers de la couronne qui ont souscrit les diplomes de Louis VI et de Louis VII (1108–1180)* (Paris, 1881), 33–34; and Lindy Grant, *Abbot Suger of St. Denis: Church and State in Early Twelfth Century France* (London, 1998), 101, 148.

14 *Cartulaire*, ed. de Lasteyrie, no. 203, p. 222–223. Prior to that he had been a canon of Étampes, which is how he appears in 1119, in a document of Louis VI, ibid., no. 185, p. 209. He was involved in the dispute with bishop Stephen of Senlis over control of the chapter. See Bautier, "Paris au temps d'Abélard," 66–67, and Stephen of Senlis, *Epistola ad Henricum Senonensem archiepiscopum*, *RHF* 15: 329–330.

15 For the chancellor, see Stephen C. Ferruolo, *The Origins of the University: The Schools of Paris and their Critics, 1100–1215* (Stanford, 1985), 189–192, and (for the later development of the office), Gaines Post, "Alexander III, the *Licentia docendi* and the Rise of the Universities," in *Anniversary Essays in Mediaeval History by Students of Charles Homer Haskins*, ed. Charles H. Taylor, John L. LaMonte (Boston, 1929), 235–278.

16 Bernard Plongeron et al., *Le diocese de Paris*. Volume 1: *Des origines à la révolution*, Histoire des diocèses de France 20 (Paris, 1987), 106.

17 Gane and Billot, *Le chapitre de Notre-Dame de Paris au XIVe siècle*, 39.

18 The documents usually end with "data per manum Alrgini cancellarii."

19 Plongeron et al., *Le diocese de Paris*, 106.

Comestor, Hilduin of St Denis, and Peter of Poitiers.[20] Algrin may well have been a master himself.

Algrin also had responsibilities and interests beyond the chapter. He was a canon at St Martin d'Étampes, where he seems to have first encountered Stephen de Garlande, who also held a canonry there. They both travelled to the papal curia in 1119 to argue for the rights of their fellow secular canons.[21] Algrin was a close ally of Stephen in the disputes of the 1120s and 1130s.[22] He became an archdeacon of the diocese of Orléans in 1124, and he held this position until his death.[23] He was also important in the Capetian court. With Stephen's backing, his influence had grown in the reign of Louis VI, when he had served as a notary and as vice-chancellor.[24] Just before the king's death, Algrin had been appointed royal chancellor.[25] Along with drafting and sealing royal documents, the chancellor's importance in government was considerable, particularly in the areas of justice and foreign diplomacy.[26]

We saw in the previous chapter that the accession of Louis VII brought about changes to the circle of royal advisers. Initially, Algrin kept his position, but by 1140, he had been replaced by Cadurc, one of the new men at court.[27] Algrin did not take the dismissal well. It is difficult to say exactly what happened, but Algrin seems to have been part of some sort of armed action, along with the king's brothers, Henry and Robert.[28] The two were reconciled following the mediation of a host of powerful figures, including Suger, Bernard of Clairvaux, Count Ralph of Vermandois, and several bishops and abbots.[29]

20 Odo of Soissons is discussed later in this chapter. For Peter Comestor's chancellorship, see chapter seven, below, 169.

21 Teske, *Die Briefsammlungen des 12. Jahrhunderts in St. Viktor, Paris*, 183; Grant, *Abbot Suger of St. Denis*, 100–101.

22 Grant, *Abbot Suger of St. Denis*, 110, 125.

23 Teske, *Die Briefsammlungen des 12. Jahrhunderts in St. Viktor, Paris*, 182.

24 Luchaire, *Remarques sur la succession des grands officiers de la couronne*, 33–34; Grant, *Abbot Suger of St. Denis*, 101.

25 Grant, *Abbot Suger of St. Denis*, 129.

26 Achille Luchaire, *Histoire des institutions monarchiques de la France sous les premiers Capétiens (987–1180)* (Paris, 1883), 1: 186–187.

27 For the dismissal, see Teske, *Die Briefsammlungen des 12. Jahrhunderts in St. Viktor, Paris*, 184–185; Luchaire, *Remarques sur la succession des grands officiers de la couronne*, 33–34; Grant, *Abbot Suger of St. Denis*, 148; and Marcel Pacaut, *Louis VII et son royaume* (Paris, 1964), 41.

28 Teske, *Die Briefsammlungen des 12. Jahrhunderts in St. Viktor, Paris*, 184; Luchaire, *Remarques sur la succession des grands officiers de la couronne*, 33–34.

29 *RHF* 16: 6–7.

The agreement refers to Algrin as archdeacon of Orléans, and the king promises peace not only with him but also with all those with him, both clerical and lay, and his property.[30] Nevertheless, Algrin did not return to his former position, and the transformation of the court was now complete: "the 'old counsellors' were no longer in control."[31] Algrin would remain, however, as chancellor of Notre Dame until 1156.

Two new men in the chapter who certainly made an impression were Henry and Philip of France, the younger brothers of Louis VII. This was quite a new departure for the canons. Members of the royal family had not been seen in the chapter in anyone's living memory.[32] Both were in their early to mid-twenties.[33] Henry appears as subdeacon in 1145, the same year that Peter Lombard became a canon.[34] The following year he relinquished his canonry, along with other clerical offices, to enter Clairvaux as a monk. A typically embellished version of the occasion appears in the *Life of St Bernard,* in one of the books written by Geoffrey of Auxerre.[35] Henry's letters reveal a noviciate that, one cannot help but feel, would not be the norm for other young Cistercians.[36] Within a year of entering Clairvaux, he left

30 "Praedictus siquidem dominus Rex Francorum bonam et plenam et firmam pacem de se et de omnibus hominibus suis et de Henrico et de Roberto fratribus suis specialiter praedicto Algrino et omnibus rebus et hominibus suis tam clericis quam laicis composuit et pacem illam perpetuo se observaturum et quod ab universis hominibus suis et a praedictis fratribus suis observaretur se facturum in manu praedictorum religiosorum promisit et firmavit." *Pactio inter Ludovicum Francorum Regem et Algrinum Aurelianensem archidiaconum, RHF* 16: 7.

31 Grant, *Abbot Suger of St. Denis,* 148.

32 None of the brothers of Louis VI were clerics.

33 Louis VII (b. 1120) was the second born son of Louis le Gros, after Philip, who died. Henry was born after that. See the family tree in Yves Sassier, *Louis VII* (Paris, 1991).

34 *Cartulaire,* ed. de Lasteyrie, no. 319, p. 296, "Henricus, frater regis, subdiaconus."

35 *Vita Prima Sancti Bernardi* 4 (PL 185: 330). It was written while Henry was bishop of Beauvais ("Henricum quoque germanum regis Francorum, qui Belvacensem hodie cathedram ornat"). See also Elphège Vacandard, *Vie de Saint Bernard,* 3rd ed. (Paris, 1902), 2: 390–392. Events in the *Vita Prima* must never be assumed to have taken place exactly as described.

36 The majority of Henry's letters were printed in *RHF* 16: 171–200. For his letter collection, including a discussion of the manuscript evidence, see Ludwig Falkenstein, "Alexandre III et Henri de France: Conformités et conflits," in *L'Église de France et la papauté (Xe–XIIe siècle): Actes du XXVIe colloque historique Franco-Allemand,* ed. Rolf Grosse (Bonn, 1993), 103–176, at 104.

due to an unspecified illness and rested at Rheims.[37] Apparently, however, the "illness" did not prevent him from riding away from Clairvaux on his own horse.[38]

Responsibilities caught up with Henry later on. He was appointed bishop of Beauvais in 1150. His initial reaction was to write to Suger of St Denis and Peter the Venerable asking that someone else be given the job.[39] Henry's tenure as bishop started disastrously when he faced a revolt from the local aristocracy.[40] Louis threatened force against him, and the two were not reconciled until the following year.[41] Even after the return to relative normality, he faced continual criticism that he was not spending enough time in his diocese.[42] The satirical poet Hugh Primas lampooned him in verse.[43] Henry also faced similar criticisms when he was archbishop of Rheims.[44] Ludwig Falkenstein, an authority on Henry's episcopate, concluded that he lacked three things in particular: a solid intellectual formation, experience, and good counsel.[45] Despite his poor record as a diocesan administrator, at the wider political level Henry developed into a key statesman. He had a close association with the new pope, Alexander III, whose full recognition he helped secure during the schism.[46] He became a regular confidant both of the pope and of his brother Louis VII, and his role as a go-between was indispensable.

37 Henry of France, archbishop of Rheims, *Ep.* 4, *RHF* 16: 172–174, in which one of the Clairvaux monks, Nicholas, writes to Henry, pleading with him to return.

38 "Cum enim equum ascenderes ... ." Ibid., 172.

39 Suger, Abbot of St Denis, *Ep.* 93, *RHF* 15: 518. Also, Peter the Venerable, *Ep.* 146, *The Letters of Peter the Venerable*, ed. Giles Constable (Cambridge, MA, 1967), 1: 362. See also, *Ep.* 145, where Bernard of Clairvaux and Peter the Venerable agree that Henry should be bishop.

40 Grant, *Abbot Suger of St. Denis*, 282–283.

41 Ibid.

42 For a full account of Henry's record as an administrator, see Falkenstein, "Alexandre III et Henri de France: Conformités et conflits," 103–176.

43 Christopher J. McDonough, "Hugh Primas and the Bishop of Beauvais," *Mediaeval Studies* 45 (1983): 399–409.

44 See Henry of France, *Ep.* 84, *RHF* 16: 184, where Peter, abbot of St Remigius writes of the disastrous consequences of Henry being away.

45 Falkenstein, "Alexandre III et Henri de France: Conformités et conflits," 170–171.

46 For their relationship, see Marcel Pacaut, *Alexandre III: Étude sur la conception du pouvoir pontifical dans sa pensée et son oeuvre* (Paris, 1956), 116–117, and Falkenstein, "Alexandre III et Henri de France: Conformités et conflits," 108–114.

Philip's career was not so illustrious. Nor is it as well documented. There is no set of letters as there is for Henry.[47] After Henry's departure for Clairvaux, Philip inherited the different positions his brother had held.[48] He appears as a *puer* in the 1145–1146 Notre Dame documents, where his name is always next to Peter Lombard's.[49] There seems to have been some association between them, perhaps the younger man's high regard for the brilliant master. As we will be arguing in the next chapter, there is no reason to reject Robert of Torigny's report that Philip helped Peter to become bishop of Paris.[50] After 1147, when he witnessed one of Louis VII's acts,[51] Philip seems to have spent some time away from Paris. It would be tempting to suggest that he accompanied his brother on crusade, but there is no evidence for this. It is more probable that he was looking after his interests outside the city. He was treasurer of St Corneille de Compiègne, a house of secular canons. This brought him into conflict with the king, who supported an attempt to replace the canons with monks of St Denis in June 1150.[52] Philip led an armed resistance against the move and was supported by his mother, Adelaide of Savoy. Louis eventually diffused the situation by promising arbitration.[53] Philip was back in Paris in 1152,[54] among the canons of Notre Dame, and before his early death in 1160–1161, he had been appointed archdeacon.[55]

47 The only document that bears his name (other than as a witness), is a diploma confirming certain rights that his father granted to the abbey of St Victor. *Diploma Philippi, fratris Ludovici regis Francorum pro monasterio S. Victoris*, in *Veterum scriptorum et monumentorum historicorum, dogmaticorum moralium, amplissima collectio*, ed. Edmund Martène and Ursini Durand (Paris, 1724–1733), 6: 228–229.

48 Henry had been dean of Tours and archdeacon of Orléans. Brady, Prolegomena 1: 33*.

49 *Cartulaire*, ed. de Lasteyrie, no. 319, p. 296, no. 321, p. 298, no. 301, p. 325.

50 Robert of Torigny, *Chronicon*, ed. Ludwig Conrad Bethmann (MGH SS 6: 510).

51 *Cartulaire*, ed. de Lasteyrie, no. 331, p. 305. The witnesses included "Philip puer, frater noster."

52 Pacaut, *Louis VII et son royaume*, 79–80; Luchaire, *Histoire des institutions monarchiques de la France sous les premiers Capétiens (987–1180)*, 1: 156; and Grant, *Abbot Suger of St. Denis*, 280–282.

53 Grant, *Abbot Suger of St. Denis*, 282.

54 *Cartulaire de l'église Notre-Dame de Paris*, ed. Guérard, 1: no. 22, 388–389. In this document he appears next to the subdeacons although the word *subdiaconus* does not actually follow his name.

55 He is archdeacon under Maurice of Sully in *Cartulaire*, ed. de Lasteyrie, no. 413, p. 361. His death is referred to in documents dated between August 1160 and April 1161. Achille Luchaire, *Études sur les actes de Louis VII* (Paris, 1885), no. 432 and no. 434, p. 239.

After the long tenure of Bernerus (c.1105–c.1140),[56] there was a new dean at Notre Dame in the 1140s, Bartholomew of Senlis.[57] The dean was elected by the other canons and he was the head of the chapter. He received a promise of obedience from the canons, and he represented the chapter at occasions.[58] The documents of the cathedral are often in the dean's name. Bartholomew does not seem to have featured among the canons before his election, which probably occurred while his uncle, Stephen of Senlis, was still bishop. The influence of Bartholomew's family, once considerable, had been eclipsed somewhat by that of the Garlandes in the early part of the century.[59] The Senlis family had traditionally held the royal office of butler.[60] Bartholomew's father, William de Loup, who died during the Second Crusade,[61] held that office from 1132 to 1147[62] and was succeeded by his son Guy. Two of Bartholomew's brothers were major figures in the church of Soissons.[63] Bartholomew left the chapter in 1147 to become bishop of Châlons, and he implied in a letter to Suger that the king recommended him for the post.[64] He

56 For Bernerus, see *Gallia Christiana* 7: 194–195. He succeeded Fulco as dean and first appears in *Cartulaire*, ed. de Lasteyrie, no. 139, p. 159.

57 For Bartholomew, see Luchaire, *Remarques sur la succession des grands officiers de la couronne*, 36–37, and *Gallia Christiana* 9: 881–882. I have not been able to consult Jean-Pierre Ravaux, "Barthélemy de Senlis: 54e évêque de Châlons-en-Champagne [Marne]," *Mémoires de la Société d'agriculture, commerce, sciences et arts du département de la Marne* 118 (2003): 23–40.

58 Gaudemet, "Les institutions ecclésiastiques en France du milieu du XIIe siècle au début du XIVe siècle," 189. For cathedral deans outside France, see, for example, David Dunford, "Dean," in *The Catholic Encyclopedia: An International Work of Reference on the Constitution, Doctrine, Discipline, and History of the Catholic Church*, ed. Charles G. Herbermann (New York, 1907–1914), 4: 659–990; and Kathleen Edwards, *The English Secular Cathedrals in the Middle Ages* (Manchester, 1949), 139–141.

59 Eric Bournazel, *Le gouvernement capétien au XIIe siècle* (Paris, 1975), 31, 40–45.

60 Ibid., 40–45, 97.

61 Ibid., 45. Guy held the office from 1149 to 1180. See also Aubert de La Chesnaye-Desbois, *Dictionnaire de la noblesse*, 3: 65–66.

62 Marcel Pacaut, *Louis VII et les élections épiscopales dans le royaume de France* (Paris, 1957), 138.

63 Peter of Senlis was archdeacon there and Stephen was dean of the cathedral. Aubert de La Chesnaye-Desbois, *Dictionnaire de la noblesse*, 3: 66.

64 Pacaut, *Louis VII et les élections épiscopales*, 67, 119. The letter is in PL 186: 1408–1409. A charter of Louis VII approving Bartholomew's election can be found in *Veterum scriptorum et monumentorum historicorum, dogmaticorum moralium, amplissima collectio*, ed. Martène and Durand, 1: 803.

died in 1152 on pilgrimage to Jerusalem.[65] He may have wished, among other things, to pay his respects to his late father.

Bartholomew was replaced as dean by Clement, who had joined the canons in the mid-1140s as a priest. Nothing is known of Clement's family background. His election was contentious. Suger of St Denis, the famous abbot and statesman, described the circumstances in a letter to Pope Eugenius.[66] The canons met repeatedly to choose a new dean, but the different factions were unable to agree, so they entrusted the election to the "more honest persons" in the chapter.[67] This was an electoral procedure known as compromise, and it was frequently used in episcopal election.[68] Four men were chosen, but, to the surprise of everyone, one of the four, Clement, was elected.[69] This was clearly some sort of coup. Suger thought that the election irregularities could have been overlooked if Clement had proved himself to be a good dean, but this was not the case. He was not a man known for "discretion, good conversation, or good repute," and under him the church would "languish rather than prosper."[70]

The canons cannot have been happy with Clement's actions, and the divisions came to a head in a very public way. The new dean clashed openly with Albert d'Étampes, cantor of Notre Dame. The cantor was the number two position in the chapter, and he represented the canons when the dean was absent.[71] Albert had held the position since at least 1142, in

65 *Gallia Christiana* 9: 881–882.

66 Suger, Abbot of St Denis, *Ep.* 61, *Epistola ad Eugenium Papam* (PL 186: 1380–1382). There is a partial translation in Wright, *Music and Ceremony at Notre Dame*, 280. The dispute is also covered, although it is a paraphrase of Suger's letter, in *Gallia Christiana* 8: 196–197.

67 "honestioribus personis ejusdem Ecclesiae." Suger, Abbot of St Denis, *Ep.* 61, *Epistola ad Eugenium Papam* (PL 186: 1380–1381).

68 Jörg Peltzer, *Canon Law, Careers and Conquest: Episcopal Elections in Normandy and Greater Anjou, c.1140–c.1230* (Cambridge, 2008), 41: "An election through compromise meant that the chapter commisioned a small, variable number of suitable men, often members of the chapter, to elect the bishop in its place."

69 Suger, Abbot of St Denis, *Ep.* 61, *Epistola ad Eugenium Papam* (PL 186: 1380–1381).

70 "nec alicujus discretionis, nec bonae conversationis, nec bonae famae existit ... sub quo languere potius quam prosperari Ecclesia valeat." Ibid.

71 Gaudemet, "Les institutions ecclésiastiques en France du milieu du XIIe siècle au début du XIVe siècle," 189. For the office, see Wright, *Music and Ceremony at Notre Dame*, 18–19 and *passim*; Günther Birkner, "Notre Dame Cantoren und Succentoren vom Ende des 10. bis zum Beginn des 14. Jahrhunderts," in *In Memoriam*

succession to Adam.[72] The cantor (or chanter) supervised liturgical music,[73] and fragments of Albert's compositions for Notre Dame have survived.[74] He was also in charge of the education of the boys in his choir. We know that in the later Middle Ages the choir school was also a grammar school.[75] In effect, the cantor was the counterpart to the chancellor. While Algrin was responsible for higher education, Albert maintained the preparatory school.

The dispute took place at some point between 1147 and 1149.[76] Suger's letter to the pope is again the source: "They had been celebrating the canonical hour in choir on a certain day, and the cantor was speaking to one of the clerics about correct pronunciation, either in singing or reading. The dean, having taken the opportunity for abuse, leapt up against the cantor and demanded silence in an ugly manner. When the cantor continued on with what he had begun, amazed at the dean's indiscreet vehemence, the dean, raging in the manner of one possessed, demanded silence of those who were

---

Jacques Handschin, ed. Higini Anglès (Strasbourg, 1962), 107–126, at 107–112; and Ferruolo, *The Origins of the University*, 189. There is also material in Margot Fassler, "Who Was Adam of St Victor? The Evidence of the Sequence Manuscripts," *Journal of the American Musicological Society* 37 (1984): 233–269. Fassler argues that Adam, Albert's predecessor as cantor of Notre Dame, should be identified with Adam of St Victor.

72 Albert first appears as cantor in *Cartulaire*, ed. de Lasteyrie, no. 291, p. 280–281. For Albert, see especially Wright, *Music and Ceremony at Notre Dame*, 277–281, and Birkner, "Notre Dame Cantoren und Succentoren," 113–114. There are no references to his and Algrin's being brothers, so it is more probable they were simply both from Étampes. The two prominent noble families of Étampes are not known before the fourteenth century. See de La Chesnaye-Desbois, *Dictionnaire de la noblesse*, 6: 151–152.

73 Peter Lombard explains the duties of the cantor and subcantor in book four of the *Sentences*: "Cantor vero vocatur, qui vocem modulatur in cantu. Huius sunt duo genera: praecentor, et succentor. Praecentor qui vocem praemittit in cantu, succentor qui subsequenter canendo respondet." *Sententiae* 2, dist. 24.12, ed. Brady, 2: 406.

74 Wright, *Music and Ceremony at Notre Dame*, 277–281, discusses his output and reproduces part of his conductus, *Congaudeant catholici*.

75 The choir school is discussed in Gane and Billot, *Le chapitre de Notre-Dame de Paris au XIVe siècle*, 33. As we have seen in chapter one, the grammar school was an essential part of education.

76 It took place after Clement's election in 1147 and before Louis returned from crusade in mid-1149, since Suger was still regent.

singing in the choir."[77] This was an extraordinary scene. Albert sought justice against the injury by appealing to his bishop, Theobald, to Joscelin, the bishop of Soissons, and to his archbishop, Hugh of Toucy of Sens. Theobald had already written to the pope about the matter.[78] Suger was writing in his capacity as regent of France, in the absence of Louis VII, who was on crusade, and he pleaded that action be taken against Clement for the good of Notre Dame: "For since it has been accustomed, up until now, to be honoured for its nobility, and to shine by the light of those famous for doctrine, but now, tottering gravely through the failure of its dean, it will hurry down a path of decline if it is not relieved."[79] Unfortunately, we do not know how this situation was resolved. Clement remained as dean until 1167, when he was succeeded by Barbe d'Or.[80] Albert continued as the cantor until the mid-1170s.[81] As the two highest dignitaries in the chapter, they must have found a way to work together. Presumably, some sort of restitution was made, brokered by Suger and Theobald.[82] But one wonders whether such gaping wounds in the chapter could ever have been fully healed.

Suger had close relations with the chapter of Paris. Two of his nephews were canons at the same time as Peter Lombard. Suger's family, obscure knights at the turn of the century, had prospered with his rising influence.[83] Hilduin and Simon of St Denis appear regularly in the documents in the 1160s

77 "Quadam die cum essent in choro horam canonicam decantantes, et cantor cuidam clerico loqueretur, quo more solet omnibus de canendis vel legendis pronuntiare, accepta inde occasione invective insiliens in cantorem, turpiter tacere imperavit, et dum cantor auditori prosequeretur quod incoeperat, admirans indiscretam decani vehementiam, decanus ipse (Clemens) more arreptitii furens choro decantanti silentium imperavit." Suger, Abbot of St Denis, *Ep.* 61, *Epistola ad Eugenium Papam* (PL 186: 1381).

78 Ibid.

79 "Cum enim venerandi status nobilitate, et famosa doctrinae lampade hactenus clarere consueverit, in defectu personatus decaniae vacillans graviter, si non ei subveniatur, declinare festinat." Ibid.

80 *Cartulaire*, ed. de Lasteyrie, no. 462, p. 392, and no. 467, pp. 394–395.

81 He was still cantor in 1174 (ibid., no. 521, p. 430), but by 1178 (ibid., no. 559, p. 457), he had been replaced by Walter. This Walter appears to have been the chaplain to Maurice of Sully. Maurice had a new chaplain in 1176, named Daniel.

82 Gérard Dubois, *Historia Ecclesiae Parisiensis* (Paris, 1690–1710), 2: 116, cited it as an example of bishop Theobald's great abilities as a reconciler.

83 For Suger's family, see John F. Benton, "Suger's Life and Personality," in *Abbot Suger and Saint-Denis: A Symposium*, ed. Paula L. Gerson (New York, 1986), 3–15, at 3. Grant, *Abbot Suger of St. Denis*, 75–76.

and 1170s.[84] Simon was a canon as early as 1150[85] and a deacon from 1159.[86] As for Hilduin, there is a *puer* by that name in 1145 and 1147. This may be the same person as the master Hilduin who was a canon in 1168 and became chancellor in 1180.[87] If it is, how do we explain his twenty-year absence? He could have left Paris to study. A more compelling reason has to do with his brother Simon, who was royal chancellor in 1150–1151.[88] For unknown reasons, the king became displeased with him and dismissed him from his post.[89] Simon went to Rome and took refuge with Pope Eugenius. John of Salisbury recalled, in his *Historia pontificalis*, that "no one could be found to protect Suger's relatives, since the King temporized and avenged himself on some of them because Simon, Suger's nephew, had incurred the King's anger."[90] John also claimed that the new abbot of St Denis, Odo, "strove to ruin [Suger's] whole family."[91] Eugenius took Simon in, out of regard for Suger, and sent him, with a letter of introduction, to Henry of France, bishop of Beauvais.[92] The letter reveals that Simon did not travel alone. His relatives accompanied him.[93] This seems to support John's claim. It was not wise for the Suger fam-

84 When the two are deacons, their names usually appear next to each other in *Cartulaire*, ed. de Lasteyrie, no. 495, p. 412 (1171), no 521, p. 430 (1174), and no. 559, p. 457 (1178). Crucially, in *Archives de l'Hôtel-Dieu de Paris (1157–1300)*, ed. Léon Brièle (Paris, 1894), 4, they are listed as brothers: "Symone de Sancto Dyonisio et magistro Hilduino fratre ejus." Two documents edited by Mortet also refer to them as brothers: Victor Mortet, "Maurice de Sully, évêque de Paris (1160–1196): Étude sur l'administration épiscopale pendant la seconde moitié du XIIe siècle," *Mémoires de la Société de l'histoire de Paris et de l'Île-de-France* 16 (1890): 105–317, at no. 19–20, pp. 296–297 .

85 *Cartulaire*, ed. de Lasteyrie, no. 366, p. 326 .

86 Ibid., no. 410, pp. 357–358 .

87 Ibid., no. 467, pp. 394–395 .

88 Jean Dufour has distinguished him from the Simon (of Crécy) who was Louis VI's chancellor from 1128–1132: *Recueil des actes de Louis VI: Roi de France (1108–1137)*, ed. Robert Henri-Bautier and Jean Dufour (Paris, 1992–1994), 3: 37–38.

89 For Simon's chancellorship, see Teske, *Die Briefsammlungen des 12. Jahrhunderts in St. Viktor, Paris*, 185–189, and Luchaire, *Remarques sur la succession des grands officiers de la couronne*, 38–39.

90 John of Salisbury, *Historia pontificalis* 44, ed. and trans. Marjorie Chibnall (London, 1956), 87–88.

91 Ibid.

92 Eugenius III, *Epistola ad Henricum Belvacensem episcopum, RHF* 15: 469. Dated 19 January 1152.

93 Ibid. There is a reference to *suos* in the letter, which usually meant kinsmen.

ily to be in Paris. Hilduin could easily have travelled with Simon. Simon also unsuccessfully pursued legal remedies against Odo.[94] He and his brother do not reappear in the documents of Notre Dame until the 1170s and 1180s, by which time Odo of St Denis had died.

Simon's replacement as royal chancellor in 1151, Hugh of Champfleury, was also a canon of Notre Dame.[95] His first act as chancellor was the reform of Compiègne, which Philip of France resisted.[96] Another of the new canons, Hugh joined the chapter in 1147.[97] His family background is somewhat elusive. Although there were lords of Champfleury in the thirteenth century, there is no evidence for an aristocratic family of that name in the twelfth.[98] He certainly managed to have a successful career. He had been archdeacon of Arras since the 1130s and was nominated for the bishopric of that diocese in 1148. Hugh owned several houses in Paris.[99] From 1159 to 1172 he was bishop of Soissons, and he held this position concurrently with the royal chancellorship.[100]

Hugh's tenure as chancellor was longer than that of Algrin d'Étampes and Simon of St Denis. He played a significant role in diplomacy, between Louis VII and Henry II, and during the papal schism of 1160. He also had close links with the papal curia throughout his chancellorship.[101] He was the longest serving of Louis's chancellors, and there is evidence for a warm relationship between the two.[102] This makes his dismissal in 1172, the reasons for which are unknown, all the more surprising.[103] Henry of France intervened on Hugh's behalf. In a letter to Louis, he warned his brother that he was worried about the matter: if he abandoned Hugh, he would offend God and the

94 Teske, *Die Briefsammlungen des 12. Jahrhunderts in St. Viktor, Paris,* 185–189.
95 For Hugh, see Teske, *Die Briefsammlungen des 12. Jahrhunderts in St. Viktor, Paris,* 115–181, which is founded on the author's study of the correspondence of his chancellorship. See also Luchaire, *Remarques sur la succession des grands officiers de la couronne,* 39–40.
96 Luchaire, *Études sur les actes de Louis VII,* 57–58.
97 *Cartulaire,* ed. de Lasteyrie, no. 327, p. 302 .
98 Pacaut, *Louis VII et les élections épiscopales,* 139.
99 Nikolaus M. Häring, "Chartres and Paris Revisited," in *Essays in Honour of Anton Charles Pegis,* ed. J. Reginald O'Donnell (Toronto, 1974), 328.
100 Some letters from his chancellorship and episcopate can be found in *RHF* 16: 201–208.
101 Teske, *Die Briefsammlungen des 12. Jahrhunderts in St. Viktor, Paris,* 120–125.
102 Ibid., 119.
103 Luchaire, *Études sur les actes de Louis VII,* 57–58.

people.[104] The king, however, was not to be moved. Hugh died three years later, but not before he had preserved the documents of his chancellorship for posterity. The letter collection of Louis VII is thought to have been collected and edited by Hugh.[105]

Hugh was also a master.[106] Along with Peter Lombard and Ivo of Chartres, he was involved in the proceedings against Gilbert of Poitiers's teachings in 1147 and 1148. Hugh took part in the first debate over Gilbert's orthodoxy, at a papal consistory in Paris in April 1147.[107] He was criticized by Otto of Freising for offering "an oath instead of an argument" there.[108] We will return to these events in chapter four. It is not clear how long Hugh actually spent teaching or if he did so in Paris. He is not mentioned in either of the two main lists of Paris-based masters in the period, by John of Salisbury and William of Tyre, respectively.[109] It seems more probable that his teaching activity took place in Arras, before his political career took off.

A surviving work by Hugh has been almost completely forgotten.[110] Although busy with the combined duties of royal chancellor and bishop of Soissons, he began to write a work during his moments of leisure. The prologue, addressed to his sister, Helwide, who was in religious life, is titled *Otium Hugonis ad Helwidem* – "the leisure moments of Hugh to his sister Helwide." It is not a work that directly reflects Hugh's period as a master, although the

104 "Super hoc negotio sollicitus sum: timeo enim ne, si ab eo recessiritis, Dei et populi offensam incurratis. Rogo, supplicio, consulo, ne ab eo recedatis." Louis VII, *Ep.* 462, *RHF* 16: 154. See also Henry's letter to Hugh: Henry of France, *Ep.* 155, *RHF* 16: 192.

105 André Wilmart, *Codices Reginenses Latini* (Rome, 1937–1945), 1: 419–430; Richard W. Southern, *Medieval Humanism and Other Studies* (Oxford, 1970), 148, 178.

106 *Cartulaire*, ed. de Lasteyrie, no. 327, p. 302. Also, Otto I, Bishop of Freising, *Gesta Frederici I imperatoris* 53 (MGH SS 46: 60), trans. by Christopher C. Mierow and Richard Emery as *The Deeds of Frederick Barbarossa* (New York, 1953), 89.

107 For the Paris consistory, see Nikolaus M. Häring, "Das Pariser Konsistorium Eugens III vom April 1147," *Studiana Gratiana* 11 (1967), 91–117, and Häring, "Chartres and Paris Revisited," 303–304.

108 See the discussion of this event in chapter four, below, 86–87.

109 See chapter five, below, 116, and Richard W. Southern, *Scholastic Humanism and the Unification of Europe* I: *Foundations* (Oxford, 1995), 232.

110 Although Dom Wilmart described the work and edited the prologue in "Les 'loisirs' ou sentiments intimes d'un chancelier de France," *Revue Bénédictine* 51 (1939): 182–204, it has remained completely neglected. The only later reference to it that I have seen is in Southern, *Medieval Humanism*, 177–178.

frequent use and occasional glossing of scripture does indicate a theological training. The prologue is predominantly a lament, filled with Hugh's sense of unworthiness, his regret for his sins, and his fear of eternal judgement: "When thinking on these things, horror invades my flesh and my soul, and whatever is in the present is made small in comparison with what is to come ... I have despaired in every way for my strengths. I hope for the help of God, but I am terrified of his judgement."[111] Although he had become bishop of Soissons and royal chancellor, these positions only increased Hugh's misery:

> I would flee and change my station gladly if I could escape my calamity, but wherever I go, it follows me, and I am made a counsellor of others when it is I who needs counsel and help.[112] ... I write to you, my sister, completely full of sorrow, because to me the whole world is a source of sorrow, such that, while I draw breath in breathing, the air itself seems to furnish sorrow.[113]

One theology master with a higher profile than Hugh of Champfleury was Odo of Soissons. He was yet another new canon in the 1140s, and he appears in the documents as *presbyter* or *sacerdos* (a priest) between 1145 and 1157.[114] Only a small number of the canons were actually priests, the rest being spread over the other orders of the church. The late-twelfth century chronicler Robert of Auxerre described Odo, Peter, and Ivo of Chartres as

111 "Haec ego recogitans horror invadit carnem et animam meam, et quidquid est in presenti levigatur in comparatione futurorum ... De meis enim viribus omnino desparavi; de adiutorio dei spero quidem; sed tamen iudicium eius maxime formido." Wilmart, "Les 'loisirs' ou sentiments intimes d'un chancelier de France," 197.

112 "Fugerem igitur et mutarem libenter loca mea, si possem effugere calamitatem meam; sed quocumque ego vado me persequitur, et factus sum consiliarius aliorum ipse egens consilio et auxilio." Ibid., 201.

113 "Haec loquor tecum soror mea, totus amaritudine plenus, nimirum quia totus mundus michi materia doloris est, ita ut, dum ipsum aerem respirando traho, totus aer subministrare amaritudinem michi videtur." Ibid., 201.

114 *Cartulaire*, ed. de Lasteyrie, no. 291, pp. 280–281, is his first appearance (as a canon in 1145). He no longer appears around the time that master Odo begins signing the documents as chancellor. On this identification, see also Ignatius C. Brady, "Peter Lombard: Canon of Notre Dame," *RTAM* 32 (1965): 277–295, at 288–289.

the three most eminent masters in France.[115] He was not, as is sometimes claimed, an early pupil of Peter Lombard.[116] It is more probable that Odo studied with Gilbert of Poitiers.[117] He and Peter began teaching at the same time.

He was appointed chancellor of Notre Dame sometime between 1157 and 1160, in succession to Algrin d'Étampes.[118] The bishop who appointed him may have been Peter Lombard, but it could also have been Theobald. He resigned the chancellorship in 1167 and left Paris to become abbot of the Cistercian abbey of Ourscamp. This provided him with a resource few other theology masters had access to: a scriptorium.[119] There he seems to have started a project of collecting his works for posterity. Most of his surviving works are known from a single manuscript, once of Ourscamp, now housed in Cambrai.[120] This contains letters (rare for a twelfth-century theologian), sermons, and *quaestiones* (reports of theological positions). Much of this material has been edited,[121] while a number of other manuscripts contain

115 "Inter magistros Francie optinatissimi habentur Petrus Lombardus, Odo Suessionensis, Ivo Carnotensis." Robert of Auxerre, *Chronicon,* ed. Oswald Holder-Egger (MGH SS 26: 219–276, at 237), quoted in Häring, "Chartres and Paris Revisited," 314.

116 Although Brady had pointed out that Odo was "aemulus, non discipulus," Prolegomena 1: 28*, both Ferruolo, *The Origins of the University,* 190, and Colish, *Peter Lombard,* 424, repeated the idea that Odo was a pupil.

117 Ludwig Hödl, *Die Geschichte der scholastische Literatur und der Theologie der Schlüsselgewalt* (Münster, 1960), 129.

118 He first signs as chancellor in *Cartulaire,* ed. de Lasteyrie, no. 410, pp. 357–358 , a document of Bishop Peter Lombard.

119 Peter Lombard's student, Herbert of Bosham, lived at Ourscamp abbey for a period towards the end of his life (after Odo's death). Smalley, *Becket Conflict,* 74.

120 Brady, "Peter Manducator," 461–462, gives a full description of the manuscript, Cambrai, Bibliothèque municipale 561. Brady shows that a second series of *quaestiones* are also included in the manuscript, not by Odo but attributed to him. This suggests that the work was done after his death.

121 Working from the Cambrai manuscript, Leclercq edited eight letters: Jean Leclercq, "Lettres d'Odon d'Ourscamp," *Analecta Monastica* 3 (1955): 145–157. Cardinal Pitra had already edited the remaining three, although he worked from transcriptions of the Cambrai manuscript: see *Analecta Novissima Spicilegii Solesmensis Altera Continuatio,* ed. Jean-Baptiste Pitra (Paris, 1885–1888), 2: xxxix–xlii. He also edited one of Odo's sermons: ibid., xlii–xlvii. The *Quaestiones,* on 3–167, are not all, as he thought, the work of Odo. It is thus essential to consult Brady, "Peter Manducator," 454–464, for what is Odo and what is not.

additional sermons and *quaestiones*.[122] Odo's life and works deserve more detailed study than can be attempted here.[123]

Preserved in this manuscript is a letter that is one of the most important documents for understanding the day-to-day running of the twelfth-century schools.[124] It was written between 1167 and 1170, the years of Odo's abbacy. In it he complains to Pope Alexander III about the fate of one his students, his *praepositus* (assistant), who was without a clerical position.[125] It is a candid and poignant letter, and it provides a rare glimpse into some of the real problems faced by those who try to make a living from scholarship. Odo clearly felt a deep sense of responsibility for his pupil. He begins by praising the truth and goes on to point out that those in ecclesiastical office should speak the truth, since their lies are sacrilegious.[126] This sets the tone for the main target of the letter, the bishop of Paris, Maurice of Sully:

> Accordingly, I am showing to your discretion, holy father, that, when preparing to leave the world, just as is fitting, I made my proposal to the bishop of Paris, asking and entreating that he might concede my canonry to one of my own, or at least provide him with some ecclesiastical benefice. I wished this for one of my students, who had been my *praepositus* in the schools and who succeeded me in the schools, a man whose knowledge is worthy of approval, but whose life is even more so. It was not flesh or blood that moved me to this wish but love for my father in heaven. For he labours in the study of the holy page courageously and catholically. And now exhibiting grey hairs, he is still not found as a prelate of the church, who could at least call him to a benefice of two-

122 For the sermons, see Ferruolo, *The Origins of the University*, 346. For the *quaestiones*, see Brady, "Peter Manducator," 454–464.

123 The best accounts of Odo's life and work are those of Hödl, who successfully identified the master and chancellor Odo of Soisssons with Odo, abbot of Ourscamp. See Hödl, *Die Geschichte der scholastische Literatur und der Theologie der Schlüsselgewalt*, 116–141, and Ludwig Hödl, "Die theologische Auseinandersetzung zwischen Petrus Lombardus und Odo von Ourscamp nach dem Zeugnis der frühen Quästionen und Glossenliteratur," *Scholastik* 33 (1958): 62–80.

124 Odo of Soissons, *Epistola ad Alexandrum Papam*, in *Analecta Novissima Spicilegii Solesmensis Altera Continuatio*, ed. Pitra, 2: xxxix–xl.

125 For the position of *praepositus*, see chapter nine, 237–238, on Adam of Wales, who was Peter Lombard's *praepositus*.

126 Odo of Soissons, *Epistola ad Alexandrum Papam*, xxxix.

> pence. For more than twelve years, as I reckon it, I have supported him materially, and now he lives elsewhere. Your prudence knows what a misery it is to live at someone else's dining table. Therefore, perceiving my proposal, the bishop attentively asked me to hide my counsel, because if it were made public knowledge, the king might threaten the idea and my chancellorship besides; the bishop also added and made the point that he would not be unmindful of me: this was his word, and it would not change.
>
> Accepting his word in good faith, and believing that he had listened to my petition, I bowed, and with my much weeping I offered my thanks. If he had responded otherwise to me, my counsel would have proceeded in another direction. For he gave his word to me that, without the king knowing, without the king seeing or giving his blessing, I might enter the cloister. In this, I confess, I was gravely at fault, and indeed I sinned, because I had originally accepted my Parisian canonry through the kindness of the king.[127]

Before departing for the cloister, Odo reminded Maurice of the matter and asked him to keep his word. The bishop replied that he retained a clear memory of their conversation and that "to his understanding he had not given his

127 "Inde discretioni vestrae, Pater sancte, significo, quod a saeculo parans exire, sicut decebat, episcopo meo Parisiensi meum scilicet manifestavi propositum, rogans et supplicans ei, ut canonicam meam alicui meorum concederet, aut alio saltem ecclesiae beneficio provideret. Quemdam vero discipulorum meorum, qui praepositus meus in scolis fuerat, michique successit in scolis, virum probatum scientia, sed probatiorem vita, volebam [provideri?]. Voluntatem illam caro vel sanguis in me non movebat, sed caritas Patris mei qui in coelis est. Laborat enim in sacra pagina viriliter et catholice. Etiam existens in canis, non invenit praelatum ecclesiae, qui saltem ad duorum nummorum beneficium eum vocaret. Plusquam duodecim annis, ut reor, mea vixit in mensa, et vivit adhuc in aliena. Novit autem prudentia vestra quam miserum sit aliena vivere quadra. Meo igitur percepto proposito, praesul attente me rogavit, ut consilium meum celarem, ne si publicaretur, rex ei super cancellaria mea praeter voluntatem suam instaret; adiiciens et contestans, quod non esset immemor mei: hoc enim fuit verbum eius, idem nec mutatum. Ego igitur simpliciter et bona fide verbum eius accipiens, credens scilicet quod meam exaudisset petitionem, inclinavi, et ei cum lacrimis gratias egi. Si enim michi aliter respondisset, alia via consilium meum processiset. Ad hoc enim me verbum eius induxit, ut praeter conscientiam regis, rege non viso, rege non salutato, claustrum intrarem. In quo me graviter errasse et peccasse confiteor, quum per regis benignitatem canonicam Parisiensem accepissem." Ibid., xxxix–xl.

word."[128] Odo then allows his scarcely concealed anger to come to the surface, quoting the Psalmist, "the lord destroys deceitful lips," and Ecclesiasticus, "the sophist is hateful to God." He closes the letter by advising the pope to force Maurice to grant a prebend to his *praepositus*.[129]

Some have assumed that Odo is referring to his chancellorship.[130] Peter Comestor, Lombard's pupil, was appointed to succeed him. But Odo does not say this. He is referring to his position as canon of Paris, which he obtained through the king in 1145. Alexander's reply, if there was one, has not survived, but we know that in 1170 he thought highly enough of Odo to make him cardinal bishop of Tusculum. In the previous year, he had asked Odo to assist with the reform of St Victor, following its decline under abbot Ernisius.[131] Odo's hope that his student would obtain his canonry failed. There are some new names among the canons of Paris at that time, but none that are known to have taught theology.[132] Alexander did do something, however. Joseph Warichez established that the *praepositus* in question was Simon of Tournai.[133] He had been a student of Odo, and soon after this letter was written, the pope authorized an increase in the number of canons at Tournai.[134] Simon became one of the new canons. Simon was apparently a difficult man who made enemies. According to John Baldwin, "his writings reveal him to have had a blunt, self-assertive personality, a characteristic which was reflected in his subsequent reputation. At the end of the twelfth and throughout the thirteenth century, stories circulated that attribute to him arrogance, blas-

128 "Positis igitur pedibus meis in compedibus Domini, cum eum rogarem verbum suum impleret, et ut beneficium aliquod cui destinaveram impenderet, respondit eo intellectu verbum illud se non accepisse seque verbum suum verum tenere, cum mei memoriam apud se retineret." Ibid.

129 "Cum odibilis sit Deo qui sophistice loquitur, disperdatque Dominus universa labia dolosa, cum ad intellectum audientis loqui debeat qui loquitur veritatem in corde, placeat iustitiae vestrae, sancte Pater, ut Parisiensem episcopum ad intellectum meum implendum moneatis, et si contempserit, cogatis, ne dolos perfecisse se rideat, et clericus ille quem praetaxavi, beneficium aliquod per pietatem vestram recipere se gaudeat." Ibid.

130 Ferruolo, *The Origins of the University*, 190.

131 Colish, *Peter Lombard*, 431.

132 *Cartulaire*, ed. de Lasteyrie, no. 467, p. 394 . These include Joscelin, a priest, Peter de Campellis, a deacon, and William, a subdeacon.

133 Joseph Warichez, *Les Disputationes de Simon de Tournai* (Louvain, 1932), xii–xvi.

134 Ibid. Warichez was archivist to the bishops of Tournai.

phemy and the possession of a concubine."[135] Such rumours indicate the presence of a climate hostile to Simon, and this may well explain his failure to obtain a prebend.[136]

The presence of Odo's *quaestiones* in a number of manuscripts backs up Robert of Auxerre's view that he was one of the most eminent masters in France. *Quaestiones* often survived because a master's position was considered to have weight. They allowed for citation of other opinions. Odo was considered to be someone worth citing. As theologians, Odo and Peter Lombard had some common ground but also distinct differences, which Ludwig Hödl has dealt with in detail.[137] Also, as a preacher, Odo may have influenced Peter. His surviving sermons help to provide a sense of the preaching tradition at Notre Dame. Like Peter, he was preaching there in the 1140s and 1150s. A sermon edited by Pitra does show some of the same stylistic features that Peter Lombard would later use, particularly the mode of address and the systematic use of scriptural quotation.[138] The problem, however, is that we do not know which of Odo's sermons date from his years as master and which from his abbacy. Certainly, Odo's Cistercian writings tend to have a different quality. The letters edited by Leclercq play much upon the stock theme of leaving the worldly knowledge of the schools for the true knowledge of the cloister,[139] a contrast that was innovative when Bernard of Clairvaux was using it but that by this time had become a mannerism.

The brothers Osmund and Simon of Poissy also featured prominently in the chapter during the time that Peter was there. Eric Bournazel has done an admirable job of disentangling the various branches of the knights of Poissy. Osmund and Simon descended from Robert of Poissy, and the family had often been chamberlains to the king.[140] Their uncle was also a canon of Notre

135 John W. Baldwin, *Masters, Princes, and Merchants: The Social Views of Peter the Chanter and His Circle* (Princeton, 1970), 44. For Simon, see also David Luscombe, "Tournai, Simon of," in *Oxford Dictionary of National Biography,* ed. Henry C.G. Matthew and Brian Harrison (Oxford, 2004), 55: 84–85.

136 Warichez, *Les Disputationes,* xviii.

137 Hödl, "Die theologische Auseinandersetzung zwischen Petrus Lombardus und Odo von Ourscamp nach dem Zeugnis der frühen Quästionen und Glossenliteratur," 62–80.

138 Odo of Soissons, *Sermo: "Egredietur virga de radice Iesse,"* in *Analecta Novissima Spicilegii Solesmensis Altera Continuatio,* ed. Pitra, 2: xlii–xlvii.

139 Leclercq, "Lettres d'Odon d'Ourscamp," 145–157.

140 For their complex genealogy, see Bournazel, *Le gouvernement capétien au XIIe siècle,* 76.

Dame.[141] Osmund entered the chapter in 1134,[142] while Simon first appeared in the 1140s.[143] Simon was another of the theologians. He does not seem to have left any written work,[144] and he was not as highly regarded as his contemporaries. John of Salisbury studied with him for a short while and recalled him as "a dependable lecturer, but more dull when it came to the dispute."[145] There is evidence that Osmund was also a master although he usually did not attach the title to his name in documents as his brother did.[146] The brothers were well connected, and they rose steadily in the chapter. They both became deacons, and Simon held one of the three archdeaconries in the 1160s and 1170s.[147] In 1164 they spearheaded the renovation of the oratory of St Denis du Pas.[148] Simon was also sometimes employed in royal service. The chronicle of Morigny records that Louis VII sent him to Rome on a diplomatic mission, accompanied by the king's chaplain, in 1141–1142.[149] As often, the presence of a master was essential to diplomacy, and this was surely not the only time that Simon had been engaged in such work. The mission took place before his entry into the chapter,[150] which may suggest that, at that time,

141 Ibid.

142 *Cartulaire*, ed. de Lasteyrie, no. 253, pp. 251–253 . The deacon named Walter in this document is presumably the uncle of Osmund and Simon.

143 Ibid., no. 319, pp. 295–296. For Simon, see Brady, "Peter Lombard: Canon of Notre Dame," 289–290.

144 Brady, "Peter Lombard: Canon of Notre Dame," 289–290, says he is "likely not" the Master Simon who authored a *De Sacramentis*.

145 "Deinde me excepit Simon Pexiacensis, fidus lector, sed obtusior disputator." John of Salisbury, *Metalogicon* 2.10, ed. John B. Hall and Katharine S.B. Keats-Rohan (CCCM 98: 72).

146 The brothers are described as *magistri* in *Cartulaire*, ed. de Lasteyrie, no. 450, pp. 381–382 .

147 Ibid., no. 451, pp. 382–383 , no. 462, pp. 390–392 , no. 521, p. 430. In these documents there are two Simons, Simon of St Denis, the deacon, and archdeacon Simon.

148 Ibid., no. 450, pp. 381–382 ; Brady, "Peter Lombard: Canon of Notre Dame," 290.

149 "Qui acceptis regalibus litteris, comitantibus secum Petro regis capellano, et magistro Simone de Pissiaco, quos pro quibusdam negotiis Romam rex dirigebat, Cluniacum venit." *Chronicle of Morigny* 3 (PL 180: 131–176, at 172). The reference to the death of Henry Sanglier, archbishop of Sens, and his replacement by Hugh of Toucy a little later dates the negotiations in 1141–1142 ("In illis quoque diebus Henricus Senonensis archiepiscopus finem vitae sortitus est, succedente sibi Hugone venerabili tunc illius Ecclesiae praecentore." Ibid., 172–173).

150 He is not listed among the canons in 1142: *Cartulaire*, ed. de Lasteyrie, no. 291, pp. 280–281 .

Simon was employed full-time in the king's service. A good impression there could have led to his canonry.

The archdeacons for most of Peter's time in the chapter were Guermund (1147–1178), Ivo of Chartres (1142–1158), and Bernard (c.1140–1155). An archdeacon was appointed by the bishop. The position was probably as prestigious as that of dean, but it concerned the wider diocese rather than the cathedral itself. We will be discussing the duties of the Paris archdeacons in more detail in the next chapter, because Peter was one himself. For now it is sufficient to point out that they administered a third of the diocese each, and their responsibilities were quite similar to those of bishops. Guermund had replaced Stephen de Garlande, and had possibly inherited his position of being the most senior of the three.[151] His area of responsibility, known as his archdeaconry, was probably west-southwest of the city.[152]

The other two, Ivo of Chartres and Bernard, were both masters. Bernard took up his post around 1140.[153] Surviving documents indicate that his archdeaconry was south-southeast of the city.[154] The Notre Dame obituary commemorates him as a master and priest.[155] He must have joined the chapter sometime between 1135 and 1140. As Häring remarks, it is "difficult to distinguish him" from another master Bernard active in Paris at the time, Bernard the Breton.[156] That Bernard was one of William of Tyre's masters.[157] The two men are not to be confused, however: their deaths are commemo-

151 See chapter four, below, 105–106.

152 Stephen was archdeacon at the same time as William of Champeaux. William mentioned, in *Cartulaire*, ed. de Lasteyrie, no. 148, p. 167 , that his archdeaconry contained Gonesse (north of the city) along with a church within the city. Bernard was responsible for the area south-southeast (see note 154 below), so Stephen and his successor Guermund must have seen to the western part of the diocese.

153 He first appears in *Cartulaire*, ed. de Lasteyrie, 280–281.

154 In the cartularies of Corbeil, *Cartulaire de Saint-Spire de Corbeil au diocèse de Paris*, ed. Emile Coüard-Luys (Rambouillet, 1882), no. 10, pp. 15–19, and Yerres, Mortet, "Maurice de Sully," 285, he appears as the only archdeacon in two documents. See the fuller discussion of the archdeaconries of the diocese in chapter four, below, 105–106.

155 "De dome sancte Marie obiit magister Bernardus sacerdos et archidiaconus." *Cartulaire de l'église de Notre Dame de Paris*, ed. Guérard, 4: 193–194. He is also a master in *Cartulaire*, ed. de Lasteyrie, no. 353, pp. 318–319 .

156 Häring, "Chartres and Paris Revisited," 298. Brady, "Peter Lombard: Canon of Notre Dame," 288, also takes no position on who Bernard is.

157 William of Tyre, *Chronicon* 19.12 (CCCM 63: 880).

rated several months apart.[158] Archdeacon Bernard last appears in Parisian documents in 1155, after which he seems to have retired.[159] Bernard the archdeacon, like Hugh of Champfleury, is simply another twelfth-century master of whose teaching no record survives.

Ivo would have been responsible for the area north of the city, a position once held by William of Champeaux.[160] Häring identified him as master Ivo of Chartres.[161] He was a native of Chartres,[162] and his brother was apparently a potter there.[163] Ivo had been a student of Gilbert of Poitiers,[164] and he is shown sitting at the feet of his master in a well-known contemporary miniature.[165] He also defended Gilbert at the council of Rheims.[166] He wrote a commentary on the Psalms, which Smalley exam-

158 The Notre Dame obituary commemorates Archdeacon Bernard on 1 December: *Cartulaire de l'église de Notre Dame de Paris*, ed. Guérard, 4: 193–194. The death of Bernard the Breton, bishop of Quimper, is commemorated on 4 August: *Cartulaire de Notre-Dame de Chartres*, ed. Lucien Merlet and Eugène de Buchère de Lépinois (Chartres, 1862–1865), 3: 148.

159 *Cartulaire*, ed. de Lasteyrie, no. 384, p. 339 , where Adèle, abbess of Montmartre, makes a concession after consulting with Bernard, archdeacon of Paris. The only reference to his retirement, noted by Brady, "Peter Lombard: Canon of Notre Dame," 288, is Dubois, *Historia Ecclesie Parisiensis*, 2: 169: "Bernardus Archidiaconus Parisiensis, cujus nomen litteris Capituli Parisiensis subscriptum legimus, amore solitariae vitae incensus et rerum humanarum taedio affectus, a munere Ecclesia Parisiensis discessit ... ."

160 William described part of his archdeaconry in *Cartulaire*, ed. de Lasteyrie, no. 148, p. 167 . See the previous notes under Bernard and Guermund for why Ivo was not responsible for the southern or western area. See also the fuller discussion of the Paris archdeaconries in chapter four, below, 105–106. This may be the same Ivo who appears as a deacon in 1124–1134: *Cartulaire*, ed. de Lasteyrie, no. 203, p. 223, no. 239, p. 244 , no. 253, p. 251.

161 Häring, "Chartres and Paris Revisited," 313–317. For the work of Master Ivo, see the excellent article by Beryl Smalley, "Master Ivo of Chartres," *English Historical Review* 50 (1935): 680–686.

162 "Magister Ivo, genere et natione Carnotensis." William of Tyre, *Chronicon* 19.12 (CCCM 63: 880).

163 The *Cartulaire de Notre-Dame de Chartres*, ed. Merlet and Lépinois, 1: 238, has a reference to "Herbertus potarius, frater Yvonis decani." Smalley, "Master Ivo of Chartres," 680–681.

164 Häring, "Chartres and Paris Revisited," 314. As was mentioned earlier, Ivo defended Gilbert at Rheims.

165 Smalley, "Master Ivo of Chartres," 680–681. For the miniature, see Southern, *Scholastic Humanism* I: *Foundations*, 203.

166 John of Salisbury, *Historia pontificalis*, ed. Chibnall, 16. See chapter four, 87.

ined.[167] She notes that he does not quote the better known commentaries, the *Glossa Ordinaria*, or Gilbert of Poitiers's gloss, which were in circulation in the 1140s.[168] She concludes that Ivo's commentary dates from the 1120s or early 1130s. It was still being referred to in the 1150s and 1160s, but after that it was supplanted by Peter Lombard's commentary.[169] When William of Tyre studied with Ivo, between 1146 and 1153, he was teaching not theology but the arts.[170] This would also seem to suggest that the commentary was an early work. Ivo retired from his archdeaconry in 1156/1157[171] and lived out the remainder of his life as dean of Chartres.[172] He died in 1165.[173]

The last colleague to examine is probably the most famous name among the canons of 1145–1160, Maurice of Sully.[174] Anyone who visits or reads about Notre Dame Cathedral will come across him, since he was the driving force behind its reconstruction during his long episcopate (1160–1196). Maurice was from a poor family in the town of Sully (near Paris), but, like Peter, his academic gifts were recognized and supported.[175] He was born around 1120, and he would have studied the arts in the 1140s. We know that he progressed to the study of theology, probably under Robert of Melun.[176] He became a deacon at Notre Dame by 1159.[177]

167 Smalley, "Master Ivo of Chartres," 681–684. The manuscripts are described on 681–682. It remains unedited.

168 Ibid., 683. She also pointed out that he does not make use of Peter Lombard's gloss, but that did not begin to circulate until after Ivo's death.

169 Ibid., 684.

170 William of Tyre, *Chronicon* 19.12 (CCCM 63: 880).

171 His last appearance as archdeacon is *Cartulaire*, ed. de Lasteyrie, no. 394, pp. 347–348.

172 Häring, "Chartres and Paris Revisited," 314. He first signs there as dean in October 1156.

173 Ibid.

174 Although two specialized studies of Maurice's sermons have appeared, and he features regularly in discussions of the renovation of Notre Dame, the best full-length study of him is still Mortet, "Maurice de Sully." It was never widely available in libraries but is now on the internet archive.

175 Mortet, "Maurice de Sully," 115–116, discusses the references to Maurice's early poverty in a number of different sources. As we have seen in chapter one, some of these same stories were told of Peter Lombard.

176 Ibid., 125. According to John of Cornwall, Maurice criticized Peter Lombard's positions, so he is unlikely to have been his student. Nikolaus M. Häring, "The *Eulogium ad Alexandrum Papam Tertium* of John of Cornwall," *Mediaeval Studies* 13 (1951): 253–300, at 268. See the discussion of John in chapter nine, 253–255.

177 "S. Magistri mauricii. S. Osmundi, diaconorum." *Charta*, ed. Brady, Prolegomena 1: 36*. He may also be the subdeacon Maurice who signs in 1147: *Cartulaire de l'église*

We also know that Maurice was teaching theology that year. When Peter Lombard became bishop of Paris, two of his students, William of Tyre and John of Cornwall, had not yet completed the course with him. They elected to continue their studies with Maurice.[178] It is difficult to evaluate Maurice as a theologian. His positions are very occasionally cited in *quaestiones*,[179] and his written work consists of sermons.[180] Since Maurice was comparatively young when he became bishop, it is not surprising that there are no theological works credited to him. His teaching career was probably just beginning.

Maurice may also have been appointed archdeacon in 1159, but the evidence is not completely convincing. Robert of Torigny described the appointment of *Mauricius archidiaconus Parisiensis* as bishop, but there are no documents of Notre Dame referring to him as such.[181] This would not be the first time that Robert confused the positions of Notre Dame dignitaries, since he described Philip of France as dean.[182] For Maurice to have been archdeacon, he would have had to have replaced Peter Lombard. On the other hand, two documents from Peter's episcopate list only two archdeacons, Guermund and Gerard.[183] Then, in the first months of Maurice of Sully's episcopate, Philip of France appears as the third.[184] It is quite possible that Philip replaced Ivo in 1157, his absence from documents at that time being explained by his other interests. For this to be the case, Archdeacon Gerard would have to be Peter Lombard's replacement. This is plausible, because Gerard was only a

---

Notre-Dame de Paris, ed. Guérard, 2: 360, and ed. Brady, "Peter Lombard: Canon of Notre Dame," 285.

178 See the discussions of William and John in part two.

179 In addition to Häring, "The *Eulogium ad Alexandrum Papam Tertium* of John of Cornwall," 268, Brady, "Peter Manducator," 458, detects another citation of Maurice's teaching.

180 For the sermons, some of which date from his episcopate, see Jean Longère, *Oeuvres oratoires de maîtres parisiens au XIIe siècle: Étude historique et doctrinale* (Paris, 1975), 1: 14–18. Longère discusses the manuscripts in *Les sermons latins de Maurice de Sully, évêque de Paris (1196): Contribution à l'histoire de la tradition manuscrite* (Dordrecht, 1988). For the non-Latin sermons, see Charles A. Robson, *Maurice of Sully and the Medieval Vernacular Homily* (Oxford, 1952). Maurice's sermons are also addressed in Ferruolo, *The Origins of the University*, 188–189, and Mortet, "Maurice de Sully," 131–136, who also discusses the significant reputation they enjoyed in the late–twelfth and early–thirteenth centuries.

181 Robert of Torigny, *Chronicon*, ed. Bethmann (MGH SS 6: 511).

182 Ibid., 510.

183 Brady, Prolegomena 1: 35*–36*. *Cartulaire*, ed. de Lasteyrie, no. 415, p. 362.

184 *Cartulaire*, ed. de Lasteyrie, no. 413, p. 361.

puer in the year that Ivo retired (1156/1157).[185] The canons could not have expected that they would face another episcopal election within a year, and Maurice could have been elected straight from the diaconate.

There is no question that Maurice was ambitious. This can be seen not just in his career but in the policies he introduced when bishop. The reconstruction of the cathedral was his major achievement, and he was able to manage it through indefatigable fundraising.[186] Maurice also increased the size of the bishop's staff by introducing a personal secretary, a staff of clerks, and a chaplain.[187] There is also some evidence that Maurice renovated the episcopal residence.[188]

Peter Lombard had other colleagues of whom we know less. A complete list follows this chapter (see table 1). These colleagues included Hervaeus, who spent twenty-three years in the lowly position of subdeacon and was never promoted, a master Walter, who became chaplain to Maurice of Sully, and Robert, who was the deputy of cantor Albert. From those we have looked at, we can certainly say that Peter was not the only member of the chapter of humble birth. Colish exaggerates when she writes that "to a man" the canons were members of the leading families of Capetian France.[189] The majority were, as we have demonstrated. The exceptions were Peter himself, Ivo of Chartres (who was from a craftsman's family), and Maurice of Sully. There could well have been more, since it is not possible to trace the family origins of all the canons. These three also rose highly within the chapter. They each became an archdeacon, a bishop, or both. Their positions as self-made men seem to have given them ambition and a sense of purpose. In their case, however, material success was not the only goal. The three were also theology masters. Studying and teaching theology did not guarantee security. Odo's student serves as a poignant reminder of this. But we will see in part two that theologians took comfort from what they saw as the special dignity of their profession. It was not a lucrative or an easy one, but it was the more worthwhile for that.

185 Ibid., no. 394, p. 347–348.
186 Mortet, "Maurice de Sully," 220–226. Maurice's efforts in this area have also recently been discussed by Nicole Bériou, "Maurice et Eudes de Sully et la cathédrale de Paris," in *Notre Dame de Paris 1163–2013*, ed. Cédric Giraud (Turnhout, 2013), 19–28.
187 Mortet, "Maurice de Sully," 203–205.
188 Ibid., 234–237.
189 Colish, *Peter Lombard*, 20.

In his letter to the pope regarding the Clement affair, Suger provides the ideal of what the chapter of Notre Dame should be. The canons should shine as an example to others for their nobility and for their doctrine. It was therefore expected that the canons would be noted masters and members of the elite. Whether they were examples is debatable. They could be prone to divisions, jealous of position, subject to power games, and fond of intrigue. But in the ceremonial arena, they had to have the appearance of unity. This comes across clearly in the documents they signed as witnesses. When Clement, the dean, interrupted Albert's choir and demanded silence, he broke that unity. He had insulted not just Albert personally but the identity and public perception of the chapter. This explains why high-ranking clerics like Suger and Bishop Theobald were moved to act against him. The unity of the cathedral chapter was vital. For fifteen years Peter Lombard was part of this unity.

Table 1: The Canons of Notre Dame, 1145–1160.

Albert d'Étampes	Precentor/Cantor, 1142–1174
Algrin d'Étampes	Chancellor, 1124–1156/1157
	Royal Chancellor, 1137–1140
Andrew	Puer, 1117–1124
	Subdeacon, 1133–1146
Anselm	Puer, 1117–1124
	Subdeacon, 1133–1146
Bartholomew	Puer, 1152–1156
Bartholomew of Senlis	Dean, c.1140–1147
	Bishop of Châlons, 1147–1152
Master Bernard	Sacerdos, c.1136–1140
	Archdeacon, c.1140–1155
Boso	Puer, 1152–1160
Clement	Presbyter, 1145–1148
	Dean, 1148–1167
Durand	Subdeacon, 1145–1152
	Deacon, 1152–1156
Gerard	Puer, 1156
	Deacon, c.1158
	Archdeacon, 1159–1180
Goslin	Subdeacon, 1124
	Deacon, 1145–1147

Table 1 (*continued*)

Guermund	Sacerdos/Presbyter, 1142–1145
	Subcantor, 1146
	Archdeacon, 1147–1178
Guy of Chelles	Deacon, 1134–1150
Henry of France	Subdeacon, 1145–1146
	Monk of Clairvaux, 1146–1149
	Bishop of Beauvais, 1150–1172
	Archbishop of Rheims, 1172–1176
Herbert	Subdeacon, 1146–1156
	Deacon, 1156
Herluin	Deacon, 1142–1160
Hervaeus	Subdeacon, 1145–1178
Master Hilduin of St Denis	Puer, 1146–1148(?)
	Deacon, 1168–1179
	Chancellor of Notre Dame, 1180–1193
Master Hugh de Champfleury	Puer, 1147(?)
	Deacon, 1147–1150
	Royal Chancellor, 1150–1172
	Bishop of Soissons, 1159–1172
Master Ivo of Chartres	Deacon, 1124–1142
	Archdeacon, 1142–1158
John	Subdeacon, 1150
Master Maurice of Sully	Subdeacon, 1147 (probable)
	Deacon, c.1158–1160
	Bishop of Paris, 1160–1196
Master Odo of Soissons	Sacerdos/Presbyter, 1145–1157
	Chancellor, 1160–1167
	Abbot of Ourscamp, 1167–1170
	Cardinal Bishop of Tusculum, 1170–1171
Master Osmund of Poissy	Puer, 1134
	Subdeacon, 1150–1156
	Deacon, 1159–1174
Master Peter Lombard	Puer, 1145–1147
	Subdeacon, 1147–1150
	Deacon, 1150–1156
	Archdeacon, 1156–1159
	Bishop of Paris, 1159–1160

Table 1 (*continued*)

Peter de Monciaco	Subdeacon, 1124–1145
	Deacon, 1145–1152
Philip of France	Puer, 1145–1147
	Subdeacon, 1152
	Archdeacon, c.1157–1161
Ralph	Deacon, 1150–1152
Robert	Sacerdos/Presbyter, 1147–c.1175
	Succentor, 1160–1175
Simon of St Denis	Canon, 1150
	Subdeacon, 1159–1160
	Deacon, 1160–1180
	Royal Chancellor, 1150–1151
Master Simon of Poissy	Deacon, 1145–1160
	Archdeacon, 1163–1177
Stephen de Garlande	Archdeacon, 1096–1147
	Seneschal, 1120–1127
	Royal Chancellor, 1106–1127, 1132–1137
Theobald	Subdeacon, 1156–1164
Urban	Puer, 1124
	Subdeacon, 1146
Walter	Sacerdos, 1156
	Capellanus, 1160–1176
Master Walter	Sacerdos/Presbyter, 1142–1180
William	Puer, 1147

CHAPTER FOUR

The Years of Achievement, 1145–1160

By 1145, Peter Lombard's accomplishments were already impressive. He had been teaching theology for at least three years, and he was gaining a reputation. In addition to the income he derived from teaching, he now had a clerical position, something that was by no means certain for masters. It was also not an obscure position. He was part of the diocesan elite at Paris. Notre Dame was a place where the ecclesiastical, the intellectual, and the political all coalesced. It was a comfortable position for him to be in.

And yet, Peter was not content simply to remain where he was. As a theologian, he would not make his mark by teaching alone. Although he left a deep impression on his pupils (which we will see in part two), he also wanted to transmit his ideas through the written word. Over this fifteen-year period, he completed his *Commentary on the Letters of Paul,* a series of over thirty sermons, and, most importantly for his reputation, the *Sentences.* These works were refined and tested among his students.

At the same time, Peter seems to have been determined to rise within the chapter. He began as a cleric in minor orders, then worked his way up through the different grades of the diaconate, and was finally appointed bishop of Paris. Each new position he attained involved a greater degree of responsibility. This meant that when he took on episcopal authority, he was already quite well prepared for it, particularly from the experience of having been an archdeacon.

As we have seen in the previous chapter, the charters of Notre Dame allow us to identify the names and positions of the canons at particular times. In these documents, a transaction or decision is usually associated with either the dean or the bishop, or very occasionally with one of the archdeacons. Peter's appearance as a witness does not mean that he was involved in a ruling. But by using the documents to show what positions Peter held and when, and by examining what those positions entailed, we will be able to say something of the duties he carried out alongside his teaching and writing.

For the liturgical role of some of the positions he held, the best place to look is in Peter's own writings. In book four of the *Sentences*, he provides a list of the different orders of the church, as part of his discussion of the sacraments.[1] It would be a mistake to see this section as relating in any way to his personal experience. The *Sentences* was built on the writings of authorities, and, in the case of the sacrament of ordination, that meant principally Isidore of Seville,[2] along with some further material taken from his teacher Hugh of St Victor.[3] Also, Peter understandably focuses on the liturgical aspects of the orders, rather than on contemporary administrative norms.[4]

For his first two years at Notre Dame, Peter was a cleric in minor orders, listed as a *puer* in the documents.[5] A cleric in minor orders could be an exorcist, a doorkeeper, a lector, or an acolyte. In the eleventh century, three acolytes always featured in the documents of Notre Dame, until this changed to the more undefined *puer* in 1107.[6] The acolyte, according to Peter, was responsible for "the preparation of the window-shutters in the sacristy. He carries the wax candles, and he prepares the vessel with the water and wine

1 *Sententiae* 4, dist. 24, ch. 5–19, ed. Brady, 2: 393–408. Peter also discusses the orders of the church in the *Commentary on the Letters of Paul.* He elaborates on Paul's treatment of bishops and deacons in 1 Timothy 3:1–6 (PL 19: 352–345) and in Titus 1:7–9 (PL 192: 386–367).

2 Direct quotations of sections of Isidore, *Etymologiae* 7.12 (always acknowledged as such) characterize this section of the *Sentences.*

3 Hugh's discussion of ordination occurs in Hugh of St Victor, *De Sacramentis Christiane fidei* 2.3, ed. Rainer Berndt (Münster, 2008), 343–360.

4 In this context it is notable that Peter of Poitiers, a representative of the generation of theologians after Lombard, considered the orders to be a subject more appropriate to canonists than to theologians: "de quinto, id est de ordinibus, nil hic dicendum eo quod decretistis disputatio de his potius quam theologis deservit." Peter of Poitiers, *Sententiae* 5:15 (PL 211: 1257). The teacher of Peter of Poitiers, Peter Comestor also omitted ordination in his short work *De Sacramentis,* a summary of book four of Peter Lombard's *Sentences.* For this work see chapter seven, 174–175.

5 Brady, Prolegomena 1: 22*–23*. For the meaning of *puer* as a cleric in minor orders, see Charles du Fresne du Cange, *Glossarium mediae et infimae Latinitatis,* ed. Léopold Favre (Niort, 1883–1887), 6: 558; Jan Frederik Niermeyer and C. van de Kieft, *Mediae Latinitatis lexicon minus,* rev. ed. Johannes W. J. Burgers (Leiden, 2002), 2: 1135.

6 Three *pueri* are listed in *Cartulaire,* ed. de Lasteyrie, no. 145, p. 165, a document of 1107. The last time the three acolytes appear as witnesses is ibid., no. 121, p. 145, from 1098.

supplied for the eucharist for the subdeacons."[7] It has been suggested that these *pueri* were the boys in the choir school.[8] Although some may have been, it seems probable that designating clerics as *pueri* was a way of indicating different minor orders. The most familiar meaning of *puer* is certainly a boy, but by the twelfth century it was also used of servants, vassals, and armed retainers.[9] While a young member of the chapter like Philip of France might carry out the acolyte's duties, someone of Peter's abilities and experience would seem to be more suited to the minor order of lector. Again, to quote the *Sentences*:

> What pertains to the lector is to read out the [Old Testament] readings and the things that the prophets prophesized, to preach to the people, so that by his office he may read the prophecies and lessons in the church .... A person promoted to this office ought to be instructed in the knowledge of letters so that he can understand the sense of the words, know the strength of the accents, and read distinctly, so that he does not mislead the understanding of those listening by a confused pronunciation .... The voice of the lector should console the hearts and ears.[10]

The lector therefore required a solid educational background, which Peter certainly had. This was especially necessary because of the obligation to preach. It would have been the first time that Peter Lombard had to preach sermons, and his surviving output in that area will be addressed in the next chapter. One did not have to be a priest or even a deacon to give sermons, but the lectors were restricted to preaching only on the Old Testament. The

7 "Ad acolytum pertinet praeparatio luminarium in sacrario; ipse cereum portat, ipse urceolum cum vino et aqua suggesta, pro eucharistia subdiaconis praeparat," *Sententiae* 4, dist. 24, ch. 8, ed. Brady, 2: 399.

8 Craig M. Wright, *Music and Ceremony at Notre Dame of Paris, 550–1550* (Cambridge, 1989), 166.

9 Niermeyer and van de Kieft, *Mediae Latinitatis lexicon minus*, 2: 1135.

10 "Ad lectorem autem pertinet lectiones pronuntiare, et ea quae prophetae vaticinaverunt, populis praedicare, ut jam ex officio in ecclesia legat prophetias et lectiones ... Qui ad hunc gradum provehitur, litterarum scientia debet esse instructus, ut sensum verborum intelligat, vim accentuum sciat, distincte legat, ne confusione prolationis intellectum auditoribus auferat. Attendat quid indicative, quid interrogative sit legendum, ubi sit in oratione facienda distinctio ... Auribus et cordi consulere debet vox lectoris." *Sententiae* 4, dist. 24, ch. 6, ed. Brady, 2: 397.

deacon, on the other hand, was expected "to preach to the people on the Gospel and the Epistles. For just as the lectors are commanded to preach on the Old Testament, so the deacons must do so for the new."[11] This has implications for dating Peter's surviving sermons. As we will see in the next chapter, the majority of his sermons have Old Testament verses as their starting points, so it is certainly plausible that he was preaching as early as 1145.

In Peter Lombard's time, no member of the chapter remained as a *puer* for more than eight years.[12] This may suggest that to retain a benefice, one was expected to be at least a subdeacon. Peter is first mentioned as a subdeacon in 1147.[13] He remained in that position until at least 1152. The subdiaconate was not a major order of the church until the time of Innocent III,[14] but it was already considered to be in some way above the minor orders. Unlike them, subdeacons were bound by the law of chastity. According to the *Sentences*, "to the subdiaconate pertains carrying the chalice and paten to the altar of Christ, handing them to the deacons, and ministering with them … . The law of continence is placed upon them because, in drawing near the altar, they carry the body and blood of Christ."[15] Peter also adds that subdeacons are "subject to the commands and duties of the deacons."[16] Material on the administrative duties of subdeacons is difficult to find, but at Notre Dame they probably assisted the deacons and the archdeacons in overseeing the clergy of the diocese. In the Roman church in this period, one of the duties of subdeacons was to be the bearers of the pope's letters. This can be seen

11 "Ad diaconem pertinet … praedicare Evangelium et Epistolam. Nam sicut lectoribus vetus Testamentum, ita diaconibus novum praedicare praeceptum est." Ibid., dist. 24, ch. 10, ed. Brady, 2: 402.

12 See Andrew, Anselm, and Boso in the table at the end of chapter three, above.

13 *Cartulaire de l'église Notre-Dame de Paris*, ed. Benjamin Guérard (Paris, 1850), 2: 360. This document is also edited by Ignatius C. Brady in "Peter Lombard: Canon of Notre Dame," *RTAM* 32 (1965): 277–295, at 285.

14 William Fanning, "Subdeacon," in *The Catholic Encyclopedia: An International Work of Reference on the Constitution, Doctrine, Discipline, and History of the Catholic Church*, ed. Charles G. Herbermann (New York, 1907–1914) 14: 320–321. For this development, see Roger Reynolds, "The Subdiaconate as a Sacred and Superior Order" in *Clerics in the Middle Ages: Hierarchy and Image* (Aldershot, 1999), chapter IV.

15 "Ad subdiaconum pertinet calicem et patenam ad altare Christi deferre, et levitis tradere, eisque ministrare … . His lex continentiae imponitur, quia altari propinquantes, vasa corporis et sanguinis Christi portant," *Sententiae*, dist. 24, ch. 9, ed. Brady, 2: 400.

16 "Qui ideo sic appellantur, quia subiacent praeceptis et officiis levitarum." Ibid.

from a number of references in the letters of Eugenius III, for example,[17] and it meant in practice that the subdeacon was a diplomat. Those who delivered medieval letters were expected to verbally pass on information that was too sensitive to put in writing.[18] References of this kind do not seem to appear in any surviving letters of the twelfth-century bishops of Paris, however.[19]

So for his first seven years in the chapter, Peter's status was not prominent, but it was reliable and a solid basis on which to build. Meanwhile his reputation as a theologian was continuing to grow, and other events in 1147–1148 allow us to glimpse this. These are well-documented years for ecclesiastical affairs in Paris, because in April 1147, Pope Eugenius visited the city. His visit formed part of the elaborate choreography of preparations for the Second Crusade. Louis VII had committed himself to the project the previous year, and the pope's visit included a number of public ceremonies that would reinforce the image of the king as a pious crusader. The canons of Notre Dame played their part in these too. We can assume that Peter Lombard would have been present at one such ceremony held at St Denis in June. The canons processed with the relic of the true cross given to them by the patriarch of Jerusalem in 1120.[20] The pope also met Peter Lombard on this visit, when he decided to consult him on a point of doctrine (the question of fraternal correction).[21] This shows that Peter already had a widely recognized authority as a master, even though the *Sentences* would not be published for another nine years.

17 Eugenius III, *Epistolae* (PL 180). Letters 128, 129, 130, and 231 all refer to being delivered by subdeacons. Letter 231 (PL 180: 1284) is the best example, since it specifies that the subdeacon will say more than is actually in the letter.

18 See the letter mentioned in chapter one, Bernard of Clairvaux, *Ep.* 551, *Sancti Bernardi opera*, ed. Jean Leclercq, Charles H. Talbot, and Henri Rochais (Rome, 1957–1977). Ferruccio Gastaldelli, "Le tre ultime lettere dell'epistolario di San Bernardo," *Analecta Cisterciensia* 50 (1994): 251–292, at 272–274. Bernard, as Bredero explains, "followed the custom of his day of writing letters that testified to his friendship and goodwill toward the addressee, while the courtier who delivered the letter was charged with orally transmitting or explaining the real reason." Adriaan H. Bredero, *Bernard of Clairvaux: Between Cult and History* (Edinburgh, 1996), 3.

19 For example, the letters of Stephen of Senlis (PL 173: 1411–1421). Nor do the letters of the archbishop, Hugh of Sens, *RHF* 15: 710–719.

20 For the ceremony, see Jonathan Phillips, *The Second Crusade: Extending the Frontiers of Christendom* (New Haven, 2007), 126. The donation by the patriarch to the chapter can be found in *Cartulaire*, ed. de Lasteyrie, no. 151, pp. 171–172.

21 Brady, Prolegomena 1: 26*–27*; Rosemann, *Peter Lombard*, 37–38.

Not all of the pope's time in Paris was devoted to preparations for the crusade. A controversy had developed concerning the theology master Gilbert of Poitiers, who had taught in Paris before becoming bishop of his native city in 1142.[22] The dispute was over the position he took on the Trinity in his *Commentary on Boethius*. He had been denounced by two of his own archdeacons, and this hints at how personal the controversy was. It is often difficult to know whether it was the position or the person that was on trial. The two archdeacons, Arnold and Kalo, were able to interest Bernard of Clairvaux in their case, knowing how important his moral authority could be.[23] Nikolaus M. Häring points to how easy it was to misunderstand Gilbert's works if not read with the proper care,[24] and also to the involvement of a group of French bishops.[25] In Paris, Eugenius convoked a meeting called a consistory to look into the matter.[26] Peter was probably in attendance, although there is no record of him saying anything.[27] The proceeding was a strange affair since "nobody had apparently thought of obtaining a copy of the controversial commentary on Boethius."[28] Instead, two theology mas-

22 For Gilbert, see Nikolaus M. Häring, "The Case of Gilbert de la Porrée, Bishop of Poitiers (1142–1154)," *Mediaeval Studies* 13 (1951): 1–40, and Theresa Gross-Diaz, *The Psalms Commentary of Gilbert of Poitiers: From 'Lectio Divina' to the Lecture Room* (Leiden, 1996), 1–25. An excellent recent treatment of the events of 1147–1148 is Clare Monagle, *Orthodoxy and Controversy in Twelfth-Century Religious Discourse: Peter Lombard's* Sentences *and the Development of Theology* (Turnhout, 2013), 32–41.

23 Otto I, Bishop of Freising, *Gesta Frederici I imperatoris* 53 (MGH SS 46: 54, 59).

24 Häring, "The Case of Gilbert de la Porrée, Bishop of Poitiers (1142–1154)," 2–3: "He wrote intricate, but excellent Latin, which requires very attentive and careful reading. Once his basic principles are properly understood, Gilbert is generally neither vague nor obscure." Elsewhere, Häring refers to Gilbert's commentary on Boethius, which "is no easy reading, and it happened that even some of his students misinterpreted his doctrine." Nikolaus M. Häring, "Chartres and Paris Revisited," in *Essays in Honour of Anton Charles Pegis*, ed. J. Reginald O'Donnell (Toronto, 1974) 303. See also Monagle, *Orthodoxy and Controversy in Twelfth-Century Religious Discourse*, xv and 32–41.

25 Nikolaus M. Häring, "Notes on the Council and Consistory of Rheims," *Mediaeval Studies* 28 (1966): 39–59, at 45–46. For their role, see John of Salisbury, *Historia pontificalis*, ed. Marjorie Chibnall (Oxford, 1956), 15–20.

26 For the Paris consistory, see Nikolaus M. Häring, "Das Pariser Konsistorium Eugens III vom April 1147," *Studiana Gratiana* 11 (1967): 91–117; Häring, "Chartres and Paris Revisited," 303–304.

27 Brady, Prolegomena 1: 29*.

28 Haring, "Notes on the Council and Consistory of Rheims," 58.

ters, Hugh of Champfleury (the canon of Notre Dame) and Adam of the Petit Pont, came forward and asserted, "as though under oath," that they had heard Gilbert take heretical positions.[29] Otto of Freising commented further that "many of those who were present were surprised that such great men, skilled in the practice of debate, should offer an oath instead of an argument."[30] Eugenius wisely deferred a decision until the matter could be looked at in more detail.

The opportunity for this arose at the council of Rheims, planned for the following year. When the council ended, after eleven days, Pope Eugenius requested that some people, mostly cardinals and bishops, remain behind to examine the controversy again.[31] At Paris, the contributions of the theologians had lacked credibility. This time, the debate was more specific. Ivo of Chartres provided a spirited defence of Gilbert, whose student he had been. The case against was taken by Peter Lombard and Robert of Melun.[32]

Why was Peter involved? It does seem as if most of the Paris theology masters took one side or the other. John of Salisbury questioned his motivation, however: "I cannot say whether they [Peter and Robert of Melun] acted out of zeal for the faith, or jealousy for [Gilbert's] fame and merit, or out of a desire to propitiate the abbot [Bernard], whose influence was then at its height."[33] Jealousy can surely be ruled out as a motive, since Peter was a canon of Paris already, and well recognized as a theologian. It was probably a combination of the other two motivations. Peter certainly owed Bernard of Clairvaux for his support in the 1130s. We should also remember that the position of theology masters may simply have been to explain each side of the argument to the dignitaries in attendance. They were certainly not the motivating force. But at the same time, Peter Lombard's criticisms were sincerely meant.

29 Otto I, Bishop of Freising, *Gesta Frederici I imperatoris* 53 (MGH SS 46: 60), trans. by Christopher C. Mierow and Richard Emery as *The Deeds of Frederick Barbarossa* (New York, 1953), 89.

30 Ibid.

31 John of Salisbury, *Historia pontificalis*, ed. Chibnall, 16. For the distinction between council and consistory, and for the proceedings against Gilbert, see Häring, "Notes on the Council and Consistory of Rheims," 39–60.

32 John of Salisbury, *Historia pontificalis*, ed. Chibnall, 16, and Brady, Prolegomena 1: 30*, addresses whether Peter was present at both council and consistory and where his intervention took place.

33 John of Salisbury, *Historia pontificalis*, ed. Chibnall, 16.

He went on to incorporate them into the *Commentary on the Letters of Paul* and the *Sentences*.[34]

As the trial continued, it became obvious that Gilbert had too much support, particularly among the cardinals, to be found guilty. Peter was probably one of the masters present at Bernard of Clairvaux's residence when the compromise of having Gilbert read a profession of faith was discussed. This was how the consistory ended.[35] The proceedings would have left an impression on Peter. He would have been made very aware of the potential risks of writing theology, and of how crucial it would be to have his positions correctly represented. In some ways, the reputation of theology masters depended on their students. They had to be able to correctly state and explain their master's positions, especially in circumstances where books were not available for consultation. Gilbert and his former students had insisted on presenting his work as a whole, while his opponents had selected passages out of context.[36] This had worked in his favour.

What impact did all of this have on Peter's reputation? The degree of bitterness that he could have faced from Gilbert's supporters would have depended on how much had been at stake. It is not clear what a guilty verdict at Rheims would have meant, beyond the condemnation of specific positions in the text. The atmosphere seems to have been less explosive than the earlier councils at Soissons (1121) and Sens (1141), where Abelard's positions had been put on trial. At those events, there had been a real threat of the proceedings spilling over into popular violence.[37] On this occasion, the pope had to request that some people remain after the council. The majority of atten-

34 Brady, Prolegomena 1: 30*. See also, *Sententiae* I, dist. 33, ch. 1, ed. Brady, 2: 240. Brady believes that "secundum hoc capitulo Magister positionem S. Bernardi defendit contra Gilbertum Porretanum." He goes on to point out that Bernard's position is outlined in *De Consideratione* 5: 8–18. However, Peter may not have seen that work yet since it dates from the end of Bernard's life. See Guy Lobrichon, "Chronologie des oeuvres de Saint Bernard de Clairvaux," in *Bernard de Clairvaux: Histoire, mentalités, spiritualité* (Paris, 1992), 32–41.

35 Häring, "Notes on the Council and Consistory of Rheims," 49–50.

36 Ibid., 45.

37 For Soissons, see Peter Abelard, *Historia calamitatum*, ed. Jacques Monfrin (Paris, 1959), 83. See also Michael Clanchy, *Abelard: A Medieval Life* (Oxford, 1997), 304–306. For Sens in this context, see Constant Mews, "The Council of Sens (1141): Abelard, Bernard, and the Fear of Social Upheaval," *Speculum* 77 (2002): 342–382.

dees were uninterested.[38] Nevertheless, some of Gilbert's followers would probably have held it against Peter.

If Peter made enemies because of his activities at Rheims, however, they did not act immediately. In his lifetime, there were no serious challenges to his work. The only documented case is from a rather obscure figure, Robert Cricklade.[39] Cricklade, an English prior and author of assorted works,[40] turned up in Paris in the 1150s, seeking to take issue with Peter Lombard over his position on Christ's human nature.[41] He claimed that Peter did not teach that Christ was God and man, but he made no specific reference to his works.[42] He also trotted out clichés like "the truth should always be loved."[43] Cricklade seemed to believe he was following in the footsteps of St Bernard, whose works he was fond of.[44] One wonders if he knew of Bernard's assistance to Peter in the 1130s. He claims that he had engaged in a debate with one of Peter's students. With all the self-satisfaction of the second rate, Cricklade recalls how he won the argument. This is in a work called *Speculum Fidei*, written years after these events: "In that city where he taught, Paris, I openly pronounced him to be a heretic. There are witnesses .... I affirmed in public

38 Häring, "Notes on the Council and Consistory of Rheims," 45.

39 In one of his works, Gerhoh of Reichersberg criticized Anselm, Gilbert, and "most recently Peter Lombard" of inserting into their glosses "falsehoods" wrongly attributed to Ambrose. This had been thought to date from 1142, but Brady, Prolegomena 1: 82*–88*, suggests that the mid-1160s is more probable. Gerhoh of Reichersberg, *De Ordine Donorum*, ed. Damien Van de Eynde, *Opera inedita* (Rome, 1955–1956), 1: 71.

40 Cricklade was prior of St Frideswide in Oxford and is best known for a life of Becket which exists now only in an Old Norse version. See M.A. Orme, "A Reconstruction of Robert of Cricklade's *Vita et Miracula S. Thomae Cantuariensis*," *Analecta Bollandiana* 84 (1966): 379–398. See also Charles H. Haskins, *Studies in the History of Mediaeval Science* (Cambridge MA., 1924), 169–171, and Anne J. Duggan, "Cricklade, Robert of," in *Oxford Dictionary of National Biography*, ed. Henry C.G. Matthew and Brian Harrison (Oxford, 2004), 14: 191–192. The debate is also covered in Monagle, *Orthodoxy and Controversy in Twelfth-Century Religious Discourse*, 88–92.

41 Richard W. Hunt, "English Learning in the Late Twelfth Century," *Transactions of the Royal Historical Society* 19 (1936): 19–42, at 32, 37–38.

42 "'In quo,' inquit, 'hereticus est magister Petrus?' 'In multis,' inquam. 'Unum,' inquit, 'proferetur.' 'Separat,' inquam, 'hominem a Deo, ut non sit una persona homo cum Deo in Trinitate, qui revera filius Dei est.'" Ibid., 37–38. Robert's interlocutor here is Roger, later bishop of Worcester.

43 "'Veritas,' inquam, 'audienda est et semper amanda.'" Ibid., 39.

44 Ibid., 31

that he was a heretic, and I debated it with some of his disciples, who, as I learned, were sent to me by Peter .... The learned men who were there openly congratulated me."[45] It is clear, however, that Peter did not take him seriously enough to debate. Cricklade is an isolated example, but after Peter's death, criticisms intensified. Indeed, Robert of Melun and Achard of St Victor, who did later take issue with some of Peter's positions, are named by Cricklade as witnesses to this debate.[46] Their attendance, however, should not necessarily be taken as a full endorsement of his arguments. The growing criticism of Peter Lombard after 1160 will be addressed in part two. It is explained partly by two factors. The *Sentences* only began to gain a reputation from 1158, two years before his death. Also, in his lifetime, his ecclesiastical dignity as archdeacon and then bishop of Paris might have dissuaded such moves.

Most authorities agree that the first version of the *Commentary on the Letters of Paul* was completed after the council of Rheims.[47] At least four manuscript copies were made, presumably authorized by Peter. In the 1150s he reworked it and produced a second version. This second version was copied with greater frequency and was the source of the sixteenth-century printed editions.[48] The com-

45 "Et in sua civitate, id est Parisius, ubi docebat, hereticum eum esse patenter pronuntiabam. Testes michi sunt ... eum hereticum esse publice affirmabam; et cum potioribus discipulis eius contuli ad me ut didici, ab eo missis ... Qui vero tunc aderant sane sapientes congratulantur michi." Ibid., 37–38.

46 Ibid., 37. See also Constant J. Mews, "Between the Schools of Abelard and Saint-Victor, in the Mid-Twelfth Century: The Witness of Robert of Melun," in *L'école de Saint-Victor de Paris: Influence et rayonnement du Moyen Âge à l'epoque moderne*, ed. Dominique Poirel (Turnhout, 2010), 121–138, at 125–128.

47 Discussions of the commentary can be found in Brady, Prolegomena 1: 62*–89*, who addresses the sources, the date of composition, and the manuscripts. The best critical assessment is by Marcia Colish, who helpfully divides Peter's approach to Paul into categories: Colish, *Peter Lombard*, 192–225. See also her earlier article, "Peter Lombard as an Exegete of St Paul," in *Ad Litteram: Authoritative Texts and Their Medieval Readers*, ed. Mark D. Jordan and Kent Emery (Notre Dame, 1992), 71–92. Mark Zier's recent article, "Peter Lombard and the *Glossa Ordinaria*: A Missing Link?" in *Pietro Lombardo: Atti del XLIII Convegno storico internazionale* (Spoleto, 2007), 361–409, is also very helpful, as is Rosemann's assessment in *Peter Lombard*, 44–48. Like the psalm commentary, however, the work lacks a modern critical edition.

48 For the two versions, see Brady, Prolegomena 1: 65*–72*. He also discusses the problems with the 1535 edition, problems which were made worse by its inclusion in the *Patrologia Latina*.

mentary is sometimes referred to as the *Collectanea*, which means "things assembled," or "materials drawn together." This title, however, was added later and was not used by Peter. It will also be discussed in some detail in chapter eight, since Peter's student Herbert of Bosham completed an edition of it after his master's death.

The commentary is clearly a product of Peter's lectures in his theology school. Certain passages have the definite character of theological instruction. In the *Commentary on Ephesians*, Peter warns his readers to "be careful that you understand in this way" and to "therefore distinguish it in this way."[49] The commentary is also characterized by a broad use of authorities and influences. In this it differs from the *Commentary on the Psalms*.[50] We can take the overall prologue as an example. Although influenced by a number of predecessors, it is very much Peter's own. For this reason, it provides a valuable example of how he approached writing an *accessus*, a prologue, and how he introduced material in his school of theology.[51]

Peter first explains the significance of where the letters appear in the New Testament: "after the Gospels, in which the order of the Christian religion and the doctrine of perfect sanctity is delivered, the useful doctrine of the Letters of Paul and the others followed, so that it could protect the church of God against wicked heretics, and free (us) from faults rising again, and exclude future questionings."[52] After this, he moves to a discussion of the author, and he sees Paul as one who provides hope: "having violently persecuted the church of God, for which he deserved the heaviest penalty, instead of malediction he attained grace, and instead of damnation he took

49 "Cave quomodo intelligas." "Ita ergo distingue." Peter Lombard, *Glossa in epistolas* (PL 192: 9–520, at 200).

50 The preface to the psalm commentary seems to have been largely borrowed from Gilbert of Poitiers, from the description of Gilbert's work in Gross-Diaz, *The Psalms Commentary of Gilbert of Poitiers*, 79–93.

51 "The Lombard's preface goes far beyond the very brief introductions found in the gloss manuscripts or even the preface of Gilbert of Poitiers's *Media Glossatura*. Peter borrows from Jerome's preface ... but with considerable freedom." Zier, "Peter Lombard and the *Glossa Ordinaria*: A Missing Link?" 366.

52 "In Novo Testamento post Evangelium, in quo Christianae religionis ordo et perfectae sanctitatis doctrina traditur, Epistolarum Pauli et aliorum perutilis secuta est doctrina, ut Ecclesiam Dei contra haereticas communiret pravitates, et suborientia vitia resecaret, et post futuras quaestiones excluderet." Peter Lombard, *Glossa in epistolas* (PL 191: 1297–1696, at 1297).

on compassion. In view of his case, our own hope is raised up to a great extent."[53]

The order of the letters symbolizes the Old and New Testaments. The ten letters to churches stand for the Old (built on the Decalogue), while the four persons represent the four gospels. Peter then deals with the authenticity of the letters, and with their chronology. He believes that the Letter to the Romans opens the collection, "not because it was written first by the apostle, but on account of the dignity of the Romans, who at that time held sway over all nations ... their reputation resonated in the mind of every man."[54] Explaining the letters in their historical context is a feature of Peter's approach in the commentary.[55]

There is a brief section on the subject matter and intention of the collection, but Peter thinks that these aspects would be best approached in terms of each individual letter. The rest of the preface is largely concerned with the Letter to the Romans rather than with the collection as a whole. He discusses where it was written, and how Paul emerges as the perfect reconciler for the competing claims of the Jews and gentiles to revealed truth.[56] Finally he addresses the subject and purpose of this letter. These sections together could be described as a second preface.

Each letter also opens with a preface that discusses the historical background, Paul's purpose in writing, the intention, and the structure. These prefaces were set apart from the commentary proper in manuscripts, but they can be easy to miss in the *Patrologia Latina* (which incorporates an imperfect sixteenth-century edition).[57] The discussion of structure is somewhat less literary than the prefaces had been in the *Commentary on the*

53 "Violenter Ecclesiam Dei persecutus, pro quo summo dignus fuit supplicio, pro maledictione consecutus est gratiam, et pro damnatione suscepit misericordiam. In quo ipso spes nostra plurimum sublevatur." Ibid., 1298.

54 "Non quod ab Apostolo prima sit scripta, sed causa dignitatis Romanorum, qui tunc temporis universis gentibus imperabant ... eorumque fama omnium hominum resonabat in ore," Ibid., 1300.

55 Colish, *Peter Lombard*, 200–207, writes well on instances of this in the commentary.

56 Peter Lombard, *Glossa in epistolas* (PL 191: 1301).

57 On the shortcomings of the printed edition incorporated in the *Patrologia Latina*, see Brady, Prolegomena 1: 72*. On the manuscript edition of the commentary prepared by Peter's student Herbert of Bosham, see chapter eight, below, 226–232.

Psalms. There, Peter had demonstrated how each psalm could be divided into a certain number of sections.[58] Here he simply summarizes each chapter, often with the word *deinde* appearing in succession ("then ... then ... then").[59] Admittedly, this has partly to do with the genre of the text he is approaching.

Since the commentary grew out of lectures in a theology school, and given Peter's later work in the *Sentences*, it is not surprising that it contains substantial sections elaborating doctrine.[60] Some of these are extended enough to be considered treatises in their own right. The best example of this occurs in the treatment of the Letter to the Romans. Peter's approach to Paul's text is extremely thorough and logical. For example, he glosses Paul's seemingly simple greeting to the Romans, "Paul, a servant of Jesus Christ, called Apostle," as follows: "In this greeting he commends the person in four ways, by his name, by his condition, by his dignity, and by his office. By name, saying 'Paul,' by condition, 'servant,' by dignity, 'apostle,' by office, 'set apart for the gospel of God.'"[61] He then goes on to explain each of the four ways in turn. Mark Zier refers to this, rightly, as "a typical scholastic division."[62] One would expect Peter to treat his text in this manner. The careful exposition of each line was an approach to texts he had learned throughout his education. But when he reaches Romans 1:3, "concerning his son who was made," things change. A theological mind like his could not let the phrase *factus est* ("he was made") pass by without extended comment. This was an opportunity for him to discuss the incarnation in detail. In the first version of the commentary, the treatment of *factus est* was so long that it was in danger of dwarfing the rest of the work. Brady edited this as a separate treatise, which he called *On the Incarnation,* and it runs to twenty-three pages.[63]

58 See, for example, on Psalm 71, "modus: septem sunt partitiones." Peter Lombard, *Commentaria in psalmos* (PL 191: 5–1297, at 657).

59 See, for example, the preface to 1 Corinthians: Peter Lombard, *Glossa in Epistolas* (PL 191: 1534).

60 "In this work, we encounter the Lombard, as it were, torn between *sacra pagina* and systematic theology." Rosemann, *Peter Lombard,* 45.

61 "In hac autem salutatione primum personam commendat quatuor modis, scilicet a nomine, a conditione, a dignitate, ab officio. A nomine, dicens, *Paulus;* a conditione, *servus;* a dignitate, *apostolus;* ab officio, *segregatus in Evangelium Dei."* Peter Lombard, *Glossa in Epistolas* (PL 191: 1302).

62 Zier, "Peter Lombard and the *Glossa Ordinaria*: A Missing Link?" 367.

63 Brady, Prolegomena 2: 54*–77*.

Brady also edited three other sections as separate works, which do not appear in the second version.[64] None of these are quite as long, however.

Working on these sections, it seems, brought Peter to the realization that a commentary was not the best place to set down thoroughly argued positions on points of doctrine.[65] These sections had the potential to be something more, if he detached them and linked them up with material in a similar format. In the second version of the commentary, the treatment of *factus est* is scaled back, and it does not interfere with the overall flow of the work.[66] But he did not completely leave aside the material he had removed. Instead, he began to make use of it. This is where we can glimpse Peter working toward a new kind of project, which would be the *Sentences*. The original treatment of Romans 1:3 became the basis for Peter's treatment of the incarnation in book three of the *Sentences*.[67]

This discussion of *factus est* also shows Peter's awareness of how much was possible in scriptural interpretation. A surviving gloss should not be seen as his last word on any particular verse. He had to take the length and the overall balance of the work into account. That does not mean he said all he had to say on it. In chapter six we will see how the task of preaching a sermon on the psalm text "o for the wings of a dove" spurred Peter on to one of his most unique sermons. It was on a completely different level to his brief treatment of this verse in the *Commentary on the Psalms*. This must have made his classroom an electrifying atmosphere at times. It also recalls Peter's patron Bernard of Clairvaux, who could construct a connected series of eight sermons from a single line in the *Song of Songs*.[68]

The early 1150s saw the return of Louis VII from crusade, and his divorce from Eleanor of Aquitane. A number of clerical giants passed away: Bernard

64 These are *De Corpore Christi*, ibid., 77*–84*, from the gloss on 1 Corinthians 11; *De Coniugo*, ibid., 84*–87*, from the gloss on 1 Corinthians 7; and *De Processione Filii et Spiritus Sancti*, Brady, Prolegomena 1: 90*–93*, from the gloss on Romans 11.

65 Rosemann, *Peter Lombard*, 45–47, writes well on this point.

66 In the second version, the explanation of *factus est* takes up five columns of the PL text. Peter Lombard, *Glossa in Epistolas* (PL 191: 1304–1309).

67 Brady, Prolegomena 1: 86*–88*.

68 The first eight of the eighty-six *Sermons on the Song of Songs* are based on verse 1.1: "Let him kiss me with the kiss of his mouth." Evans refers to this approach as "ruminating" on the text "until every vestige of flavour and meaning have been extracted from it." Gillian R. Evans, *Bernard of Clairvaux* (New York, 2000), 58.

of Clairvaux, Pope Eugenius, and Suger of St Denis. Among the canons of Notre Dame, however, the 1150s presented continuity rather than change. There were few canons that had not been there at the close of the 1140s. If we take a list of the canons from 1156–1157 as an example, the only new faces are the three *pueri* and two subdeacons (which would be expected).[69] Those who had been there for some time were all in the same positions. The exception is Peter Lombard, who between 1150 and 1159, appears as first a subdeacon, then archdeacon, and finally bishop. This advancement meant that he was given greater administrative responsibilities. It is actually remarkable that he was able to balance this workload with his most productive period in teaching and writing. It was not until he became bishop that he had to leave the schools behind.

Peter was still a subdeacon in 1152, but he had been appointed archdeacon by 1156. In the intervening years, he must have spent some time as a deacon, since it was not possible to skip that step. In the *Decretum*, Gratian, citing a council of Pope Urban II, stated that no one could be promoted to the archidiaconate (or the episcopate) without being first a deacon or priest.[70] It is unlikely that Peter became one of the priests because the documents of Notre Dame always list the same three people in that office between 1147 and 1156 (Odo of Soissons, Robert, and Walter).[71] As a deacon, Peter's responsibilities as a preacher changed. He would now be required to preach sermons on the New Testament.[72] Traditionally, deacons also had two long-established roles. They oversaw church property, and they assisted the bishop with the management of the diocese.[73] In the classic phrase, the deacon

69 *Cartulaire*, ed. de Lasteyrie, no. 394, pp. 347–348.

70 "Nullus episcopus in ecclesia sua, nisi diaconus sit, archidiaconum instituere, nec archipresbiterum aut decanum, nisi presbiteri sint, ordinare presumat." Gratian, *Decretum*, dist. 60, ch. 1. ed. Emil Friedberg, *Corpus iuris canonici* (Leipzig: Bernhard Tauchnitz, 1879–1881), 1: 226.

71 See the table at the end of chapter three, above.

72 See the discussion of the lector's duties, above, 83–84.

73 Herbert Thurston, "Deacons," in *The Catholic Encyclopedia*, 4: 647–653. For the development of the office in the medieval church, see for example Georg Scheibelreiter, "Church Structure and Organization," in *New Cambridge Medieval History*, ed. Paul Fouracre (Cambridge, 1995–2005), 1: 690; Christopher Brooke, *Churches and Churchmen in Medieval* Europe (London, 1999), 119; and Herbert E.J. Cowdrey, "The Structure of the Church, 1024–1073," in *New Cambridge Medieval History*, ed. David Luscombe and Jonathan Riley-Smith (Cambridge, 1995–2005), 4.1: 229–267, at 251.

should be "the eye of the bishop, a roving eye" that "shines a light, with discretion, on the affairs of the whole church."[74] He was expected to refer potential problems to the bishop.[75] This description, from the ninth-century Pseudo-Isidoran decretals, had become standard by the twelfth century, where it is found in Gratian.[76] By this time, however, such duties were carried out as much by the archdeacons as by deacons.[77]

Peter was almost certainly a deacon by 1154. In that year, we find him assisting his bishop by accompanying him on a trip to Rome.[78] Bishop Theobald had a number of matters to attend to there, among them receiving papal confirmation of his rights over the church of St Geneviève.[79] The influential archdeacon Stephen de Garlande had been dean of the church, and the bishops of Paris had not attempted to enforce their rights over it while he lived.[80] Since Stephen's death in 1148, attempts had been made to scale back the independence of the canons of St Geneviève.[81] Theobald and his clerics were in Rome from late November 1154 to early 1155.[82] While they were there, Pope Anastasius (who had succeeded Eugenius III the previous year) died on 3 December, and Adrian IV was elected on the following day.

Peter's familiarity with the country meant he was a good choice to accompany bishop Theobald, particularly for the journey down the *Via Francigena*. This may well have been the first time he had visited Italy after leaving twenty years prior. We are left in no doubt, however, that Peter was a scholar first and a clerical career man second. He used his time in Rome to familiarize

74 "Diaconi vero Ecclesiae tanquam oculi sint episcopi, oberrantes et circumlustrantes cum verecundia actus totius Ecclesiae." Pseudo-Isidore, *Decretalium Collectio* (PL 130: 23).

75 "ut referant haec ad episcopum." Ibid.

76 Gratian, *Decretum*, dist. 93, ch. 6, ed. Friedberg, 321–322.

77 See the discussion of archdeacons, below, 102–103.

78 Brady, "Peter Lombard: Canon of Notre Dame," 292–293, established beyond doubt that Peter's journey to Rome must have been in Theobald's retinue. See also his more detailed discussion of the Italian journey in Brady, Prolegomena 2: 13*–19*.

79 Brady, "Peter Lombard: Canon of Notre Dame," 292–293.

80 For Stephen de Garlande, see chapter three, above, 53–54.

81 For these events, see Robert Henri Bautier, "Paris au temps d'Abélard," in *Abélard en son temps*, ed. Jean Jolivet (Paris, 1981), 58, 77, and Lindy Grant, *Abbot Suger of St. Denis: Church and State in Early Twelfth Century France* (London, 1998), 166.

82 Brady, "Peter Lombard: Canon of Notre Dame," 291–293; Brady, Prolegomena 2: 16*–17*.

himself with at least one text not yet available in Paris, *De fide orthodoxa* ("On Orthodox Faith") by the Greek father John Damascene. This work had recently been given a new Latin translation by Burgundio of Pisa. Since John provided a summary of theological doctrine based on all available authorities, *De fide orthodoxa* is often seen as a precursor to the work of sentence theologians like Lombard. In Rome, Peter spent as much time as he could studying this text,[83] and it helped him to refine his Christological positions in the *Sentences*.[84] He must have either brought a working version of the *Sentences* with him to Rome or had portions of the translation copied while there. While it is certainly probable that Peter checked other references while in Rome, the work on John Damascene stands out because he told his students about it later. When one of them wrote his own commentary on the *Sentences*, he noted beside a reference to Damascene that "the master consulted this while he was in Rome."[85]

The two years following his return from Rome would have represented intensive work on the *Sentences*, since it was released for publication and introduced in Peter's classroom in 1156.[86] Peter had now been studying theology since he arrived in France twenty years before, and the *Sentences* was the product of that consistent focus. We have seen that he incorporated discarded sections from the *Commentary on the Letters of Paul* into it and that his lectures in the 1140s probably also furnished material.[87] The *Sentences*, however, represented his most recent and considered positions. Brady points out that a number of sermons must antedate the *Sentences* because they treat subjects in a very different way.[88]

83 Brady, Prolegomena 1: 121*; Rosemann, *Peter Lombard*, 38.
84 Rosemann, *Peter Lombard*, provides an accessible demonstration of this on 123 and 126.
85 "A libro isto sumpsit Magister hanc auctoritatem dum Romae esset." This is the Pseudo-Peter of Poitiers gloss on the *Sentences*, quoted in Brady, "Peter Lombard: Canon of Notre Dame," 292. For a discussion of this student, see chapter seven, below, 192–194.
86 For the date of composition for the *Sentences*, Brady, Prolegomena 1: 122*–129*, is absolutely essential.
87 See chapter two, above, 45.
88 For example, Brady, Prolegomena 1: 105*, notes that the treatment of the Eucharist in sermon 35 has "no affinity" with book four of the sentences. Even a New Testament sermon, on John 12: 32 (composed after 1152), takes a different approach to Christological questions, ibid., 106*.

The *Sentences* was not the first of its genre. We have seen in chapter two that Peter was exposed to this kind of theological writing in his first years in France, at the school of St Victor. In the 1140s and 1150s, Robert Pullen and Robert of Melun published their own *Sentences*. Peter's work was marked by coherence and a thorough use of authorities. He divided it into four books, the first on the Trinity, the second on creation, the third on the incarnation, and the fourth on the sacraments and last things. This idea for this structure came from Augustine's statement in *On Christian Doctrine* that "all teaching is about signs or things, but even things are learned through signs."[89] Peter then quotes Augustine again to explain that "in the case of things, we must consider that there are some things to be enjoyed, others which are to be used, and yet others which are to be used and enjoyed."[90] Book one represents the things to be enjoyed, book two the things to be used, and book three the things to be used and enjoyed. Finally, book four deals with signs.[91]

The subjects of the four books are vast, and Peter made them manageable by breaking them down. He includes a table of contents, through which, as he put it, "one may more easily find what one seeks."[92] This concern to make the text as accessible as possible can also be seen throughout the text. Although it is conventional to refer to the *Sentences* by distinctions (i.e., for each new subject), this method of organizing the text is not found in the earliest manuscripts. The distinctions were added in the thirteenth century, when the work had become part of the theology curriculum at Paris.[93] Peter's own method was to highlight new chapter headings, citations, and subdivisions (often in the form of questions) with marginal notes known as rubrics.[94] This

89 "Ut enim egregius doctor Augustine ait in libro de Doctrina christiana, 'omnis doctrina vel rerum est vel signorum: sed res etiam per signa discuntur.'" *Sententiae* 1, dist. 1, ch. 1, ed. Brady, 1: 55; Peter Lombard, *The Sentences*, trans. Giulio Silano (Toronto, 2007–2010), 1: 5.

90 "Res aliae sunt quibus fruendum est, aliae quibus utendum est, alia qua fruuntur el utuntur." *Sententiae* 1, dist. 1, ch. 2, ed. Brady, 1: 56; *The Sentences*, trans. Silano, 1: 6.

91 See Rosemann, *Peter Lombard*, 57–61, for a more thorough treatment of the structure of the work.

92 "Ut autem quod quaeritur facilius occurrat, titulos quibus singulorum librorum capitula distinguuntur praemisimus." *Sententiae*, preface, ed. Brady, 1: 4. See also Rosemann, *Peter Lombard*, 64.

93 Ignatius C. Brady, "The Distinctions of Lombard's Book of Sentences and Alexander of Hales," *Franciscan Studies* 25 (1965): 90–116.

94 Brady has discussed the rubrics extensively in "The Rubrics of Peter Lombard's Sentences," *Pier Lombardo* 6 (1962): 5–25, and in Prolegomena 1: 143*–144*. He was

helped to make the *Sentences* a work that could be used for reference, for teaching, or for individual study. Furthermore, Peter passed these methods on to his students. As we will see in chapter eight, the use of rubrics and desire to make the text manageable comes across very prominently in the manuscripts of Peter's works prepared by Herbert of Bosham.

It was also coherent and manageable because Peter knew when to stop. He concentrated on the information that was necessary to his project. He aimed to resolve questions with reference to authorities. If he could not, he simply moved on, stating on one such occasion, "this is a complicated question, nor can it be fully resolved by us as we move to other matters."[95] When Peter taught the *Sentences* in 1156–1157 and again in the following academic year, he dealt with subjects in greater detail in the classroom. Surviving reports of his teaching reveal this, showing him giving his opinion and expressing hesitation.[96] But when he released the *Sentences* for publication, he made sure he included only positions (matters of which he was sure).

A comprehensive treatment of the *Sentences* is beyond the aims of this book. That is something that Colish and Rosemann have already done. Their books, along with Silano's English translation, have made the *Sentences* much more accessible. But it is still important to provide some sense of the character of the work. Book three, which Silano calls "the most congenial in which to become immersed,"[97] illustrates aspects of Peter's life and thought that run through this study. It follows on from the *Commentary on the Letters of Paul*, illustrating Peter's creative method, and it also exhibits a chronological approach to structure, which Peter had learned from his master Hugh of St Victor.

---

also the first to comprehensively incorporate them into a printed edition of the *Sentences*. Rosemann, *Peter Lombard*, 64–65 also provides a very good explanation of "the consultation aids with which Peter deliberately and meticulously equipped his work."

95 "Verumtamen latebrosa quaestio est haec, nec a nobis plene absolvenda, properantibus ad alia." *Sententiae* 3, dist. 29, ch. 2, ed. Brady, 2: 176; *The Sentences*, trans. Silano, 3: 125

96 These are covered in part two of this book. The central work on the subject is Brady, "Peter Manducator," 454–490. Rosemann, *Peter Lombard*, 40–41, discusses the oral teachings and includes translations of the most representative passages.

97 Peter Lombard, *The Sentences*, trans. Silano, 3: xl.

The title of book three is "The Incarnation of the Word," and thus Christ is the firm focus. Peter begins on a note of humility: "Let us now readily attend, with the whole consideration of our mind, to understanding and treating those things which pertain to the mystery of the word made flesh, so that, with God revealing, we may be able to utter some little thing on these ineffable matters."[98] He first considers the incarnation in the context of the Trinity. The chapters within this distinction, as is Peter's method, often take the form of questions, such as "why the Son took on flesh and not the Holy Spirit." In distinction two, "what is understood by the term humanity, or human nature," Peter shows how important his trip to Rome was by leaning heavily on John Damascene.[99] Peter then looks deeply into difficult Christological questions, grappling with the meaning of the central phrases "the word was made flesh" (John 1:1) and "He was made" (Romans 1:3).[100] Peter here makes extensive use of his earlier work on *factus est*, now detached from the *Commentary on the Letters of Paul*. Peter's teaching on the two natures of Christ became controversial after his death. We will examine this criticism in part two. The later controversy, however, revolved more around reports of Peter's oral teaching rather than around the text of the *Sentences*.

Peter then turns to Christ's taking on of man's defects: "It is also not to be passed over that the Son of God took a human nature that was capable of suffering, and flesh that was capable of suffering and mortal. And so that he should be shown to have a true body, he took on the defects of the body: hunger and thirst and suchlike; and so that he should be shown to have a true soul, he took on the defects of the soul, namely sadness, fear, pain and suchlike."[101] From here he moves to Christ's passion and resurrection, and a chronological structure is beginning to emerge. Rosemann is right to point

98 "Iam nunc his intelligendis atque pertractandis, quae ad Verbi incarnati mysterium pertinent, integra mentis consideratione intendamus, ut de ineffabilibus vel modicum aliquid fari, Deo revelante, valeamus." *Sententiae* 3, preface, ed. Brady, 2: 23; *The Sentences*, trans. Silano, 3: 3.

99 *Sententiae* 3, dist. 2, ch. 1–2, ed. Brady, 2: 27–31.

100 *Sententiae* 3, dist. 2–10, ed. Brady, 2: 27–74.

101 "Illud quoque praetermittendum non est, quod Dei Filius naturam hominis accepit passibilem: animam passibilem et carnem passibilem et mortalem .Ut enim probaretur verum corpus habere, suscepit defectus corporis, famem, sitim et hujusmodi. Et ut veram animam probaretur habere, suscepit defectus animae, scilicet tristitiam, timorem, dolorem et hujusmodi." *Sententiae* 3, dist. 15, ch. 1, ed. Brady, 2: 92–93; *The Sentences*, trans. Silano, 3: 57.

out that in distinction nineteen, Peter's tone changes, sounding "like part of a homily."[102] When Peter discusses the passion and death of Christ, he switches to using the second person, which is unusual in this work: "To what end, then, did he will to suffer and die, if his virtues were sufficient to merit those things? For your sake, not his own ... so that his passion and death should be a model and cause to you: the model of virtue and humility."[103] This is a tone which occurs often in Peter's sermons.

The idea of Christ as an example explains the rest of book three. Peter deals with faith, hope, and charity by asking "whether Christ had faith and hope as he had charity."[104] He then moves on to a detailed discussion of charity, including the four principal virtues, the seven gifts of the Holy Spirit, and how the ten commandments are contained in the two commandments of charity. This structure has sometimes been criticized as a deviation from the Christological focus of the rest of the book.[105] This is because the "virtues and vices" (in the conventional uses of the terms) are usually considered separately from Christological questions. But Rosemann is surely correct when he says that the structure "represents a logical consequence of Peter Lombard's understanding of human nature in its fallen state, and of his conviction that the human being needs to emulate the exemplary perfection of Christ."[106]

The structure of book three could also be explained in broadly chronological terms. Peter discusses first the incarnation, and then Christ as a man (by providing examples of his human weaknesses and attributes). He covers his passion and death, and he views him as an example for those who live after him. In fact, one can also apply a chronological structure quite neatly to the *Sentences* as a whole. Book one deals with the existence of the Trinity, prior to creation, leading into the creation of the angels, the earth, and man in book

102 Rosemann, *Peter Lombard,* 138.

103 "Ad quid ergo voluit pati et mori, si ei virtutes ad merendum illae sufficiebant? Pro te, non pro se ... ut ipsius passio et mors tibi esset forma et causa. Forma virtutis et humilitatis; causa gloriae et libertatis; forma Deo usque ad mortem obediendi; et causa tuae liberationis ac beatitudinis." *Sententiae* 3, dist 18, ch. 5, ed. Brady, 2: 116; *The Sentences,* trans. Silano, 3: 77.

104 *Sententiae* 3, dist. 23, ch. 1.

105 Colish, *Peter Lombard,* 471–472. See Rosemann's discussion of her views, along with those of Otto Baltzer: *Peter Lombard,* 119–121.

106 Rosemann, *Peter Lombard,* 121.

two. Book three covers the coming of Christ, while the sacraments of the church and the end of the world are the subjects of book four. This was, as is suggested above, a structural approach that Peter may have learned from Hugh of St Victor.[107] Both saw the outline of universal history as fundamental to their theological works.

By the time he taught the first version of the *Sentences*, Peter was definitely an archdeacon.[108] Bishop Theobald appointed him to the position, either before or after the Rome trip. It is interesting that Peter does not discuss archdeacons at all in the *Sentences*, even while he was holding the office himself. This is probably because he did not think it was necessary in a discussion of ordination. The archdiaconate was not considered to be one of the seven orders. Archdeacons were not ordained as such, but were simply senior deacons, which is how the office had arisen. This is another example of Peter ensuring that the *Sentences* would be concise as well as coherent, by eliminating unnecessary material. One of Peter's main sources for ordination, Hugh of St Victor's *On the Sacraments*, provides a description of the office, however. As Hugh explains it,

> the archdeacon commands the subdeacons and deacons, and their duties pertain to him. He is responsible for the care of parishes, ordination, and [the settlement of] disputes. He advises the priests on restoring diocesan churches, he inquires into the parishes, by order of the bishop, and into the state of the church or parish items; he refers matters of the freedom of churches to the bishop, he accepts money collected from the communion and offers it to the bishop. He also dispenses other duties of episcopal providence, under the bishop, like an advocate in part of his care of examining church business.[109]

107 See chapter two, above, 38–39.
108 *Cartulaire*, ed. de Lasteyrie, no. 394, pp. 347–348.
109 "Archidiaconus imperat subdiaconis et levitis, ad quem ista pertinent ministeria. Sollicitudo parochiarum et ordinatio, et jurgia ad ejus pertinent curam. Pro reparandis dioecesanis basilicis ipse suggerit sacerdoti, ipse inquirit parochias cum jussione episcopi, et ornamenta vel res basilicarum, vel parochiarum; gesta libertatum ecclesiasticarum episcopo idem refert, collectam pecuniam de communione ipse accipit et episcopo defert, et caetera quaedam episcopalis providentiae ministeria sub episcopo quasi in partem curae advocatus, in causis ecclesiasticis examinandis dispensat." Hugh of St Victor, *De Sacramentis Christiane fidei* 2.3, ed. Berndt, 357.

This was clearly a serious responsibility. The diocese of Paris had three archdeacons, and they each had a particular area of responsibility, their archdeaconry.[110] The dividing of dioceses into territorial archdeaconries had definitely taken place by the eleventh century in France[111] and reflected the general expansion of the eleventh and twelfth centuries: there were more people, more clerics, and more churches. Archdeacons had to supervise the clergy in their archdeaconries. This included visiting parish churches, assessing the condition of liturgical items, interviewing the clergy, and examining finances. Their role was especially important when they deputized for the bishop in his absence.[112]

Peter Lombard was actually very well suited to some of the archdeacons' duties. On their parish visits, they were supposed to examine the doctrinal knowledge of the clergy and their understanding of the sacraments.[113] They also inspected the condition of the liturgical books and assessed the ability of the clergy to preach.[114] In practice this would have meant that Peter often explained theology outside of his school, and perhaps gave advice on preaching sermons. We have seen in the previous chapter that the two other archdea-

110 The eleventh and twelfth century documents always list no more than three archdeacons in any one period.

111 Jean F. Lemarignier, "Les institutions ecclésiastiques en France de la fin du Xe au milieu du XIIe siècle," in *Histoire des institutions Françaises au moyen âge III: Institutions ecclésiastiques*, ed. Robert Fawtier and Ferdinand Lot (Paris, 1962), 1–139, at 20; Christopher Brooke, "The Archdeacon and the Norman Conquest," in *Tradition and Change: Essays in Honour of Marjorie Chibnall*, ed. Diana Greenway, Christopher Holdsworth, and Jane Sayers (Cambridge, 1985), 1–19, at 8–9. The use of the term *archidiaconatus* (an archdeaconry) appears in a document of Notre Dame from 1108, *Cartulaire*, ed. de Lasteyrie, no. 148, pp. 167–168.

112 An excellent overview of this office is A. Amanieu, "Archdiacre," in *Dictionnaire de droit canonique* (Paris, 1935–1965), 1: 948–1004. Victor Mortet, "Maurice de Sully, évêque de Paris (1160–1196): Étude sur l'administration épiscopale pendant la seconde moitié du XIIe siècle," *Mémoires de la Société de l'histoire de Paris et de l'Île-de-France* 16 (1890): 105–317, at 162–165, discusses the duties of the archdeacons of Paris. See also Winston Black, "The Medieval Archdeacon in Canon Law with a Case Study of the Diocese of Lincoln" (PhD diss., University of Toronto, 2008), which discusses their appearance in twelfth-century canon law in detail.

113 Amanieu, "Archidiacre," 971–973. Interestingly, Rosemann is of the view that a passage in the *Sentences* where Peter complains of the lack of knowledge of some of the clergy is a rare occasion where "the master allows us to catch a glimpse of his personality, his voice is tinged with emotion." Rosemann, *Peter Lombard*, 166.

114 Amanieu, "Archidiacre," 971–973.

cons in the period 1147–1158, Ivo of Chartres and Bernard, were also theology masters.[115] This is surely not coincidental. Bishop Theobald, who appointed Ivo and Peter, must have taken the view that a full theological training was a necessary asset for the position.

Past divisions may also have played a part in Theobald's choice. In the 1120s and 1130s, the archdeacons of Paris had been difficult to control. Two in particular, Stephen de Garlande and Theobald Notier, had often quarrelled with the bishop, Stephen of Senlis.[116] They were also well-connected members of aristocratic families. When Notier excommunicated a priest in 1127, Bishop Stephen appealed the matter to Rome. Since he had been in the diocese at the time, he believed that he should have been consulted. Pope Honorius issued a ruling stating that archdeacons could not appoint, depose, excommunicate, or suspend priests without the authorization of their bishop. If bishops were absent for three months or more, however, archdeacons could, in emergencies, promote clerics.[117] It is interesting that Hugh of St Victor was writing *On the Sacraments* in the same period, and emphasizing in it that archdeacons must be *sub episcopo* in all their duties.[118] At the same time, the pope's ruling was a compromise. He also outlined the financial rights and responsibilities of archdeacons. A bishop could not collect money from the parishes without the archdeacon, and "as is the custom," the archdeacon would obtain a third of the amounts collected.[119] The two archdeacons appointed by Bishop Theobald, Ivo and Peter, form a complete contrast with those days. They were not from powerful local families, but from humble non-Parisian origins.

Where was Peter Lombard's archdeaconry? This is a difficult question. Despite their substantial role, systematic record keeping of the work of archdeacons in Paris did not take place until well after the time of Peter Lom-

115 For Ivo and Bernard, see chapter three, above, 73–75.

116 For these conflicts, see Bautier, "Paris au temps d'Abélard," 66–68, and Grant, *Abbot Suger of St. Denis*, 124–132.

117 *Cartulaire de l'église Notre-Dame de Paris*, ed. Guérard, 1: 28. This was after all a deal brokered by bishops. See also Lindy Grant, "Geoffrey of Lèves, Bishop of Chartres: Famous Wheeler and Dealer in Secular Business," in *Suger en question*, ed. Rolf Grosse (Munich, 2004), 45–56, at 54.

118 Hugh of St Victor, *De Sacramentis* 2.3, ed. Berndt, 357.

119 "Collectas vero episcopus, absque archidiacono, per parrochiam ipsius non faciet." *Cartulaire de l'église Notre-Dame de Paris*, ed. Guérard, 1: 28.

bard.[120] The three archdeaconries are usually stated to be Paris (the great archdeaconry, including the area north of the walled city), Josas (broadly west-southwest), and Brie (broadly east-southeast).[121] This was certainly the case from the late thirteenth century.[122] In the twelfth century, however, the archdeacons are never named as being from one or the other. They are simply styled "archdeacon of Paris," and there are no references at all to Josas or Brie until 1268.[123] Furthermore, the diocese was reorganized in the 1190s. At that time were introduced two urban archpriests, who had responsibility for the churches within the city of Paris.[124] We do know that territorial units of the diocese did exist before 1190, because of references to *archidiaconati*, archdeaconries. In a document from 1108, the archdeacon William of Champeaux (who later retired to found the abbey of St Victor) donated the revenues from three of the churches in his *archidiaconatus* to the chapter of Notre Dame, including St Peter in Gonesse and St Gervaise in Paris.[125]

There was a senior archdeacon, and in Peter's time this was Guermund. He had replaced Stephen de Garlande and held the office from 1147 until

120 Jean Favier, *Les Archives Nationales: État général des fonds* (Paris, 1978), 1: 315, 316, and 330 lists some documents dating from as early as 1170, but regular records do not start until the thirteenth century at least.

121 Bernard Plongeron et al., *Le diocese de Paris*. Volume 1: *Des origines à la révolution*, Histoire des diocèses de France 20 (Paris, 1987), 111–116. See also the maps following 483.

122 Auguste Longnon, "L'ancien diocèse de Paris et ses subdivsions," *Bulletin du Comité d'histoire et d'archéologie du diocèse de Paris* 1 (1883): 10–19, at 15–17. Longnon dates the first appearance of these names to 1268. However, the names are sometimes projected back into earlier periods, by, for example, Mortet, "Maurice de Sully," 120–121, and Jacques Boussard, *Nouvelle histoire de Paris*. Volume 1: *De la fin du siège de 885–886 à la mort de Philippe Auguste* (Paris, 1970–2001), 135.

123 Longnon, "L'ancien diocèse de Paris et ses subdivsions," 15–17.

124 Adrien Friedmann, "Notre-Dame et les paroisses de Paris aux XIIIe siècle," *Revue d'histoire de l'église de France* 50 (1964): 27–33, at 29. Up until this point, the archdeacons also had responsibility for the city.

125 *Cartulaire*, ed. de Lasteyrie, no. 148, p. 167. It is clear from this document that the rule whereby the archdeacon retained one third of the revenues (mentioned in the papal document above) was in effect at this time: "Ego Guillelmus, dei gratia Parisiensis archidiaconus, notum facio tam posteris quam presentibus quia terciam partem altaris Sancti Gervasii Parisiensis, et terciam partem altaris Sancti Petri, apud villam que vocatur Gonessa, terciam quoque partem altaris Sancti Martini apud villam que nuncupatur Erlebatum, has, inquam, tres tercias partes iure archidiaconatus nostri possidebam, et in dominio meo tanquam proprias habebam."

1178.[126] In the documents of the 1120s and 1130s, Stephen's name always follows the dean and chancellor in the lists of witnesses, and his name is sometimes prominent in the text. Where then did Peter and Ivo of Chartres fit in? Victor Mortet was of the view that they were the archdeacons of Josas and Brie respectively, but failed to provide satisfactory evidence.[127] Peter, who was archdeacon for a fairly short period, only features in documents as a witness along with the other two. However, we know that Peter had replaced Bernard. There are a number of documents either issued in Bernard's name or featuring him as the only archdeacon present. In one, he was involved in a decision of Henry of France, who was acting as abbot of the royal church of St Spire in Corbeil.[128] This was sometime between 1145 and 1152.[129] Bernard also witnessed a donation at the abbey of Yerres in 1142.[130] Corbeil and Yerres were within the boundaries of what became the archdeaconry of Brie, whose borders were marked by the Seine and the Marne rivers.[131] In the twelfth century, however, archdeacon Bernard also seemed to have had responsibility for St Victor. Positioned just outside the city walls, it was not part of the later medieval archdeaconry of Brie. In one document, Bernard made a donation to the abbey.[132] He also witnessed both a ruling of Abbot Gilduin[133] and the transfer of Victorine canons to St Geneviève.[134] These findings seem to situate Peter Lombard's area of responsibility south-southeast of the walled city of Paris.

126 See chapter three, above, 73.
127 Mortet, "Maurice de Sully," 121, who projects the thirteenth-century archdeaconries back into the twelfth, states that Bernard and Peter were archdeacons of Josas, and Ivo of Chartres of Brie. He says this is evident from the printed charters and from those he edited in the valuable appendix to his work. I can find no reference in them, however, to Ivo signing as archdeacon of Brie as he claims: "Yves, qui souscrivait avant 1159 comme archidiacre de Brie." See the further discussion of Ivo's archdeaconry in chapter three, 73–75.
128 *Cartulaire de Saint-Spire de Corbeil au diocèse de Paris*, ed. Emile Coüard-Luys (Rambouillet, 1882), no. 10, pp. 15–19.
129 It must be prior to 1152 because Durand signs as subdeacon. He became a deacon after 1152. See the table at the end of chapter three, above.
130 The cartulary of the abbey of Notre Dame in Yerres remains unedited, but this document was printed by Mortet, "Maurice de Sully," 285.
131 Corbeil would later be the site of one of two rural deaneries within the archdeaconry.
132 *Cartulaire*, ed. de Lasteyrie, no. 366, p. 326.
133 Ibid., no. 370, pp. 330–331.
134 Ibid., no. 353, pp. 318–319.

Although busy with these duties, Peter continued to teach. In 1157–1158 he again gave a course on the *Sentences*. He made changes, particularly in the form of marginal notes. This is why there are two editions of the work.[135] He then lectured on his *Commentary on the Psalms* in 1158–1159. Apparently his students had asked him to do this, and he began to put the text in final shape as he taught it.[136] But in January 1159 Bishop Theobald died, and several months passed before a successor was elected. The election had the potential to be contentious. It was the first real test for the canons since the disastrous events of twelve years before, when the "four honest men" had elected Clement. The recent retirement of Ivo of Chartres meant that Peter was well placed to succeed Theobald. The other archdeacon, Guermund, already held the senior archdeaconry and was presumably quite comfortable in that role.

Peter Lombard, the master of sentences, becoming a bishop was not as strange as it might seem. Twelfth-century canonists tended to stress intelligence and theological expertise as necessary qualifications for a bishopric.[137] After at least three years as an archdeacon, he had the necessary experience of responsibility for a large part of the diocese. He had also been involved in diocesan administration in Paris since 1147. His election now requires close consideration. According to the chronicler Robert of Torigny, Peter "obtained the bishopric of Paris with the support of Philip, the King's brother, dean of the same church, who, as they say, conceded his own election to the same Peter."[138] Robert's view

135 Brady, Prolegomena 1: 126*–129*; Rosemann, *Peter Lombard*, 55.

136 That Peter taught the Psalms commentary just before becoming bishop is clear from the words of Herbert of Bosham. Herbert of Bosham, *Praefatio*, in *History of the Vulgate in England*, ed. Hans H. Glunz (Cambridge, 1933), 342–346, at 343. See also Brady, Prolegomena 1: 126*–129*. For Herbert's testimony, see chapter eight, 213.

137 Jörg Peltzer, *Canon Law, Careers and Conquest: Episcopal Elections in Normandy and Greater Anjou, c.1140–c.1230* (Cambridge, 2008), 48–50. See especially 48–49: "Gratian named intelligence, aptness in learning, a moderate temper, a chaste and abstemious life, a sense of responsibility for his affairs, kindness, compassion, profound learning, knowledge of canon law, an awareness of the meaning of the Scriptures, training in ecclesiastical doctrines and above all the Catholic faith."

138 "Magister etiam Petrus Lombardus Parisiensem episcopatum adeptus est, conivente Philipo eiusdem ecclesiae decano, fratre regis Francorum; qui, ut dicunt, electionem suam concessit eidem Petro." Robert of Torigny, *Chronicon*, ed. Ludwig Conrad Bethmann (MGH SS 6: 510). The text is the same in the two later printed editions of the chronicle: *Chronique de Robert de Torigni, abbé de Mont Saint-Michel*, ed. Léopold Delisle (Rouen, 1872–1873), 1: 324; *Chronicles of the Reigns of Stephen, Henry II, and Richard I*, ed. Richard Howlett (London, 1884–1889), 4: 3–316, at 204.

found its way into later authors. The humanist Paulus Aemilius of Verona, commissioned to write a history of the French kings in 1499 (and himself a canon of Notre Dame), incorporates it, describing Peter as "a citizen of Novara, called the Lombard, and easily pre-eminent among theologians."[139] Two seventeenth-century French historians, Dubois and Du Boulay, citing Paulus, repeat the assertion. Dubois even quotes Paulus directly in his *History of the Church of Paris*.[140] Du Boulay adds that Peter's election was favoured by "the majority of the canons."[141] By the time the *Gallia Christiana* was compiled, Philip had become a former student of the Lombard.[142] Benjamin Guérard, in his edition of the Notre Dame cartulary, repeats the idea that Philip had been Peter's student,[143] and from there it found its way into modern authors such as Marcel Pacaut.[144]

Brady advises against believing the story of Philip's involvement.[145] He points out that he was not dean, as Robert claimed, since Clement still held that office. Nor does he seem to have even been in Paris at the time.[146] Brady concludes that Robert's account deserves as little credence as Walter of St Victor's allegation that Peter had obtained his bishopric through simony.[147]

139 "Franci regis frater Philippus Ecclesiae Parisiensis Archidiaconus, cum sacra ea vacante sede Pontifex eligeretur, Petro civi Novarensi cognomine Longobardo Theologorum facile principi cessit: isque Episcopus ab rege salutatus." Paulus Aemilius Veronensis, *De Rebus Gestis Francorum* (Paris, 1566), fol. 110.

140 Gerard Dubois, *Historia Ecclesiae Parisiensis* (Paris, 1690–1710), 2: 121. Dubois also mentions Robert of Torigny as a source.

141 "Hoc anno [1159] M.Petrus Lombardus post longam litterarum tam secularium quam divinarum professionem episcopatus Parisiensis adiit possessionem ex spontanea Philipi archidiaconi et Ludovici regis fratris cessione, qui a maiori canonicorum parte electus fuerat, ut notat Paulus Aemilius in *Vita Ludovici*." César-Égasse du Boulay, *Historia Universitatis Parisiensis* (Paris, 1665, repr. Frankfurt, 1966), 2: 287.

142 "Electus est episcopus. At quae Philippi virtus erat et modestia, in gratiam Petri quondam praeceptoris dignitati lubens renunciavit." *Gallia Christiana* 7: 68. The authors of this work pointed out that Philip was an archdeacon, not the dean.

143 "Anno 1157 in episcopatum electus, sedem Parisiensem recusavit, quam, loco eius, suscepit Petrus Lombardus, olim eiusdem Philippi praeceptor." *Cartulaire de l'Église Notre Dame de Paris*, ed. Guérard, 1: 389 n1.

144 Marcel Pacaut, *Louis VII et son royaume* (Paris, 1964), 110; Marcel Pacaut, *Louis VII et les élections épiscopales dans le royaume de France* (Paris, 1957), 119.

145 Brady, Prolegomena 1: 33*–35*.

146 "Proinde tempore electionis Magistri Petri Philipus nec decanus fuit Parisiensis ecclesiae nec etiam, ut videtur, Parisius inveniabatur." Ibid., 33*.

147 "His omnibus perpensis, prudentius nobis videtur inter fabulas ac legendas connumerandum quod Robertus de Monte reportat." Ibid., 34*. For Walter's pamphlet, the *Contra Labyrinthos*, see chapter nine, below, 246–248.

But that is an unfair comparison. Walter was writing a polemical pamphlet against Peter Lombard, almost twenty years after his death. Character assassination was part of his mandate. Robert of Torigny, on the other hand, was at least trying to be a reliable chronicler. In 1159 he had been abbot of Mont St Michel in Normandy for five years. Much of the information in his chronicle was relayed to him by visitors to his monastery, which, as a site for pilgrimage, had a high turnover of guests.[148]

There seems to be no reason to disbelieve Robert's assertion that Philip supported Peter's election. Although he tends to be vague about the positions held by individual canons, the substance of his story should not be rejected. Brady's point about Philip being absent from Paris during the election does not stand up to scrutiny. After he died, his brother Louis VII issued a number of documents concerning the substantial property Philip had held in the city.[149] Whether he was also in the running for the bishopric is not something we can say for certain, although, if he had been archdeacon since Ivo's departure, then it is plausible.[150] Either way, Philip's backing would have been important for a candidate. Peter's status as an outsider may also have worked in his favour. In ideal circumstances, a cathedral chapter was supposed to unanimously elect a bishop.[151] His candidacy would not reignite long-standing rivalries between the elite families of Capetian France, and Philip could well have put him forward to spare the chapter yet another divisive election.

Peter's tenure as bishop was brief. The new position did not radically alter the pattern of his life. He continued to live in the house he had occupied as a canon.[152] He continued to work closely with the chapter. As archdeacon he had already grown accustomed to having responsibility for part of the diocese. That responsibility was now simply on a larger scale, both territorially

148 Howlett, introduction to *Chronicles of the Reigns of Stephen, Henry II, and Richard I*, xvii. For more on Robert as a historian, see David Spear, "Torigni, Robert de," in *Oxford Dictionary of National Biography*, 55: 46–47, who points to Robert's "relatively few factual errors."

149 Achille Luchaire, *Études sur les actes de Louis VII* (Paris, 1885), no. 432 and no. 434, p. 239. The documents are dated between August 1160 and April 1161.

150 See the discussion in chapter three, above, 58, 76–77.

151 Peltzer, *Canon Law, Careers and Conquest*, 38.

152 For Peter's house, which the chapter inherited on his death, see Brady, Prolegomena 1: 19*–21*.

and also in the sense of his duty to the people as a whole. He was also part of a wider clerical world. One of his surviving acts gives a sense of this. Peter makes a ruling in favour of Remigius, dean of St Germain d'Auxerre, and refers to consultations with Henry of France, bishop of Beauvais, and Samson Mauvasin, archbishop of Rheims, both of whom were powerful, seasoned prelates. This is an interesting piece, because in contrast with the formulaic style of the two other acts (one of which is a concession to St Victor[153]), it sounds a lot like Peter:

> Let those here present and those afterwards know that I, Peter, by the grace of God bishop of Paris, have removed a complaint made against Remigius, dean of the church of St Germain d'Auxerre, concerning the treasury of the same church. For I had doubts, following the suggestions of certain others, whether he obtained the position of treasurer by a donation of my predecessor Theobald. At length, having carefully looked into, listened to, and become acquainted with the truth of the matter, that Remigius possessed the treasury along with the deanery, by the donation and allowance of my predecessor Theobald, justly and by the law of the church, and also because the deans of that church had obtained the treasury along with the deanery, with the assistance and counsel of Samson, archbishop of Rheims, Henry, bishop of Beauvais, and Robert, bishop of Chartres, also of Peter, abbot of Troyes, and William, prior of St Martin des Champs, and especially for the sake of the truth, I dismiss altogether the complaint that has been made now and in perpetuity.[154]

153 Brady, Prolegomena 1: 36*.

154 "Sciant presentes et posteri quod ego Petrus, Dei gracia Parisiensis episcopus movi querelam adversus Remigium, decanum ecclesiase [sancti] Germani autissiodorensis, pro capiceria eiusdem ecclesie. Dubitavi enim, quorundam suggestione, utrum dictam capiceriam donatione predeccessoris nostri Theobaldi optineret. Demum vero diligenter inquisita rei veritate et audita et cognita, scilicet quod predictus R. ipsam capiceriam cum decania, donacione et tradicione predecessoris nostri Th., et iuste et canonice possidebat, et quod eciam iamdicte ecclesie decani ipsam capiceriam cum decania optinuerant; interventu quoque et consilio Sansonis Remensis archiepiscopi, Henrici Belvacensis episcopi, et Roberti Carnotensis episcopi, Petri quoque Trecensis abbatis, et Willermi prioris Sancti Martini de Campis, et maxime pro recognitione veritatis, querelam inceptam ex toto et imperpetuum dimisi." *Cartulaire*, ed. de Lasteyrie, no. 415, p. 362.

We can also turn to what else was happening during the period of Peter's episcopate. There is no question that the dominant issue in ecclesiastical affairs was the papal schism. Two months after Peter's election, Adrian IV died. Peter would have had a limited role in the decisions of the French church on this matter. The archbishops, and the king, quickly decided in favour of Alexander III. Only two letters survive from Alexander III to Peter, and neither hint at any sort of personal relationship. The first, from November 1159, is an eloquent, sometimes strident statement of his legitimacy,[155] and the second is an authorization for the number of canons in a Parisian house to be increased.[156] The decision of Louis VII (and Henry II of England) to support Alexander was formalized at the council of Beauvais in July 1160,[157] by which time Peter had died. Had he lived, he probably would have taken part in the flurry of diplomatic activity that aimed to persuade Frederick Barbarossa to support Alexander. But this process, which did involve a lot of bishops, was concentrated in the period between 1161 and 1163.[158]

Peter was around sixty years old when he died. We do not know the cause, but his decline is likely to have been brief, if not sudden. The other twelfth-century bishops of Paris were in office for at least seven years, and Peter would not have been elected if he had been showing signs of ill health. Herbert of Bosham remarked wistfully that he was "removed from human affairs."[159] This was on 20 July 1160. Peter's achievement in Paris was certainly remarkable. He had arrived in the mid-1130s, dependent on the support of others and with no works to his name. He had managed to obtain a position in the cathedral of Notre Dame and to rise within it. Clearly there was something about Peter that impressed people and caused them to make room for him, assist him, listen to him, and defer to him. But perhaps that is to make him

155 *Acta Pontificum Romanorum inedita*, ed. Julius von Pflugk-Harttung (Tübingen, 1884), 2: 364–366, addressed to Peter and "dilectiis filiis maioris ecclesie et universo clero Parisiensi."

156 *Cartulaire*, ed. de Lasteyrie, no. 412, p. 360. The church in question was St Opportune.

157 For the council, which Henry of France hosted, see Lambert of Waterlos, *Annales Cameracenses*, ed. Georg H. Pertz (MGH SS 16: 509–554, at 534), and Robert of Torigny, *Chronicon* (MGH SS 6: 511).

158 Yves Sassier, *Louis VII* (Paris, 1991), 307–330.

159 "Post in brevi humanis rebus exemptus." Herbert of Bosham, *Praefatio*, ed. Glunz, 343.

sound passive. He went from *puer* to subdeacon, to deacon, to archdeacon, to bishop in the space of a mere fifteen years. This would seem to suggest that he wanted those positions and that he actively sought them.

His impressive clerical career, however, was only part of his achievement. It was his written works that caused him to be remembered. He understood the necessity of circulating his works in Paris, the "scholastic metropolis of Northern Europe," as R. W. Southern describes it.[160] It was not enough simply to teach. Peter was clearly concerned with disseminating his works, but in a form of which he approved. He revised the *Sentences* and the *Commentary on the Letters of Paul* before becoming bishop. When he taught his *Commentary on the Psalms* to his students, he made it clear that it was not yet a finished work.

Becoming bishop meant he had to cease teaching. He would still have been somewhat available to his former students. After Odo of Soissons left Paris to become an abbot, his former *praepositus* was still receiving his patronage.[161] Peter's students felt his loss keenly, especially those who had not completed the course when he left the schools to become bishop. The students often described him simply as "the master," and what united all of them was a desire to speak highly of Peter Lombard and to make his works as available and accessible as possible. The unexpectedness of Peter's death may have partly motivated this effort. They were continuing the work that he had been unable to finish. This will be the subject of part two of this book.

160 Richard W. Southern, *Scholastic Humanism and the Unification of Europe* I: *Foundations* (Oxford, 1995), 198.
161 See chapter three, above, 68–70.

PART TWO

The Master and His Students

CHAPTER FIVE

Master and Student in the Mid–Twelfth Century: A Prologue

While Peter Lombard may have been involved in some kind of teaching for much of his adult life, his period of renown as a theology master was fairly concentrated, lasting less than twenty years (1142–1159). His teaching career was carried out alongside the production of theological works and his responsibilities to the church of Paris. The last chapter examined the achievements of those years, but one vital area was left out – how he inspired his students. Those students made their master's legacy a priority after he was gone. They were determined that his works would be read and understood by the widest audience possible. They also had to deal with a sustained and persistent opposition to his teaching. How they responded to this challenge, in the 1160s and 1170s, is the other theme of the chapters that follow.

Peter set up a school of theology in the early 1140s after obtaining a licence to teach from the chancellor of Notre Dame, as we have seen in chapter two. The chancellor still retained a certain control over higher education in Paris, but there were now many more students than could be accommodated within the kind of cathedral school common to other episcopal cities.[1] Just as student life had changed, so had the role of the master. In the first three decades of the twelfth century, the person of the master had been far more important than where he was teaching. Students went to Laon because Master Anselm was teaching there. They went to Rheims (as Peter had done) to hear Alberic. Abelard was even followed into the wilderness by some of his students.[2] There was considerably less institutional apparatus surrounding

1 See chapter two, above, 48.

2 There are individual studies for these masters: John R. Williams, "The Cathedral School of Reims in the Time of Master Alberic, 1118-1136," *Traditio* 20 (1964): 93–114; Valerie I.J. Flint, "The 'School of Laon': A Reconsideration," *RTAM* 43 (1976): 89–110. Abelard informs us of his following in Abelard, *Historia calamitatum*, ed. Jacques Monfrin (Paris, 1959), 92.

these masters than there would be in the thirteenth century, when university statutes formalized their duties.

By the 1140s, the master could no longer depend on students coming to him. If he wanted to have a significant reputation, to develop his ideas and to make them widely known, he had to go to Paris. It had superseded other locations for a number of reasons. The ready availability of accommodation had facilitated a large influx of students.[3] Also, the number of renowned masters there, known for both their reputation and their written works, had created a snowball effect.

There was undoubtedly a huge demand for higher instruction in Paris, particularly in the arts. Peter Lombard, however, taught theology. Fewer masters were teaching this subject and their classes were much smaller. Students could only take theology after they had spent several years studying the arts. This is evident from the works of John of Salisbury and William of Tyre, both of whom wrote accounts of their study years.[4] Theology was one of three advanced subjects, along with medicine and the law.[5] Unlike those subjects, it did not guarantee employment, and this gave its practitioners a unique sense of identity. We will encounter this in the chapters that follow. Theology itself was not new. The Christian tradition had been shaped by works of a theological character, while the word itself derives from Greek antiquity.[6] However, the theological works that come down to us from the twelfth cen-

3 Richard W. Southern, *Scholastic Humanism and the Unification of Europe* I: *Foundations* (Oxford, 1995), 198–231. See also Richard W. Southern, "The Schools of Paris and the School of Chartres," in *Renaissance and Renewal in the Twelfth Century*, ed. Robert L. Benson and Giles Constable (Cambridge, MA, 1982), 113–137, at 119–121, and Stephen C. Ferruolo, *The Origins of the University: The Schools of Paris and their Critics, 1100–1215* (Stanford, 1985), 11–27.

4 John of Salisbury, *Metalogicon* 2.10, ed. John B. Hall and Katharine S.B. Keats-Rohan (CCCM 98: 72); William of Tyre, *Chronicon* 19.12, ed. Robert B.C. Huygens, Hans Eberhard Mayer, and Gerhard Rösch (CCCM 63: 879–880). See the excellent discussion of these accounts in Southern, *Scholastic Humanism* I: *Foundations*, 212–220, 230–231.

5 On the origins of theology as an advanced subject, and its image contrasted with the other advanced subjects, medicine and the law, see Smalley, *Becket Conflict*, 18–21.

6 For the word *theologia* and the development of theology up to the twelfth century, see Raymond Winling, "Théologie," in *Dictionnaire de spiritualité ascétique et mystique: doctrine et histoire* (Paris, 1932–1995), 15: 463–500. The pre-twelfth century situation is also admirably described in Rosemann, *Peter Lombard*, 8–25.

tury – commentaries, *quaestiones*, and the doctrinal collections known as *Sentences* – are the products of a teaching environment. The teaching of theology in the twelfth century was dedicated to producing a body of Christian doctrine through the reconciling of authorities.[7]

The masters in theology were a new group, and their profession required years of apprenticeship.[8] Peter Lombard regarded their work very highly, and he did not publish works in any other genre. His wholehearted belief in theology must have been stimulating to his students, but at the same time intimidating. None of them, as far as we know, quite measured up to the exclusive theological focus of their master, although this partly had to do with where they found employment. Peter Comestor came the closest, by teaching at Notre Dame, giving sermons with substantial theological content, and writing works based on the *Sentences*. He is best known, however, for the *Historia Scholastica*, his retelling of the bible that, among other things, amalgamates the four gospels into a single narrative. Herbert of Bosham composed a commentary on the Psalms, but his method is very different from that of Peter Lombard. His major literary work was his *Life of St Thomas Becket*. William of Tyre, after his return from the schools of the West, became a bishop and the official historian of the Latin Kingdom of Jerusalem. Adam of Wales, although he taught privately for some time, is better known as the bishop of the turbulent diocese of St Asaph.

And yet, Peter's theological training stayed with them. There are echoes of Peter's schoolroom in William of Tyre's *Historia*. Herbert of Bosham could not resist inserting theological sections into his works in praise of Becket. Peter Comestor's sermons, although individual, bear the influence of his master in their method and content, and even the *Historia Scholastica* borrows substantially from the *Sentences*. We can also point to a sustained effort by this group to ensure that their master would not be forgotten by posterity. Herbert of Bosham supervised the production of illuminated editions of his master's commentaries, which were designed to make them as accessible as possible. Peter Comestor attempted to make the *Sentences* better known

7 Rosemann, *Peter Lombard*, 25–33; Colish, *Peter Lombard*, 33–76.

8 Professionalization is the word most often used to describe this development. See Colish, *Peter Lombard*, 90–91, and Rosemann, *Peter Lombard*, 25–26. On the theology masters, see also John W. Baldwin, "Masters at Paris from 1179 to 1215: A Social Perspective," in *Renaissance and Renewal in the Twelfth Century*, ed. Benson and Constable, 138–172, at 147–148.

through teaching and commentary, while Adam of Wales defended Peter's teaching in the run-up to the Third Lateran Council. William of Tyre's contributions have gone unrecorded, but he provided a glowing description of Peter in his *Historia*, emphasizing his "sound doctrine" and the activities of his devoted followers.

Before dealing with the students in detail, we should say something about numbers. In addition to these four, who all studied with Peter for a considerable period, five others are known. These include a master Udo, who wrote an early abridgement of the *Sentences*, and three other anonymous disciples who prepared commentaries on their master's work. The fifth is John of Cornwall, who spent only two or three years in Peter's school. Unlike the other students, he did not complete the course with Peter.

It may seem surprising that there are only nine documented students of Peter Lombard, given that he taught for seventeen years. It is important to remember, however, that his school was a very select group. The teaching career of Peter Abelard was considerably longer, and, in his case, according to David Luscombe, "the names of some twenty-one disciples and sometime pupils ... are known."[9] Enrollment in theology was strictly controlled. This is in keeping with its status as an advanced subject. While hearing different masters, and picking and choosing lectures, was common in the arts, William of Tyre and John of Salisbury do not mention this happening in theology.[10] Students enrolled with one theology master, and probably required a recommendation or interview to do so. This was important for masters. The students who regularly attended became trusted disciples and would be able to correctly explain their master's positions. In the later Middle Ages, theology schools numbered around twenty students.[11] This would be a reasonable estimation for the twelfth century also. Only some of the arts graduates would continue with the three advanced subjects, and those pursuing theology would be divided among several active masters.[12]

9 David Luscombe, *The School of Peter Abelard: The Influence of Abelard's Thought in the Early Scholastic Period* (Cambridge, 1969), 14. Those followers are discussed on 14–59.

10 Southern, *Scholastic Humanism* I: *Foundations*, 213–214.

11 Jacques Verger, "Teachers," in *A History of the University in Europe*: Volume 1: *Universities in the Middle Ages*, ed. Hilde de Ridder-Symoens (Cambridge, 1992), 144–168, at 159.

12 It is true that one text, *The Dialogue of Ratius and Everard*, makes reference to Gilbert of Poitiers lecturing to three hundred students in Paris. For this, see Nikolaus M.

As part of the settlement of 1127, a hall had been constructed at Notre Dame that could accommodate large lectures.[13] This would be suitable for the arts courses and for special occasions. It could also be used for smaller groups of masters and students. Some twelfth-century masters also held classes in their houses,[14] so the numbers would have to be small. Peter, as a canon of Notre Dame, was able to afford a house near the cathedral.[15] He probably held his classes there, since he kept the books he would have needed for his teaching in it. As we have seen in chapter two, these books were his own copy of the *Sentences*, Gratian's *Decretum*, and glossed books of the Bible.[16] With a school of less than twenty students, most of whom remained for seven or eight years, Peter would have taught between forty and fifty students in total.

There is no question that out of such proximity a close relationship would develop between a master and his students. Masters often tried to help their students find positions, as we have seen with Odo of Soissons. In Peter Lombard's case, we know that he continued to discuss theology with former students. In Peter Comestor's description of such gatherings, "he was speaking to safe ears, that is to those he had taught."[17] This emphasizes again that masters were wary of their positions being misinterpreted. Former students were "safe ears" because they could be trusted not to spread rumours. This would give a

---

Häring, "A Latin Dialogue on the Doctrine of Gilbert of Poitiers," *Mediaeval Studies* 15 (1953): 243–289, at 252. However, in addition to theology, Gilbert also taught grammar and logic in Paris (which would attract more students), and there are questions over whether this work (a fictional dialogue) represents actual events. On these issues, see Nikolaus M. Häring, "The Cistercian Everard of Ypres and His Appraisal of the Conflict between St. Bernard and Gilbert of Poitiers," *Mediaeval Studies* 17 (1955): 143–172; Theresa Gross-Diaz, *The Psalms Commentary of Gilbert of Poitiers: From 'Lectio Divina' to the Lecture Room* (Leiden, 1996), 15–20; and Southern, *Scholastic Humanism I: Foundations*, 225–230.

13 Gross-Diaz, *The Psalms Commentary of Gilbert of Poitiers*, 20. For a sense of how such lectures would appear, see the illustration in Maurice Keen, *A History of Medieval Europe* (London, 1967), facing page 86 (Plate 3), showing a master, several note takers, and eighty-five students (though not at Paris). The plate, from an MS of Eadwine of Canterbury, is only found in the original Routledge & Keegan Paul edition of this book. The more common Penguin edition does not contain as many illustrations.

14 Verger, "Teachers," 157–159; Rosemann, *Peter Lombard*, 40.

15 On Peter's house, see Brady, Prolegomena 1: 19*–21*.

16 Ibid., 21*. See the discussion in chapter two, above, 42–43. Peter donated the house to the chapter of Notre Dame, and this inventory was made after his death.

17 "tutis auribus loquebatur, id est illis quod instruxerat." Note he says "'to those he had taught,'" not those he was teaching. Brady, "Peter Manducator," 473.

master a certain freedom in airing his opinions and in discussing difficult questions before he came to a firm position. After Peter's death, his students spoke up for him, defended his works, and made sure they were read, copied, and disseminated.[18] They had a filial relationship with him, governed by the very strict rules of loyalty and obligation that bound people in the Middle Ages.

The majority of Peter's sermons were preached to his students and colleagues, and they provide an idea of how he presented theological material to an audience and of how he related to his students. In order to give a sense of Peter as a master, and to retain a connection with his intellectual personality, the second part of this book opens with an examination of these texts. It is not an exaggeration to say that they have been neglected. There has not been an extended treatment of them since 1881. The structural features of the sermons and the character of their spiritual advice will receive consideration. Peter's sermons, even if they do not appear so at first glance, are the most self-revealing things he wrote.

In the discussion of Peter's school, the chronological focus shifts to include the two decades following Peter's death. Five students are looked at in detail: Peter Comestor, William of Tyre, Herbert of Bosham, John of Cornwall, and Adam of Wales. With the exception of John, they all studied with Peter for a considerable period of time. This is a somewhat different approach than is usually taken for examining a twelfth-century school. A tendency that has proven fruitful is to use the term "school" loosely to mean anyone influenced by a particular master. This is a profitable approach for the history of theology or philosophy, since it allows one to perceive the transmission of ideas. One of the best examples of this approach is David Luscombe's excellent book *The School of Peter Abelard,* which examines the influence of Abelard's thought. The study is not limited to those who actually studied with Abelard, although Luscombe does provide a useful list of his students.[19] The only previous discussion of Peter Lombard's school in this sense was by Lauge-Olaf Nielsen.[20] Nielsen restricts himself to the authors of early commentaries and abridgments of the *Sentences,* not all of whom studied with

18 Verger, "Teachers," 158–159.
19 Luscombe, *The School of Peter Abelard,* 14–59.
20 Lauge-Olaf Nielsen, *Theology and Philosophy in the Twelfth Century: A Study of Gilbert Porreta's Thinking and the Theological Expositions of the Doctrine of the Incarnation During the Period 1130–1180* (Leiden, 1982), 243–362.

Peter.[21] He prefers to describe them as belonging to Peter's "immediate sphere of influence."[22]

Peter Lombard's school has an advantage for historians. We know precisely where and when he taught. The focus can be kept on his students in a particular time and place, and the functioning of a twelfth-century school can be examined more closely than is usually possible. This approach to Peter Lombard's school is also helpful because it shows the students of a theology master working in a variety of fields. Limiting the focus to the students that made careers as theologians would not provide the full story of Peter's school. The material they learned there had a practical application for their careers, whether they were masters, diplomats, bishops, advisers, or freelance writers. The students are examined with respect to three areas in particular: their study years in Peter's school, how those years are reflected in their careers and writings, and how they defended or increased awareness of Peter's teaching. It will also become clear that the students, like Peter himself, were not from illustrious families. This did not deter them from pursuing a relatively new subject that offered no instant rewards. In Peter's school, the theologians' sense of identity was very strong.

Although the chapters are divided by the students themselves, they also address particular points of Peter's image and reception, and a coherent narrative emerges. Chapter seven, on Peter Comestor and William of Tyre, is especially concerned with Peter's influence on the writings of his students, how his work was transmitted, and his posthumous image. It also includes a discussion of a group of disciples who William of Tyre refers to as a *chorus*. The members of this group are all anonymous, but they seem to have regarded clarifying, elaborating, and disseminating Peter's work as a priority. The two chapters on Herbert of Bosham, Adam of Wales, and John of Cornwall, also address these themes, but here the particular focus is on the Christological controversy that enveloped Peter's work in the 1160s and 1170s. Examining the students' role in the controversy will provide a fresh outlook. Previous treatments have looked at a gradual buildup of opposition, not at how it was surmounted.

21 See chapter seven, below, 191–192.

22 Nielsen, *Theology and Philosophy in the Twelfth Century*, 281. On his shortcomings in this respect, see also Marcia Colish, "Christological Nihilianism in the Second Half of the Twelfth Century," *RTAM* 63 (1996): 146–155, at 155.

The students have received considerable scholarly attention, but their training under Peter Lombard has sometimes been pushed into the background. Their careers are discussed here only insofar as they show the broad application of a theological training. A discussion of their study years and careers precedes an examination of Peter's influence on their works. The exception to this is Adam of Wales, who has received very little attention, and who left no written works to evaluate. For this reason, it is necessary to provide as much detail about him as is possible. In any case, it has considerable bearing on how he ended up in Rome, defending his master.

CHAPTER SIX

The Master: Peter Lombard in His Sermons

Without letters, without any sort of extended recollection of him, it is always going to be difficult to talk about Peter Lombard, "the man." If we try to search for traces of Peter Lombard's personality, the best starting point might be his sermons. Peter did not intend his sermons to be openly self-revelatory. In fact, he rarely brings himself or his experience into them. And yet he is there in every line, from the very personal choice of text to preach on,[1] to the gently reassuring tones of his opening paragraphs, to the skillfully conceived structures, which are notable for the interplay and development of themes. Moreover, he was giving these sermons to his students. He was preaching to them, but, at the same time, not haranguing them. Peter appears in the sermons as a *magister* in full control of his material. They also reveal that he could connect on a more personal level with his students by providing them with spiritual guidance. It might go too far to call him a spiritual director, but he was keen to see that his students took the observance of their religion seriously.

Looking at Peter's sermons in this way is new, and before doing so, it is worth examining what *has* been written about them up to now. Although the vast field of sermon literature has taken off in the past fifteen to twenty years,[2] there have been no new studies of Peter's work in the genre. In general terms, scholars have come to the sermons with preconceived ideas: the almost off-putting length and scope of the *Sentences* has coloured the picture of the sermons, as it has the man. Furthermore, there has perhaps also been a tendency

1 Peter did not have complete freedom to choose a text. Readings had to follow the liturgy. The preacher, however, would choose a particular sentence to focus on.

2 For example, the journal *Medieval Sermon Studies*. Also *Preacher, Sermon and Audience in the Middle Ages*, ed. Carolyn Muessig (Leiden, 2002), and *The Sermon*, ed. Beverly M. Kienzle (Turnhout, 2000). A renewed interest in sermons has been stimulated partly by Schneyer's collection of sermon incipits: Johannes B. Schneyer, *Repertorium der lateinischen Sermones des Mittelalters: Für die Zeit von 1150–1350* (Münster, 1969–1990).

to assume that Peter's sermons should be assessed as one would assess a sermon today.

Louis Bourgain was the first author to provide a critical assessment of Peter's sermons in 1879. His work was inspired by the pioneering overview of thirteenth-century scholastic Latin sermons by Albert Lecoy de la Marche.[3] Lecoy's tripartite structure of preachers, sermons, and society was both original and influential, and it is still used today as an approach.[4] Bourgain closely followed Lecoy's structure and method when he prepared a similar volume for the twelfth century.[5] But he lacked the balance and fairness of his exemplar. In a supposedly comprehensive work, Peter Lombard receives a mere two pages. Bourgain dismisses Peter as "cold and stiff,"[6] "a famous theologian, but a mediocre preacher."[7] He detects only "one passage worthy of interest,"[8] and includes it. It was from a sermon for Ash Wednesday, which is indeed one of the more accessible sermons, but the paragraph quoted by Bourgain is not necessarily the best one. There is no sense that he had anything more than a surface familiarity with Peter's sermons.

A more careful assessment appeared two years later, in the abbé Félix Protois's fine monograph, *Pierre Lombard.*[9] Protois made notes on the sermons he had consulted in two manuscripts at the Bibliothèque nationale de France.[10] It remains the most extended treatment of the sermons to date. He deals with the main points of each sermon, the quality of Peter's Latin, and the question of who the audience might have been. He also includes

3 Albert Lecoy de la Marche, *La chaire française au moyen âge, spécialement au XIIIe siècle, d'après les manuscrits contemporains,* 2nd ed. (Paris, 1886).

4 For example, Carolyn Muessig, "Sermon, Preacher and Society in the Middle Ages," *Journal of Medieval History* 28 (2002): 73–91.

5 Louis Bourgain, *La chaire française au XIIe siècle d'après les manuscrits* (Paris, 1879). Bourgain also used the subdivisions "Les prédicateurs; les sermons; la société d'après les sermons."

6 Ibid., 46–47: "Ses homélies sont des dissertations régulières, nourries de l'Écriture sainte et particulièrement des Prophètes, mais froides et compassées."

7 Ibid., 46: "Pierre Lombard, célèbre théologien, fut un prédicateur médiocre."

8 Ibid., 47.

9 Félix Protois, *Pierre Lombard: Évêque de Paris dit le maître des Sentences: Son époque, sa vie, ses écrits, son influence* (Paris, 1881), 123–148.

10 Protois consulted Paris, Bibliothèque nationale de France, lat. 18170, which contains 20 sermons, and lat. 3537, which contains 28 sermons, and is described in *Bibliothèque nationale: Catalogue général des manuscrits latins* (Paris, 1939–1988), 6: 6–7.

samples and translations of passages he particularly enjoyed – because of their literary qualities, because of a felicitous phrase or two, or because of an impressive, original way of making a point. He singles out these over others and is slightly puzzled by the apparently varying quality of the sermons.[11] Protois assumes that the sermons all dated from Peter's episcopacy, and this is no longer accepted. However, his other finding regarding the possible audience is strengthened by later scholarship. From an attentive reading of the sermons, Protois establishes that the majority were preached to clerics and monks.[12]

After Protois, important work was carried out in the area of identifying and cataloguing Peter's sermons.[13] The majority were already in print in the *Patrologia Latina*, there mistakenly attributed to Hildebert of Lavardin. This was demonstrated in 1888 and 1890[14] by Hauréau, whose work on identification laid the groundwork for many similar studies in the first half of the twentieth century. Later, Van den Eynde added to his findings.[15] Brady reca-

11 Protois, *Pierre Lombard*, 124–125: "Il y a beaucoup d'inégalité dans les sermons de Pierre Lombard. Les uns n'offrent rien de remarquable; l'on trouve au contraire dans les autres de véritables mouvements d'éloquence ... le latin en est toujours correct, quelquefois même élégant."

12 Ibid., 147–148, 190.

13 In this sense, work on Peter sermons followed a pattern common to the early twentieth century of identifying, cataloguing, and disentangling misattributions. The *Patrologia Latina* volumes purporting to contain the works of Hildebert and Peter of Blois were the main culprits. The work of scholars such as Châtillon and Lebreton was then incorporated into Schneyer's *Repertorium*. His list of Peter's sermons only contains 29 sermon incipits, suggesting that he was not aware of or had not had a chance to consult Brady's work: Schneyer, *Repertorium der lateinischen Sermones des Mittelalters*, 4: 700–704.

14 Barthélemy Hauréau, "Notice sur les sermons attribués à Hildebert de Lavardin," *Notices et extraits des manuscrits de la Bibliothèque nationale* 32 (1888): 107–166. Antoine Beaugendre, in his edition, *Venerabilis Hildeberti primo cenomanensis episcopi, deinde Turonensis archiepiscopi opera, tam edita quam inedita* (Paris, 1708), believed that the collection of 26 anonymous sermons in Paris, Bibliothèque nationale de France, lat. 12415, was a work of Hildebert. Migne incorporated Beaugendre's edition into the *Patrologia Latina* wholesale. See Brady, Prolegomena 1: 95*. It is essential to consult Hauréau's article for a number of corrections and additions to the Beaugendre/Migne text.

15 Damien Van den Eynde, "Deux sermons inédits de Pierre Lombard," in *Miscellanea Lombardiana* (Novara, 1957), 75–87. He also discussed the question of dating in "Essai chronologique sur l'oeuvre littéraire de Pierre Lombard," in *Miscellanea Lombardiana*, 45–63, at 58–60.

pitulated all of this work and compiled a valuable list of all the sermons.[16] He also made brief notes on each sermon, centering usually on how the sermons relate to Peter's other works, and, occasionally, to other works of the period.

While they are more accessible to readers than before, Peter's sermons have yet to receive extensive or sympathetic attention. In recent assessments of them, authors seem to be in agreement that, as a preacher, Peter lacks certain qualities. Jean Longère, in his study of the sermons of Parisian masters, is impressed with Peter's doctrinal content, but he thinks that Peter lacked warmth.[17] Unhappily, in his general book, *La prédication médiévale*, he is content to quote Bourgain.[18] Lorenzo Fantini, in an article published in *Pier Lombardo*,[19] sees him as ultimately "unsuccessful,"[20] although he does make some original points about structure. Brady took issue with these views in 1981, noting that they were based on the erroneous assumption that the sermons represented Bishop Peter preaching to his flock. Rather, he concludes that this was Peter the canon, preaching to his students and colleagues.[21] This awareness led to a modification of the negative view. Colish provides a good two-page assessment in 1994,[22] describing the sermons as "grave and cool in

16 Brady, Prolegomena 1: 95*–112*. He listed 33 sermons, one dubious sermon, and one spurious. He added two more in Prolegomena 2: 34*–35*, one definite and one possible. Brady also lists manuscript and, where applicable, print references to the sermons. He also lists the titles, opening verse, and incipit. This is essential, since the sermons that appear in print in the *Patrologia Latina* were often given speculative or incorrect titles by their original editor, Dom Antonius Beaugendre. The sermons are cited in this book by Brady's titles, along with the applicable print or manuscript reference. They are also listed individually in the bibliography.

17 Jean Longère, *Oeuvres oratoires de maîtres parisiens au XIIe siècle: Étude historique et doctrinale* (Paris, 1975), 1: 83–88, 293–295. His assessment, on 295, is "il apparaît homme de doctrine, plus que pasteur. On ne saurait lui reprocher de faire plus appel à la raison qu'aux sentiments, cependant sa prédication manque un peu de chaleur."

18 Jean Longère, *La prédication médiévale* (Paris, 1983), 70.

19 Lorenzo Fantini, "I Discorsi di Pier Lombardo," *Pier Lombardo* 5 (1961), 69–80.

20 Ibid., 80: "E veramente la nota caratteristica di ogni discorso del Nostro è la monotonia, la freddezza e l'aridità, la mancanza di vita e di animazione, di movimento: un pensatore privo quasi completamente di fantasia, di immaginazione, di sensibilità, di communicativa: doti senza le quali non ci può essere arte oratoria. ... un oratore fallito, in poche parole; la sua vera ed autentica grandezza deve cercarsi altrove."

21 Brady, Prolegomena 2: 33* n2.

22 Colish, *Peter Lombard*, 26–27. She also included a list of Peter's sermons in PL 171. There is one misprint: sermons 57 and 58 in PL 171 are sermons of Peter Lombard, not 67 and 68.

their voice," appealing "more to the intellect than to the heart."[23] Southern, while finding them impressive in their very intensity, remarks that "there is no lightness of touch in them: all is weighty, solemn, solid."[24] Rosemann provides probably the most positive impression in his brief description of the sermons, remarking that "Peter was competent and calm as a preacher, preferring affectionate exhortation and charitable compassion to violent diatribes."[25]

The image of austerity must have deterred serious consideration of Peter's sermons. Bourgain's judgement of "mediocrity" would have convinced countless readers who turned to it as a work of reference for the period. Protois's book, however, which had a limited circulation when it came out, is rarely cited and rarely read.[26] There are four main reasons besides these, however, that explain why the sermons have not received systematic attention. Scholars who have dealt with the sermons of Parisian masters have not really known what to do with Peter Lombard. In the first place, there is the reason of chronology. Peter was active just before the period when masters began to see preaching as an important part of their routine. This has been called the "new emphasis on preaching."[27] The Third Lateran Council of 1179, and the importance it gave to preaching, was decades away. Even further off were the clearly defined duties of a master in thirteenth-century university statutes. A second reason, following on from that, has to do with the structure and layout of his sermons. In the late twelfth century, there was a growing demand for guidelines on how to write a sermon. This resulted in manuals on the art of preaching, which were sometimes complex (aimed at masters) and sometimes very simple (prepared for parish priests).[28] But Peter's sermons do not

23 Ibid., 27.

24 Richard W. Southern, *Scholastic Humanism and the Unification of Europe* II: *The Heroic Age* (Oxford, 2001), 140.

25 Rosemann, *Peter Lombard*, 49. I had already completed a draft of this chapter when Rosemann's book appeared and was pleased to see that the tide was beginning to turn in the reception of Peter's sermons.

26 It was a version of his doctoral thesis.

27 For this development, see Zier, "Sermons of the Twelfth Century Schoolmasters and Canons," in *The Sermon*, ed. Kienzle, 325–362. Also, Richard H. Rouse and Mary A. Rouse, *Preachers, Florilegia and Sermons: Studies on the Manipulus Florum of Thomas of Ireland* (Toronto, 1979), ch. 5: "The New Emphasis on Preaching," 43–64.

28 On the *Artes Praedicandi*, see, for example, Longère, *La prédication médiévale*, 195–202.

fit into these schemes. His structure is his own, deriving from his early rhetorical training and his knowledge of the material. He does not have that much in common with the older homiletic approach either, which was a step-by-step investigation of a substantial scriptural passage.[29] So it is all too easy to assume his sermons are structurally unsound.

Thirdly, Peter's sermons cannot be mined for details about Parisian society in this period.[30] He does not use the sermons to discuss contemporary issues or lament moral failings. He only hints at the occupation of his audience in two passages that seem to show a very high regard for the work of theologians.[31] Presumably all of this would leave the sermons as fertile ground for those inquiring into Peter's theology or the interpretation of the Bible in this period. However, anyone wishing to do that immediately turns to the *Sentences* or to the commentaries. Books on Peter Lombard tend to treat the sermons very briefly before moving on to the bigger works. That is the fourth reason.

What Peter Lombard's sermons can do, however, is show him interacting, and connecting, with an audience. Students made up the majority of this audience. That Peter preached in the milieu of the schools must be proven from internal evidence. Unlike late–twelfth century sermons, his do not have subtitles like *ad scolares* or *habitus in scholis*. However, Protois, Van Den Eynde, and Brady, who read the sermons attentively, note that they were quite definitely aimed at an audience of educated clerics.[32] Brady points especially to the use of theological concepts and language that would not have been famil-

29 For the definition of a homily, see Kienzle, "Introduction," in *The Sermon*, 144–168; Louis Jacques Bataillon, "Approaches to the Study of Medieval Sermons," *Leeds Studies in English* 11 (1980): 19–35, repr. in *La prédication au XIIIe siècle en France et Italie* (Aldershot, 1993), chapter 1, at 28; and Muessig, "Sermon, Preacher and Society in the Middle Ages," 77. For a concise definition of preaching, see Longère, *La prédication médiévale*, 12.

30 This approach to sermons was pioneered by Lecoy de la Marche: "He went a long way in highlighting how sermons could uncover the social history of the Middle Ages. He demonstrated that the content of sermons could reveal details related to church reform, politics, trade, religious devotion, women and marriage." Muessig, "Sermon, Preacher and Society in the Middle Ages," 74.

31 Peter Lombard, *Sermo de adventu* (PL 171: 370–376, at 374) and *Sermo in epiphania* (PL 171, 401–409, at 403). See below for a discussion of these passages.

32 Protois, *Pierre Lombard*, 147–148, 190; Van den Eynde, "Essai chronologique," 59; Brady, Prolegomena 2: 33*.

iar to people outside the schools.[33] This will also be evident as this chapter continues. Brady concludes that Peter preached as a canon of Notre Dame on specific occasions (typically during Advent or Lent, or on feast days like the Epiphany or Ascension). Some of Peter's fellow canons would certainly have also attended. We have seen in chapter three how important liturgical occasions were to their identity. The students of the school in attendance would not just include Peter's own students but also the students of other masters. Peter's audience was therefore a select group, not a large congregation.

Moving to when they were preached, Bourgain and Longère assumed that the sermons dated from Peter's episcopacy. However, there are at least thirty-four sermons we know of, and Peter was bishop for only eleven months. Most of the main manuscript collections contain between twenty-four and twenty-eight sermons, in sequence according to the liturgical year.[34] Certain feast days are represented by more than one sermon.[35] He was a canon of Notre Dame for fourteen years (1145–1159), and, as we have seen in the previous chapters, preaching had been one of his duties from the beginning.[36] Brady suggests that any sermon that treats issues also discussed in the *Sentences* and yet bears little resemblance to that work must date from before 1155, when the first version was produced.[37] This is certainly valid, but

33 Brady, Prolegomena 2: 33*. He noted the recurring idea of the *regio dissimilitudinis* and also the reference to *theologia* in the *Sermo in epiphania*. Brady was convinced that the audience was therefore the students and canons of Notre Dame. One thinks also of the technical discussion of the Trinity in Peter Lombard, *Sermo de trinitate et de pascha partim* (PL 171: 435).

34 For a list and description of the manuscripts containing Peter's sermons, see Brady, Prolegomena 1: 96*–98*. The most important collections are those termed by Brady "C" (Paris, Bibliothèque Mazarine, 1708), "D" (Paris, Bibliothèque nationale de France, lat. 3537), "E" (Paris, Bibliothèque nationale de France, lat. 12415), "F" (Paris, Bibliothèque nationale de France, lat. 13374), "K" (Prague, Codex Lobkowicz 444), and "L" (Vatican City, Biblioteca Apostolica Vaticana, Vat. lat. 1275). "K," though attributed to "Petrus Baeolardus" (i.e., Abelard), contains 31 sermons, including the two preached to the clergy.

35 Brady, Prolegomena 1: 99*–112*. There are two sermons each for the purification, Good Friday, and Palm Sunday, and at least three for Easter.

36 For the dating of the sermons, see Brady, Prolegomena 2: 34*–35*, and Van den Eynde, "Essai chronologique," 58–60.

37 Brady, Prolegomena 1: 37*. See also his notes on the sermons on 99–112, which concern their relation to the *Sentences*. Or, Colish, *Peter Lombard*, 27, who points out that some of them must date from the 1140s and early 1150s because "they do not manifest the more pointed doctrine and the crisper theological vocabulary found in the final edition of the *Sentences* on those subjects."

Brady's other argument in that context – that a sermon that does resemble the *Sentences* must date from 1155 or later – is problematic. Peter Lombard could easily have refined his ideas in lectures and sermons.[38]

None of the sermons can be definitively dated within Peter's episcopacy, and Brady admitted this.[39] He raised the possibility, however, that as many as eight were.[40] These include a sermon on penitence, which is concise, direct, and warm.[41] Another two were sermons to the clergy, emphasizing themes such as the necessity of preaching.[42] These would certainly date either from Peter's archidiaconate or from his episcopacy, when instructing the clergy was one of his duties. The grounds for considering any other sermons as episcopal are very slim, however, since they are usually based on affinity with the *Sentences*.[43] The first version of the *Sentences* had been completed by 1154, a full five years before Peter became bishop. Brady also suggested that an anonymous sermon may be the work of Peter the bishop.[44] Prefixed *ad populum* ("to the people"), it begins:

> You see, my brothers, that the will of our Lord is such as to appoint me, although an unworthy sinner, not through my merits but through his compassion, to guard the church and to entrust your custody, and that of others pertaining to this see, to me. A bishop or archbishop must attentively guard those entrusted to him and educate them in the commandments of God.[45]

38 This point has been noted by Peter Harris Tibber, "The Origins of the Scholastic Sermon, c.1130–c.1210" (Dphil diss., University of Oxford, 1983), 31.

39 Brady, Prolegomena 1: 112*.

40 Ibid., 37*. See also the brief notes on the individual sermons on 99–112.

41 Peter Lombard, *Sermo in receptione poenitentium* (PL 171: 524–530). Brady pointed to a tradition of the bishop of Paris exhorting the faithful to penitence on Holy Thursday at the cathedral. Prolegomena 1: 37* n2.

42 For example, fol. 112a, "Praedicamus igitur et commodemus mysticum, moralem et historialem intellectum," quoted in Brady, Prolegomena 1: 109*.

43 Ibid., 37*.

44 *Sermo ad populum* (PL 171: 921–924). The suggestion is in Prolegomena 2: 35*.

45 "Videtis, fratres, talem fuisse voluntatem Domini nostri, ut me, licet indignum peccatorem, non per merita mea, sed per misericordiam suam, ad regendam Ecclesiam istam constituerit, et mihi custodiam vestram, et aliorum ad hanc sedem pertinentium commendaverit. Debet enim quisque episcopus, vel archiepiscopus, populos sibi commissos attente custodire, in mandatis Domini erudire." Ibid. (PL 171: 921).

Although this sermon provides a valuable description of the expected role of bishops, it was probably not preached by Peter. As we will soon see, Peter never begins his sermons by placing the focus on himself like that. That was more characteristic of the generation following him.

The majority of the sermons then were preached to the canons and students of Notre Dame, between 1145 and 1159. Peter himself prepared the text of the sermons.[46] This is consistent with the care Peter usually took over his works. As we have seen, none of them originated as *reportationes* (notes taken by students).[47] He made two editions of the *Sentences* and the *Commentary on the Letters of Paul.* He also stressed to his students that his *Commentary on the Psalms* was not finished.[48] Headings or rubrics denoting the different sections of the sermons appear in the margins.[49] The authorities are also carefully noted. These procedures typify his other works.[50]

The following discussion of the sermons revolves around certain distinctive features that characterize them. First, the sermons tend to begin with a reassuring tone, or with a note of celebration. It is also at the beginning that Peter tends to refer to his audience most frequently. Secondly, the character of the spiritual advice – sometimes very straightforward, sometimes quasi-monastic – will be considered. Thirdly, it is important to examine certain recurring structural features. Peter's sermons have been sometimes analyzed solely as an exposition of the opening text, but alongside this, the feast day in question operates as an equally important theme. Finally, the use of visual imagery is an occasional, though not dominant, feature of the sermons.

When preaching became common in the schools in the late twelfth century, a fashion developed for beginning a sermon with protestations of unsuitability. The preacher would often claim he was unworthy of his text.[51] In rheto-

46 Brady, Prolegomena 1: 112*, was adamant on this point.

47 See chapter two, above, 43. For problems surrounding later twelfth-century sermons that are *reportationes,* see Bataillon, "Approaches to the Study of Medieval Sermons," 21, and Augustine Thompson, "From Texts to Preaching: Retrieving the Medieval Sermon as an Event," in *Preacher, Sermon and Audience in the Middle Ages,* ed. Muessig, 15–20.

48 See chapter four, above, 107.

49 Brady, Prolegomena 1: 95*–97*, 112*. I have observed the use of rubrics in Paris, Bibliothèque nationale de France, lat. 13374, fol. 1–49v.

50 Brady, Prolegomena 1: 112*, 138*–141*. See also Brady, "The Rubrics of Peter Lombard's Sentences," *Pier Lombardo* 6 (1962): 5–25, and Rosemann, *Peter Lombard,* 65.

51 Tibber, "The Origins of the Scholastic Sermon," 123–124.

ric this was known as *captatio benevolentiae*, where the speaker would try to gain the goodwill of the audience by flattery, or by reference to his record, or by a display of humility. Such techniques were already well established in letter writing by Peter Lombard's day, but had not yet found their way into sermons. Instead, Peter usually begins his sermons gently, by praising the feast day for which they have gathered or the text on which he is preaching. For example, he describes one of his opening verses in this way: "a sweet and gentle trumpet of promise sounds to the hearts of the faithful through the prophet Obadiah, and, like the music of salvation, and the harmony of the heavens, widens the minds of the faithful to spiritual exaltation and perfect love."[52] Rather than talking about himself, Peter focuses on the text and refers to the inspiration of the Holy Spirit in the words. This is especially true when he preaches on texts from the prophets, for example, "This is not the counsel of a man, this is the counsel of the Holy Spirit, who urges us to conversion through the prophet Jeremiah."[53] He brings in the Holy Spirit like this to comfort his audience. He leaves out the stern judge: "We must not be diffident, we must not despair, because the Holy Spirit will come to the aid of our infirmity. He speaks to us through the prophets, telling us that now we are sons, and friends, not slaves, for we are regenerated by grace."[54]

52 "Suavis et mitis promissionis buccina cordibus fidelium insonuit per prophetam Abdiam, qui velut musica Salvatoris, et harmonia coelistis, fidelium mentes spirituali exsultatione, atque perfecta dilectione dilataret." Peter Lombard, *Sermo in circumcisione Domini* (PL 171: 394–401, at 394). The text being preached on is "In monte Sion erit salvatio, et erit Sanctus, et possidebit domus Jacob eos qui se possederant, et erit domus Jacob ignis, et domus Joseph flamma." (Obad. 1.17). This sermon will be further discussed below. Hauréau notes that one manuscript has "suavis et dulcis," rather than "suavis et mitis."

53 "Non est hoc hominis, sed Spiritus sancti consilium, qui per prophetam Jeremiam nos admonet ad conversionem." Peter Lombard, *Sermo de trinitate et de pascha partim* (PL 171: 432). Other sermons beginning this way are *Sermo de Sancto Joanne evangelistae* (PL 171: 723–727, at 723); *Sermo in epiphania* (PL 171: 401); *Sermo in prima dominica quadragesimae* (PL 171: 443–451, at 443); *Sermo in ramis palmarum* (PL 171: 491–502, at 491); *Sermo de annuntiatione* (PL 171: 605–610, at 605); *Sermo in coena Domini* (PL 171: 510–524, at 510); *Sermo in parasceve* (PL 171: 796–806, at 796); *Sermo de paschali tempore* (PL 171: 871–873, at 871); and *Sermo sine rubrica*, ed. Henri M. Rochais, "Une collection de textes de S. Bernard dans le manuscrit Tours 343," *RTAM* 29 (1962): 106–111, at 106.

54 "Non igitur diffidamus, non desperemus, quia spiritus adjuvat infirmitatem nostram. Nobis enim ipse per prophetas loquitur, quia jam filii sumus et amici, quia ejus gratia regenerati, non servi." *Sermo de trinitate de pascha partim* (PL 171: 433).

In this, Peter may have been characteristic of his generation in the schools. Odo of Soissons seems also to have begun his sermons with a similar tone.[55] Another master, Geoffrey Babion, directly influenced Peter in that area.[56] The opening of Peter's sermon *In receptione poenitentium* ("on the reception of penitents") is almost identical to one of Geoffrey's: "Listen, brethren, to how that most gentle of fathers, that father of compassion, the God of all consolations, recalls us with a sweet voice, with such paternal affection ... he does not alienate you, he does not frighten you off, but rather, with a paternal voice, he invites you to correction."[57] Otherwise, however, Geoffrey's sermons do not have the rigorous structure or skillful interweaving of themes that are characteristic of Peter's. This was partly because they were not preached in the milieu of the schools, but instead date from his episcopacy in Bordeaux.[58]

Passages in this vein will occur throughout the sermons, and not always at the opening. In one of the sermons, Peter proclaims, "How wonderful and worthy of love is that promise! How sweet and faithful it is, and worthy of wholehearted acceptance!"[59] It is very important to understand how such

55 Odo of Soissons, *Sermo*: "Egredietur virga de radice Iesse," in *Analecta Novissima Spicilegii Solesmensis Altera Continuatio*, ed. Jean-Baptiste Pitra (Paris, 1865–1888), 2: xlii–xlvii.

56 For Geoffrey as a preacher, see Jean-Paul Bonnes, "Un des plus grands prédicateurs du XIIe siècle: Geoffroy du Louroux, dit Geoffroy Babion," *Revue Bénédictine* 56 (1945–1946): 174–215. Many of Geoffrey's sermons, like those of Peter, were attributed to Hildebert of Lavardin by Beaugendre.

57 "Attendite, fratres, quam dulci voce, quam paterno affectu, revocat nos Pater mitissimus, Pater misericordiarum, Deus totius consolationis ... non vos alienat, non vos exterritat, set paternali voce, ad emendationem invitat." Peter Lombard, *Sermo in receptione poenitentium* (PL 171: 524–525). Compare this with how Babion begins one of his sermons: "Audistis, fratrres charissimi, quam dulci voce, quali affectu revocat vos mitissimus pater; non vos alienat, non exterritat vos, sed patria voce vos ad emendationem invitat." (PL 171: 505).

58 For this, and assessments of Babion's preaching, see Bonnes, "Un des plus grands prédicateurs du XIIe siècle: Geoffroy du Louroux, dit Geoffroy Babion," 186; Guy-Marie Oury, "Les sermons de Geoffroi Babion et la chrétienté Bordelaise," *Cahiers de civilisation médiévale* 22 (1979): 285–297.

59 "Quam dulcis et amanda promissio! Quam suavis et fidelis sermo, et omni acceptione dignus!" Peter Lombard, *Sermo de Adventu* (PL 171: 379), text corrected by Hauréau, "Notice sur les sermons attribués à Hildebert de Lavardin," 114. Peter is referring to a verse from Isaiah, 'Non elongabitur, et salus mea non morabitur; dabo in Sion salutem, et in Jerusalem gloriam meam' (Isa. 46:13). There is a similar passage in the *Sermo de Sancto Joanne evangelistae* (PL 171: 723): "O quam grata, quam dulcis, quam magna est ista promissio." There he is referring to the opening text.

passages function in the structure as an emotional release. We will say more of this presently. Early on in another sermon, he reminds his audience to "look at the compassion and truth of God, and understand the goodness of God."[60] Later on, just before recapitulating the main text, he comes back to this: "Love God, my brothers, not the world, with all your heart, and your neighbour as yourselves."[61] This Peter Lombard hardly seems to resemble the image in Bourgain and Longère at all: the mediocre preacher who was too cold and stiff to reach his audience.

The only time Peter begins a sermon on a less than reassuring note is in the *Sermo in die cineris*, a sermon for Ash Wednesday, preached on a verse from Proverbs about rising from sleep[62]: "Just as the kingdom is promised to those staying awake, so the wise man threatens those sleeping with eternal punishment. Such a sleep is perverse, my brothers, and it must be strongly avoided. It is not a sleep of the body, but of the mind. It does not stand for calmness of mind, but brings in oppression."[63] Distinctions between different kinds of sleep, and different kinds of night, appear throughout. Subsidiary quotations refer to sleeping and rising, and later to converting. The beginning of Lent furnished the tone. Peter presumably wanted his audience to make a fresh start and to take their religion more seriously. The sermon is also unusual in that, for once, theology, commentary, and structure are reduced, and simple exhortation takes their place. To modern eyes, it has more in common with what is considered an effective sermon, and this may have been the reason why it was singled out by Bourgain as a better sermon than the others.[64]

As he often does, Peter holds back the subject of the sermon until comparatively late. After devoting a considerable amount of time to what

60 "Attendite ergo Dei misericordiam et veritatem. Intelligite Dei bonitatem." Peter Lombard, *Sermo in dominica ante palmas* (PL 171: 456–463, at 457).

61 "Diligite fratres, toto corde Deum, non mundum, et proximos sicut vosmetipsos." Ibid., 461.

62 "Usquequo, piger, dormies? Quando consurges e somno tuo? Paululum dormies, paululum dormitabis, paululum conseres manus, ut dormias, et veniet tibi quasi viator egestas, et pauperies quasi vir armatus." Prov. 6: 9–11.

63 "Sicut vigilantibus promittitur regnum, ita dormientibus Sapientia minatur aeturnum interitum. Pervesa est dormitatio, et ideo, fratres, vehementer est fugienda. Non est iste somnus corporis, sed mentis; nec mentis praestat quietem, sed ingerit oppressionem." Peter Lombard, *Sermo in die cineris* (PL 171: 451–456, at 451).

64 Bourgain, *La chaire française*, 47.

should be avoided, Peter urges conversion, and here the sermon resolves into something very gentle: "Consider, my brothers, how compassionate and how patient our redeemer is, who, daily, continuously, warns us – who are falling – that we can rise. He recalls those who stray to life. We may abandon him, but he will not abandon us, whom he redeemed."[65] Peter outlines what is necessary: compunction, open confession, and true penitence.[66]

Usually – as in this Ash Wednesday sermon – Peter Lombard, as a preacher, was content to provide straightforward spiritual advice for his hearers. He reminded them of the basics, such as prayer, confession, fasting, almsgiving, good works, and turning away from sin. Most of the sermons refer to these themes. And yet, occasionally, the sermons do show that Peter was certainly acquainted with the writings on the spiritual life by his contemporaries in monastic houses, even though he did not seek to imitate them. This is apparent in a sermon on the Ascension.[67] It is built around the ways in which Christ ascended to heaven and descended to earth, and how this may be imitated. It is a remarkable sermon, which alternates between a theological exposition of the incarnation and meditations on the spiritual life. It also includes celebratory prose and gently shifting images of new life arising and the old law vanishing in a sunset.[68]

Peter contrasts "the good cloud in which Jesus ascended" with "the bad cloud in which man descends."[69] His discussion of the bad cloud is unmistakably influenced by monastic writing, particularly in its diagnostic approach to the spiritual life. He describes three spiritual states, the clouds of passion, iniquity, and fantasies.[70] Those in the cloud of iniquity may be able to fend off

65 "Attendite, fratres, quantae misericordiae, quantae patientes est Redemptor noster, qui nos quotidie cadentes incessanter admonet ut surgamus, aberrantes revocat ad vitam. Nos [ipsum] deserimus, sed ipse nos non deserit, quos redemit." Peter Lombard, *Sermo in die cineris* (PL 171: 454).

66 Ibid., 455–456.

67 Peter Lombard, *Sermo in ascensione*, ed. Damien Van den Eynde, in "Deux sermons inédtis de Pierre Lombard," in *Miscellanea Lombardiana*, 80–87.

68 Even Brady, rarely given to subjective statements, wrote that in this sermon, Peter "beautifully illustrates" (*pulchre illustrat*) in what way Christ's example of descent and ascent is to be followed. Prolegomena 1: 109*.

69 "Triplex autem est nubes bona in qua Iesus ascendit, sicut triplex est nubes mala in quo homo descendit," Peter Lombard, *Sermo in ascensione*, ed. Van den Eynde, 84.

70 "alia voluptatis, alia iniquitatis, alia phantasiarum." Ibid.

passion, but "they retain avarice, pride, and other spiritual illnesses."[71] Those who have put aside passion and iniquity still face problems: "they are disturbed in their prayers by fantasies, and they are influenced by weariness, so that their souls gradually waste away in what is wrong."[72] What is rare here is the discussion of spiritual progress. Peter presents it as a long journey, with a succession of obstacles that must be conquered. Usually he would not go into such detail.

It is also significant that Peter shows the direct influence of Bernard of Clairvaux in this sermon, while discussing the imitation of Christ's descent. This can be done by following three "steps of humility." This idea immediately brings Bernard to mind, since one of his best known works is *The Steps of Humility and Pride*. However, Peter's model here is not that work, but one of Bernard's own sermons on the Ascension. Though considerably shorter, Bernard's sermon is also built on the idea of imitating Christ's ascent and descent. It contains the following passage:

> Let us descend by the road of humility, and let its first step be set up by us, that is, the first step of progress: not to desire to dominate; second: to desire to be subject; third: in that very subjection to bear with a quiet mind whatever insults or injuries are laid upon us. Lucifer missed that first step in heaven by saying in his heart, "I will ascend the heavens, I will exalt my throne above God's stars ..." (Isa. 14:13–14). By saying these things he fell from heaven irretrievably, and perhaps it was for this reason that pride, which is the desire to dominate, is altogether intolerable. The first human beings missed the first step in paradise .... Let us listen to the prophet seeking how he may be lifted up. "Who," he says "shall ascend the mountain of the Lord, who shall stand in his holy place? The man with clean hands and pure heart who has not received his soul in vain nor sworn deceitfully to his neighbour" (Psa. 23:3–4). Let us note in these

71 "Nubes iniquitatis est malitiosa, haec est spiritualis nequitia quam multi incurrunt qui voluptatis postponunt et [minus] tolerabilior est eorum nequitia quam quorumdam immunditia. Praesumunt enim de se aliosque contemnunt et, dum voluptatem fugiunt, avaritiam superbiam aliasque spirituales nequitias quasi licitas retinent." Ibid.

72 "Et sunt nonnulli qui voluptatis et iniquitatis nubes evadunt, phantasiis tamen in orationibus perturbantur et taedio afficiuntur ut in malis anima eorum contabescat." Ibid.

> verses the three steps he set up to be climbed. The first step is integrity (innocence) in deeds, the second is purity of heart, the third is the fruit of devotion.[73]

Peter Lombard's treatment of the steps of humility relies heavily on this passage, although it is not a direct copy.

> Let us descend therefore by the road of humility which Christ proposed for us. There are three steps: the first is sufficient [humility], the second abundant, the third all-encompassing. The first is to subject oneself to those greater, and not to place oneself above equals, the second to subject oneself to equals and not to place oneself before those below, third to be under those below, in which there is all justice. Christ made this clear when he came to John the Baptist. Lucifer missed these steps in heaven, as did the first human beings in paradise, and so they fell headlong to ruin. And just as we ought to descend by these three steps, so by another three we ought to ascend, namely purity of heart, innocence of deeds, and the fruits of justice. The prophet in seeking recommended this order – "who shall ascend the mountain of the Lord?" – and he responded, "the man with clean hands and pure heart" (Psa. 23:3–4).[74]

73 "Descendamus per viam humilitatis, ponaturque nobis primus eius gradus, id est primus profectus, nolle dominari; secundus, velle subici; tertius, in ipsa subiectione quaslibet contumelias et iniurias illatas aequanimiter pati. Primo illo gradu caruit in caelo Lucifer ille, qui dixit in corde suo: 'In caelum ascendam, super astra Dei exaltabo solium meum' ... Haec dicens irreparabiliter cecidit de caelo, et hoc ideo forte, quia omnino intolerabilis superbia est, velle dominari. Secundo gradu caruerunt primi homines in paradiso .... audiamus Prophetam quaerentem quomodo ascendendum sit. 'Quis,' inquit, 'ascendet in montem Domini? aut quis stabit in loco sancto eius? Innocens manibus et mundo corde, qui non accepit in vano animam suam, nec iuravit in dolo proximo suo.' Ubi notandum quod triplicem ascendendi gradum constituit. Primus gradus est innocentia operis; secundus, munditia cordis; tertius, fructus devotionis." Bernard of Clairvaux, *Sermo de Ascensione Domini* (*Sermones de Diversis* 40), in *Sancti Bernardi opera*, ed. Jean Leclercq, Charles H. Talbot, and Henri Rochais (Rome, 1957–1977), 6: 292. The translation is by Grace Forster, "Three Short Sermons on the Ascension by St Bernard of Clairvaux," *Cistercian Studies* 25 (1990): 3–8, at 4–5. Bernard's ascension sermons are discussed by Jean Leclercq, "The Mystery of the Ascension in the Sermons of Saint Bernard," *Cistercian Studies* 25 (1990): 9–16.

74 "Descendamus ergo per viam humilitatis quam Christus nobis proposuit. Cuius sunt tres gradus: primus sufficiens, secundus abundans, tertius consummans. Primus enim est subdere se maiori et non praeferre se aequali, secundus subdere se aequali

Peter refers to this again in another sermon, explaining, with great conciseness, that Christ "made the first step of humility in flesh, the second on a cross, the third in death. His whole life is our doctrine and his every action is our lesson."[75]

Similarities with the works of Bernard also occur in a sermon on the Annunciation. Here Peter views the passion as something that can draw humanity toward the love of God: "There was not a more convenient way to cure our misery. For in such a way he awakened our love towards him, and he commended charity to us."[76] He then addresses his audience directly: "what better way was there for him to show his love for you, and encourage your love for him?"[77] He ends in the hortatory style common to many of the sermons: "let us love the compassion by which we are redeemed."[78] This idea is expressed prominently by Bernard in his sermon on the three qualities of love (no. 20) from the Sermons on the Song of Songs: "I think this is the principle reason why the invisible God willed to be in the flesh and to converse with men as a man. He wanted to recapture the affections of carnal men who were

---

et non praeferre se minori, tertius subesse minori, in quo omnis iustitia; hunc Christus implevit qui ad Ioannis baptismum venit. His gradibus caruerunt Lucifer in caelo, et primi homines in paradiso, unde praecipites corruerunt. Et sicut his gradibus descendere, ita aliis tribus ascendere debemus, scilicet munditia cordis, innocentia operis, iustitiae fructibus. Quem ordinem propheta quaerenti: 'Quis ascendit in montem Domini?' Insinuat respondens: 'Innocens manibus et mundo corde.'" *Sermo in ascensione*, ed. Van den Eynde, 83. The themes of descent and ascent by means of steps also occur in an unedited sermon, *Sermo in ramis palmarum*, Paris, Bibliothèque nationale de France, lat. 13374, fol. 47, where the rubrics "de tribus gradibus ascencionis" and "de tribus gradibus descensionis" can be seem in the margin.

75 "Et fecit primum gradum humilitatis in carnem, secundum in crucem, tertium in mortem. Eius tota vita doctrina nostra est, et omnis actio est nostra lectio." *Sermo sine titulo* (PL 171: 942–944, at 943). This sermon is based on John, 8:36: "If the son frees you, you will truly be free." It is also discussed below. Bernard also makes this point: "Et in descendendo primus quidem gradus est a summo caelo usque ad carnem; secundus usque ad crucem; tertius usque ad mortem." Bernard of Clairvaux, *Sermo de Ascensione Domini*, in *Sancti Bernardi opera*, ed. Leclercq, Talbot, and Rochais, 6: 291.

76 "Sed nullus fuit convenientior modus sanandae nostrae miseriae. Sic enim et nostram erga se plurimum excitavit dilectionem, et suam nobis commendavit chari tatem." Peter Lombard, *Sermo in annuntiatione B. Mariae* (PL 171: 610).

77 "Quomodo posset melius etiam suam vobis dilectionem intimare, et vestram circa se incitare?" Ibid.

78 "Diligamus misericordiam qua redempti sumus." Ibid.

unable to love in any other way, by first drawing them to the salutary love of his own humanity, and then gradually raise them to a spiritual love."[79] It was a view that Peter also incorporated into his Sentences.[80]

The *Sermo communis* is another of Peter's sermons that deals with spiritual progress.[81] It opens with the soul in the "region of dissimilitude,"[82] and arrives ultimately at "internal peace and eternal peace."[83] The idea of the *regio dissimilitudinis* comes up again and again in the sermons[84] and is also found in Peter's *Commentary on the Psalms.*[85] It was by no means a commonplace of the day, however, and once again there could be a monastic influence. In his masterful article on the concept of *regio dissimilitudinis,* Pierre Courcelle

79 "Ego hanc arbitror praecipuam invisibili Deo fuisse causam, quod voluit in carne videri, et cum hominibus homo conversari, ut carnalium videlicet, qui nisi carnaliter amari non poterant, cunctas primo ad suae carnis salutarem amorem affectiones retraheret, atque ita gradatim ad amorem perduceret spiritualem." Bernard of Clairvaux, *Sermones super canticum canticorum* 20, in *Sancti Bernardi opera,* ed. Leclercq, Talbot, and Rochais, 1: 118, translated by Kilian Walsh in *On the Song of Songs* (Spencer, MA, 1971–1980), 1: 152. This idea can also be found in Bernard of Clairvaux, *De Diligendo Dei* 3.7, in *Sancti Bernardi opera,* ed. Leclercq, Talbot, and Rochais, 3: 124. On the significance of this passage, see also Richard W. Southern, *The Making of the Middle Ages* (London, 1953), 222.

80 *Sententiae* 3, dist. 19, ch. 1, ed. Brady, 2: 118, and *Sententiae* 3, dist. 27, ch. 1, ed. Brady, 2: 162. On this, see also Colish, *Peter Lombard,* 463: "As with Bernard of Clairvaux, Abelard, Roland, and Robert of Melun, Peter sees this love, both as extended to man, and as responded to by man, as a force that changes man from within, energizing him and enabling him to reorder his own loves, to accept the grace of God, and to reorient himself, as justified, in charity to his fellow man."

81 Peter Lombard, *Sermo communis,* in *Notices et extraits de quelques manuscrits latins de la Bibliothèque Nationale* 3, ed. Barthélemy Hauréau (Paris, 1891), 44–49. The title, meaning "general sermon," or "sermon for general use," means that it is not for a specific liturgical day.

82 "Videntur haec verba esse peccatoris qui longius advolavit in regionem longinquam, in regionem dissimilitudinis." Ibid., 45.

83 "de pace interna ad pacem aeternam." Ibid., 49.

84 In addition to this one, it occurs in *Sermo in die paschae* (PL 171: 352–363, at 354); *Sermo in circumcisione Domini* (PL 171: 397); *Sermo in epiphania* (PL 171: 404); *Sermo de trinitate et de pascha partim* (PL 171: 434); *Sermo in prima dominica quadragesimae* (PL 171: 445); *Sermo in annuntiatione B. Mariae* (PL 171: 610); *Sermo in parasceve* (PL 171: 798); *Sermo de septuagesima* (PL 171: 845–853, at 850); and *Sermo in laetare Ierusalem* (PL 171: 853–864, at 856–857). See also Brady, Prolegomena 1: 95*–112*.

85 Peter Lombard, *Commentaria in psalmos* (PL 190: 61). This is the commentary on Ps. 1:1, *beatus vir*: "'Beatus' dicitur cui omnia optata succedunt, vir scilicet contra prospera et adversa firmus, 'qui non abiit' a Deo in regionem dissimilitudinis."

shows how it was originally used by Plato and then Plotinus. It reached the twelfth century especially through Augustine. Peter Lombard's scholastic predecessors Anselm of Laon and Gilbert the Universal used it on one occasion each. However, the twelfth-century authors who referred most frequently to the *regio dissimilitudinis* were William of St Thierry, Bernard of Clairvaux, and Peter Lombard himself.[86]

The *Sermo communis* is built around the well-known text from Psalm 54, *Quis dabit mihi pennas sicut columbae et volabo et requiescam*, "Who will give me the wings of a dove that I may fly away and find rest."[87] Peter Tibber, who discusses this sermon, believes that Peter was selective in his treatment of the text. The concepts of wings and flight were certainly covered, but not the rest: "In the very last sentence of this sermon, Lombard turned to the words 'dove' and 'rest,' which he had as yet barely mentioned, and swiftly placed them in the symbolic canvas he had sketched."[88] In the first place, this is not entirely true. The *requiescam* motif is present: the sermon deals with the journey of a soul away from the *regio dissimilitudinis* and towards internal peace. The word *requiescam* ("that I may find rest") functions as the goal to be attained. But more importantly, in this sermon, Peter visualizes what is happening in the first part of the text. He gives his audience an image to think about: "These seem to be the words of the sinner who, long before, had flown into that distant region, the region of dissimilitude, where, with wicked and disordered living, he wasted his inheritance, his innate goodness, which, no matter how deep into sin someone may fall, even right into the middle of Babylon, is still not completely worn away, so that a certain good disposition and natural will remain by which the soul at least wants to wish to be good."[89] The sermon begins in the *regio dissimilitudinis* and refers to how the sinner arrived there in

86 Pierre Courcelle, "Tradition néo-platonicienne et traditions chrétiennes de la 'région de dissemblance,'" *Archives d'histoire doctrinale et littéraire du moyen âge* 25 (1958): 5–33. Courcelle's list of references to the *regio*, on 24–33, is especially useful. Colish discusses Peter's use of the term in *Peter Lombard*, 174.

87 Ps. 54:7.

88 Tibber, "Origins of the Scholastic Sermon," 129.

89 "Videntur haec verba esse peccatoris qui longius advolavit in regionem longinquam, in regione dissimilitudinis, ubi prave et inordinate vivendo dissipavit substantiam suam, id est bona naturalia, quae, in quantumcumque profundum peccatorum, usque in mediam etiam Babylonem, aliquis perveniat, non sunt tamen ex tota attrita quin maneat quidam bonus affectus et voluntas naturalis ex qua vult saltem se velle bonum." *Sermo communis*, ed. Hauréau, 44–45.

the first place, but after that it gradually moves upwards. Spiritual ascent is again the main idea. Peter isolates two words, *alae*, "the wings," and *volabo*, "I will fly," and brings them up constantly. There are four "fatal wings" leading down to the *regio*: worldly happiness, worldly sorrow, hypocrisy, and pride.[90] But there are also four, "which are the opposite of the fatal wings, in which there is life, and by which the soul can return and fly back to the place he came from."[91] Those four – spiritual happiness, healthy sorrow, true piety, and humility – bring the soul to a certain point. Beyond that, six more wings, the wings of virtue, take the soul further[92] and arm him against adversaries. These are fear, hope, penance, confession, humility, and love. It is only by means of these that the soul can find rest.[93] Peter explains the different wings through distinctions and subdivisions. A diagram illustrating this structure is included below (see figure 1). It is a shorter sermon than most, however. There are no digressions or sub-themes. It is concise, strongly integrated, and contains nothing extraneous. The integrated structure is the result of the image. And this is to say nothing of the emotional impact. At the end of the sermon, the hope for the attainment of peace is moving: "The saints find rest within the mind; from that peace, souls are about to pass to the peace of God, from internal peace to eternal peace, and to receive peace upon peace."[94]

This approach is very different from Peter's handling of the same text in his earlier *Commentary on the Psalms*. There, he merely deals with each aspect in turn.[95] Comparing the *Sermo communis* to the commentary only reinforces how inspired Peter was by the concepts of flight and wings, and by the image of the sinner calling out from the *regio*. Like many original conceptions, however, the germ of the idea can be found much further back. In the commentary, Peter refers to the "wings of virtue, with which he could fly away into solitude and climb the heights of contemplation."[96]

90 Ibid., 46–47.

91 "Istis autem quatuor alis mortiferis aliae quatuor pennae, in quibus est vita, contrariae sunt, quibus revertendum et revolandum unde advolavit." Ibid., 47.

92 "Sunt et sex pennae quibus assumptis reditur ad patriam." Ibid.

93 Ibid., 49.

94 "Intus in mente requiescunt sancti; de qua pace animi transituri sunt ad pacem Dei, de pace interna ad pacem aeternam, pacem super pacem accepturi." Ibid., 49.

95 Peter Lombard, *Commentaria in psalmos* (PL 191: 508).

96 "Unde et petit pennas virtutum, quibus possit avolare in solitudinem et in altum contemplationis conscendere." Ibid. Peter provides a slightly more detailed, but less

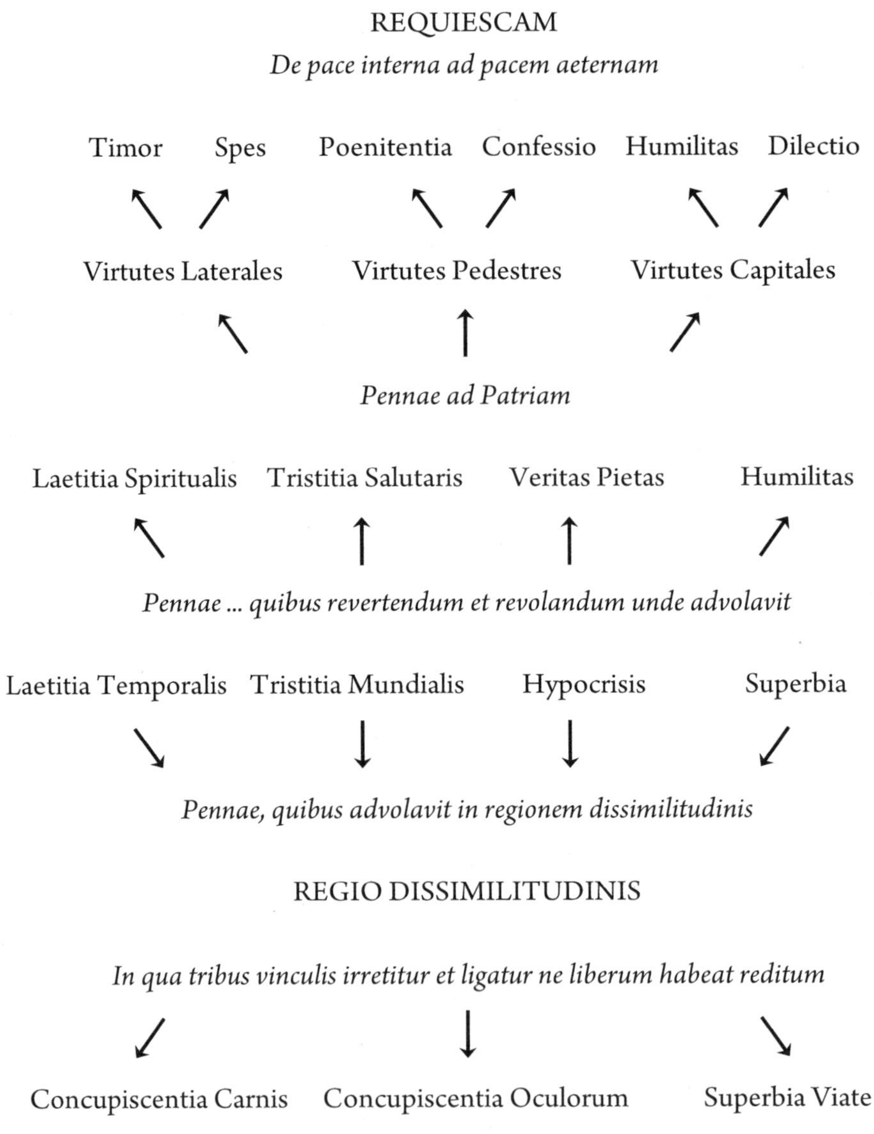

Figure 1: A Diagram Displaying the Structure of Peter Lombard's *Sermo Communis.*

While Peter dealt with the wings of virtue idea in the *Sermo communis*, he did not address "the heights of contemplation." He does do this, however, in a sermon on a text from the Gospel of John, *si filius vos liberaverit*, "If the son frees you, you will truly be free."[97] Any discussion of contemplation, the monastic ideal, is rare and unexpected in Peter Lombard's sermons, and is thus all the more valuable. This sermon contains an almost visionary section toward the end that seems to take up where the *Sermo communis* leaves off. Again, Peter is talking about ascent through the "wings of virtue": "We ascend through contemplation, while the mind, winged by virtues, rises above, and disdaining the earthly dwelling, or certainly forgetting it, says with Moses 'Lord, if I have found grace in your sight, show me your face.' He ascended the mount of contemplation, like Abraham and the boy, leaving in the valley the servant and the ass."[98]

Contemplation is discussed in more detail in a sermon for Easter, which begins with the verse "set up a watchtower for yourself" (Jer. 31:21). Peter describes a "spiritual watchtower," which should be built "in the innermost depths of the mind, where it has so many uses. This is the watchtower of contemplation and discretion."[99] The watchtower signifies remaining on guard, "lest we walk on the road unclothed and bare and unprepared."[100] For Peter this also meant watching out for "false brothers who enter by stealth under the habit of peace and religion,"[101] a problem he associated with the present ("and now"). Late in the sermon he returns to the opening text and speaks again in the hortatory style: "let us then erect a watchtower for ourselves, let us stand in front of it; for he that stands in a watchtower touches neither earth

---

satisfying, treatment of the idea of the four wings in *Sermo sine rubrica*, ed. Rochais, 106–111. This sermon was similar enough to Bernard of Clairvaux to be attributed to him by Henri Rochais, editor of the Saint's works. Note also 111 n345, where Rochais points out similarities with Bernard's other works.

97 John 8:36. Peter Lombard, *Sermo sine titulo* (PL 171: 942–944).

98 "Per contemplationem ascendimus, dum mens virtutibus pennata, erigit se super se, et terrenam habitationem exosa, vel penitus oblita, dicit cum Moyse: 'Domine, si inveni gratiam in oculis tuis, ostende mihi te ipsum' (Exod. 33:13). Ascendit et haec anima in montem contemplationis cum Abraham et puero, relictis in valle servis cum asino." Peter Lombard, *Sermo sine titulo* (PL 171: 944).

99 "Bona est haec specula, et ideo in penetrali mentis statuenda, quae tam multiplicem tenet usum. Haec est specula contemplationis et discretionis." Peter Lombard, *Sermo de paschali tempore* (PL 171: 872).

100 "ne nudi et vacui in via ambulemus." Ibid.

101 "Et nunc enim falsi fratres subintrant sub habitu pacis et religionis." Ibid.

nor sky ... let us touch neither the earth through concupiscence of the flesh or eyes nor the sky through elation of the mind."[102]

These sermons show that Peter was certainly aware of what his monastic contemporaries were doing and that as a preacher he was capable of taking a diagnostic approach to the spiritual life. In other sermons, he was content to remind his audience of their day-to-day duties as Christians. At the same time, he brought an original approach to the basics. The substantial doctrinal and intellectual content of the sermons allows Peter to show his audience that their individual observances are related to the highest mysteries of their faith.

A sermon for Lent is a good example.[103] Peter reminds his hearers of the necessity of confessing their sins, and of fasting and almsgiving. The advice is often straightforward: "Fasting restrains the flesh, almsgiving refreshes one's neighbour. Therefore give to others what, in fasting, you have denied yourself."[104] He underlines the importance of right intention: "Whoever, therefore, wishes to be heard by God, whose seat is in heaven, should strive all the more to raise the intention of his heart to God ... rather than to raise a great clamour of his voice."[105] But the succession of ideas, and the handling of scriptural texts, is complex. The sermon is preached on a text from Lamentations: *Bonus est Dominus sperantibus in eum, animae quaerenti illum*, "The Lord is good to them that hope in him, to the soul that seeks him."[106] At the beginning of the sermon, Peter focuses on the word *quaerenti* (seeking) by seeing Lent as a time "especially intended" for seeking God.[107] Later, he examines

102 "Statuamus nobis speculam, stemus super eam; qui enim stat in specula nec terram tangit nec coelum ... nec terram contingamus per concupiscentiam carnis vel oculorum, nec çoelum per mentis elationem." The *Patrologia Latina* text of *the Sermo de paschali tempore* is incomplete, and the (substantial) remainder was edited by Hauréau, "Notice sur les sermons attribués à Hildebert de Lavardin," 152–158, from which this extract comes (154).

103 Peter Lombard, *Sermo in letaniis* (PL 171: 567–572).

104 "Jejunium (carnem) castigat, eleemosyna proximum reficit. Aliis ergo da (quod) tibi jejunio denegasti." Ibid., 569.

105 "Qui ergo vult audiri a Deo, cujus sedes coelum est, magis enitatur levare ad Deum cordis intentionem, et manus operationem, quam vocis clamorem." Ibid., 571.

106 Lam. 3:25.

107 "Sunt tamen quidam dies specialiter ad Deum quaerendum nobis propositi, qui dies Litaniarum dicuntur." Peter Lombard, *Sermo in letaniis* (PL 171: 571)

other scriptural references to seeking.[108] In another section, he compares the need for confession before prayer with the bridegroom in the *Song of Songs* who would not approach the bride without myrrh and incense.[109] This comparison leads him on to other texts dealing with betrothal: "Christ is the bridegroom, the church the bride, which he pledged to himself in three ways, just as Hosea says, 'I will betroth you to me in eternity, and I will betroth you to me in justice and compassion, and I will betroth you to me in faith.'"[110] This gives rise to an intricate description of this "threefold betrothal," which washes away sin, first through the patriarchs, then through the prophets, and then with the advent of the Son.[111] At the end, Peter returns to his initial exhortation to penitence: "and thus our prayer will be directed unhindered to God, if the myrrh of bitterness, that is penitence, is added to it – and it is not true penance without fasting and almsgiving."[112] Peter's treatment of confession in this sermon is very similar to the *Sentences*.[113]

Peter's goal in this sermon was to show his audience why their day-to-day duties were important. To take another example, there is the sermon *De purificatione* ("on the purification").[114] Again, we have a commonplace of Christian teaching, that each person must carry a cross. Yet Peter illustrates this for his audience in a way that makes use of his theological training: "we ought to imitate the length (*longitudo*), breadth (*latitudo*), depth (*profundum*), and height (*sublimitas*) of the cross. Breadth can be found in the amplitude of his charity, for when he had been placed on the cross, he prayed for his enemies."[115] Likewise *longitudo* should be imitated "by the very length of charity, so that, until death, we love God with the whole heart and our neigh-

108 Ibid., 570. Forms of *quaero* occur 19 times in the sermon.

109 Ibid., 568.

110 "Christus est sponsus; sponsa Ecclesia, quam sibi desponsavit tertio, sicut per Osee ait: 'Sponsabo te mihi in sempiternum, et sponsabo te mihi in justitia et misericordia, et sponsabo te mihi in fide' (Hos. 2:20)." Ibid.

111 Ibid., 568–569.

112 "Et sic dirigitur oratio nostra ad Deum velut incensum, si ei additur amaritudinis myrrha, id est poenitentia, quae sine jejunio et eleemosyna non est vera." Ibid., 569. This sermon is unusual for Peter in that the opening text is barely used.

113 Brady, Prolegomena 1: 108*.

114 Peter Lombard, *Sermo de purificatione* (PL 171: 623–627).

115 "Hoc lignum est crux Christi, cuius latitudinem et longitudinem, profundum et sublimitatem imitari debemus. Latitudinem, in amplitudine charitatis, ut sicut ipse in cruce positus, pro inimicis oravit." Ibid., 624–625.

bour as ourselves."[116] Height can be imitated by reflecting on heavenly things, and depth by doing good after the foundation laid by Christ.[117] In this passage, Peter is able to explain the image of the crucifixion to his audience with a sense of its profound implications. This is influenced predominantly by Ephesians 3:19 when St Paul refers to the length, breadth, depth, and height of charity. Peter had also made the connection between this passage and the cross of Christ in his *Commentary on the Letters of Paul,*[118] and it recurs in two other sermons.[119]

We can observe Peter offering personal guidance to his audience in the reassuring tone of his sermons, in the exhortations, and in the spiritual advice. The treatment of the passion, of confession, and of the cross underlines how close the connection can be between Peter's preaching, his classroom lectures, and his other works. Although there may be similarities of content, structurally the sermons are very different.

The key thing to grasp about the structure of Peter Lombard's sermons is that most of them are built around the interplay of two themes. One is the opening scriptural text, which is usually a sentence or two from one of the readings. The other is either the feast day being celebrated or, for Sunday sermons, more general themes related to the season (such as Lent or Advent). It is not the old homiletic approach where the entire sermon was a step-by-step exposition of a substantial block of text.[120] But, at the same time, the text is not dispensed with. Peter does not use the opening text as a nod to convention to then proceed with a treatise on a doctrinal issue.[121] Instead, the two aspects are developed together, resulting in an integrated whole.

116 "Longitudinem vero in longanimitate charitatis, ut usque ad mortem Deum ex toto corde, et velut nos, proximos diligamus." Ibid., 625.

117 "Sublimitatem vero, ut in spe omnium quae agimus, sola coelestia meditemur. Profundum vero, ut super Christi fundamentum, omne bonum nostrum constituamus." Ibid.

118 Peter Lombard, *Glossa in epistolas* (PL 192: 9–520, at 193–195).

119 Peter Lombard, *Sermo de paschali tempore,* in "Notice sur les sermons attribués à Hildebert de Lavardin," ed. Hauréau, 156. Peter Lombard, *Sermo in ramis palmarum,* Paris, Bibliothèque nationale de France, lat. 13374, fol. 48.

120 For the homily, see Muessig, "Sermon, Preacher and Society in the Middle Ages," 76–77; Kienzle, "Introduction," in *The Sermon,* 161–162; and Tibber, "The Origins of the Scholastic Sermon," 115–120.

121 Tibber, "The Origins of the Scholastic Sermon," 20: "Although the *thema* supplied the subject and point of departure for the scholastic preacher, it was, in itself, much

The handling of the two themes, and Peter's favoured technique of breaking the text into fragments, can be clearly seen in the sermon on the Circumcision.[122] The three emotional high points are the opening comment on the text, the eventual appearance of the other theme (the Circumcision), and the return to the opening text at the end. As often, Peter finds particular resonance in a verse from the Prophets: *In monte sion erit salvatio, et erit sanctus et possidebit domus Jacob eos qui se possederant, et erit domus Jacob ignis, et domus Joseph flamma,* "Upon Mount Sion will be salvation, and there will be holiness: and the house of Jacob will possess their possessions. And the house of Jacob will be a fire, and the house of Joseph a flame."[123] We have already seen that he begins this sermon gently, with a sense of warmth: "a sweet and gentle trumpet of promise sounds to the hearts of the faithful through the prophet Obadiah ... 'there will be,' he says, 'on Mt. Sion, salvation, and there will be holiness ... before he was conceived he was called Jesus, that is, the saviour."[124] By mentioning Jesus at the beginning, Peter foreshadows the theme of the circumcision without referring to it directly. He then turns to a text from the book of the Apocalypse, which functions as a sub-theme. It refers to a vision of an angel with a face like the sun and feet like pillars of fire.[125] The unifying thread is the word *ignis* (fire) from the opening text. The pillar of fire, *columna ignis,* also occurs in Exodus, leading Moses to the promised land,[126] and it is

---

less important to the substance and structure of the sermon than was the equivalent biblical passage for the homily." For Tibber, the *thema* is the opening text. For more on his view, see below.

122 Peter Lombard, *Sermo in circumcisione Domini* (PL 171: 394–401).

123 Obad. 1:17.

124 "Suavis et mitis promissionis buccina cordibus fidelium insonuit per prophetam Abdiam, qui velut musica Salvatoris, et harmonia coelestis, fidelium mentes spirituali exsultatione, atque perfecta dilectione dilataret. 'Erit,' inquit, 'in monte Sion salvatio, et erit sanctus.' Ideo scilicet salvatio erit, quia sanctus. Hic est Sanctus sanctorum, quo veniente, cessat unctio Judaeorum, qui antequam conciperetur, vocatus est Jesus, id est salvator." Peter Lombard, *Sermo in circumcisione Domini* (PL 171: 394).

125 Apoc. 10:1–2: "Vidi angelum fortem descendentem de coelo amictum nube, et iris in capite ejus, et facies ejus erat ut sol, et pedes ejus tamquam columnae ignis, et habebat in manu sua libellum apertum."

126 "Hic est Angelus ille, qui filios Israel commeantes praecedebat in columna nubis in die, et columna ignis in nocte." *Sermo in circumcisione Domini* (PL 171: 395). Peter is citing Exod. 13:2.

the fire that goes before us "in the night of sins and faults."[127] Peter then returns to the Apocalypse text, explaining this *columna ignis,* the feet of the angel, as "those firm in faith, who minister necessary things to others."[128] The face of the angel, on the other hand, is those who engage in contemplation.[129]

The second half of the sermon takes the angel's little book (*libellus apertus*) as its point of departure. This is holy scripture and it leads into a new section built around a verse from Wisdom: "This," explains Peter, "is the almighty word that came, 'when peaceful stillness compassed everything, and night in its swift course was half-spent, from heaven's royal throne."[130] Peter deals with the three aspects in turn, a threefold silence, a threefold night, and the almighty word. This also relates to what has gone before. In the first place, we have already had a treatment of the night, when the pillar of fire led the way. But, more importantly, in the chapter of the book of Wisdom, from which this quotation comes, there is also mention of the pillar of fire.[131] The logical, systematic character of Peter's thought process is obvious. There is also a growing sense, in this sermon, that the appearance of Christ, and redemption, is imminent.

At this point the sermon embarks on a previously unheard note of celebration, as the almighty word leads into the subject of the day, the Circumcision:

> The almighty word, the unique son of the father, came from the royal throne ... to flesh, to a cross, and to death; from the light of heaven, to the shadows of darkness. At this, heaven is amazed, and earth marvels; man trembles in fear ... . For this is a deed without any precedent, a humility

127 "ergo qui peccatores ita conflat et colat, in columna ignis nos praecedere dicitur, et hoc in nocte peccatorum et vitiorum." Ibid., 397. There is also brief mention of a reference to fire in Mal. 3:2–3.

128 "Pedes vero dicti sunt firmi in fide, aliorum necessitati ministrantes." Ibid., 397.

129 "Facies angeli intelliguntur illi quibus relucet Dei imago et similitudo, ut in contemplativis, qui sunt ut sol, quia eorum consideratio est in coelis, qui lucent in medio hujus pravae et perversae nationis, tanquam luminaria fixa in firmamento coeli." Ibid.

130 "Hic omnipotens Sermo Patris, qui dum medium silentium tenerent omnia, et nox in suo cursu medium iter haberet, a regalibus sedibus venit." Ibid., 397–398. The Wisdom text, virtually the same, is 18:14.

131 "Propter quod igni ardentem columnam ducem habuerunt ignotae viae et solem sine laesura boni hospitii praestitisti." Wis. 18:3.

> beyond measure, an unexpected grace, a gift without reward. For he, of whose magnitude there is no limit, allowed himself to be so humbled for us that not only was he born of a woman but he even became subject to the law, undertaking the custom of circumcision, so that he could bring about a spiritual circumcision in us, and free us from the burden of the law.[132]

Peter then recommends following Christ's example, and he explains the "spiritual circumcision." He calls for an interior as well as exterior circumcision, which must occur,

> not just in that one part of the body where actual circumcision takes place, but it must be observable in every part of the body, so that we display our limbs, not to sin by the arm of iniquity, but to God by the arm of justice. We circumcise our hearts, lest we dwell on what is harmful and malignant, and our eyes, lest we look on what is empty; our ears, lest we listen to dangerous voices; the nose, lest we are enchanted by sordid, harmful odours; our tongues and mouths, lest we spit out malicious words .... We circumcise our feet, lest they are quick to spill blood, and the hands, lest they are touched by forbidden things stretching out toward them. All of this is true and healthy circumcision, by which the interior man is made to live.[133]

132 "Sermo Altissimi, unicus Patris Filius regis a regalibus sedibus venit ... ad carnem, ad crucem, ad mortem; de lumine coeli usque ad tenebras inferni. Super hoc coelum stupet, terra miratur, homo contremiscit .... Hoc est enim opus sine exemplo, humilitas sine modo, gratia sine merito, donum sine pretio. Ille enim, cujus magnitudinis non est finis, in tantum pro nobis humiliari dignatus est, ut non solum pro nobis fieret de muliere, sed etiam sub lege fieret, circumcisionis signaculum suscipiens, ut spiritualem in nobis circumcisionem perficeret, et ab onere legis sicut ab aliis poenis nos solveret." Peter Lombard, *Sermo in circumcisione Domini* (PL 171: 399). There is a similar passage in another sermon, *In parasceve* (PL 171: 799).

133 "Illam generalem futuri temporis circumcisionem spiritualis et interior circumcisio, quae non modo in exteriori, sed etiam in interiori homine servando est, nec in una tantum parte corporis, ut illa circumcisio carnalis, sed in singulis membris est exhibenda, ut membra nostra, non arma iniquitatis peccato, sed arma justitiae Deo exhibeamus. Circumcidamus ergo corda nostra, ne noxia et maligna cogitemus, et oculos, ne vanitatem videamus; aures, ne voces sanguinum audiamus; nares, ne immunditiae sordibus delectemur; linguam ac labia, ne in verba malitiae prorumpamus .... Circumdicamus et pedes, ne ad effundendum sanguinem sint veloces, et manus, ne ad vetitiorum tactum sint porrectae. Haec est vera et salubris circumcisio, qua vivificatur homo interior." Peter Lombard, *Sermo in circumcisione Domini* (PL 171: 400).

The sermon ends with an explanation of the opening text in its entirety. There is an emphasis again on the fire and flame.[134]

This circumcision passage bears the unmistakable imprint of the house of St Victor, where Peter Lombard had stayed when he first came to Paris. We have already seen in chapter two that his attendance at mealtimes would have exposed him to the particular atmosphere of the house.[135] There, and in the houses of regular canons in general, there was a strong emphasis on outward display, in dress, in facial expressions, at table, while walking, and so on. Caroline Bynum has explained how important this was for regular canons, since they aimed to teach by example.[136] The Victorine environment can be sampled in the *Liber Ordinis,* which details the rules and customs of the order.[137] Hugh of St Victor's *On the Formation of Novices,*[138] which is geared toward introducing new recruits to the essentials of the Victorine way of life, is another source for it. Hugh includes chapters on *disciplina* in appearance, in gesture, in speech, and at mealtimes. Like Peter in his treatment of the circumcision, Hugh makes a connection between outward discipline and inner well-being: "just as inconstancy of mind can give rise to irregular bodily movement, so also since the body is held fast through discipline, the soul is made firm in its stability. And little by little, the inner mind is brought to quiet."[139] Hugh warns against speech that is harmful, dishonest, or without use. Hugh's advice is also far more strict and detailed. In dealing with cathedral school students, Peter recalls the Victorine atmosphere, without actually demanding the observance of their rule. It is also worth mentioning here that Peter's technique of breaking down scriptural

134 Ibid., 401.

135 See chapter two, above, 39–40.

136 Caroline W. Bynum, "The Spirituality of Regular Canons in the Twelfth Century: A New Approach," *Medievalia et Humanistica* 4 (1993): 3–24. Caroline W. Bynum, *Docere verbo et exemplo: An Aspect of Twelfth-Century Spirituality* (Missoula, 1978). For the Victorine environment, see also C. Stephen Jaeger, "Humanism and Ethics at the School of St. Victor in the Early Twelfth Century," *Mediaeval Studies* 55 (1993): 51–79, especially 62–63.

137 *Liber ordinis Sancti Victoris Parisiensis,* ed. Lucas Jocqué and Ludovicus Milis (CCCM 61).

138 Hugh of St Victor, *De institutione novitiorum* (PL 176: 925–952).

139 "Sicut enim de inconstantia mentis nascitur inordinata motio corporis, ita quoque dum corpus per disciplinam stringitur, animus ad constantiam solidatur. Et paulatim intrinsecus mens ad quietem componitur." Ibid., 935.

passages into threefold distinctions, which occurs in this and other sermons, was also a feature of Victorine authors.[140]

A sermon on St John the Evangelist follows the same structural technique of waiting to introduce the subject of the feast day until after a substantial working out of other motifs.[141] John is not mentioned until the last third of the sermon. This is not arbitrary, however. Peter delays his appearance until it will make sense in the structure. The text is *secundum dies ligni erunt dies populi mei ... quia semen benedictorum Domini est, et nepotes eorum cum eis, eritque, antequam clament, ego exaudiam,* "as the days of a tree, so shall be the days of my people ... for they are the seed of the blessed of the Lord, and their posterity with them. And it shall come to pass, that before they call, I will hear."[142] Peter focuses in particular on the word *lignum,* a tree (or simply wood). As often, other scriptural occurrences of this word help to give the sermon forward momentum. He explains that "this is not the tree of good and bad knowledge, in which we fell, but the tree of life,"[143] and this introduces the first main section, on the fall. This quite literal treatment of Genesis is followed by a section that uses a verse from Ezechiel as the focal point: "I the Lord have brought down the high tree, and have dried up the green tree, and have caused the fig tree to flourish."[144] This section is on the redeeming work of Christ. The Ezechiel verse is intertwined with one from Kings about the prophet Eliseus, who cast a piece of wood into the water to retrieve a sinking axe head: "Into that turbulent and bitter water the axe head of humankind fell through the sin of the first man, and our Eliseus came, i.e., Christ, called by

140 For this, see Beryl Smalley, *The Study of the Bible in the Middle Ages,* 3rd ed. (Oxford, 1983), 86–87, and Mark Zier, "Preaching by Distinction: Peter Comestor and the Communication of the Gospel," *Ephemerides Liturgicae* 105 (1991): 301–329, at 307–308. Peter's use of threefold distinctions has been discussed in Protois, *Pierre Lombard,* 126–130. It should be pointed out that Peter frequently also uses fourfold distinctions.

141 Peter Lombard, *Sermo de Sancto Joanne evangelista* (PL 171: 723–727).

142 Isa. 65:22.

143 "Non est hoc lignum scientiae boni et mali, in quo cecidimus, sed lignum vitae in medio paradisi plantatum." Peter Lombard, *Sermo de Sancto Joanne evangelista* (PL 171: 723). The tree planted in paradise is also a reference to Psalm 1, which is discussed more fully later in the sermon.

144 "Ego Dominus humiliavi lignum sublime, et siccavi lignum viride, et frondere feci lignum aridum." Ezek. 17:24.

the prayer of the prophets, and he cast the wood (*lignum*) into the water."[145]

The tree and the water turn Peter's attention to Psalm 1: "'when the tree is planted near running waters, it brings forth fruit in due season.' This is the tree of life, i.e., the wisdom of the father, which is planted near running waters, and in the middle of paradise."[146] This allows him to continue his treatment of Christ: "Near running waters, because the son was made man following the operation of the Holy Spirit, whose grace is not extinguished by the uncertainty of sin, just as thirst by water, and in the middle of paradise, because Christ is in the middle of the church."[147] The final *lignum* text is from Job: "the tree ... if it is cut, grows green again, and the boughs sprout."[148] This stands for the passion and resurrection of Christ. We can see how Peter Lombard uses the appearance of the word *lignum* in scriptural texts to once again indicate the central narrative of the fall and redemption. The sermon then follows a scriptural/historical framework just as the *Sentences* does, and this continues when Peter moves from the resurrection to the apostles.

The opening Isaiah text, he believes, contains a "tripartite distinction": the blessed, the seed of the blessed, and their descendants.[149] Explaining the blessed as the apostles, the seed as those converted by them, and the descendants as those born of the converted,[150] Peter finally has an appropriate place for introducing John. This allows for an almost celebratory note, previously

145 "In illam vero aquam turbulentum et amarum ferrum humani generis decidit per peccatum primi hominis, et venit noster Elizaeus, id est Christus, precibus prophetarum vocatus, lignumque in aquam misit." Peter Lombard, *Sermo de Sancto Joanne evangelista* (PL 171: 724). The Eliseus story is from 2 Kings 6:4.

146 "Cum lignum plantatum secus decursus aquarum, dedit fructum suum in tempore suo (Ps. 1). Hoc est lignum vitae, id est Sapientia Patris, quae plantata est secus decursus aquarum, et in medio paradisi plantata est." Ibid., 725.

147 "Secus decursus aquarum quia humanatus est Dei Filius secundum operationem Spiritus sancti, cujus gratia aestus peccati exstinguitur, sicut sitis aqua, et in medio paradisi, quia Christus in medio Ecclesiae tanquam caput et princeps." Ibid.

148 "Lignum si praecisum fuerit, rursus virescit, et pullulant rami ejus." Job 14:7.

149 "Tripartita est hac distinctio, scilicet benedictio, et semen benedictorum, et nepotes eorum." Peter Lombard, *Sermo de Sancto Joanne evangelista* (PL 171: 725). There is probably a transcription error here: "benedicti" would make more sense than "benedictio." In Paris, Bibliothèque nationale de France, lat. 13374, fol. 7v, it is "benedicti."

150 "Benedicti ergo merito intelliguntur apostoli, qui benedictionis atque gratiae primitias perceperunt. Semen eorum sunt ei quos in fide genuerunt. Nepotes vero eorum, qui ab eorum filiis in fide geniti sunt." Ibid., 726.

unheard in the sermon: "And among those sons, certainly the blessed of God, the most holy evangelist John, whose feast is celebrated today, stands out for the grace of chastity, the singular privilege of his love, the gift of immense wisdom."[151] The sermon, in common with many others, ends with an image of future eternal happiness, "the blessed of the Lord, and the seed of the blessed, and their descendants will rejoice with them in eternity, shining like the sun in the kingdom of the father."[152] Peter's achievement in this sermon is remarkable. By making use of scriptural occurrences of the word *lignum*, he has summarized the biblical narrative of universal history. The marginal rubrics in the sermon manuscripts draw further attention to this. Although in some sermons they highlight subsections and theological questions, here they consist of the word *lignum* (at the opening), followed by all of the scriptural references.[153]

In some sermons Peter dealt with the feast day straightaway. The sermon on the Ascension begins with a celebratory passage:

> That day we have longed for, my most beloved brethren, the day of our Lord's ascension, has arrived, whereby the glorification of our saviour was made perfect, and humankind was freed from their captivity. Joyful and venerable is the solemnity of this day, by which Hell, along with its prince, will grieve for its pillaging, and the heavenly army will rejoice at their restoration. ... Today a new and permanent way has been initiated, about which the Apostle speaks: "Having therefore, brethren, a confidence in the entering into the holies by the blood of Christ, a new and living way which he has dedicated for us."[154]

151 "Inter autem [filios], scilicet benedictos Domini, eminet sanctissimus evangelista Joannes, cuius hodie festivitas celebratur, virginitatis gratia, dilectionis singularis privilegio, immensae sapientae dono" Ibid.

152 "Benedicti Domini, et semen eorum, et nepotes eorum cum eis in aeternum gaudebunt, fulgentes sicut sol in regno Patris." Ibid., 727.

153 Peter Lombard, *Sermo de Sancto Joanne evangelista*, Paris, Bibliothèque nationale de France, lat. 13374, fol. 7–7v. Rubrics highlighting subsections and questions can be seen for example in the *Sermo in ramis palmarum*, ibid., fol. 47, highlighting the steps of ascent and descent, and in the *Sermo de trinitate et de pascha*, ibid., fol. 43, highlighting the threefold distinctions in the trinitarian section (see below, 157–159).

154 "Optatus nobis, dilectissimi, dominicae ascensionis dies advenit, quo salvatoris nostri clarificatio est consummata et humani generis captivitas soluta. Iucunda ergo et venerabilis huius diei solemnitas, qua de exspolitione sua dolet cum principe suo

There is a similar mood early on in sermons on the Epiphany,[155] and the Nativity.[156] The openings of Peter's sermons therefore alternate between the feast day and the opening text.

The sermons were not all preached on a particular feast day. Some were intended for different Sundays during Lent, and in these Peter would reflect the season by building a structural framework around the opening text and a particular piece of moral advice. The sermon *In dominica ante palmas* ("on the second Sunday before Easter")[157] is a good example, and it also shows Peter again taking a highly sophisticated approach to basic religious guidance. The advice centres around doing works of charity, and the opening text is from Hosea, *seminate vobis justitiam in veritate, et metite in ore misericordiae. Innovate vobis novale, tempus enim requirendi Dominum*, "Sow for yourselves in justice, and reap in the mouth of mercy; break up your fallow ground, for it is the time to seek the Lord."[158] This text is the initial theme, providing the structure to all that follows and building the second theme from its parts. Rather than gloss the opening text in its entirety straightaway, Peter fixates on key fragments, isolating the words *veritas* (truth), *justitia* (justice), and *misericordia* (compassion). From these words, he will eventually construct the second theme. He dwells on them for some time, seeing them as essential to the love of God and the love of neighbour. He also brings up subsidiary verses that contain the isolated words, a favourite technique: "The spirit of God commends and promises these two things especially for us, namely, truth and compassion, which are all the ways of

---

tartarus et de restauratione sua gaudet caelestis exercitus. ... Hodie initiata est nova via et permanens, de qua dicit Apostolus: 'Habentes, fratres, fiduciam in introitum sanctorum, in sanguine Christi, quam initiavit nobis viam novam et viventem' (Heb 10:19–20)." Peter Lombard, *Sermo in ascensione*, ed. Van den Eynde, 80.

155 "Exsultat ergo et laetatur solitudo gentium, quae hodie facta est sicut lilium inter spinas, et amica inter filias. Hodie namque Ecclesia gentium olim sterilis coepit parere plurimos, quando suas primitias in tribus Magis Regem regum adorare misit." Peter Lombard, *Sermo in epiphania* (PL 171: 402).

156 "Laetentur ergo coeli, et exsultet terra, quia Verbo sociata est nostra natura, et quae in terris sunt, et quae in coelis restaurata, et pace hominibus in terra data, facta est Deo in excelsis gloria, dum angelicae ruinae reparantur dispendia." Peter Lombard, *Sermo in natali* (PL 171: 381–388, at 382). This mood of celebration recurs at the end of the sermon, ibid., 388.

157 Peter Lombard, *Sermo in dominica ante palmas* (PL 171: 456–463). The title in the *Patrologia Latina* (*de bonis operibus*) is a later addition by Beaugendre.

158 Hos. 10:12.

God. By the witness of the prophets, 'all the ways of the Lord are compassion and truth.'"[159]

The way of the Lord brings Peter to two new words, *dilectio* (love) and *timor* (fear), which help to move the argument forward: "Consider, my brothers, the way of the Lord, by which he deigned to come to us. First, in compassion, in giving to us the gifts of grace; second, in justice, in driving out from us what should be driven out, and through this, my brothers, learn to fear him as God and love him as a father."[160] Love and fear motivate observance of the commandments and love of neighbour. The secondary theme of charitable works has now emerged, and Peter develops it, advising his audience that "no one can flatter himself by saying he loves God, if he does not show love to his neighbour."[161] A new section then begins, where the two themes are addressed together. Here, Peter returns to isolating fragments of the main text, this time *seminate* (sow) and *metite* (reap). His focus now is to build up to a re-emergence of the main text, where there will be a more thorough exposition, involving the joining together of the fragments. He brings up other references to sowing and reaping, foreshadowing the return to the main text.

When it does return, it receives extended treatment. Peter advises sowing "in the spirit, not in the flesh, in doing good, not in being sparing, in persevering, not in giving up,"[162] and discusses "what must be sown, and in what way."[163] This reintroduces the secondary theme, for the sowing of justice means doing "good works, charitable works, and works of peace."[164] This time Peter lends more weight to the secondary theme by relating the stories of Zacchaeus, and the poor widow in the temple. The watertight structure is

159 "Duo nobis promittit, et spiritualiter [f. specialiter] Spiritus Dei commendat; scilicet, veritatem et misericordiam, quae sunt universae viae Domini, 'Universae viae Domini,' testante Propheta, sunt 'misericordia et veritas' (Ps. 24:10)." Peter Lombard, *Sermo in dominica ante palmas* (PL 171: 456).

160 "Considerate igitur, fratres, vias Domini, quibus ad nos venire dignatus est. Primo, in misericordia, largiendo nobis dona gratiae; secundo, in justitia, exigendo a nobis debita, et per hoc discite timere eum ut Dominum, et diligere ut patrem." Ibid., 458.

161 "Nemo igitur sibi blandiatur, dicens se Deum diligere, si non diligit et proximum." Ibid., 459.

162 "Seminate non in carne, sed in spiritu, non parce, sed in benedictionibus; non deficientes, sed perseverantes." Ibid., 461.

163 "Sed quid seminandum est, et quomodo, audite." Ibid., 461.

164 "Non igitur rapinam, non iniquitatem, sed justitiam seminate, id est opera bona, opera charitatis, opera pacis." Ibid., 462.

also coupled with a real sense of urging an audience. The sermon closes with an appeal based on the main theme:

> And so you must sow justice in the truth, that is in charity that is not feigned, with a love of compassion, so that you might invite others to compassion through your own, so that the virtue of justice may remain fixed as a root in your mind and may be uttered in speaking by a voice of justice. In this way the secrets of intention may be pleasing to the hidden observer, and the observances of good speech may delight your neighbours. And in this way we may ascend to God through compassion and truth, just as through certain other ways, who wished to descend to us, as has been written, so that we may sing to him of compassion and justice.[165]

What might be surprising, at first glance, is that Peter barely touches on the second half of the text, *innovate vobis novale, tempus enim requirendi Domini.* He only mentions it at the very end,[166] and he has been criticized for this tendency. Peter Tibber compares him to a student writing an exam, "who has spent fifty minutes discussing one point and who suddenly realizes he has only ten minutes left in which to deal with four more."[167] But Tibber analyzes the structure of twelfth-century sermons around the treatment of the *thema,* the opening text. This misunderstands Peter's structures. They are not organized as step-by-step explanations of the main text. Peter was able to do that if the need arose, as his commentaries show. A sermon was designed in a different way. There are two or more themes, and their interplay allowed him to better reach his audience. Peter chose the part of the text which would work best in the structure, and which would best express the day (or season) in question.

165 "Seminate ergo justitiam in veritate, id est in charitate non ficta, amore misericordiae, ut ex misericordia alios idem invitetis, ut sit virtus justitiae infixa radici mentis, et pronuntietur voce justitiae loquentis, quatenus occulto inspectori placeant arcana intentionis, et proximos iuvent officia locutionis, et ita per misericordiam et veritatem, quasi quibusdam viis ascendamus ad Dominum, qui ad nos eisdem descendere voluit, sicut supra dictum est, ut nos ei misericordiam et judicium cantemus." Ibid., 463.

166 "Quaerite ergo faciem Domini; 'innovate vobis novale'. Ab omni specie mali abstinete vos. 'Seminate justitiam in veritate et in ore misericordiae' .... Amen." Ibid., 464.

167 Tibber, "The Origins of the Scholastic Sermon," 129.

Peter could also use the opening text to build a highly complex structure, with several constituent parts. One of his longest sermons demonstrates this, preached on the text *Convertimini, filii, revertentes, dicit Dominus, quia ego, vir vester; et assumam vos, unum de civitate, et duos de cognatione, et introducam vos in Sion* (Jer. 3:14).[168] This verse has been subjected to some appallingly unhelpful English translations, such as "return o ye revolting children" (Douay-Rheims) and "turn ye backsliding children" (King James). Ronald Knox's translation, "wandering hearts the Lord bids you to come back to him," is more true to the sense in which Peter Lombard explained the words.[169] From the opening text he derives two main subjects, penitence and the Trinity. He provides a subsidiary verse to reflect both of these subjects, which then allows for further argument. Peter shows great structural ability in handling these five main points and in bringing them together into a unified whole, particularly in the conclusion. It is worth looking at his method in this sermon.

Peter begins the sermon with *convertimini filii revertentes,* by examining the position of someone needing to repent. He illustrates this by bringing up Ephraim's captivity *(transmigratio)* in Jeremiah 31:13, a captivity that is for Peter akin to the *regio dissimilitudinis.*[170] Thus far we are in similar territory to the *Sermo communis.* After describing and lamenting this "wretched transmigration,"[171] Peter returns to the opening text to point the way out and begins the exposition of *assumam vos,* "I will take you." For Peter, "he took us up through grace, so that he could restore the honour that we squandered and the glory that we lost."[172] The honour was that man was made in the image of God,[173] not "as the father, or the Son, or the Holy Spirit, but of the three

168 The text printed in PL 171: 432–439 is incomplete with the remainder edited by Hauréau in "Notice sur les sermons attribués à Hildebert de Lavardin," 120–124. Brady, Prolegomena 1: 108*–109*, titles the sermon as *de trinitate et de pascha partim,* which has manuscript authority, although he believes *de trinitate et de poenitentia* would be a more appropriate title. One of the manuscripts has the title *de contritione et poenitentia.*

169 *The Holy Bible: A Translation from the Latin Vulgate in the Light of the Hebrew and Greek Originals,* trans. Ronald Knox (London, 1956), 683.

170 Peter Lombard, *Sermo de trinitate et de pascha partim* (PL 171: 433–434).

171 "Infelix transmigratio" Ibid., 434.

172 "Assumpsit itaque nos per gratiam, ut honorem quem perdidimus, et gloriam quam amisimus, restauraret." Ibid., 435.

173 "Sed quis ille est honor, quae gloria illa? Fecit Deus hominem ad imaginem et similitudinem suam." Ibid.

at the same time."[174] The sermon then briefly takes on the explicit character of theological instruction: "The three hypostases [in the Trinity] are distinct properties, but are one, because they are one essence."[175] This proves how man is created in the image of the Trinity: "in the mind there are three properties, memory, intellect, and love, and these three are in one substance ... rightly therefore man can be said to be put together in the image and likeness of the ineffable Trinity."[176]

From the Holy Trinity, Peter moves to the general sense of the word *trinitas* (anything with a threefold quality). He blends this with the opening theme of penitence when calling for the conversion of the sinner who "transmigrated" to the "base and horrendous trinity ... the trinity of concupiscence of the flesh, concupiscence of the eyes, and pride of life. To this trinity all evils are indebted, just as all goods are to the highest Trinity. This trinity is the region of dissimilitude where memory is dissipated, intellect is blinded, and the will is polluted."[177] The integration of the different elements of the sermon is admirable, and Peter is also looking forward at this point to the exposition of *unum de civitate, et duos de cognatione*, "one out of a city and two from a kindred." Those add up to three, and Peter includes further discussion of the Trinity in this section. The fifth and final section details how "three are taken up, by the three, and are offered threefold to the three,"[178] using a verse from Samuel: "you shall come to the oak of Thabor, and there you shall meet three men going up to God to Bethel, one carrying three kids, and another three loaves of bread, and another carrying a bottle of wine" (1 Samuel 10:3). He examines the significance of the different elements of this text, and this could almost be a sermon in itself. One of the most interesting parts is the explanation of the three loaves of bread, which stand for the three ways of interpret-

174 "factus est homo ad imaginem Dei, non Patris tantum, vel Filii, vel Spiritus sancti, sed horum trium simul." Ibid.

175 "Tres sunt hypostases suis proprietatibus distinctae, sed unum sunt, quia unius essentiae sunt." Ibid.

176 "Ita in mente tres proprietates sunt, memoria, intellectus, dilectio, et haec tria in una substantia sunt ... . Recte igitur ad ineffabilis Trinitatis imaginem et similitudinem conditus homo dicitur." Ibid.

177 "Incidit in trinitatem horrendam et foedam ... scilicet in concupiscentiam carnis, concupiscentiam oculorum, superbiam vitae. Cui trinitati obnoxia sunt omnia mala, sicut summae Trinitati omnia bona. Haec trinitas ... est regio dissimilitudinis, ubi memoria dissipatur, intellectus caecatur, voluntas foedatur." Ibid., 436.

178 "Tres ergo assumuntur, et a Trino assumuntur, et Trino trina offerunt." Ibid., 438.

ing sacred scripture, a section discussed already in chapter two.[179] But Peter shows in the conclusion that the different sections can be drawn together, and the Samuel verse is actually fused with the opening text: "Behold, three men offer a threefold gift to the one and to the three; he, the prince of the people who they found at the oak of Thabor, takes them up, one from the city and two from a kindred. They would not have found him if he had not taken them up."[180] Peter then finally deals with the last part of the opening text, *introducam vos in Sion*, "I will bring you into Sion." This is "a heavenly Sion ... where there is eternal peace and glory."[181] As in the *Sermo communis*, Peter leaves the last part of the text to the very end, not because he is being unsystematic, but because it functions as the goal of the entire sermon.

Before we leave these structural aspects of the interplay of themes, and the breaking up into fragments, we should mention that Peter's technique of isolating words and using them as motifs to propel the argument forward does not always depend on the opening text. A sermon on Advent[182] begins with the same verse from the book of the Apocalypse that Peter deals with in the *Sermo de circumcisione*. For this sermon, however, he leaves out the section about the pillars of cloud and of fire. Referring to the text, Peter explains that John "heard secret things, saw new things, and understood signs."[183] He goes on to set his vision in the context of Jeremiah and Isaiah. All three saw new things (*nova*) and understood signs (*signata*). These two words now govern the whole sermon, allowing for an easy-to-follow structure. The Nativity and the virgin birth were equally *novum* and *significatum*. In the first thirty lines, the words *novum* and *signatum* each occur ten times. Only at the conclusion, does Peter go back to glossing the opening text.[184]

179 See chapter two, above, 44–45.

180 "Ecce tres viri quorum tria offerunt singuli et trino offerunt, quos assumit, unum de civitate scilicet et duos de cognatione, princeps populi quem invenerunt apud quercum Thabor. Non enim invenissent nisi eos ipse assumissent." Peter Lombard, *Sermo de trinitate de pascha partim*, ed. Hauréau, 123.

181 "Non ista Syon terrena ... sed coelestis et aeterna ... ubi est pax sempiterna et gloria." Ibid.

182 Peter Lombard, *Sermo de adventu Domini*, ed. Van den Eynde, 75–79.

183 "Filius tonitrui, in exstasi raptus positus et extra immo supra hominem factus, in spiritu audivit occulta, vidit nova et intellexit signata." Ibid., 75.

184 Ibid., 78–79. The interpretation here has little in common with the treatment of the same text in the circumcision sermon. This could indicate an earlier origin (material not fully worked out) or a later origin (a desire not to revisit old material). A later origin might explain why Peter would choose not to isolate parts of the text.

Peter was also susceptible to visualization, and his sermons are occasionally structured around an image. He tends to use the image as a starting point, before investigating and illuminating the surrounding landscape. This certainly applies to the *Sermo communis*, as we have already seen, with the image of the soul in the region of dissimilitude. More often, however, Peter allows a structure to develop around an image from the Bible. In the Easter sermon, which refers to the watchtower of contemplation, Peter dwells on the image of the three crosses on Calvary. One, the cross of penitence (*crux poenitudinis*), was on the right of Christ: "the thief crucified to the right of Christ carried this cross in knowledge of his crime, and he testified to the truth. This cross stands out in three ways, namely by genuine sorrow, by open confession, and by satisfaction in deed. In these virtues together the thief on the right shone forth when he shouted that he had received what he deserved."[185] To the left was the cross of agitation (*crux exercitationis*) where the unrepentant thief spent his time "grumbling and in detraction."[186] In the centre was the cross of charity (*crux caritatis*), and Peter divided this further into breadth, length, height, and depth, as he had in the *Sermo de purificatione*. He explained that Christ's love is present in all of these dimensions. Unusually, however, Peter departed from his Calvary image to describe a fourth cross, the cross of forced service (*crux angariationis*), "which sad hypocrites carry ... for popular favour."[187] He had to take the story back to Simon of Cyrene to fit in the fourth cross. Another sermon contains an almost identical treatment of the four kinds of cross, although the Calvary image is far less prominent.[188]

Peter's sermon on the Epiphany is also very visual.[189] This time Peter dwells on an image that is not the opening text. Rather, he focuses on the Magi, and an investigation of them constitutes the main part of the sermon.

185 "Hanc crucem portavit latro a dexteris Christi crucifixus, in ipso scandalo passionis veritatem protestatus. Haec crux in tribus consistit, scilicet in gemitu cordis, confessione oris, satisfactione operis. His cunctis virtutibus dexter latro emicuit, qui digna factis in cruce se recepisse clamavit." Peter Lombard, *Sermo de paschali tempore*, ed. Hauréau, "Notice sur les sermons attribués à Hildebert de Lavardin," 156.

186 "in murmure et detractione." Ibid.

187 "portant hypocrites tristes qui demoliunt facies suas ut videantur hominibus, quos addicit cruci non amor, non religio Dei, sed favorem populi." Ibid.

188 Peter Lombard, *Sermo in ramis palmarum*, Paris, Bibliothèque nationale de France, lat. 13374, fol. 48.

189 Peter Lombard, *Sermo in epiphania* (PL 171: 402–409).

He asks his hearers to "look carefully at who came, at how many came, what led them, where they came from, where they were going, and what they brought."[190] A discussion of each question in turn follows. We can easily imagine that the starting point for this inquiry was simply a picture in Peter's mind of the Magi on the road to Bethlehem. The most extended of the questions is the treatment of what the Magi brought. This includes the significance of the gifts and how to imitate their offering of gifts to Christ. The discussion of the Magi is framed by two shorter sections dealing with the opening text. Unlike other sermons, the opening text can easily be paralleled with the feast day. It is *congregabuntur filii Juda et filii Israel pariter, et ponent sibimet caput unum, et ascendent de terra, quia magnus dies Israel,* "and the children of Juda, and the children of Israel, shall be gathered together: and they shall appoint themselves one head, and shall come up out of the land: for great is the day of Israel" (Hos. 1:11). This brings to mind the Epiphany because "on this day, the church, once sterile, began to bring forth many peoples, when it sent out the first fruits in the persons of three Magi to adore the King of Kings."[191]

What really stands out from this sermon, however, is the section on who the Magi were. It is fascinating, because Peter seems to be drawn to them as fellow scholars, people for whom the spirit of inquiry is the dominant force in their lives. It is worth quoting in full:

> The Magi were not necromancers or magicians, as some claim, but Chaldean philosophers, who applied themselves to philosophy alone, who learned to weigh things signified to them and to recognize the future by the changing circumstances of things in the present. It is said they came from the tribe of Baalam, and that they were successors of his doctrine, who predicted that "there shall step forth a star out of Jacob, and a sceptre shall rise out of Israel, and shall smite through the corners of Moab," and that they came from Persia, where the river Saba is, from which the region takes its name. All of these things have an allegorical significance and point to a spiritual sense. Spiritual kings, therefore, such

190 "Attendite ergo diligenter qui venerint, et quot, quo duce, nec non unde, et quo venerint, et quid obtulerint." Ibid., 402.

191 "Hodie namque Ecclesia gentium olim sterilis coepit parere plurimos, quando suas primitias in tribus Magis Regem regum adorare misit." Ibid.

as they were, signify those who rule others (and themselves) in virtue, who safeguard their hearts in every way, who dispose their hearts to virtue – that is in charity – so that they have not only the appearance of virtue, but also virtue itself, about which scripture says, "The king's heart is in the hand of the Lord. He turns it wherever He will," and Jeremiah says, "Man's way is not his own; it is not in man to direct his steps as he walks." Therefore it was right to call these kings heavenly, and spiritual, for they paid homage to the King of Kings, who the star had shown, about which the prophet says "Now therefore, O you kings, be wise; be admonished, you judges of the earth." It is as if to say: heavenly men, who now rule in hope, and who will rule in reality in the future, since you will shine as the sun in the reign of the father, you who judge lands – i.e., you accuse and condemn worldly things – understand him, the one whom the star points to, you who are Magi and philosophers, not through following worldly philosophy that deceives, as the apostle says, "take care lest you are deceived by philosophy and inane falsehood," but through heavenly theology by which you discern the mysteries of the kingdom of God. Therefore, those who are kings must rule well and judge rightly, and those who are Magi, that is theologians, must understand in what way they come, and where they come to the new king, and how many come.[192]

192 "Fuerunt autem Magi non utique nigromantici [necromantici], vel malefici, ut quidam dicunt, sed philosophi Chaldaeorum, de singulis philosophantes, qui ex [eis] significata perpendere didicerant, et ex circumstantiis rerum futuros eventus agnoscere. Et dicuntur fuisse de genere Balaam, et successores doctrinae ipsius qui praedixerat: 'Orietur stella ex Jacob, et consurget virga de Israel, et percutiet duces Moab (Num. 24:17); 'et venisse de terra Persarum, ubi est Saba fluvius, a quo regio nominatur: quae omnia allegoricae serviunt significationi, spiritualemque sensum efflagitant. Spirituales igitur reges, quales et ipsi erant, in eis significati sunt, qui se et alios in virtutibus regunt, qui cor suum muniunt omni custodia, qui corda supponunt [f. disponunt] in virtute, id est in charitate, ut non solum speciem virtutis habeant, sed etiam virtutem [ipsam,] de quibus ait Scriptura: 'Cor regis in manu Domini, et quocunque voluerit vertet illud (Prov. 21:1).' Ut enim Jeremias ait: 'Non est hominis via ejus, nec viri est ut ambulet, et dirigat gressus suos (Jer. 10:23).' Reges ergo coelestes et spirituales merito dicuntur, qui Regi regum, quem stella demonstrat, adhaerent, quibus Propheta dicit: 'Et nunc, reges, intelligite; erudimini, qui judicatis terram (Ps. 2:10).' Ac si dicat: Viri coelestes, qui jam regnatis in spe, et regnaturi estis in re futura, quando fulgebitis ut sol in regno Patris, qui judicatis terram, id est accusatis et damnatis in nobis terrena, intelligite illum, scilicet quem stella declarat, qui Magi estis et philosophi, non utique secundum terrenam philosophiam

So much of Peter Lombard is contained in this passage. There is the student who was a lifelong searcher, who travelled to France to learn more. In the reference to the allegorical and spiritual sense, there is the master of the holy page, who taught students how to interpret the scriptures. There is the man who was helped by the Victorines and by St Bernard, both of whom emphasized a connection between outer conduct and inner virtues.[193] There is the canon of Notre Dame who was intimately acquainted with the Capetian court, and the idea of kings having a divine mission. But most of all, there is the theologian. Peter grants the Magi the title of theologians, and in so doing he stands up for the dignity of his profession. The point can hardly have been lost on his audience of students, or on his colleagues. They were aware that what they were doing was important, but theology was also a relatively new discipline. Peter showed them here how devoted he was to it, and he must have been a tremendous example for younger theologians. The idea of theology's special place is something we will encounter again in his pupils.

Peter Lombard's sermons are like any artistic works that demand close attention: those who study them will be rewarded. They do not betray their secrets at first glance. They show that Peter was an accomplished teacher of theology, but they also show a side to him that the other works do not. The discussion of spiritual progress is unexpected as is the personal reassurance of the openings. The innovative approach to structure also stands out in the combining of feast day and opening text. Finally, the technique of isolating a word in the opening text and pointing to its use elsewhere depended on a deep knowledge of scripture. This came from the years spent comprehensively glossing the Bible in his classroom. Peter was able to bring up the different appearances of words like *lignum* and also discuss the interpretation of these passages and put them to use in the sermon's argument.

---

quae decipit, unde ait Apostolus: 'Videte ne quis vos decipiat per philosophiam et inanem fallaciam (Col. 2:8),' sed per coelestem theologiam qua cognoscitis mysterium regni Dei. Qui ergo reges sunt, bene regant, et recte judicent; et qui Magi sunt, id est theologi, intelligant quomodo veniant, et unde ad regem novum, et quot veniant." Ibid., 402–403.

193 For some distinctions between Bernard and the Victorines on this point, see C. Stephen Jaeger, *The Envy of Angels: Cathedral Schools and Social Ideas in Medieval Europe, 950–1200* (Philadelphia, 1994), 269–270.

Peter's sermons also met a need. He had to preach once he became a canon at Notre Dame. We do not know if he had thought of preaching before, or whether he approached it with reluctance. He does not tell us. But it is very clear from the sermons that he wanted to reach his audience. He preached to them because he cared about their spiritual welfare. Peter's sermons set a tone for the increased interest in preaching in the schools, later in the century. The motivation for the increase in preaching was not simply utilitarian. It was born not only of a recognition that training was necessary for students who would one day be preachers. The students themselves also needed to hear sermons.

CHAPTER SEVEN

Peter Comestor, William of Tyre, and the *Chorus*

Peter Comestor (c.1115–1180/1)

Peter Comestor[1] was as famous as Peter Lombard in the Middle Ages. Both are mentioned in Dante's *Paradiso*.[2] Comestor's fame rested on his *Historia Scholastica* ("Scholastic History"). He was nicknamed the master of histories, just as Lombard was the master of sentences. The *Historia* is a narrative treatment of biblical events up to the Acts of the Apostles. It is now found in eight hundred manuscripts, a quite staggering number.[3] The work was also translated into several vernacular languages.[4] Peter Comestor had a significant influence over what was taught in the schools of Paris. From 1169 until his death in 1178, he was the chancellor of Notre Dame, and it was his responsibility to grant masters the *licentia docendi*, the licence to teach. It was also a lucrative position. Peter charged a fee for the licence, which some considered excessive.[5] While the large numbers of masters and students in Paris may have limited the authority the chancellor had, Comestor would have ensured that criticism of Peter Lombard did not gain the ascendancy. Before he became chancellor, Comestor's activity as a master was immensely important for Peter Lombard's reputation. He was the first theology master to produce a commentary on the *Sentences*. By doing this, he inaugurated the tradition of teaching the *Sentences* in the schools of Paris. He also attempted to make the

1 French authors usually call him Pierre le Mangeur. English-speaking authors prefer Peter Comestor or Peter Manducator.

2 Dante Alighieri, *The Divine Comedy: Paradise*, trans. Dorothy L. Sayers and Barbara Reynolds (Baltimore, 1962), 138.

3 Agneta Sylwan, "Petrus Comestor: *Historia Scholastica*, une nouvelle édition," *Sacris Erudiri* 39 (2000): 345–382, at 345.

4 James H. Morey, "Peter Comestor, Biblical Paraphrase and the Medieval Popular Bible," *Speculum* 68 (1993): 6–35; Beryl Smalley, *The Study of the Bible in the Middle Ages*, 3rd ed. (Oxford, 1983), 178–180.

5 For the chancellor of Notre Dame, see chapter three, above, 54–55.

treatment of the sacraments in book four widely accessible by producing an abbreviation for parish use.

Comestor has been receiving significant scholarly attention lately, and our knowledge of him continues to steadily evolve.[6] Work has been done on the identification and interpretation of his works, the chronology of his life, and the positions he held.[7] Ignatius Brady firmly established that he had studied with Peter Lombard and then taught theology in Paris in the 1160s.[8] A collection of *quaestiones* (oral reports of a master's teaching) was his crucial piece of evidence, one of which reads "Master Comestor, having the solution from Peter Lombard, says."[9] Similar reports have since been published, which show that Comestor had knowledge of Peter Lombard's oral teachings.[10]

Comestor's career, like that of his master, was largely concentrated in Paris. He began his studies, however, at Tours, under master John at the cathedral school.[11] John of Tours taught theology and had attended Anselm of Laon's school.[12] Comestor then arrived in Paris while Abelard was still teaching. Since Abelard died in 1141, Comestor must have studied with John

6 The most recent examples are a collection of articles called *Pierre le Mangeur ou Pierre de Troyes: Maître du XIIe siècle*, ed. Gilbert Dahan (Turnhout, 2013), and Mark J. Clark's landmark study *The Making of the* Historia scholastica, *1150–1200* (Toronto, 2015).

7 Key articles for identifying Comestor's works are Raymond M. Martin, "Notes sur l'oeuvre littéraire de Pierre le Mangeur," *RTAM* 3 (1931): 54–66; Artur Landgraf, "Recherches sur les écrits de Pierre le Mangeur," ibid., 292–306, 341–372; and Marie-Madeleine Lebreton, "Recherches sur les manuscrits contenant des sermons de Pierre le Mangeur," *Bulletin d'information de l'Institut de Recherche et d'Histoire des Textes* 2 (1953): 25–44; 4 (1955): 35–36. Two very good articles on his life are Saralyn R. Daly, "Peter Comestor: Master of Histories," *Speculum* 32 (1957): 62–73, and David Luscombe, "Peter Comestor," in *The Bible in the Medieval World: Essays in Memory of Beryl Smalley*, ed. Katharine Walsh and Diana Wood (Oxford, 1985), 109–129. Luscombe, in particular, is essential reading. See also David Luscombe, "The Place of Peter Comestor in the History of Medieval Theology," in *Pierre le Mangeur ou Pierre de Troyes: Maître du XIIe siècle*, ed. Dahan, 27–48, which covers similar ground to his earlier article.

8 Brady, "Peter Manducator," 479–490.

9 Ibid., 486, "Magister Petrus Comestor habens solutionem a magistro Petro Lombardo, dicit." For Brady, "the solution, however, goes beyond anything found in the *Sentences*; hence the Comestor must have heard Lombard."

10 Beryl Smalley, "Some Gospel Commentaries of the Early Twelfth Century," *RTAM* 45 (1978): 147–180; Brady, Prolegomena 2: 20*–21*, 39*–44*.

11 Brady, "Peter Manducator," 484–485.

12 Ibid., 485.

of Tours in the early to mid-1130s. He would have joined Peter Lombard's school in the 1140s, making him one of the older pupils to be discussed here. Comestor probably remained in the school for much of that decade, since he was later to be a *magister* himself. Even after his departure he continued to discuss theology with Peter and other former students.[13] It is clear that their discussions took place while Peter was working on the *Sentences*, since Comestor describes Peter explaining a topic covered in book three.[14]

Comestor would have set up his own school of theology at some point during the 1150s. We have already seen, from Brady's research on the *quaestiones*, that he was teaching in the 1160s. Also, we know that when Comestor became a theology master, one of his most outstanding pupils was Peter of Poitiers. Comestor appointed him his *praepositus*.[15] According to Alberic of Trois Fontaines, Peter of Poitiers taught theology from 1167 until 1205.[16] Comestor must therefore have been teaching him throughout the 1160s if not before. Mark Clark has also recently discussed Comestor's teaching activity in the 1160s and suggests that he taught Stephen Langton at that time.[17] Peter Lombard's departure to become bishop in 1159 increased the importance of Comestor's school. As we will see later in this chapter, he attracted students who had not completed their training with Peter Lombard. By studying with Comestor, they could continue to be in Peter Lombard's tradition. Comestor lectured on his master's *Sentences*, and perhaps the *Commentary on the Psalms*,[18] and discussed his master's positions on other books of the Bible.[19]

13 See chapter five, above, 119.

14 Brady, "Peter Manducator," 473. For further discussion of this passage, see chapter eight, below, 206–207.

15 "Et Pictavini, prepositi scolarum Petri Comestoris." Walter of St Victor, *Contra quatuor labyrinthos Franciae* 4.7, ed. Palémon Glorieux, *Archives d'histoire doctrinale et littéraire du moyen âge* 19 (1952): 187–335, at 274–275.

16 "Obiit Petrus Pictavinus cancellarius Parisiensis qui per annos 38 theologiam legerat Parisius." Alberic of Trois Fontaines, *Chronicon*, ed. Paul Scheffer-Boichorst (MGH SS 23: 631–950, at 886).

17 Clark, *The Making of the* Historia scholastica, *1150–1200*, 163–172, 193–198. Clark refers to "a direct pedagogical line between Peter Lombard, who taught Peter Comestor in the 1150s, and Stephen Langton, whom Comestor taught and mentored" (256).

18 Luscombe, "Peter Comestor," 116–117, points to glossed copies of the commentary, attributed to Peter Comestor in two thirteenth-century manuscripts. His lectures on the *Sentences* are discussed below, 172–174.

19 See chapter two, above, 42–43.

Two thirteenth-century writers, Stephen of Bourbon and Caesar of Heisterbach, recorded a story that Comestor and Maurice of Sully were both in the running to succeed Peter Lombard as bishop of Paris.[20] Some scholars have repeated this without question.[21] But their accounts can hardly be trusted as reliable sources. Comestor was still building a reputation at that point. He was not a canon of Paris,[22] and the bishops of the city usually had that position prior to their elevation. He had become dean of Troyes in 1147. He continued to hold that position even while chancellor of Paris (1169–1178).[23] This would not imply continuous residency at Troyes, however. It was quite common for clerics to teach at Paris while retaining the income from a post elsewhere.[24] Comestor also seems to have become a canon of the abbey of St Loup at Troyes at some point.[25]

Ten years later, however, he was much better known in Paris. He was probably the most highly regarded of the Paris theology masters, and this made him a natural choice to succeed Odo of Soissons as chancellor. As noted in chapter three, the chancellor of Notre Dame was in charge of preparing and sealing official documents and acted as the cathedral librarian.[26] He also

20 Stephen of Bourbon, *Tractatus de diversis Materiis Praedicabilibus*, ed. by Albert Lecoy de la Marche as *Anecdotes historiques, légendes et apologues tirés du recueil inédit d'Etienne de Bourbon, Dominicain du XIIIe siècle* (Paris, 1877), 418. For the similar story in Caesar of Heisterbach, see ibid., 418 n2.

21 Marcel Pacaut, *Louis VII et les élections épiscopales dans la royaume de France* (Paris, 1957), 119, is sceptical, but Yves Sassier, *Louis VII* (Paris, 1991), 337, takes Stephen at his word. Daly, "Peter Comestor: Master of Histories," 65, also repeats the story.

22 Comestor first appears in the documents of Notre Dame as chancellor in 1169. *Cartulaire*, ed. de Lasteyrie , no. 467, pp. 394–395.

23 Brady, "Peter Manducator," 483–484. As late as 1178, Cardinal Peter Chrysogonus describes him as *decani Trecensis* in a letter to Alexander III (PL 200: 1370–1372, at 1371). The context of this letter will be further discussed below. For his position at Troyes, see also Pierre Gandil, "Pierre le Mangeur, doyen du chapitre cathédral de Troyes," in *Pierre le Mangeur ou Pierre de Troyes: Maître du XIIe siècle*, ed. Dahan, 17–25.

24 Stephen C. Ferruolo, *The Origins of the University: The Schools of Paris and their Critics, 1100–1215* (Stanford, 1985), 64, uses the example of Robert Pullen. Other examples, including Comestor, are mentioned in Richard W. Southern, "The Schools of Paris and the School of Chartres," in *Renaissance and Renewal in the Twelfth Century*, ed. Robert L. Benson and Giles Constable (Cambridge, MA, 1982), 113–137, at 125–126.

25 An obituary there describes him as "dean of St Peter's, and canon of St Loup." Brady, "Peter Manducator," 484; *Obituaires de la Province de Sens*, ed. Auguste Longnon and Auguste Molinier (Paris, 1902–1923), 4: 233.

26 Bernard Plongeron et al., *Le diocese de Paris*. Volume 1: *Des origines à la révolution*, Histoire des diocèses de France 20 (Paris, 1987), 106.

had overall responsibility for masters teaching in Paris.[27] He granted them their licences to teach, and he could take them away. Given the large numbers of masters and students in Paris, this gave Comestor considerable power. Within the next half-century, a new organizational structure, the university, would spring up around the schools. In Comestor's day, the chancellor was that structure. Comestor also charged a fee for granting the licence to teach. This practice was becoming controversial. Pope Alexander III wrote to all the French bishops in 1172, urging that a fee should not be charged.[28] The pope used strong language: chancellors who did not cease this practice, a "sin of rapacity and cupidity," should be threatened with excommunication.[29] This suggests that in some cathedral towns, a climate of corruption had set in around the granting of licences. Alexander hoped that if his decree was enforced, "suitable and learned men" would now be able to conduct schools, "without trouble or exaction."[30]

It was up to Alexander's legates to see that the decree was enforced, and one, Cardinal Peter Chrysogonus,[31] provoked a storm when he tried to make the chancellor of Paris comply. Protests were made, and Alexander quickly

27 For this aspect of the chancellor's duties, see Ferruolo, *The Origins of the University*, 189–192, and Daly, "Peter Comestor: Master of Histories," 66–67.

28 Alexander III, *Epistola ad episcopos per regnum Francorum constitutos* (PL 200: 741–742). For an account of the policy and its effect on the development of Paris as an intellectual centre, see Gaines Post, "Alexander III, the *licentia docendi* and the Rise of the Universities," in *Anniversary Essays in Mediaeval History by Students of Charles Homer Haskins*, ed. Charles H. Taylor and John L. LaMonte (Boston, 1929), 235–278.

29 "Nos quoque, qui licet immeriti, dispensante clementia Conditoris, suprema fungimur potestate, tantae cupiditatis et rapacitatis vitium nolentes inemendatum relinqui, fraternitati vestrae per apostolica scripta mandamus, quatenus sub anathematis interminatione prohibere curetis, ne qui dignitate illa, si dignitas dici potest, fungentes, pro praestanda licentia docendi alios ab aliquo quidquam amodo exigere audeant vel extorquere." Alexander III, *Epistola ad episcopos per regnum Francorum constitutos* (PL 200: 741). Anathema was excommunication imposed by the pope directly.

30 "Sed eis districte praecipiatis, ut quicunque viri idonei et litterati voluerint studia regere litterarum, eos sine molestia et exactione qualibet scholas regere patiantur, ne scientia de caetero pretio videatur exponi, quae singulis debet gratis impendi." Ibid.

31 For Peter Chrysogonus, see Marcel Pacaut, "Les légats d'Alexandre III, 1159–1181," *Revue d'histoire ecclésiastique* 50 (1955): 835, 837, and Marcel Pacaut, "Louis VII et Alexandre III, 1159–1180," *Revue d'histoire de l'église de France* 39 (1953): 5–45, at 44–45.

called him off.[32] Comestor was given an exemption, and the pope noted that he had been swayed by the counsel of many "worthy and honest persons,"[33] including the two most powerful prelates of the kingdom, Henry of France, archbishop of Rheims, and William of the White Hands, archbishop of Sens.

William of the White Hands[34] had good relations with at least two of Peter Lombard's students. One was Herbert of Bosham, who worked for William in the 1170s. Herbert also claimed he had known William as a little boy and had watched him grow up.[35] William's association with Comestor may have begun when he was a canon of Troyes, where Comestor was dean.[36] Comestor also dedicated the *Historia Scholastica* to William. William had ultimate authority over the clergy of Paris in the 1170s, since the city was part of his archdiocese. This placed him at the centre of the debates over Peter Lombard's Christological teaching. As we will see in the next chapter, William did what he could to keep this controversy from boiling over.[37] It was undoubtedly important that he knew Comestor and Herbert well, since they would have been able to correctly explain their master's positions. William was an

32 Alexander III, *Epistola ad Petrum cardinalem S. Chrysogoni, apostolicae sedis legatum: De mercede pro scholarum regimine* (PL 200: 999). The letter is also printed and discussed in Post, "Alexander III, the *licentia docendi* and the Rise of the Universities," 273.

33 Alexander III, *Epistola ad Petrum cardinalem S. Chrysogoni* (PL 200: 999).

34 For William, the two most recent studies are by Ludwig Falkenstein: "Wilhelm von Champagne, elekt von Chartres (1164–1168), Erzbischof von Sens (1168/9–1176), Erzbishof von Reims (1176–1202), Legat des apostolischen Stuhles, im Spiegl päpstlicher Schreiben und Privilegien," *Zeitschrift der Savigny-Stiftung für Rechtsgeschichte, Kanonistische Abteilung* 89 (2003): 107–284, and "Guillaume aux Blanches Mains, archevêque de Reims et légat du siège apostolique (1176–1202)," *Revue d'histoire de l'eglise de France* 91 (2005): 5–25. See also the useful short monograph by Jules Mathorez, *Guillaume aux Blanches Mains, évêque de Chartres* (Chartres, 1911), and John R. Williams, "William of the White Hands and Men of Letters," in *Anniversary Essays in Medieval History by Students of Charles Homer Haskins*, ed. Taylor and LaMonte, 365–387.

35 "Nam qui te a parvulo Christi diligebam in Christo, eo amplius inflammavit me zelus tuus, quod cernebam te in dies evacuare que parvuli erant, crescere in augmentum Christi, et proficere in virum perfectum." Herbert of Bosham, *Praefatio*, ed. Hans H. Glunz, *History of the Vulgate in England* (Cambridge, 1933), 342–346, at 342. See chapter eight, below, 211–212, for more on Herbert's association with William.

36 Smalley, *Becket Conflict*, 65, cites the Troyes archives which show that "William ... on his election to the bishopric of Chartres agreed to renounce his *praepositura* at Troyes in return for an annual rent."

37 For the controversy, see chapter eight, below, 202–212.

influential person to have on one's side. He was the brother of Henry the Liberal, count of Champagne. He would later be regent of France, when his nephew, Philip Augustus (the son of Louis VII and Adela of Champagne) went on crusade.[38] William was once thought to have also been a student of Peter Lombard, but there is no evidence for this.[39] Furthermore, it would not be probable, since he was only twenty-four when Peter stopped teaching in 1159. He probably did frequent the schools for a period in the 1150s, but not for long enough to advance to theology. He would therefore have been aware of Peter Lombard, and he could have heard Peter preach or debate. But he had no reason to follow the long path of the theology students. Rather like Philip and Henry of France, his birth guaranteed him a high ecclesiastical position. His father had tried to gain clerical positions for him when he was still an adolescent,[40] and he became bishop of Chartres shortly after turning thirty.[41]

Peter Comestor remained as chancellor throughout the 1170s, the decade when the controversy over Peter Lombard's teachings was at its height. It has been suggested that he attended the Third Lateran Council of 1179 and that it would have presented him with an excellent opportunity for showcasing the *Historia Scholastica*.[42] It would be nice to imagine that Comestor was there, and that his voice, combined with those of William of Tyre and Adam of Wales, made a formidable defence for Peter Lombard's teachings. However, we have no categorical evidence for this.[43] Although

38 For his considerable importance in Philip's reign, see Mathorez, *Guillaume aux Blanches Mains*, 217–254, and John W. Baldwin, *The Government of Philip Augustus: Foundations of French Royal Power in the Middle Ages* (Berkeley, 1986), 32.

39 Mathorez, *Guillaume aux Blanches Mains*, 192, cites the *Gallia Christiana* 8: 1145, for the information. Williams, "William of the White Hands," 366, points out that he does not provide "confirmatory evidence of a satisfactory kind."

40 Mathorez, *Guillaume aux Blanches Mains*, 293–294. Bernard of Clairvaux refused to use his influence to help the count in *Epistolae* 271, *Sancti Bernardi opera*, ed. Jean Leclercq, Charles H. Talbot, and Henri Rochais (Rome, 1957–1977), 8: 181–182.

41 Mathorez, *Guillaume aux Blanches Mains*, 199–200; Pacaut, *Louis VII et les élections épiscopales*, 50; Robert of Torigny, *Chronicon*, ed. Ludwig Conrad Bethmann (MGH SS 6: 514).

42 Sylwan, "*Historia Scholastica*, une nouvelle édition," 348.

43 Sylwan was relying on Jean Châtillon, "Latran III et l'enseignement christologique de Pierre Lombard," in *Le Troisième Concile de Latran (1179): Sa place dans l'histoire*, ed. Jean Longère (Paris, 1982), 77. He was relying on Augustin Fliche, Raymonde Foreville, and Jean Rousset de Pina, *Du Premier Concile du Latran à l'avène-*

some have dated his death at October 1178 (before the council), he was in fact still alive.[44] Comestor is mentioned in a document relating to Notre Dame in August 1180.[45] In the same year, Hilduin succeeded him as chancellor.[46] This seems to show that Comestor had resigned the office and retired to the abbey of St Victor (where he was buried and commemorated as *noster canonicus*).[47] By 1182 he had also been replaced as dean of Troyes.[48]

Peter Comestor laid much of the groundwork for the transmission of Peter Lombard's writings, and David Luscombe provides an excellent treatment of this.[49] First, he lectured on the *Sentences* in his school of theology. As we will see later in this chapter, a number of students refer to Comestor discussing parts of Peter Lombard's *Sentences* in the classroom. Comestor also wrote a commentary on the *Sentences*, of which only the prologue now sur-

---

ment d'Innocent III, Histoire de l'église (Paris, 1953), 9: 157, 159. The authors of this work do not cite a source for the information, and the primary documents dealing with the council, which they list, make no mention of Comestor. Also, Mansi does not list him among those attending the council, although admittedly his list of prelates might not have included him anyway. The chancellor of Notre Dame, if he attended, would go as part of the retinue of the bishop of Paris or the archbishop of Sens. Giovanni Domenico Mansi, *Sacrorum Conciliorum Nova et Amplissima Collectio* (Florence and Venice, 1759–1798), 21: 209–217 and 464–467.

44 Brady, "Peter Manducator," 484, cites the Notre Dame obituary which commemorates his death for 22 October: *Cartulaire de l'église de Notre-Dame de Paris*, ed. Benjamin Guérard (Paris, 1850), 4: 172. "22 Oct. Eodem die obiit magister Petrus Manducator, cancellarius." There is no year given, but the previous entry is from 1177. This does not prove anything, however, since the entry after Comestor is for someone that died in 1243. Nor does "Petrus Manducator, cancellarius" imply that he died in office, as Brady claims. One would expect the Notre Dame obituary to mention the office he had once held.

45 "Ad universos igitur Sanctae Matris Ecclesiae filios volumus pervenire nos, precibus Barbedauri decani, et Philippi archdiacioni, et magister P. Manducatoris, et quorandam aliorum de capitulo Parisiensi." *Archives de l'Hôtel-Dieu de Paris (1157–1300)*, ed. Léon Brièle (Paris, 1894), 8. This document is mentioned by Daly, "Peter Comestor: Master of Histories," 72.

46 *Chartularium Universitatis Parisiensis*, ed. Heinrich Denifle (Paris, 1889–1897), 1: no. 50, pp. 49–50. Dated 1180. *Cartulaire*, ed. de Lasteyrie, no. 574, pp. 467–468 has the date 1180, 20 April–4 April 1181. For the foundation, see Ferruolo, *The Origins of the University*, 284.

47 Brady, "Peter Manducator," 484; *Obituaires de la Province de Sens*, ed. Longnon and Molinier, 1: 593, 4: 233.

48 Brady, "Peter Manducator," 484: "Peter's successor as dean of Troyes, Haicus or Bartholomew de Plancy, is not recorded as exercising that office earlier than 1182."

49 Luscombe, "Peter Comestor," 116–118.

vives.[50] This prologue substantially influenced later commentaries on the *Sentences.*[51] Raymond Martin and Artur Landgraf provide examples of late–twelfth century prologues closely dependent on that by Comestor. The conclusion is inescapable that Comestor began a tradition of lecturing on the *Sentences.* By doing this, and by encouraging his student Peter of Poitiers to do the same, he set a process in motion that culminated with the *Sentences* becoming a set text at the University of Paris. Other masters in Paris owed their positions to Comestor as chancellor. That gave him enormous influence over what they were actually teaching.

Comestor begins his prologue with the image of Moses at Mount Sinai, from Exodus 19.[52] For Comestor, Mount Sinai is "the truth of sacred scripture,"[53] while the boundaries of the mountain are the writings of the fathers.[54] Peter Lombard (referred to as "the master") prepared an entry to the mountain by pruning these boundaries.[55] Although it is not openly stated, Comestor's prologue contains the implication that his master was like Moses, as someone who was able to go further than others. This brings out the deep impression Peter Lombard made on his students. But as the prologue continues, something else begins to happen. We have seen that Peter Lombard was devoted to theology, and that it must have been a source of inspiration to his students. In Comestor's prologue, this devotion is translated to self-importance. The idea that theologians constitute an elite is prominent. He refers

50 The prologue is contained in Martin, "Notes sur l'oeuvre littéraire de Pierre le Mangeur," 61–62. For its authenticity, see ibid., 61–65, and Landgraf, "Recherches sur les écrits de Pierre le Mangeur," 350–353. See also Luscombe, "Peter Comestor," 116–117. It is also discussed, with the first half translated, in Nancy Spatz, "Approaches and Attitudes to a New Theology Textbook: The *Sentences* of Peter Lombard," in *The Intellectual Climate of the Early University*, ed. Nancy Van Deusen (Kalamazoo, 1997), 27–52, at 35. Ricardo Saccenti has very recently argued that the text is not a prologue to a lost commentary but an introduction for the teaching of the *Sentences* in Comestor's school. "The *Materia Super Liber Sententiarum* Attributed to Peter Comestor: Study of the Text and Critical Edition," *Bulletin de Philosophie Médiévale* 54 (2012): 155–215.

51 Martin, "Notes sur l'œuvre littéraire de Pierre le Mangeur," 62–65; Landgraf, "Recherches sur les écrits de Pierre le Mangeur," 350–357.

52 Peter Comestor, *Materia super librum Sententiarum*, ed. by Raymond M. Martin in "Notes sur l'oeuvre littéraire de Pierre le Mangeur," *RTAM* 3 (1931): 61–62, at 61.

53 "Per montem istum sacre scripture veritas, id est utriusque testamenti canon significatur." Ibid.

54 "Termini circa montem positi sunt agiographi, id est, sanctorum patrum scripta, utriusque testamenti intellectum nobis aperiencia." Ibid.

55 "Propter hec tria genera hominum, Magister videns terminos illos iam in magnas arbores excrevisse, ut faciolorem ... incessum nobis prepararet." Ibid.

to the elders of Israel, who approached the limits of Mount Sinai but then retreated to the camp: "As for the elders, reaching the boundaries, and then retreating, they are the learned who draw near to read the volumes of the fathers, but frightened as much by the magnitude as by the quantity of the books, as if despairing, they transfer to the shallower arts, to medicine, law and such like."[56] Medicine and law were the branches of advanced study that guaranteed a secure income. Theology did not. Comestor, understandably, had to make his students feel that they were doing something worthwhile, and this picture also found its way into future prologues.

The commentary was not the only work by Comestor to be directly founded on the *Sentences*. He compiled a work, called *On the Sacraments*, for a very different audience.[57] In doing this he aimed to make the *Sentences* accessible for parish priests. It is an abridged version of Peter's treatment of the sacraments in book four. This section of the *Sentences* would be the most useful to priests in their day-to-day duties. Raymond Martin, who edited the work, preferred to characterize it as an "abrégé mixte," rather than an "abrégé simple."[58] The distinction is that, unlike some abridgements, which appeared later in the century, Comestor makes changes to the arrangement of material and adds further references to authorities.[59] With this text, as Luscombe puts it, a priest "would find, for example, advice not to say Mass more than once a day, how to distribute the Eucharist, and how to administer the sacrament of penance."[60] R. W. Southern, in *Scholastic Humanism and the Unification of Europe*, points out how the work of the late–twelfth century schools filtered down to the popular level much more quickly than might be expected.[61] In

56 "Per seniores quidem ad terminos pervenientes, sed postea regredientes, designantur docti accedentes ad legenda patrum volumina, sed tam magnitudine quam numerositate librorum exterriti, quasi desperantes, ad breviores artes se transferunt, ut ad phisicam, leges et huiusmodi." Ibid.

57 Peter Comestor, *De Sacramentis*, ed. by Raymond M. Martin in *Maitre Simon et son groupe: De sacramentis*, ed. Henri Weisweiler (Louvain, 1937), 3–105.

58 Ibid., xxiv–xxv.

59 Ibid.

60 Luscombe, "Peter Comestor," 117.

61 "The wide distribution of scholastically trained masters in positions of pastoral and administrative authority, at every level of importance from parochial vicarages and rectories up to the very highest positions in the Church, all brought the secular world into touch with the results of scholastic teaching in everyday life." Southern, *Scholastic Humanism and the Unification of Europe* I: *Foundations* (Oxford, 1995), 131–134.

On the Sacraments, Comestor aimed to make the *Sentences* accessible, so that it might have an influence on the day-to-day lives of ordinary Christians. He would go much further in popularizing the work of the schools when he produced his *Historia Scholastica*. Unlike that work, however, *On the Sacraments* did not attain rapid popularity. It survives in complete form in only three manuscripts, with fragments appearing in others.[62] Comestor then seems to have been more successful in ensuring the future of Peter Lombard's works within the schools.

The influence of Peter Lombard can also be seen in Comestor's other works. Recently, Mark Clark has written illuminatingly on the relationship between the *Sentences* and Comestor's *Historia Scholastica*.[63] Since the structure of the *Sentences* is broadly chronological, and also governed by the narrative of the Bible, common ground would be expected. For Clark, this influence is most overt when Comestor discusses the creation story. In this section, he "systematically mined the second book of the *Sentences*."[64] There Peter Lombard deals with the work of the six days of creation.[65] Comestor follows his master's chapter titles ("on the work of the second day," "on the work of the third day," etc.), and is indebted to their theological content.[66] For Clark, "the *Sentences* lie just beneath the surface of this part of the *History*."[67] In his recent monograph, Clark shows that Peter Lombard was an important mentor to Comestor and the *Sentences* was a source of inspiration to him.[68]

62 Landgraf, "Recherches sur les écrits de Pierre le Mangeur," 341–350.

63 Mark J. Clark, "Peter Comestor and Peter Lombard: Brothers in Deed," *Traditio* 60 (2005): 85–142.

64 Ibid., 89.

65 Peter Comestor, *Scholastica historia: Liber Genesis*, ed. Agneta Sylwan (CCCM 191). Clark also provides his own working version of this section on 123–142 of his article.

66 Clark, "Peter Comestor and Peter Lombard," 113–118. For each of the six days, Clark shows how Comestor followed his master's outline or relied primarily on the *Sentences* over other texts.

67 Ibid., 89. The influence of the *Sentences* on this section of the *Historia* is also discussed in Mark J. Clark, "Stephen Langton and Hugh of St. Cher on Peter Comestor's *Historia scholastica*: The Lombard's *Sentences* and the Problem of Sources Used by Comestor and His Commentators," *Recherches de théologie et philosophie médiévales* 74 (2007): 63–117.

68 Clark, *The Making of the* Historia scholastica, *1150-1200*, 15–22, 46, 256–258.

Comestor, like his master, also preached sermons in the milieu of the schools.[69] Mark Zier has provided the best assessment of his preaching, based on a reading of an Advent sermon. Among the features he points to are structural symmetry, the use of distinctions (often threefold), and "a creatively imaginative elaboration of visual images."[70] This seems to suggest a strong similarity with the sermons of Peter Lombard, from what we have observed in the previous chapter. Zier detects a Victorine influence in Comestor's use of threefold distinctions.[71] Certainly that influence is well attested throughout his works, but it seems highly probable that the sermons of his master also made an impression on Comestor in this context.

The influence of Peter Lombard's preaching on Comestor's warrants further investigation. Comestor preaches on the same text as his master in only three of his sermons.[72] Of these three, he only uses one for the same occasion as Lombard, a sermon on Advent.[73] The choice of text was limited to the readings prescribed for the liturgical day. But the preacher still had to select a particular sentence or two from those readings. To compare the two men as preachers, we can examine them dealing with the text from the Song

69 Lebreton, "Recherches sur les manuscrits contenant des sermons de Pierre le Mangeur," 25–44; Johannes B. Schneyer, *Repertorium der lateinischen Sermones des Mittelalters* (Münster, 1969–1990), 4: 636–646; Tibber, "The Origins of the Scholastic Sermon, c.1130–c.1210" (Dphil diss., University of Oxford, 1983), 32–37, also appendix; Mark Zier, "Preaching by Distinction: Peter Comestor and the Communication of the Gospel," *Ephemerides Liturgicae* 105 (1991): 301–329; Franco Morenzoni, "L'*Ars praedicandi* de Pierre le Mangeur," in *Pierre le Mangeur ou Pierre de Troyes: Maître du XIIe siècle*, ed. Dahan, 225–242. Many of Comestor's sermons remain unedited. Some are in print in PL 198, and two others have been edited by Mark Zier, one in the above article and the other in Mark Zier, "Sermons of the Twelfth Century Schoolmasters and Canons," in *The Sermon*, ed. Beverly M. Kienzle (Turnhout, 2000), 352–362.

70 Zier, "Preaching by Distinction," 301–316. The quotation is from 305.

71 Ibid., 307–308.

72 These are, according to Schneyer's list, no. 11, *Aspiciebam in visu noctis*, Troyes 1515, f. 113v; no. 44, *Egredimini filiae sion* (PL 198: 1772–1775); and no. 133, *Tempus requirendi Domini*, Troyes 1515, f. 115v. The Lombard sermons are, respectively, no. 1, *In adventu*; no. 24, *In die pascha*; and no. 15, *In dominica ante Palmas*.

73 The opening is "Manifestam vobis de adventu Domini Salvatoris prophetiam Danielis protulimus." Schneyer, *Repertorium der lateinischen Sermones des Mittelalters*, 4: 637. This would appear to contradict Tibber's claim that "the advent sermons of Lombard, Comestor and Peter of Poitiers, to take three preachers at random, have no themae in common." Tibber, "The Origins of the Scholastic Sermon," 121–122. By *thema* he means the opening text.

of Songs, *egredimini filiae Sion, et videte regem Salomonem in diademente, quo coronavit eum hodie mater sua* ("daughters of Jerusalem, come forth and look upon King Solomon, in the crown with which his mother has crowned him").[74] Peter Lombard's sermon on the text, for Easter, is one of his longest and is built on the visual image of the opening text.[75] Comestor uses the text for the Annunciation. His sermon shows him learning from his master, but also producing an independent creation. We have seen that it was characteristic of Lombard to open either on a soothing note or in celebration of the occasion. The beginning of Comestor's sermon has a very different quality and is almost theatrical. He talks about himself. He wonders if he is up to the task: "Glorious things are often spoken about the glorious mother of God. And maybe, 'if I speak with the tongue of angels and men,' my work may turn out to be worthless, because 'the well is deep,' and I have nothing wherein to draw. All the same, I can hardly be speechless, since every creature has speech: at least my speech may be joyful, and it will not be unfruitful."[76] Comestor first turns to the daughters of Sion who come out to see Solomon crowned. Peter Lombard takes these merely to refer to people who are asked to come out (*egredimini*), because they are being held back: "they do not want to come out from the darkness of ignorance and blindness to the light of faith and truth."[77] He continues with a discussion of the seven deadly sins and the devil, both of which prevent them from coming out. Comestor takes this passage differently. He makes a distinction between the daughters of Jerusalem, who are laypeople, and the daughters of Sion, a more select group. They are called out especially from the rest of the people in this quotation because they are the educated: "These words are especially directed to us, to educated people, those, I say, to whom 'it is given to know mysteries, but to the rest in para-

74 Song of Sol. 3:11.

75 Peter Lombard, *Sermo in die paschae* (PL 171: 352–363).

76 "Gloriosa dicta sunt saepe de gloriosa matre Dei. Et ego forte, 'si linguis hominum loquar et angelorum' (2 Cor. 13), tamen in irritum cedet labor meus, quia 'puteus altus est' (John 4), et in quo hauriam non habeo. Verumtamen obmutescere non possum, unde omnis loquitur creatura: tantum jucundum sit eloquium meum, et non erit infructuosum." Peter Comestor, *Sermo in annuntiatione B. Virginis* (PL 198: 1772). Comestor was certainly not unusual in taking this approach. For the popularity of beginning sermons in this way, see Tibber, "The Origins of the Scholastic Sermon," 123–124.

77 "Nolunt egredi de tenebris caecitatis et ignorantiae ad lucem fidei et veritatis." Peter Lombard, *Sermo in die paschae* (PL 171: 353).

bles.'"[78] He identifies the educated (*litterati*) in this way because of "the eminence of their knowledge" and "their guarding and instruction of others."[79] Comestor was preaching to fellow scholars and students,[80] and, as in the prologue to his commentary on the *Sentences,* he exalts the work of theologians and sounds an unmistakable note of self-congratulation.

To be fair to Comestor, he has not forgotten that he is a preacher. The sermon is not just an exercise in backslapping. If his comments about the *litterati* had lulled his audience into complacency, they would have been jolted back again by this: "What is the world anyway, and all its vain desire, except mud and faeces?"[81] He refers to things building up "in the filth of dung pits,"[82] Adam "stained with filth,"[83] and "faeces heaped upon faeces."[84] This kind of language, and the general tone of haranguing the world's vanity, was not characteristic of Peter Lombard.

Despite these differences, Comestor actually makes use of one of his master's favourite techniques to bring his sermon to this point. He isolates the word *egredimini* in the opening text and points to its use in another biblical passage, *egredere de terra tua, et de cognatione tua, et de domo patris tui* ("go forth from your country, and from your kindred, and from your father's house").[85] Unlike Peter Lombard, who could almost be too subtle about it, he signposts this device for his audience: "The same word was said to Abra-

78 "Ad nos sane praecipue dirigitur sermo, ad litteratos, inquam, quibus 'datum est nosse mysteria, caeteris autem in parabolis' (Luke 8)." Peter Comestor, *Sermo in annuntiatione* (PL 198: 1773).

79 "Per filias Sion litteratos, tum propter scientiae eminentiam, tum propter aliorum custodiam et instructionem, tum quia Sion *speculatio* interpretatur." Ibid. Southern also dealt with this passage, remarking that "Symbolically therefore, Jerusalem is Christendom; the schools are its watch-tower; the daughters of Zion are the scholars in the schools, and the townsfolk are the people in the world .... Here in a single passage we have the whole function of the schools expressed in a biblical image which makes use of the long tradition of the allegorical interpretation of the Bible."Southern, *Scholastic Humanism* I: *Foundations,* 120–121.

80 The "ad nos" makes that clear, as does the heading "habitus in scholis."

81 "Quis est iste mundus, et omnis concupiscentia ejus, nisi lutum et faeces?" Peter Comestor, *Sermo in annuntiatione* (PL 198: 1773).

82 "Quantis autem sordibus sterquilinium hoc cumuletur in evidenti est." Ibid.

83 "Adam primus et maximus omnium gigas sordes inobedientiae supernos evomuit, cujus tanta fuit labes, ut universam posteritatem miserabiliter macularet." Ibid.

84 "faeces faecibus cumulaverunt." Ibid.

85 Gen. 12:1–2.

ham."[86] Comestor then begins his section on "going forth" from the world and "all its vain desire." There is even clearer dependence on Peter Lombard when Comestor returns to the opening text. He refers to the significance of the three names for Solomon (*Salomon, Ecclesiastes,* and *Idida*), which correspond to the three books of the Old Testament traditionally ascribed to him.[87] Peter Lombard's treatment of the three names in his sermon on this text is almost identical,[88] even if the idea itself goes back much further.[89]

Comestor's explanation of Solomon's diadem is highly individual. A diadem, he tells us, differs from a regular crown: "A simple crown is a circle of gold, used by Kings in minor solemnities. A diadem is like a twofold crown, where almost a second, twin crown is added to the first and placed above."[90] The diadem represents the four natural affections (fear, hope, joy, and grief) crowned by the four principal virtues (justice, prudence, temperance, and fortitude).[91] Peter Lombard does refer to the four natural affections in connection with the crown, but not in the same way.[92] Comestor also cites Virgil ("as the poet says") for the four natural affections,[93] and the use of classical authors occurs in some of his other sermons.[94] This is another difference. While Peter Lombard was well versed in classical authors, he did not cite them

86 "His, inquam, dicitur: 'Filiae Sion,' quibus Dominus aperuit sensum, ut intelligeretis Scripturas, 'egredimini.' Idipsum dictum Abrahae homini Dei: 'Egredere' … ." Peter Comestor, *Sermo in annuntiatione* (PL 198: 1773).

87 Ibid., 1774.

88 Peter Lombard, *Sermo in die paschae* (PL 171: 361–362).

89 Hugh of St Victor, for example, refers to it in his overview of the books of the bible in *Didascalicon* 4.7, ed. Charles H. Buttimer (Washington, DC, 1939), 80.

90 "Corona simplex est circulus aureus, quo utuntur reges in minoribus solemnitatibus. Diadema est quasi duplex corona, cum ipsi coronae quasi alius circulus gemmis superpositus superadditur." Peter Comestor, *Sermo in annuntiatione* (PL 198: 1774).

91 "His autem si superponantur quatuor principales virtutes ordinate, diadema fit animae." Ibid.

92 Peter Lombard, *Sermo in die paschae* (PL 171: 363). "Corona ista quasi ex quatuor lapidibus pretiosis constat, scilicet, quatuor mentis affectionibus, quae sunt gaudium, amor, tristitia et timor. Has affectiones Christus de matre suscepit, et ordinatas habuit. Unde et Dominus: Coronavit me corona justitiae, quia justitia est affectio ordinata." He then goes on to discuss each in the context of the life of Christ.

93 "Quatuor sane sunt naturales affectiones, timor, spes, gaudium, dolor, unde poeta: 'Cupiunt, metuunt, gaudentque dolentque.'" Peter Comestor, *Sermo in annuntiatione* (PL 198: 1774). The reference is to Virgil, *Aeneid* 6.733.

94 Martin, "Notes sur l'oeuvre littéraire de Pierre le Mangeur," 55, notes also occasional citing of Horace and Ovid in Comestor's sermons. The use of Ovid was quite unusual in Comestor's period.

in sermons. The passage on Solomon's diadem leads Comestor into the feast day he is preaching on, the Annunciation: "On this day then, the day of the Lord's conception, Christ the man was crowned with a diadem in the womb of his mother."[95] As in Peter Lombard's sermons, the treatment of the feast day is the culmination of a carefully worked out structure.

Comestor's sermon on the Annunciation reveals that in temperament he was quite different to his master. He places the emphasis on himself at the beginning, and as the sermon progresses, he is blunter than Peter Lombard in urging his audience to mend their ways. However, it is also clear that he had learned from his master. The sermon shows Comestor to be adept at setting up and following a clear structure. He also makes use of Peter's favoured structural technique of breaking the text into fragments and using them to carry the argument forward. This shows us what kind of master Peter Lombard was. His students did not copy him. Instead, they learned how to handle and structure material, and to argue cases. Although the content, and indeed tone, of the works of the students may be different, the ability to develop their points and produce a satisfying whole was something they learned from their master.

It may seem as if Comestor has appeared in an almost uncomplimentary light, with his insistence on maintaining his licence fees, his playing of power games, or his self-important view of his profession. He was in fact a very typical member of medieval society. His quarrel with Peter Chrysogonus over the licence to teach represents merely an unwillingness to part with an existing privilege. He spoke highly of theology, but it was his profession, and he was aware that few others could do it. Like his teacher, he attained prestigious positions, and he did this through skill and meaningful support. Indeed, with his assertion of privilege and his pride in a particular profession, Comestor resembles a craftsman more than anything. And, like any craftsman, he was devoted to his master, under whom he had spent years of apprenticeship. Hand in hand with that devotion went obligation. Like Peter Lombard's other pupils, Comestor knew he had a part to play in keeping Peter's name alive. His contribution to this was twofold. He lectured on the *Sentences* to a select audience of theology students, but also prepared an abridgement of that work, *On the Sacraments*, for wider use. It is quite probable that he also used his

95 "In hac ergo die Dominicae conceptionis, Christus homo hoc diademate coronatus est in utero matris." Peter Comestor, *Sermo in annuntiatione* (PL 198: 1775).

influence as chancellor to ensure that masters taught theology in Peter Lombard's tradition.

William of Tyre (c.1130–1186)

William of Tyre is as familiar to students of medieval history as Peter Lombard himself.[96] His *History* is known to anyone who has read about the Crusades. It is the only work by a student of Peter Lombard to have received a modern translation,[97] and today it is certainly more widely read than the *Sentences*. The *History* is a vital source for the twelfth-century history of crusading, beginning with the First Crusade and ending with events in the East that William had personal knowledge of. It also includes a chapter, which was lost until 1962, about William's study years in France and Italy.[98] In this chapter, William remembers his theology master Peter Lombard in fond terms. William never taught or wrote theology, but that should not remove him from our attention. His career helps to illustrate the wide range of activities carried out by Peter's students and the importance of a theological education for clerics.

96 Modern scholarship on William really began with Hans Prutz, "Studien über Wilhelm von Tyrus," *Neues Archiv der Gesellschaft für Ältere Deutsche Geschichtskunde* 8 (1883): 93–132, who established the chronology of William's career and considered the dates of the composition of the *Historia* and its sources. His conclusions were given some fine tuning by Hans Eberhard Mayer, "Zum Tode Wilhelms von Tyrus," *Archiv für Diplomatik* 5/6 (1959–1960): 182–201, and Rudolf Hiestand, "Zum Leben und zur Laufbaun Wilhelms von Tyrus," *Deutsche Archiv für Erforschung des Mittelalters* 34 (1978): 345–380. More interpretative works are David W.T.C. Vessey, "William of Tyre and the Art of Historiography," *Mediaeval Studies* 35 (1973): 433–455, and Ralph H.C. Davis, "William of Tyre," in *Relations Between East and West in the Middle Ages*, ed. Derek Baker (Edinburgh, 1973), 64–76. Peter Edbury and Gordon J. Rowe, *William of Tyre: Historian of the Latin East* (Cambridge, 1988) is a comprehensive treatment of William as a historian, while Rainer C. Schwinges, *Kreuzzugsideologie und Toleranz: Studien zu Wilhelm von Tyrus* (Stuttgart, 1977), situates William within the intellectual climate of the twelfth century.

97 William of Tyre, *A History of Deeds Done Beyond the Sea*, trans. Emily A. Babcock and August C. Krey (New York, 1943).

98 The lost chapter first appeared in Robert B.C. Huygens, "Guillame de Tyr étudiant," *Latomus* 21 (1962): 811–829. It was then incorporated into the new edition, William of Tyre, *Chronicon*, ed. Huygens (CCCM 63, 63A). Huygens preferred the title "chronicon," but "historia," or "history of deeds done beyond the sea," is also in frequent use.

William was born in the Latin Kingdom of Jerusalem to a middle-class family who had settled there after the First Crusade.[99] They would hardly have been able to fund his entire education because William spent almost twenty years in France and Italy. He claims that he lived in "voluntary poverty,"[100] but this may be somewhat exaggerated. He was probably often short of money, but he must have had some kind of patronage to afford living expenses and the fees that masters customarily charged.[101] It is reasonable to assume that his intellectual promise would have been recognized and supported by the nobility or clerical elite of the Latin Kingdom. They would have understood the need for a learned class that was native-born but trained in the West. It has been estimated that his birth took place some time between 1128 and 1134, based on internal evidence in the *History*.[102] The lost chapter suggests that William went abroad for studies in 1146 or 1147.[103] This would place his birth at between 1128 and 1130. William could then have been as young as sixteen when he went to Paris.

Before enrolling with Peter, William studied the arts. The autobiographical chapter of the *History* provides very strong evidence that William was a student at Notre Dame. At least three of his masters, Peter, Maurice of Sully, and Ivo of Chartres, were canons there. On the other hand, he only heard Robert of Melun and Alberic de Monte now and again in disputations.[104] Those masters were outside the orbit of the chancellor of Notre Dame because they taught at St Geneviève.[105] William added the autobiographical

99 Prutz, "Studien über Wilhelm von Tyrus," 93–94. Prutz thought that it was William's parents that had come during the First Crusade, but Hiestand, " Zum Leben und zur Laufbaun Wilhelmus von Tyrus," 348–349, modified this by suggesting that it had been his grandparents.

100 "Fuerunt autem nobis hoc media tempore, quo in partibus transmarinis nostram in disciplinis transegimus adolescentiam, in paupertate voluntaria literarum studiis etatis nostras dedicavimus dies." William of Tyre, *Chronicon* 19.12 (CCCM 63: 880).

101 Edbury and Rowe, *William of Tyre*, 15, also raise the question of patronage.

102 Prutz, "Studien über Wilhelm von Tyrus," 94–95. In describing the deposed Patriarch, Randulph of Antioch, William remarks that he saw him as a child. Since Randulph was only patriarch from 1136–1142, Prutz pointed out that to be a child then, William would have had to been born between 1128 and 1134. He had no access to the lost chapter, however.

103 Huygens, "Guillame de Tyr étudiant," 815.

104 William of Tyre, *Chronicon* 19.12 (CCCM 63: 880).

105 For the question of where Robert of Melun taught, see Constant J. Mews, "Between the Schools of Abelard and Saint-Victor in the Mid-Twelfth Century: The Witness

chapter to his *History* to show his credentials as a writer and to give his masters credit. For the arts, he is quite matter-of-fact, merely providing the names of his masters and the subject they taught. William reserves his longest description for Peter Lombard:

> In theology, however, for six years uninterrupted, I studied diligently under a man unparalleled in that discipline, whose surviving works a group of prudent followers embraces with veneration and cultivates with reverence, a man of sound doctrine commendable in every way, namely Master Peter Lombard, who afterwards was bishop of Paris.[106]

He stayed in the school until Peter ceased teaching to become bishop, meaning that he must have enrolled with Peter in 1153. He would have stayed longer, too, for we know that he did not consider his theological training complete. He continued it with Maurice of Sully. In those six years, Peter Lombard lectured twice on the *Sentences* and once on his *Commentary on the Psalms.*[107] It was a good time to be one of his students.

After Maurice of Sully left the schools to succeed Lombard as bishop, William decided that he had learned all he could in Paris. He went to Italy and studied law with different masters at Bologna.[108] He returned to the Latin Kingdom in 1164 and immediately attained a prebend at the Acre cathedral, thanks to the bishop there, William the Lombard.[109] Little is known of this bishop. He was later killed in bizarre circumstances by a member of his ret-

---

of Robert of Melun," in *L'école de Saint-Victor de Paris: Influence et rayonnement du Moyen Âge à l'epoque moderne*, ed. Dominique Poirel (Turnhout, 2010), 122–126, and Dale M. Coulter, *Per Visibilia ad Invisibilia: Theological Method in Richard of St. Victor* (Turnhout, 2006), 244–246.

106 "In theologia autem virum in ea scientia singularem, cuius opera que exstant prudentum chorus cum veneratione amplectitur et colit cum reverentia, virum sana doctrina per omnia commendabilem, magistrum videlicet Petrum Lonbardum, qui postea fuit Parisiensis episcopus, annis sex continuis diligenter audivimus." William of Tyre, *Chronicon* 19.12 (CCCM 63: 880).

107 See chapter four, above, 97, 99, 107.

108 William of Tyre, *Chronicon* 19.12 (CCCM 63: 880–881).

109 "Postquam ergo auctore domino ad propria reversi sumus, dominus Willelmus, pie memorie Acconensis episcopus, natione Lonbardus, vir providus et discretus, ex archidiaconatu Tyrensi ad illam ecclesiam translatus, statim post ingressum nostrum mera caritatis liberalitate cum voluntate et consensu totius capituli in ecclesia sua beneficium, quod prebenda dicitur, nobis concessit" Ibid., 881.

inue on returning from a mission to Constantinople with King Amalric.[110] William's studies under Peter Lombard and in Northern Italy can only have commended him to the bishop, and this is the impression he certainly intends to give the reader when he specifies the bishop as *natione Lonbardus.*[111]

William's career from then on is well known and need not be repeated in detail here.[112] It is certain that his education in the West helped him to advance. His training in the arts and the law would be an asset for diplomatic missions to the Byzantine Empire on behalf of the crown of Jerusalem. In 1175 he was appointed archbishop of Tyre, and he would have put his theological training to use in that position. He had also been appointed royal chancellor the previous year. None of Peter's other students managed to become such powerful statesmen. They were not even in the running for those kinds of positions. William is more reminiscent of figures like Hugh of Champfleury or William of the White Hands in terms of the influence he had.

He was undoubtedly at too much of a distance from Western Europe to have taken part in the debates of the 1160s and 1170s over Peter Lombard's Christological positions. As archbishop of Tyre, however, he did attend the Third Lateran Council, and we can assume that he would have defended his master, given his high regard for him. In the autobiographical chapter, probably written after the council, he underlines Lombard's *sana doctrina*, his sound doctrine.[113] It may well have been at the council that he had learned of the *chorus*, the "group of prudent followers" who were continuing Lombard's tradition. He also wrote an account of the council "at the request of the holy fathers who were present."[114] He deposited it in the cathedral library at Tyre, but there is no trace of it today.

110 William of Tyre, *Chronicon* 20.25 (CCCM 63: 948); Charles du Fresne du Cange, *Les Familles d'Outre Mer*, ed. Emmanuel G. Rey and Nicolas R. Taranne (Paris, 1869), 777.

111 "Perhaps Bishop William, himself a Lombard, was anxious to recruit someone trained in the Bolognese school of civil law to his staff." Edbury and Rowe, *William of Tyre*, 14. For some more detail on the position at Acre, see Hiestand, "Zum Leben und zur Laufbahn Wilhelmus von Tyrus," 364–365.

112 For his career, see Edbury and Rowe, *William of Tyre*, 13–32.

113 William of Tyre, *Chronicon* 19.12 (CCCM 63: 880).

114 "Cuius siquis et statuta et episcoporum nomina, numerum et titulos scire desidera, relegat scriptum quod nos ad preces sanctorum patrum, qui eidem synodi interfuerunt, confecimus diligenter, quod in archivo sancte Tyrensis ecclesie inter ceteros, quos eidem ecclesiae contulimus libros, cui iam sex annis prefuimus, iussimus collocari." William of Tyre, *Chronicon* 21.25 (CCCM 63: 998).

William's *History*, which he wrote between 1170 and 1184,[115] is undoubtedly a product of his wide education, but it does not immediately suggest years spent in the theology school of Peter Lombard. Allusions and quotations from the classics occur, and his method in writing history was shaped by classical and early-medieval predecessors.[116] We have already seen that Peter Lombard allowed a historical-chronological approach to govern the structure of the *Sentences.*[117] William was in the school during the two years that Peter taught the *Sentences,* and he would certainly have taken this aspect on board. But, unlike Peter Comestor's *Historia Scholastica,* William's historical work was too limited in scope to be marked by the approach to history in the *Sentences.* As Edbury and Rowe make clear, William's aims were comparatively modest. He was writing the deeds of the kings of Jerusalem, and even in his introduction, he does not attempt to view those deeds within a larger context of universal history.[118]

William was at pains to single out Peter as the most illustrious of his teachers, however. Does this come across in the text of the *History*? William's version of Pope Urban's speech at the council of Clermont is worth examining in this context. It is certainly William's own creation. Since it was written much later than the other accounts of the council, his version of the speech is rarely discussed or included in anthologies of documents. It is often called a sermon, but William prefers to use the name *exhortatio* (exhortation), and it cannot therefore be directly compared with Peter Lombard's sermons.[119] Nevertheless, there are echoes of William's years in the theology school, where Peter comprehensively glossed the Bible with his students. William's use of scriptural quotation to illustrate or reinforce points is effortless, particularly in the early part of the exhortation where he picks out verses about the holy land or Jerusalem.[120] Although he would have undoubtedly been capable of breaking down the significance of these texts, this was unnecessary. His main task was to present a plausible reconstruction of what Pope

115 Edbury and Rowe, *William of Tyre,* 29. They point out that as a result of attending Lateran III William's "appreciation of his potential audience had greatly increased."

116 For the influence of William's training in the arts on his work, see Schwinges, *Kreuzzugsideologie und Toleranz,* 46–51, and Edbury and Rowe, *William of Tyre,* 32–60.

117 See chapter four, above, 101–102.

118 Edbury and Rowe, *William of Tyre,* 40.

119 William of Tyre, *Chronicon* 15 (CCCM 63: 131–135).

120 Ibid., 131–132.

Urban had said. Still, the first words of the speech quite closely resemble the kind of gentle, comforting openings favoured by Peter Lombard in his sermons:

> You know, dearest brothers, and it is right for your love to know, how the redeemer of the human race, putting on flesh for our salvation, lived as a man among men and illuminated the land of promise with his own presence, which he had formerly promised to the fathers, and made it especially illustrious, through abundant miracles ... the books of the Old and New Testament teach this in almost every syllable.[121]

This opening is not similar to the earlier versions of the speech by Fulcher of Chartres, Robert the Monk, and others.[122] William, as a student at Notre Dame, would have heard Peter preach regularly for several years before he entered his school.[123] This similarity suggests that his own sermons, which have not survived, may have been influenced by those of his master.

R.C. Schwinges discusses how William's education shaped his *History* and formed his outlook.[124] In this context, he examines the influence of his years in theology, especially under Peter Lombard.[125] At one point in the *History*, William describes an occasion when King Amalric asked him whether "besides the doctrine of the saviour and of the saints who follow Christ (concerning which he did not doubt), any reason could be found by which a future

121 "Nostis, fratres dilectissimi, et vestram nosse id expedit caritatem, quomodo humani generis reparator, pro nostra omniumque salute carnem assumens et homo inter homines conversatus, Terram Promissionis, quam pridem patribus promiserat, propria illustravit presentia et assumpte dispensationis operibus et crebra simul miraculorum exhibitione reddidit specialiter insignem: id enim et Veteris et Novi pene in omnibus sillabis docet series Testamenti." Ibid., 131.

122 *Recueil des historiens des croisades.* Volume 1: *Historiens occidentaux* (Paris, 1844–1895), 3: 323 (Fulcher of Chartres), 491 *(Gesta Francorum),* 727 (Robert the Monk), 4: 12–13 (Baldric of Dol), 137 (Guibert of Nogent).

123 For Peter's role as a preacher at Notre Dame, see chapter six, above.

124 Schwinges, *Kreuzzugsideologie und Toleranz,* ch. 3: "Toleranz und Bildung," 46–64.

125 "Doch welchen Einfluss mag die scholastische Theologie und mehr noch ihre Methode unter dem Aspekt der Korrelation von Toleranz und Bildung auf ihren Studenten ausgeübt haben." Ibid., 51.

resurrection can be proved by reliable and authoritative arguments."[126] They then debated the issue, with William playing the role of teacher, and the king the pupil. Schwinges believes that this passage displays the scholastic techniques of *quaestio* and *disputatio,* and he puts the exchange in the form of dramatic dialogue to prove his point.[127] William concludes that "God cannot be an unjust paymaster. Therefore there will be another life, and a resurrection of the flesh, where the person who has merited either good or evil should receive his reward and be recompensed."[128] Schwinges notes that this proof is closely founded on John Damascene's *De Fide Orthodoxa,* and he wonders whether William learned it from Peter Lombard.[129] This, however, is unlikely. Schwinges himself admits that the *Sentences* have no relation to Damascene here.[130] Peter deals with the resurrection toward the end of book four. He does not set out to prove it in detail, but briefly recounts the patristic and scriptural evidence.[131] He concludes that "by these words, both the truth of the resurrection and the cause and order of those who rise again are indicated most clearly."[132] With regard to the translation of Damascene by Burgundio, we have seen that Peter was able to incorporate material from it into book three during his trip to Rome in 1154.[133] The Christological chapters of Damascene's text had already been translated into Latin by Cerbanus. In Rome, Peter checked Burgundio's translation against this one, but he did not make

126 "Si praeter doctrinam Salvatoris et sanctorum qui Christum secuti sunt, de qua non dubitabat, posset ratio inveniri, qua posset probari argumentis evidentibus et necessariis, resurrectionem futuram." William of Tyre, *Chronicon* 19.3 (CCCM 63: 886–888).

127 Schwinges, *Kreuzzugsideologie und Toleranz,* 54–55.

128 "'Ergo in alia vita fiet; quia non potest deus non esse iustus retributor. Ergo alia vita erit et huius carnis resurrectio, in qua meruit quis bonum vel malum, in ea debet recipere premium et remunerari." William of Tyre, *Chronicon* 19.3 (CCCM 63: 868).

129 "Petrus Lombardus, dessen Übungen Wilhelm sechs Jahre lang in Paris besucht hatte, gehörte zu den ersten, die es benützen. Dort mag Wilhelm auf Johannes-Burgundio aufmerksam geworden sein." Schwinges, *Kreuzzugsideologie und Toleranz,* 57. Damascene's proof is in *De fide orthodoxa: Versions of Burgundio and Cerbanus,* ed. Eligius Buytaert (New York, 1955), 378–379.

130 Schwinges, *Kreuzzugsideologie und Toleranz,* 57 n38.

131 *Sententiae* 4, dist. 43, ch. 1, ed. Brady, 2: 510. The passages are Augustine, *Enchiridion* 84, Isa. 26:19, and 1 Thess. 4:13–17.

132 Peter Lombard, *The Sentences,* trans. Giulio Silano (Toronto, 2007–2010), 4: 234.

133 See chapter four, above, 97.

use of any further chapters of *De fide orthodoxa.*[134] There is no evidence that he brought a copy of Damascene-Burgundio back to Paris. William must have encountered Damascene during his further studies in Italy.[135]

William said that "his heart was deeply wounded" to see Amalric, "an orthodox prince," having doubts on this matter.[136] This passage provides another example of the wide use of theological education. Students who went on to clerical careers would encounter questions, and sometimes doubts. Herbert of Bosham, another Lombard student, inserted a proof of God's existence into his *Liber melorum* (a work in praise of Thomas Becket). His proof is partly an exposition of the psalm text "the foolish man says in his heart 'there is no God'" (Ps. 13).[137] Peter Lombard recounts four proofs for God's existence in book one of the *Sentences.*[138] Their inclusion reveals that he wanted his students to know them. It was partly for such reasons that William was sent to have a Western education in the first place. His years in Peter Lombard's theology school gave him an authority few others in the Latin Kingdom had, and an ability to deal with questions.

Schwinges also addresses the possible influence of Peter Lombard in William's depiction of the Syrian ruler Nur ad-Din.[139] When William first introduces him, in the *History,* as Zengi's successor, he describes him as "a wise and prudent man, and according to the superstitious traditions of his people, fearing God."[140] Later, marking his death, William adds, "Nur ad-Din, a great persecutor of the Christian faith and name, but a just prince,

134 John Damascene, *De fide orthodoxa,* ed. Buytaert, xii n26.

135 Although it may be wondered whether William had consulted the original Greek version, the idea that he knew Greek has been challenged. See Edbury and Rowe, *William of Tyre,* 45 n2.

136 "Tum quia animo graviter vulnus imprimebat si princeps ortodoxus et ortodoxorum filius in re tam certa pateretur scrupulum et in conscientia dubitaret." William of Tyre, *Chronicon* 19.3 (CCCM 63: 867).

137 Herbert of Bosham, *Liber melorum* (PL 190: 1294–1404, at 1355–1362). See also Smalley, *Becket Conflict,* 79. In addition, Herbert freely admitted having doubts himself and was disturbed enough at their persistence to seek Becket's advice, ibid., 74–75. Herbert's *Liber melorum* is addressed in chapter eight, below, 234–235.

138 *Sententiae* 1, dist. 3, ch. 1, ed. Brady 1: 68–70. See the discussion of this section in Rosemann, *Peter Lombard,* 75.

139 Schwinges, *Kreuzzugsideologie und Toleranz,* 129–134. Also "Exkurs I: Zum Heil Nur-ad-dins," 290–291, "Exkurs III: *Noradinus Felix,*" 292–293.

140 "Noradinus, vir providus et discretus, et iuxta traditiones illius populi supersticiosas, timens deum." William of Tyre, *Chronicon* 16.7 (CCCM 63: 723).

valiant and wise, and according to the traditions of his people, religious, died."[141] This is certainly a positive portrayal, and Schwinges raises the question of whether William was extending a doctrine of Peter Lombard by viewing Nur ad-Din as worthy of salvation.[142] As he himself admits, this can only be speculation.[143] He does, however, make the relevant point that Peter Lombard acknowledged the idea of natural virtue in ethics and might have communicated it to William.[144] In the *Sentences,* Peter states that "if someone, a Jew, or a bad Christian, for example, should see to the needs of his neighbour, led by natural piety, he does good, and he does it with a good will."[145] However, neither he nor William of Tyre seems to have taken a firm position on the question of the salvation of the virtuous pagan.[146] In any case, the awareness of virtue in non-Christians was as much a response to William's environment as it was a reflection of Peter Lombard's classroom. Unlike in some crusader towns, the non-Christian population of Tyre had been allowed to remain after it was conquered, and Jewish and Muslim com-

141 "Noradinus, maximus nominis et fidei Christianae persequutor, princeps tamen iustus, vafer et providus, et secundum gentis sue traditiones religiosus, regni eius anno vicesimo nono, mense Maio, defunctus est." Ibid., 20.31 (CCCM 63: 956).

142 Schwinges, *Kreuzzugsideologie und Toleranz,* 290–291: "Aber es sei darauf aufmerksam gemacht, dass Wilhelm mit seiner Ansicht sogar die Doktrin seines Lehrers Petrus Lombardus erweitert." Schwinges uses a quotation from the *Sentences* out of context: "dici potest nullum fuisse justum vel salvum, cui non esset facta revelatio vel distincta vel velata, vel in aperto, vel in mysterio." This occurs during a discussion of the faith of simple (i.e., uneducated) Christians, and how they can be saved. See *Sententiae* 3, dist. 25, ch. 2, ed. Brady, 2: 154–155.

143 "Ich will mich freilich nicht in eine theologisch-dogmatisch Diskussion um die Evidenz dieses Heiles einlassen." Schwinges, *Kreuzzugsideologie und Toleranz,* 290.

144 "Petrus Lombardus, der die 'Güte' ausserchristlicher Ethik durchaus anerkannte, mag Wilhelm vielleicht die Grundlagen zu seiner positiven Einstellung gegenüber den Tugenden der Muslime vermittelt haben?" Ibid., 291.

145 "Nam, si quis iudaeus vel malus Christianus necessitatem proximi relevaverit naturali pietate ductus, bonum fecit, et bona fuit voluntas qua illud fecit." *Sententiae* 2, dist. 41, ch. 2, ed. Brady 1: 564.

146 "He opens up the concept of natural virtue and the possible existence of the virtuous pagan or non-Christian." Colish, *Peter Lombard,* 484. "Yet, Peter does not come to grips expressly with the problem of the virtuous pagan." Ibid., 515. Colish further points out that Peter was aware of his own inability to pronounce firmly on who might be saved. She describes his position on baptism as follows: "While God instituted baptism as the path to be followed by mankind in ordinary cases, He Himself is not bound by the order of salvation that He lays down for man." Ibid., 539.

munities were prominent in commerce there.[147] William would have had regular dealings with them.

When William, presumably back in the East after attending the Lateran Council, wrote of the *chorus*,[148] the group of disciples who had devoted themselves to Peter Lombard's works, he was also showing an acute awareness of his own disassociation from them. They were "cultivating" his works "with reverence," elaborating on them in lectures and commentaries, providing new editions, and promoting them in the schools and beyond. He was not one of them. But William is a good example of a student whose career took him in a different direction. He was not part of the process of transmitting and elaborating on Peter Lombard's work. However, he demonstrates what the schools were all about. Those years in Paris gave him a solid grounding, first in the arts, and then, under Peter, in theology. He could draw on this experience when needed, as in the debate with the King, or presumably in preaching a sermon, or in assessing the theological knowledge of his clergy, or in any aspect of episcopal activity that required a cathedral school training. His training in Paris made him stand out in the Latin Kingdom.

The Chorus of Disciples

The attention paid to Peter Lombard's work in the 1160s and 1170s was certainly a recognition of his achievement. It was also motivated by other factors. Peter completed the second edition of the *Sentences* only three years before his death. The unexpectedness of this event meant that it was essential for his students to clarify his positions and make his work accessible. In the same period, criticism of his work became more frequent, and this would intensify as the 1160s and 1170s progressed. This is the context in which the work of Peter Comestor, and the group William of Tyre referred to as "a *chorus* of prudent followers," must be viewed.[149] This *chorus* includes the students whose careers are not known. Usually, even their names are absent. These students cannot therefore demonstrate the importance of a theological education for clerical careers, or for unrelated writings. However, it is important to examine them in the context of the third

147 Christopher Tyerman, *God's War: A New History of the Crusades* (London, 2007), 219–220; Jonathan Riley-Smith, *The Crusades: A Short History* (London, 1987), 63.
148 William of Tyre, *Chronicon* 19.12 (CCCM 63: 880).
149 Ibid.

central aim of this part of the book: their role in increasing awareness of Peter's teaching and writings.

The only one of these students whose name is known is Master Udo. His *Sentences* represents the first attempt at making a shorter version of all four books of Peter's work.[150] Udo was not writing a commentary, so his work does not refer to Peter's oral teaching. However, because his work dates from 1160–1165,[151] he is usually assumed to have been a student of Peter.[152] There is no firm evidence for this, but his knowledge of Peter's work at such an early stage makes it probable. He presumably would have studied with him in the 1150s, and then perhaps taught in the following decade. Udo's work is not comprehensive. While he follows the order of Peter's *Sentences*, some topics are not included.[153] It is also important to point out that although Udo was contributing to the process of disseminating Peter's work, he did not intend his work "to serve as a tool for the study of the Lombard."[154] What he offers instead is a *Sentences* of his own, which is based completely on Peter's work.

Other late–twelfth century figures sometimes feature in discussions of Peter Lombard's school. It has not been suggested that they actually studied with Peter. These are Master Bandinus, Gandulf of Bologna, and Odalric of Verdun.[155] All

150 Odon Lottin, "Le premier commentaire connu des *Sentences* de Pierre Lombard" *Recherches de théologie ancienne et médievale* 11 (1939): 64–71. Udo is also discussed by Artur Landgraf in "Udo und Magister Martinus," *RTAM* 11 (1939): 62–64, and *Einführung in die Geschichte der theologischen Literatur der Früscholastik* (Regensburg, 1948), 98, and by Marcia Colish, "From the Sentence Collection to the Sentence Commentary and the *Summa*: Parisian Scholastic Theology, 1130–1215," in *Manuels, programmes de cours et techniques d'enseignement dans les universités médiévales*, ed. Jacqueline Hamesse (Louvain, 1994), 9–29, at 17–18.

151 Lottin, "Le premier commentaire connu des *Sentences* de Pierre Lombard," 64–71.

152 Brady, "Peter Manducator," 480–481, cites Udo as a Lombard student.

153 Lottin, "Le premier commentaire connu des *Sentences* de Pierre Lombard," 71.

154 Rosemann, *Peter Lombard*, 249.

155 For Bandinus, see Philipp W. Rosemann, *The Story of a Great Medieval Book: Peter Lombard's* Sentences (Peterborough, ON, 2007), 28–33. His work can be found in PL 192: 964–1111. For Gandulf's work, see *Sententiarum libri quatuor*, ed. Joannes de Walter (Vienna, 1924). These authors are also discussed in Colish, "From the Sentence Collection to the Sentence Commentary," 18–20. Odalric was noticed by Martin Grabmann, "Le breviloquium sententiarum artis theologiae du chanoine Odalric de Verdun," *RTAM* 8 (1936): 296–299. Gandulf and Bandinus are discussed as representatives of Peter's school in Lauge-Olaf Nielsen, *Theology and Philosophy in the Twelfth Century: A Study of Gilbert Porreta's Thinking and the Theological Expositions of the Doctrine of the Incarnation During the Period 1130–1180* (Leiden, 1982), 287–361.

presented abbreviations of the *Sentences*, none dating from earlier than 1170. There is no evidence that they were Peter's students. It is possible that they saw themselves as being in Peter's tradition, but they do not mention him by name. This is in contrast to the writings of his actual students, who refer to Peter as "the master." Bandinus, Gandulf, and Odalric should be seen not as members of the school of Peter Lombard but as late–twelfth century theologians who made extensive use of the *Sentences* in their own works.

In addition to Comestor, we know of three early commentators on the *Sentences* who certainly had studied with Peter Lombard. They aimed to explain and clarify (rather than abbreviate) Peter's positions. Crucially, they also refer to specific occasions when they heard him teach. One of these students is the author of the first extant commentary on the *Sentences*, which was once ascribed to Peter of Poitiers.[156] It is complete in two twelfth-century manuscripts and partially complete in another, and it was also copied in the thirteenth century.[157] This commentary is usually credited to "Pseudo-Peter of Poitiers," and it has received considerable attention. Some sections have been edited,[158] and the

156 Questions were first raised against Peter of Poitiers's authorship by Artur Landgraf, "Notes de critique textuelle sur les Sentences de Pierre Lombard," *RTAM* 2 (1930): 80–99, at 81–82, who printed a letter he received on the subject from Odon Lottin. Philip S. Moore, in *The Works of Peter of Poitiers: Master in Theology and Chancellor of Paris (1193–1205)* (Notre Dame, 1936), 146–162, adds to this with further convincing grounds that the gloss was by somebody else.

157 The two twelfth-century manuscripts are Naples, Biblioteca nazionale, VIII C14, and Paris, Bibliothèque Mazarine, lat. 758. Book 1 of the commentary is also present in Bamberg, Staatsbibliothek, Cod. Patr. 128. This was established by Artur Landgraf, "Problèmes relatifs aux premières gloses des Sentences," *RTAM* 3 (1931): 140–157. He also discussed his findings in "The First Sentence Commentary of Early Scholasticism," *New Scholasticism* 13 (1939): 101–132, and "Drei Zweige der Pseudo-Poitiers Glose zu den Sentenzen des Lombarden," *RTAM* 9 (1937): 167–204. Moore, *The Works of Peter of Poitiers*, 147–150, discusses the thirteenth-century manuscripts.

158 Pseudo-Peter's commentary on book 1, dist. 25, ch. 3 of the *Sentences* (on the persons of the Trinity) was edited by Ludwig Hödl in "Die Sentenzen des Petrus Lombardus in der Diskussion seiner Schule," in *Mediaeval Commentaries on the Sentences of Peter Lombard: Current Research*, ed. Gillian R. Evans and Philipp W. Rosemann (Leiden, 2002–2015), 1: 37–40. Landgraf edited selected sections and provides a full table of contents for the commentary in "Problèmes relatifs aux premières gloses des Sentences," 147–151. The prologue is printed in Martin, "Notes sur l'oeuvre littéraire de Pierre le Mangeur," 64–65, and in Lottin, "Le prologue des Gloses sur les Sentences attribuées à Pierre de Poitiers," *RTAM* 7 (1935): 70–73.

prologue has been translated.[159] The student relies very heavily on Comestor's prologue.[160] Although his prologue is not copied word for word, it is certainly paraphrased. We have noted that Comestor took a self-important view of theology by referring to the "shallower arts" of medicine and the law.[161] Pseudo-Peter's paragraph is very similar, although he does not specify the two other faculties. Instead he borrows a verse from Proverbs (26:11): "There are those who draw near the limits, but go back tired, since they despair of their own abilities after noticing the sheer number of books involved in the study of the holy page. And so they return to the other faculties, like dogs that return to their vomit."[162] For Pseudo-Peter, medicine and the law might as well be vomit by comparison with theology.

The similarity of the two prologues makes it quite probable that the rest of the work is modelled on Comestor's now lost gloss. This hypothesis can be strengthened by examining the reports of Comestor's teaching on the *Sentences*, preserved in anthologies of *quaestiones*. Since the gloss was a record of such teaching, the reports may represent fragments of it. Brady points especially to Comestor's treatment of "whether the son also has the power of begetting" (*Sentences* 1, dist. 7, ch. 2). He showed that Pseudo-Peter's discussion of this point in his commentary is almost identical.[163] In addition, Pseudo-Peter cites Comestor's theological opinions "a dozen or more times."[164]

159 Rosemann, *The Story of a Great Medieval Book*, 41–46, contains a complete translation of the prologue. A new assessment by Marcia Colish has also recently appeared: "The Pseudo-Peter of Poitiers Gloss," in *Mediaeval Commentaries on the Sentences of Peter Lombard*, ed. Rosemann, 2: 1–33.

160 "The Pseudo-Peter proem paraphrases and expands upon Peter Comestor's text rather than citing it literally but the dependence is clear." Rosemann, *The Story of a Great Medieval Book*, 47.

161 Ibid.

162 "Sunt qui usque ad terminos accedunt, sed fatigati redeunt, utpote qui librorum sacre pagine numerositatem attendentes de seipsis diffidunt, ideoque ad ceteras facultates tanquam canes ad vomitum recurrunt," Pseudo-Peter of Poitiers, *Glossae super Sententias: Prologus*, ed. by Raymond M. Martin in "Notes sur l'oeuvre littéraire de Pierre le Mangeur," 64. Prov. 26:11 is "Sicut canis qui revertitur ad vomitum suum sic inprudens qui iterat stultitiam suam."

163 Brady, "Peter Manducator," 466–469. He comments further, on 482, that Pseudo-Peter's gloss is "quite evidently itself in debt to [Peter Comestor]." Nielsen, *Theology and Philosophy in the Twelfth Century*, 280, agrees in his discussion of Peter Lombard's school.

164 Brady, "Peter Manducator," 487.

The student indicates that he also studied with Peter Lombard himself.[165] He includes the vital information that Peter consulted Burgundio's translation of John Damascene while he was in Rome.[166] Additionally, he witnessed Peter Lombard writing marginal notes. Some of these were short, such as the single word *cave* (take care), but there were also longer notes, which provide further argument. Pseudo-Peter describes these as "flying glosses."[167] Finally, he mentions that Peter sometimes explained positions orally, but did not include them in his text: "The master used to explain this solution in debate, but he did not commit it to writing."[168] This is very significant. It again proves that Peter was very careful about his positions. As we have seen in chapter four, he does not always provide answers to the questions in the *Sentences*, but instead advises his readers to ponder them further. After witnessing, and taking part in, the trial of Gilbert of Poitiers,[169] Peter knew that any positions he included must be absolutely clear and capable of withstanding challenges.

Pseudo-Peter's commentary has considerable value because it shows how Peter's students interpreted and handled his theological positions. What also stands out, as it does in all of the students, is an obligation to Peter Lombard. Pseudo-Peter's goal was to explain and clarify his master's work. Like Comestor and Herbert of Bosham, he wanted to make it accessible. That does not mean that he always agrees with Peter.[170] But commentary, for Pseudo-Peter, is not "a platform for ... his own personal views," but is geared toward "the clarification and reinforcement of the Lombard's own theology."[171]

165 "Only infrequently does this gloss speak of Lombard's actual teachings in the school room, though these few testimonies are most precious," Ibid., 466.

166 The text, "a libro sumpsit magister hanc auctoritatem dum Romae esset" is in Naples, Biblioteca nazionale, VIII C14, fol. 14, and Bamberg, Staatsbibliothek, Cod. Patr. 128, fol. 43. Ignatius C. Brady, "Peter Lombard: Canon of Notre Dame," *RTAM* 32 (1965): 277–295, at 292.

167 Pseudo-Peter's references to marginal notes are printed in Brady's edition: *Sententiae,* 1: 61–62, 1: 227. The note *cave* is on 1: 121, and the flying glosses ("glossa volatila in margine") on 1: 91, 107. References are there given to both the Naples and Bamberg manuscripts.

168 "Hanc solutionem Magister ita explicabat in disserendo, sed non ita aperta scripsit eam." Naples, Biblioteca nazionale, VIII C14, fol. 9, quoted in Brady, "Peter Manducator," 469.

169 See chapter four, above, 87–89.

170 Rosemann, *The Story of a Great Medieval Book*, 51, finds him "uneasy" with one of Peter's positions but offers no further examples.

171 Colish, "From the Sentence Collection to the Sentence Commentary and the *Summa*," 20–21.

There are two other distinct commentaries on book four of the *Sentences* that refer to Peter's oral teaching.[172] We will refer to the authors of these commentaries as student one and student two for convenience. Although these glosses are closely related to Pseudo-Peter's, they are distinct works.[173] Like him, they witnessed Peter making marginal notes. They were both present when Peter was discussing the sacrament of marriage and the distinction between the terms *sponsa* (spouse) and *coniunx* (marriage partner).[174] They noticed that "he placed a certain note in the margin of his book" to clarify his point.[175] Notably, this observation is not found in the Pseudo-Peter gloss.[176] The two students also refer to Peter's involvement in a debate on one of the questions covered in book four of the *Sentences*. In distinction twenty-two, as part of his discussion of the sacrament of penance, Peter inquires "whether sins once forgiven may return." He concludes, "both sides of the question are favoured by esteemed doctors. Therefore, not passing judgement on either side, I leave it to the studious reader to decide."[177] Student two, however, notes in his commentary that "although the master did not agree with either side here, in debate, however, he allowed that forgiven sins may return."[178]

172 Landgraf, "Problèmes relatifs aux premières gloses des Sentences," 144–145, uncovered the anonymous gloss on book 4, found in Bamberg, Staatsbibliothek, Cod. Patr. 128 (this is the same MS that contains the first book of the Pseudo-Peter gloss). The gloss on book 4 in Munich, Bayerische Staatsbibliothek, Clm 22288, was discovered by Heinrich Weisweiler, "Eine Neue frühe Glosse zum Vierten Buch der Sentenzen des Petrus Lombardus," in *Aus der Geisteswelt des Mittelalters: Studien und Texte*, ed. Albert Lang (Münster, 1935), 360–386.

173 Moore, *The Works of Peter of Poitiers*, 147. Colish, "The Pseudo-Peter of Poitiers Gloss," 1, views these commentaries as later versions of the Pseudo-Peter gloss, rather than distinct works. This approach is at variance with earlier scholarship, and the question will have to be further investigated.

174 *Sententiae* 4, dist. 27, ch. 9, ed. Brady, 2: 429. For the terms, see also Giulio Silano, "Introduction," in Peter Lombard, *The Sentences*, trans. Silano, 4: xlvii.

175 "Posuit tamen postea in margine libri sui quandam notam ubi sponsa potest intelligi pro coniuge," Munich, Bayerische Staatsbibliothek, Clm 22288, fol. 90v. Student one writes similarly: "posuit tamen m. (magister) P. (Petrus) in margine hanc notam: et predicto modo potest intelligi ut coiunx." Bamberg, Staatsbibliothek, Cod. Patr. 128., 19a, as quoted in *Sententiae*, ed. Brady, 2: 429.

176 *Sententiae*, ed. Brady, 2: 429.

177 "Utrique parti quaestionis probati favent doctores. Ideoque alicui parti non praejudicans, studioso lectori iudicium relinquo." *Sententiae* 4, dist. 22, ch. 1, ed. Brady, 2: 389.

178 "Licet magister neutri parti hic suum prebeat assensum, in disputacione tamen fatur redeant peccata dimissa." Brady, "Peter Manducator," 479. The text is from Munich, Bayerische Staatsbibliothek, Clm 22288.

Student one and Pseudo-Peter report the same information, and this suggests that the debate took place in Peter's classroom. Pseudo-Peter explains the oral position in more detail: "the master, however, in debate said that sins may return according to their guilt, not with respect to the actions returning or the exact same guilt, but a similar guilt."[179] These extracts again reveal that Peter discussed theology with a certain degree of freedom in his classroom, but was extremely careful in his written work.

We have considered these three distinct commentaries to be the work of three individuals. It is equally possible that more people were involved. William of Tyre's words imply that "cultivating" Peter's work was a collective effort. The possibility has already been raised that several people worked on each of the glosses.[180] It must also be made clear that Peter Comestor played a vital part in this enterprise. Pseudo-Peter makes clear on a number of occasions that he also studied with Comestor.[181] When Peter Lombard became bishop, some of his students (like Adam of Wales) had studied with him for long enough to attain the title of *magister*. But there were others who would not have considered their theological training to be complete. William of Tyre and John of Cornwall were both in this situation and enrolled with Maurice of Sully. It seems that Pseudo-Peter joined Peter Comestor's school, and this would have been a more sympathetic environment for Peter's students. Bishop Peter, one assumes, would have made arrangements for some of his students to do so.

The work of Comestor and the *chorus* was pioneering. They began a process which lasted throughout the Middle Ages. There was a continuing demand for copies of the *Sentences* and for abridged versions.[182] In the thirteenth and fourteenth centuries all the major theologians in Paris lectured on

179 "Magister tamen in disputatione dicebat peccata redire quantum ad reatum, non quoad actiones redire vel reatus illi singulares, sed reatus consimiles." Ibid. In this case Brady transcribed the text from Paris, Bibliothèque Mazarine, lat. 758.

180 Moore, *The Works of Peter of Poitiers,* 151; Weisweiler, " Eine Neue zum Vierten Buch der Sentenzen des Petrus Lombardus," 391.

181 Brady, "Peter Manducator," 466–469. He comments further, on 482, that Pseudo-Peter's gloss is "quite evidently itself in debt to [Peter Comestor]."

182 For abridged versions in the thirteenth century, see Franklin T. Harkins, "*Filiae Magistri*: Peter Lombard's *Sentences* and Medieval Theological Education 'On the Ground'," in *Mediaeval Commentaries on the Sentences of Peter Lombard,* ed. Rosemann, 3: 26–78.

the *Sentences* and produced commentaries, including Bonaventure, Thomas Aquinas, Duns Scotus, and William of Ockham. Those are only the most famous. The number of commentaries extends into the thousands.[183]

183 Friedrich Stegmüller, *Repertorium commentariorum in Sententias Petri Lombardi* (Würzburg, 1947).

CHAPTER EIGHT

Herbert of Bosham

Herbert of Bosham has long been remembered chiefly for the devoted service he gave to two more famous figures. Peter Lombard, his master in theology, influenced him deeply. He was also a close confidant of Thomas Becket. He was initially appointed as the bishop's theologian, and he remained at his side throughout the quarrels with Henry II. After Becket's death, Herbert found purpose in devoting himself to the two men who had influenced him most. For Becket, in the immediate, he continued to write letters to popes and prelates, arguing his case and demanding justice. As a more lasting memorial, he produced a large scale "life." For Peter Lombard, Herbert supervised lavish new editions of his master's commentaries on the Psalms and the Letters of Paul. These were designed to make the works as accessible as possible, through marginal notes, tables of contents, and illustrations. The overall purpose of the editions was to underline Peter's achievement and orthodoxy at a time when his reputation was under attack. More recently, however, Herbert's individual achievements have been receiving substantial attention.[1] Herbert was a prominent Hebraist, and his commentary on the Hebrew text of the Psalms, written toward the end of his life, owes much to rabbinical treatments.[2]

1 Beryl Smalley paints an unforgettable picture of him, principally in *The Becket Conflict and the Schools.* Drawing on scattered details and recollections in saints lives, commentaries, and letters, she shows his profound individuality, his sense of independence, and his self-doubt: Smalley, *Becket Conflict,* 59–86. See also Beryl Smalley, "A Commentary on the *Hebraica* by Herbert of Bosham," *RTAM* 18 (1951): 29–65. How far she surpasses earlier studies can be measured by comparing her chapter with the entry for Herbert in the *Catholic Encyclopedia,* which is of interest as a rare publication by F.F. "Sligger" Urquhart.

2 The earlier work of Lowe and Smalley on this subject has been substantially added to in recent years. See the following works by Deborah L. Goodwin: "Herbert of Bosham and the Horizons of Twelfth-Century Exegesis," *Traditio* 58 (2003): 133–173; "A Study of Herbert of Bosham's Psalms Commentary (c.1190)" (PhD diss.,

The older view of the *Life of Becket* as an overlong and meandering work has been reassessed and his *Liber melorum* has also received a full length treatment.[3]

Herbert's intellectual formation under Peter Lombard, however, has been pushed somewhat into the background. It has been stated that Herbert's "theological thinking" owes "very little" to Peter Lombard.[4] Herbert's own Psalms commentary is certainly radically different from his master's. Herbert chose to use the Hebrew text, and he restricted himself to the literal sense of the Psalms.[5] That, however, is only one of several works. Herbert completed it after he had edited his master's *Commentary on the Psalms*, which he may have considered the definitive treatment of the Vulgate text, given how much care he took over it. His theological training under Peter was in fact essential to the specialized skills that he brought to his employers, and it played as much a part as anything in shaping the character and structure of his other works.

Herbert studied with Peter Lombard as early as, if not earlier than, Peter Comestor. Smalley places his birth between 1115 and 1120,[6] and he first appears in a document from 1157.[7] By that time, he was in the service of Henry II and was a *magister*. Henry sent him on a diplomatic mission to the

University of Notre Dame, 2001); and "*Take Hold of the Robe of a Jew": Herbert of Bosham's Christian Hebraism* (Leiden, 2006). See also Eva de Visscher, *Reading the Rabbis: Christian Hebraism in the Works of Herbert of Bosham* (Leiden, 2014). The earlier works are Raphael Loewe, "Herbert of Bosham's Commentary on Jerome's Hebrew Psalter," *Biblica* 34 (1953): 44–77, 159–192, 275–298, and Smalley, "A Commentary on the *Hebraica*," 42–58.

3 C. Stephen Jaeger, *The Envy of Angels: Cathedral Schools and Social Ideas in Medieval Europe, 950–1200* (Philadelphia, 1994), 301–309; Jessica L. Weiss, "Herbert of Bosham's *Liber melorum*: Literature and Sacred Sciences in the Twelfth Century" (PhD diss., Harvard University, 2003).

4 Goodwin, "Herbert of Bosham and the Horizons of Twelfth-Century Exegesis," 171. See also how she introduces Herbert on 134: "a scholar and exegete closely associated with the circle of Thomas Becket and with the School of St Victor."

5 See the prologue printed by Smalley in "A Commentary on the *Hebraica*," 32. Smalley comments on 35 that "to restrict oneself to the literal sense, of the Psalter particularly, was a strange procedure. I know of no other such attempt in the twelfth century."

6 Smalley, *Becket Conflict*, 59. He is referred to as *senex* in a letter of 1173–1176 to him from William le Mire, abbot of St Denis. The letter forms the preface to Herbert's edition of Lombard's commentary on the Letters of Paul. See *Epistola Guillelmi Medici Abbatis ad Herbertum de Boseham*, in *History of the Vulgate in England*, ed. Hans H. Glunz (Cambridge, 1933), 347. Herbert's relationship with William is further discussed in Smalley, "A Commentary on the *Hebraica*," 39–40.

7 Smalley, *Becket Conflict*, 60.

court of Frederick Barbarossa. Herbert and his fellow negotiator were to bargain with Frederick over a relic, the arm of St James.[8] It was a delicate situation. The relic had been brought to England by the Empress Matilda thirty years before. Frederick wanted the relic back, but Henry was unwilling to take it away from its new home, Reading Abbey, where it "had begun to attract pilgrims."[9] He would hardly have sent an inexperienced newcomer on such a mission. That means Herbert must have already been in royal service for at least two or three years. He studied with Peter for long enough to gain the title of *magister*. Although the use of this title in Henry's letter could refer to his general arts qualification, we will see that Herbert set up a school of theology in the 1170s. He would therefore have enrolled in Lombard's school around 1145, making him one of Peter's early pupils, and remained for between eight and ten years. His training in the arts subjects, which was not necessarily at Paris, must then have taken place between around 1135 and 1145.

Herbert's years in Peter's school influenced him deeply. He recalled him fondly in later writings, describing him as "my master of pleasant memory, Peter, bishop of Paris."[10] In the preface to his edition of the *Commentary on the Psalms*, an almost filial loyalty comes across: "The intention of my weak abilities is not to attach any mark of ignorance or negligence to that great doctor, the man who first taught me in such things, or to obscure the splendour of such a light of the church with mean-spiritedness."[11] Herbert is keen to

8 "De manu beati Iacobi, super qua nos scripsistis, in ore magistri Herberti et Willelmi clerici nostri verbum prosuimus." Henry's letter to Frederick, which the messengers carried, is printed in *Gesta Frederici I imperatoris* (MGH SS 46: 171–172). The incident is discussed in detail in Karl Leyser, "Frederick Barbarossa, Henry II and the Hand of St James," *The English Historical Review* 90 (1975): 481–506.

9 Smalley, *Becket Conflict*, 60. See also Leyser's discussion of the political importance of Reading Abbey, "Frederick Barbarossa, Henry II and the Hand of St James," 497–499.

10 "occasione magistri mei suavis recordationis Petri Parisiensis episcopi." Herbert of Bosham, *Epistola ad Henricum comitem Tricensem* (PL 190: 1416–1422, at 1418). Although a recipient or title is not listed in Migne's edition, Smalley brings up manuscript evidence to show that it was addressed to Henry, count of Champagne: "A Commentary on the *Hebraica*," 37.

11 "Nec igitur parvitatis meae intentio est tanto doctori, et qui me precipue in hac doctrina instituit, ullam ignorancie vel negligencie inuere notam seu tanti luminis ecclesie vel in modico obscurare splendorem." Herbert of Bosham, *Praefatio*, in *History of the Vulgate in England*, ed. Glunz, 342–346, at 343.

point out how much he owes "to the author of that work, and to the work of that author."[12] When Herbert speaks of how much he owes to Peter Lombard, he is not just being pious. His time in the schools was crucial for his later employment. Being a *magister* was a requirement for his first job, a messenger/diplomat for the royal court. He seems not to have had any interest in teaching, at least at that time. The kind of diplomatic missions that Herbert was sent on required somebody with an intellectual training, somebody who could say the right thing in the right way. Certainly, Herbert's initial training in rhetoric was essential, but his skills in debate would have been sharpened in Peter Lombard's theology school.

His theological training was even more important for his next position. In 1162, he joined the household of the new archbishop of Canterbury, Thomas Becket.[13] His position was that of secretary, but he was also to be a kind of private tutor. He was to aid Becket "in the study of the holy page."[14] De Hamel's phrase, "theological consultant," describes the position perfectly.[15] Becket, as archbishop, had a recognized authority. Herbert was his advisor, and we can imagine Becket turning to him whenever he needed answers on subjects like the sacraments, the principal virtues, or (especially if he was preparing a sermon) the interpretation of a particular scriptural passage. Herbert, as a graduate of Peter Lombard's school, was well versed in the positions of the fathers and in those of more recent authorities.

Herbert followed Becket into exile in December 1164.[16] They met Pope Alexander III at Sens, where he had been residing after the disputed election of 1159. The pope supported Becket's actions and refused to accept his resignation.[17] Their appearance at the papal court coincided with a debate over an issue that was becoming controversial. The annals of Reichersberg claim that on Christmas Eve of that year, the pope, along with assembled scholars and men of letters, "condemned and forbade in every way, all undisciplined arguments and questions in theology" and ordered Maurice of Sully, bishop

12 "quantam habeam ad auctorem operis gratiam, et ad opus auctoris." Ibid., 344.
13 Smalley, *Becket Conflict*, 61.
14 Ibid.
15 Christopher de Hamel, *Glossed Books of the Bible and the Origins of the Paris Booktrade* (Woodbridge, 1984), 42.
16 See Smalley, *Becket Conflict*, 63, and Frank Barlow, *Thomas Becket* (Berkeley, 1986), 117–125.
17 Barlow, *Thomas Becket*, 121–123.

of Paris, to enforce this throughout France.[18] The annals continue: "Opinions concerning the glory of man assumed in God and born in God were there openly approved and strengthened by the pope."[19] Alexander did not name Peter Lombard, and the annals are our only source for this event, but allegations about his teaching on Christ's human nature were already in the air.

It is now necessary to introduce the debates over Peter Lombard's Christological teachings.[20] We have seen that despite his involvement in the attempt to condemn Gilbert of Poitiers, there were no serious criticisms made of his work during his lifetime.[21] This began to change after his death. Gerhoh of Reichersberg, a veteran of theological debate, took serious issue with Peter in the 1160s.[22] While a number of critics would later claim that Peter down-

18 "Ipso anno ... Alexander Papa convocatis in unum scholasticis et quibusque litteratis in ipsa vigilia nativitatis Domini ... condemnavit et omnino interdixit omnes tropos et indisciplinatas questiones in theologia, Parisiensique episcopo sub obedientia praecepit, ut per totam Franciam eas compesceret." *Annales Reicherspergenses*, ed. Wilhelm Wattenbach (MGH SS 17: 443–476, at 471).

19 "Sententia autem de gloria hominis in Deum assumpti et in Deum nati approbata est ibi coram papa ac roborata." Ibid.

20 Excellent and comprehensive treatments are Joseph de Ghellinck, *Le mouvement théologique au XIIe siècle*, 2nd ed. (Bruges, 1948), 250–277; Jean Châtillon, "Latran III et l'enseignement christologique de Pierre Lombard," in *Le Troisième Concile de Latran (1179): Sa place dans l'histoire*, ed. Jean Longère. (Paris, 1982), 75–90; Lauge-Olaf Nielsen, *Theology and Philosophy in the Twelfth Century: A Study of Gilbert Porretas Thinking and the Theological Expositions of the Doctrine of the Incarnation During the Period 1130–1180* (Leiden, 1982), 243–362; Colish, *Peter Lombard*, 398–417 (background), 418–427 (Peter Lombard's position), 428–438 (the opposition); Marcia Colish, "Christological Nihilianism in the Second Half of the Twelfth Century," *RTAM* 63 (1996): 146–155; Pietro B. Rossi, "*Contra Lombardum*: Reazioni alla Cristologia di Pietro Lombardo," in *Pietro Lombardo: Atti del XLIII Convegno storico internazionale* (Spoleto, 2007), 123–191; Clare Monagle, "Christological Nihilism in the Twelfth Century: The Contested Reception of Peter Lombard's *Sententiae*" (PhD diss., Johns Hopkins University, 2007); and Clare Monagle, *Orthodoxy and Controversy in Twelfth-Century Religious Discourse: Peter Lombards Sentences and the Development of Theology* (Turnhout, 2013), 73–137. As mentioned in chapter five, these works often tend to focus on the opposition not how it was surmounted.

21 See chapter four, above, 89–90.

22 He had previously attacked positions of Abelard, Gilbert of Poitiers, their pupils, his bishop Eberhard, and even Bernard of Clairvaux. See Nikolaus M. Häring, "Introduction," in *Gerhoh of Reichersberg: Letter to Pope Hadrian about the Novelties of the Day* (Toronto, 1974), 11–14. On Gerhoh's critiques of Peter Lombard, see Châtillon, "Latran III et l'enseignement christologique de Pierre Lombard," 79–80, especially, 79 n18; Colish, *Peter Lombard*, 428–429; and Monagle, *Orthodoxy and Con-*

played (or negated) Christ's humanity, Gerhoh believed that he ignored his divinity. He based this on Peter's discussion of what devotion was appropriate for Christ in the *Commentary on the Psalms*. The two technical terms, *latria* (worship) and *dulia* (veneration), are probably most familiar regarding the distinction whereby saints are venerated but not worshipped as God is. Gerhoh believed that Christ deserved both veneration and worship. Peter Lombard, he claimed, only advocated veneration. He urged in one of his works that the "perverse doctrine" of Peter Lombard on this issue should be condemned,[23] and he accused Peter, along with "the scholastics and schoolmen," of imitating the old Nestorian heresy.[24] He also made the point in letters to the pope[25] and his bishop, Eberhard of Bamberg.[26] But Gerhoh had failed to take account of Peter's positions on the subject in the *Sentences*,[27] and Eberhard pointed this out to Gerhoh when he replied to his letter.[28] Although Gerhoh's criticisms were largely ignored, they do show that in the 1160s, Peter Lombard's work was now considered fair game for opponents. This was also happening in the schools of Paris. John of Cornwall, whom we will hear more of in the next chapter, claimed that Maurice of Sully and Robert of Melun both openly criticized Peter's Christological positions in their classrooms.[29]

---

troversy in Twelfth-Century Religious Discourse, 92–100. The standard works on Gerhoh are Damien Van Den Eynde, *L'oeuvre littéraire de Géroch de Reichersberg* (Rome, 1957), and Peter Classen, *Gerhoch von Reichersberg: eine Biographie* (Wiesbaden, 1960).

23 "Haec dicens ille magister Petrus, egregius multarum et diversarum ecclesiasticarum et scholasticarum tam antiquarum, quam et novarum sententiarum collector, non suam hanc sententiam esse indicat, sed aliorum de Nestorii faece aliquid habentiam, Cujus quidem perversa doctrina condemnata est." Gerhoh of Reichersberg, *Liber de Gloria et Honore Filii Hominis* (PL 194: 1143).

24 "Hoc testimonium ejus (sancti Hieronymi) nemo accepit inter scholasticos et scholares, Paulum samosatenum, Photinum, Nestorium simulque Bonosum haeresiarchas imitantes in doctrina sua." Ibid., 1141.

25 PL 193: 565

26 Ibid., 547–548. He also made the point in another work: Gerhoh of Reichersberg, *Utrum Christus homo sit Filius Dei, Opera Inedita*, ed. Damien Van den Eynde (Rome: 1955–1956), 1: 284.

27 Colish, *Peter Lombard*, 428–429.

28 PL 193: 562. Nielsen, *Theology and Philosophy in the Twelfth Century*, 278, points out that by this time Eberhard "was thoroughly tired of Gerhoh's christological conflicts, in which he had been involved from time to time since 1147."

29 "Multis eorum lectionibus et disputationibus interfui, in quibus et de homine assumpto et de aliis quibusdam magistri Petri Lumbardi doctrinam falsitatis arguebant, ne dicam erroris." Nikolaus M. Häring, "The *Eulogium ad Alexandrum Papam Tertium* of John of Cornwall," *Mediaeval Studies* 13 (1951): 268.

The most damaging allegation made was not at first directed at Peter Lombard, at least not publicly. This was what has been termed Christological nihilism. Opponents of the doctrine summarized it as *Christus secundum quod homo non est aliquid*, "Christ, insofar as he is a man, is not something." Achard, a theology master at St Victor, described those who taught this position as "enemies of the truth" and "the blind leading the blind."[30] This was in a sermon written in the first half of the 1150s, before Achard succeeded Gilduin as abbot in 1155.[31] An anonymous author wrote a work to refute the position in the 1160s, the *Objectiones contra eos qui dicunt quod Christus non est aliquid secundum quod est homo*.[32] John of Cornwall claimed that it was condemned by the pope at the 1163 council of Tours, although no other source mentions this.[33] We have seen that the *Annals of Reichersberg* report a papal condemnation in 1164, which was directed against theologians straying from orthodoxy. While the pope did not specify nihilism on this occasion, it is clear from the annals that he was referring to Christological questions.[34] But none of these sources associated the position with Peter Lombard. That did not happen until 1170, when the pope did so.[35] Nevertheless, even before this he may well have been associated with it in verbal exchanges.

30 "Sunt adhuc quidam inimici veritatis qui dicunt quod quando Verbum factum est homo, non est factum aliquid, nec in eo quo est homo est aliquid quod nos sumus ... ceci, duces cecorum." Achard de Saint Victor, *Sermons inédits*, ed. Jean Châtillon (Paris, 1970), 61–62. Châtillon, ibid., 62 n55, raises the possibility that Peter Lombard is the target of this statement. A translation of this work can be found in Hugh Feiss, *Achard of St Victor: Works* (Kalamazoo, 2001), 133.

31 Jean Châtillon, *Théologie, spiritualié, et métaphysique dans l'oeuvre oratoire d'Achard de Saint-Victor: Études d'histoire doctrinale précédées d'un essai sur la vie et l'oeuvre d'Achard* (Paris, 1969), 141–142. See also 202–206.

32 This is the title of the work, as Häring points out in his edition, in surviving manuscripts, but it has more recently been known by the title *Apologia de Verbo Incarnato*. The author cannot be identified, and Häring believes it dates from the early 1160s. Nikolaus M. Häring, "The So-Called *Apologia de Verbo Incarnato*," *Franciscan Studies* 16 (1956): 102–143.

33 Häring, "The *Eulogium ad Alexandrum Papam Tertium* of John of Cornwall," 257. See also Châtillon, "Latran III et l'enseignement Christologique de Pierre Lombard," 80, and Robert Somerville, *Pope Alexander III and the Council of Tours (1163): A Study of Ecclesiastical Politics and Institutions in the Twelfth Century* (Berkeley, 1977), 61.

34 "Sententia autem de gloria hominis in Deum assumpti et in Deum nati approbata est ibi coram papa ac roborata." *Annales Reicherspergenses*, ed. Wattenbach (MGH SS 17: 471).

35 Alexander III, *Epistola ad Willelmum Senonensis archiepiscopum* (PL 200: 685). See below, 210.

Why did it happen? It is not in the *Sentences*. Peter examines the nihilist position thoroughly in book three. Distinction ten begins, "It is also usual for some to ask whether Christ, according to his being a man, is a person, or even is anything."[36] As we have seen, posing questions, or dealing with questions posed in the past, is central to what the *Sentences* is all about. In this case, Peter first rehearses the arguments, making use of Boethius's definition of "person":

> There are arguments on each side of the question. That he is a person, they argue with the following reasons: If he is anything according to his being man, then he is either a person, or a substance or something else, so he is either a person or a substance. But if he is a substance, then he is either a rational one or an irrational one. But, if according to his being man, he is a rational substance, then he is a person, because this is the definition of a person: "A rational substance of individual nature." And so, if he is anything according to his being man, then he is a person according to his being man. But conversely, if according to his being man, he is a person, then either he is the third person of the Trinity or some other person; but he is not some other person; and so he is the third person in the Trinity. But if, according to his being man, he is the third person in the Trinity, then he is God.[37]

Peter finds problems with these arguments, calling them "unsuitable conclusions," and he believes that they do not fully grasp the sense of the term *secundum*, "insofar as," "according to."[38]

Why then would Peter Lombard be accused of taking a position which he refutes? Why would the statement "Christ, insofar as he is a man, is not something" be attached to his name when it is not embraced in his work? It is possible that some misread the *Sentences* or misunderstood its method by mistaking the rehearsing of the arguments of others for Peter's own position. We should remember that this kind of theological work was only thirty years old at this point, so those who had not gone to theology schools might have had difficulty with it, especially if they had read or heard about sections out of context. Rose-

36 "Solet etiam a quibusdam inquiri utrum Christus secundum quod homo, sit persona vel etiam sit aliquid." *Sententiae* 3, dist. 10, ed. Brady, 2: 72

37 *Sententiae* 3, dist. 10, ch. 2, ed. Brady, 2: 72; Peter Lombard, *The Sentences*, trans. Giulio Silano (Toronto, 2007–2010), 3: 41

38 *Sententiae* 3, dist. 10, ch. 3, ed. Brady, 2: 72; *The Sentences*, trans. Silano, 3: 41

mann points to another area that might lead to misunderstanding. While Peter refutes arguments in this section, he does not show "a viable alternative to christological nihilianism ... we do not learn what Christ could be positively."[39]

Word of mouth is also a strong possibility. We have seen in the previous chapter that Peter often went into more detail on doctrinal topics in his classroom, or when talking to former students. Reports of his oral teaching would not always be accurate, especially since Peter does not seem to have had an official notetaker. Charging a student with compiling *reportationes* of lectures was not yet standard practice for masters.[40] However, the testimony of Peter Comestor, preserved in *quaestiones*, is worth serious attention. As we have seen, Comestor referred to an occasion when Peter spoke to "safe ears." These were not students in his school but former students, those who had completed the course with him.[41] That would presumably mean Comestor and a few others who were still in Paris. With this group, Peter engaged in further discussion about the implications of the neuter noun *aliquid* – "something," "anything": "For he said that although nouns of the neutral gender may be taken as designating a nature, in the majority of cases therefore they designate a person."[42] To use *aliquid* in relation to Christ then depended on how the noun was taken: "He therefore conceded that 'Christ, insofar as he is a man is something' that is some other nature. But he denied it because 'something' seems to be taken here to designate a person. For Christ, insofar as he is man, is not some other person."[43]

This was Peter talking among trusted fellow theologians. Such a discussion of the sense of the Latin word *aliquid* may seem today almost arcane or excessively semantic, and hardly something requiring a safe environment. But

39 Rosemann, *Peter Lombard,* 132. See also Colish, *Peter Lombard,* 423–424.

40 See chapter two, above, 43.

41 "Tutis auribus loquebatur, id est illis quod instruxerat." Brady, "Peter Manducator," 473.

42 "Dicebat enim, quia quamvis nomina neutri generis soleant accipi in designatione nature, plerumque tamen accipuntur in designatione persone." Ibid. Rosemann also provides a translation and discussion of this passage in *Peter Lombard,* 133.

43 "Ideo quoque concedebat: 'Christus in quantum est homo est aliquid,' id est alicuius nature. Negabat tamen, quia 'aliquid' ibi videtur accipi in designatione persone. Christus enim non, in quantum est homo est aliqua persona." Brady, "Peter Manducator," 473. Rosemann translates "'aliqua persona"' in the last line as "a person," but the use of *aliqua* seems to imply that the *persona* here is not the third person of the Trinity, which picks up Peter's discussions of the issue in the *Sentences.* Rosemann deals with this issue in his next paragraph anyway.

it is important to remember that this was not just a matter of theological vocabulary in one language as opposed to others. At this time, in the West, Latin and Greek were the only languages considered capable of expressing theological concepts with clarity. Also, focusing on the meanings of words was a characteristic method of theologians like Peter.[44] It was therefore critical that he would be understood correctly. Comestor's report of this occasion shows that Peter was unable to come up with a firm solution, so he did not express a position in the *Sentences*. But, after his death, when Comestor and perhaps others mentioned this while teaching the *Sentences*, rumours could easily ensue. We have to assume, from the virulence of some of the critics,[45] that Peter Lombard had enemies, and to attach a few words to his name, without any context, was an easy way of criticizing him after his death. This was dangerous to his reputation, and his students grasped this.

There has also been some discussion of whether Peter had taught what was known as the *habitus* theory, the idea that Christ's humanity was like a suit of clothes, which could be taken on and off.[46] In the *Sentences*, Peter does not embrace the *habitus* position. He details it, along with the other main schools of thought on the incarnation, but finds problems with it.[47] John of Cornwall, in his treatment of nihilism, states that Peter accepted the *habitus* theory as an opinion from other masters. He argues that the *habitus* position led to nihilism.[48] This is not repeated by anyone else. At the time, the allegation made more frequently against Peter was nihilism alone. John's statement has, however, led to a debate in modern scholarship, which involves evidence from Peter's *Commentary on the Letters of Paul* and some of the early abridgements of the *Sentences* by non-students.[49]

44 Monagle, *Orthodoxy and Controversy in Twelfth-Century Religious Discourse*, xv, writes illuminatingly of this approach in the schools and how it often led to criticism.

45 See the discussion of Walter of St Victor in chapter nine, below, 246–250, who even claimed that Peter obtained the bishopric of Paris through simony.

46 For this position, see Colish, *Peter Lombard*, 401–403, 426, and Nielsen, *Theology and Philosophy in the Twelfth Century*, 323–340.

47 Peter Lombard, *Sententiae* 3, dist. 1–10, ed. Brady, 2: 24–83. See also Colish, *Peter Lombard*, 418–427, and Rosemann, *Peter Lombard*, 118–133.

48 Häring, "The *Eulogium ad Alexandrum Papam Tertium* of John of Cornwall," 264–265.

49 See Colish, *Peter Lombard*, 401–403, 426; Colish, "Christological Nihilianism in the Second Half of the Twelfth Century," 148; David Luscombe, *The School of Peter Abelard: The Influence of Abelard's Thought in the Early Scholastic Period* (Cambridge, 1969), 272–273; and Nielsen, *Theology and Philosophy in the Twelfth Century*, 323–340.

There was clearly a growing climate of criticism of Peter Lombard's work in the 1160s, and Herbert of Bosham found himself amid such debates in Sens that Christmas (1164). A more pressing matter was that Becket's household needed somewhere to live in exile, and arrangements were made for them at the Cistercian abbey of Pontigny. The abbey had, by Herbert's own account, an excellent library of the fathers, and it also had a scriptorium.[50] Here Herbert seems to have first planned a new edition of his master's *Commentary on the Psalms*.[51] It is usually claimed that Becket ordered him to do so,[52] but does Herbert state this directly? In the preface to the edition he mentions the library at Pontigny and his study of the Psalms there. He also comforts himself against those criticizing the work by remembering that Becket wished it to be done.[53] So he situates at least the idea for the work in Pontigny. But what was accomplished there?

It used to be thought that much of the work on the commentary had been done at Pontigny. Art historians, noting the elegant lettering and frequent use of illustration, termed it a deluxe manuscript.[54] Because the monks at

50 Herbert of Bosham, *Praefatio*, ed. Glunz, 342: "Pontiniaci scilicet, ubi locuples scripturarum armarium." For the library at Pontigny, see Monique Peyrafort-Huin, *La bibliothèque médiévale de l'abbaye de Pontigny (XIIe–XIXe siècles): Histoire, inventaires anciens, manuscrits* (Paris, 2001). Becket's exile there is dealt with on 108–110. Eva de Visscher also shows how the contents of the library would have allowed Herbert to begin preliminary work on the commentary: de Visscher, *Reading the Rabbis: Christian Hebraism in the Works of Herbert of Bosham*, 18–19.

51 Smalley, *Becket Conflict*, 82.

52 Ibid., 82. Also, Barlow, *Thomas Becket*, 129, and Christopher de Hamel, "A Contemporary Miniature of Thomas Becket," in *Intellectual Life in the Middle Ages: Essays Presented to Margaret Gibson*, ed. Lesley Smith and Benedicta Ward (London, 1992), 179–184. De Hamel provides the most detail on Becket's role in encouraging the work, although he rejects the idea of it being done at Pontigny.

53 "Quod si hydra multorum capitum necdum sibilare cessaverit, preter ea que iam diximus, contra ipsius venenatos aculeos duplex mihi consolationis antidotum est, quod christus domini, summus sacerdos christi, neomartyr noster sanctus thomas, ita fieri voluit." Herbert of Bosham, *Praefatio*, ed. Glunz, 344. Herbert also mentions studying the Psalms with Becket at Pontigny in his *Life of Becket*. Herbert of Bosham, *Vita Sancti Thomae archiepiscopi et martyris* 1, ed. James C. Robertson in *Materials for the History of Thomas Becket, Archbishop of Canterbury* (London, 1875–1885), 3: 155–534, at 358, 379.

54 Thomas R. Boase, *English Art, 1100–1216* (Oxford, 1953), 185–218; Charles R. Dodwell, *The Canterbury School of Illumination* (Cambridge, 1954), 105–109. See also, Smalley, *Becket Conflict*, 82–83.

Pontigny excelled in the production of illuminated manuscripts, it was an easy step to claim that the commentary had been produced there. However, Christopher de Hamel, in comparing it with other manuscripts known to be produced at Pontigny, shows that there are significant differences between the two styles.[55] For him the manuscript is probably the work of "professional illuminators" in Paris.[56] This makes sense in the context of Becket's stay. While the Cistercians were certainly happy to provide the exiles with food and shelter, putting the resources of the scriptorium at their disposal would have required a change in routine at the house.

There was another reason for the idea to take shape, and that was in response to external factors. After being at Sens, Herbert would have been aware of the allegations against his master. By editing one of his works, he could help shield him from attacks. Although a considerable amount has been written about Herbert's edition, the connection has rarely been made between it and the growing criticisms of Peter Lombard.[57] While the exiles were at Pontigny, however, matters were not as urgent as they would become. It is clear from the final version that Herbert knew the text extremely well, and his editions represent an attempt to make it as accessible and manageable as he could. This was partly born from the experience of using the text with Becket. Herbert's work on the commentary at Pontigny must then have been restricted to checking the references in the library.

Herbert and Becket stayed at the abbey for two years. In retaliation for their residence there, Henry II threatened the Cistercians in his own domain. As a result, the exiles were obliged to leave.[58] They spent the remainder of the 1160s at various locations, such as the monastery of Ste Colombe, and Paris. Their story is well known: apparent reconciliation followed by cold-blooded murder. Becket's death, on 27 December 1170, "knocked the bottom

55 De Hamel, *Glossed Books of the Bible,* ch. 4: "The so-called Pontigny School of Illumination," 45–54.

56 Ibid., 53–54.

57 Glunz makes the suggestion, but his characterization of the Christological debate as "a dispute between the rigorous ecclesiastical party and that of the philosophers" is now very out of date. *History of the Vulgate in England,* 223. More recently Goodwin situates the edition "in the period when Lombard's reputation was under attack." Goodwin, "A Study of Herbert of Bosham's Psalms Commentary," 44. There is a good overview of the controversy and Herbert's place in it on 40–46.

58 Barlow, *Thomas Becket,* 157.

out of Herbert's world."[59] He sought refuge in working on the commentary, which must have brought him back to less contentious days of intellectual debate and high pursuits. There was also another, more pressing reason for working on it. Six months before Becket's murder, Alexander III had been persuaded to take a stand on the Christology issue. He wrote to William of the White Hands, now archbishop of Sens, on 28 May 1170, and condemned Peter Lombard by name:

> When you had been in my presence, I asked that you, together with your Parisian suffragans, should aim at the annulment of the vicious doctrine of Peter Lombard, at one time bishop of Paris, that Christ, in so far as he is a man, is not something, and that you should accomplish this efficiently. Now I command by apostolic letter, just as I directed when you had been in my presence, that you assemble your Parisian suffragans, and that, along with other religious men, you try to erase the aforesaid doctrine completely; and that you direct that this is to be taught by masters and by scholars engaged in the study of theology: that Christ, just as he was perfect God, was also perfect man, and a true man consisting of soul and body.[60]

Alexander had been residing in and around Rome since the schism ended in 1165, and he wrote from Veroli. The tone of this letter is intriguing. The pope had met William in person and asked him to do something about this issue. William had failed to do so. Alexander followed up the 28 May letter with a similar one five days later to the archbishops of Bourges, Rouen, Tours, and Rheims. In that letter he does not actually name Peter Lombard, but the spec-

59 Smalley, *Becket Conflict*, 70.

60 "Cum in nostra olim esses praesentia constitutus, tibi viva voce injunximus ut, suffraganeis tuis Parisiis tibi ascitis, abrogationem pravae doctrinae Petri quondam Parisiensis episcopi, qua dicitur quod Christus, secundum quod est homo, non est aliquid, omnino intenderes, et efficacem operam adhiberes. Inde siquidem est quod fraternitati tuae per apostolica scripta mandamus, quatenus, quod tibi, cum praesens esses, praecepimus, suffraganeos tuos Parisios convoces, et una cum illis et aliis viris religiosis et prudentibus, praescriptam doctrinam studeas penitus abrogare; et a magistris et scholaribus ibidem in theologia studentibus, Christum, sicut perfectum Deum, sic et perfectum hominem, ac verum hominem ex anima et corpore consistentem, praecipias edoceri." Alexander III, *Epistola ad Willelmum Senonensi archiepiscopum* (PL 200: 685).

ified doctrine is the same.[61] Paris was clearly his main worry. He was especially concerned about masters teaching Christological nihilism and citing the teaching of Peter Lombard as their source. To what extent this was actually happening is difficult to say. John of Cornwall and the author of the *Objectiones* were adamant that nihilism was being taught. The pope was at something of a distance from things, and it is also possible that there were elements in the curia that were hostile to Peter Lombard.

William of the White Hands had to perform a delicate balancing act. He was a seasoned politician, but how much power did he have over the schools? His close association with Peter Comestor, the chancellor of the schools, is relevant.[62] Comestor had authority over masters in Paris, and had been trying to safeguard Peter's reputation. The pope, according to his letter, was apparently calling for a large-scale public denunciation of Peter Lombard's doctrine in Paris, presided over by William and his bishops, with masters and students looking on. This would have the potential for disaster. An event like that could even turn violent, and William would have wanted to avoid the kind of contentious situations that had developed in the 1140s, over Abelard especially.[63] Peter would certainly have had some defenders. A number of his students were in Paris at this point, including Comestor, Herbert, and Adam of Wales, and several former colleagues were still canons of Notre Dame.[64] Archbishop William needed something to show the pope and other luminaries that would reinforce the Lombard's orthodoxy. This is where Herbert's edition of the *Commentary on the Psalms* becomes relevant.

Herbert dedicated the finished version to William. Because it is addressed to him as archbishop of Sens, and remembers Becket as a "martyr," it can easily be dated between 1171 and 1176. What role had William played in the production of the work? The dedication alone does not prove that he com-

61 Alexander III, *Epistola ad venerabilis fratris Bituricensi, Remensi, Turonensi, Rothomagensi archiepiscopis et eorum suffraganeis* (PL 200: 684–685). On the two letters, see also Châtillon, "Latran III et l'enseignement christologique de Pierre Lombard," 82.

62 For this, see chapter seven, above, 170–171.

63 Constant Mews, "The Council of Sens (1141): Abelard, Bernard and the Fear of Social Upheaval," *Speculum* 77 (2002), 342–382, discusses how "social tensions within urban communities" could interact with the reception of the work of theologians.

64 These included Albert the Cantor, the archdeacons Guermund, Gerard, and Simon of Poissy, the priests Walter and Robert, and the deacons Simon and Hilduin of St Denis. *Cartulaire*, ed. de Lasteyrie, no. 467, p. 394, no. 521, p. 430.

missioned it, since eminent men received dedications frequently, often more in hope than anything else.[65] However, as we have seen, the manuscript was produced by the "professional illuminators of Paris."[66] Herbert could not have afforded to pay them. He spent the 1170s trying to find work (and purpose) in the aftermath of the martyrdom. His property in England remained confiscated.[67] William seems to be the strongest candidate for meeting this expense. We know that Herbert worked for him in various capacities at that time.[68] In the prefaces, Herbert clearly anticipates that William's secretaries will have the work copied.[69] Moreover, there is evidence that Herbert was living in Paris at that time.[70]

Herbert's completed edition of Peter's *Commentary on the Psalms* is the most striking and tangible monument to the relationship between Peter and his students.[71] In the case of the other students, we must rely on glowing recol-

65 John R. Williams, "William of the White Hands and Men of Letters," in *Anniversary Essays in Medieval History by Students of Charles Homer Haskins*, ed. Charles H. Taylor and John L. LaMonte (Boston, 1929), 365–389, details some of the dedications, while John F. Benton, "The Court of Champagne as a Literary Centre," *Speculum* 36 (1961): 551–591, looks at dedications to other members of the family of Champagne.

66 De Hamel, *Glossed Books of the Bible*, 53–54. In his later article "A Contemporary Miniature of Thomas Becket," 184, de Hamel downplays the role of William in favour of Becket. His idea that the preface is general, and, other than the title, "not specifically for William," is contradicted by the fact that Herbert specifically mentions how long he has known William. Herbert of Bosham, *Praefatio*, ed. Glunz, 342. See chapter seven, above, 170.

67 Smalley, *Becket Conflict*, 70–74.

68 Ibid., 70–71.

69 Herbert of Bosham, *Praefatio*, ed. Glunz, 346.

70 He acted as an assessor in a dispute: *Cartulaire*, ed. de Lasteyrie, no. 519, p. 429; Smalley, *Becket Conflict*, 71.

71 Volume 1 of Herbert's edition is now housed in the library of Trinity College, Cambridge, as MS B.5.4, and Volume 2 in the Bodleian library, Oxford, as MS Auct. E. inf. 6. A detailed description of B.5.4 can be found in Montague Rhodes James, *The Western Manuscripts in the Library of Trinity College Cambridge: A Descriptive Catalogue* (Cambridge, 1990–1994), 1: 188–194. Walter Cahn, *Romanesque Manuscripts: The Twelfth Century* (London, 1996), 2: 107–109, provides an excellent description of both volumes, including the locations of each illustration and psalm. For sample pages, which show clearly the marginal referencing of authorities and the innovative page layout, see, for B.5.4, *The Cambridge Illuminations: Ten Centuries of Book Production in the Medieval* West, ed. Paul Binski and Stella Panayotova (London, 2005), 92–94; De Hamel, *Glossed Books of the Bible*, pl. 12; Pamela R. Robinson, *Catalogue*

lections of a sentence or two, or trace Peter's influence in their works. In this case, Herbert's regard for his master is visible on every page. Herbert was not the scribe or the illuminator of the edition but the person who directed and supervised their work. This entailed three main areas: filling out the references to authorities, providing a clear organizational framework, and illustration. These three areas are not exclusive, and work toward the same goal. Herbert wanted to underline Peter's achievement by making his work accessible and available.

First, it was necessary to note all the authorities. As we have seen in chapter two, Peter had started the commentary as a study aid.[72] He only lectured on it in the schools just before being elected to the bishopric of Paris. Hence, he left the commentary unfinished and references to authorities are not always mentioned. This much we know from Herbert's own preface to his edition.[73] Aware of these deficiencies, Herbert was at pains to point out that his master should not be blamed for anything in the text:

> Nothing, however, should be said against the judgement of the famous doctor who glossed these books, and who was my principal teacher in this subject … . If he left something in his works that was not quite polished to the nail, he is not to be blamed for it but completely cleared. For

of Dated and Datable Manuscripts, c.737–1600 in Cambridge Libraries (Cambridge, 1988), 2: pl. 84; and C. Michael Kaufmann, "Manuscripts," in *English Romanesque Art, 1066–1200*, ed. George Zarnecki et al. (London, 1984), pl. 69, 124. For Auct. E. inf. 6, see Lesley Smith, *Masters of the Sacred Page: Manuscripts of Theology in the Latin West to 1274* (Notre Dame, 2001), 45–48; Christopher de Hamel, "Manuscripts of Herbert of Bosham," in *Manuscripts at Oxford*, ed. Albina C. de la Mare and B.C. Barker-Benfield (Oxford, 1980), 38; Andrew G. Watson, *Catalogue of Dated and Datable Manuscripts, c.435–1600, in Oxford Libraries* II (Oxford, 1984), pl. 78; and Mary Carruthers, *The Book of Memory: A Study of Memory in Medieval Culture* (Cambridge, 1990), fig. 5 (between 220 and 221). For isolated reproductions of some of the illuminated figures, see Stella Panayotova, "Tutorial in Images for Thomas Becket," in *The Cambridge Illuminations: The Conference Papers*, ed. Stella Panayotova (London, 2007), 77–86; Cahn, *Romanesque Manuscripts*, 1: pl. 211–214; Otto Pächt and Jonathan J.G. Alexander, *Illuminated Manuscripts in the Bodleian Library Oxford 3: British, Irish and Icelandic Schools* (Oxford, 1973), pl. 20, fig. 201a–c; Boase, *English Art*, pl. 67c; and de Hamel, "A Contemporary Miniature of Thomas Becket," 182. An excellent selection of images from MS Auct. inf. 6 (both detailed figures and full pages) is available (at time of writing) at the online Bodleian library's collection of digitized medieval manuscript images: http://bodley30.bodley.ox.ac.uk:8180/luna.

72 See chapter two, above, 36–37.

73 Herbert of Bosham, *Praefatio*, ed. Glunz, 343.

when he was writing these works, just as I learned from talking to him, it never entered his mind that they might be read publicly in the schools.[74]

Herbert also worked on making the structure and material of the commentary as clear as possible. Peter, in common with his predecessors, viewed the Psalms as falling into particular subject groups.[75] The penitential psalms would be a well-known example. They, like the moral psalms and psalms of lamentation, have an immediately apparent subject, but they do not appear in sequence. Theologians like Peter prepared commentaries and used them in their teaching partly so the Psalms could be understood in this sense. In his edition, Herbert ensured that it would be easy for the reader to find psalms by subject. To take an example, in Psalm 18, Peter states that it is "the first psalm that deals with the first advent of Christ"[76] (i.e., the nativity). Herbert here provides a list of other psalms on the same subject in the margin.[77] This is a hallmark of the edition, and he usually also provides a note written directly above the main text drawing attention to the marginal list. Additionally, Herbert's tables of contents in the edition include not just the psalm numbers and opening verses, but also the subjects where applicable.[78] This is a good example of Herbert's method. He did not change his master's text, but instead made it more accessible. In doing this, he was following his master's example, since Peter had included tables of contents and marginal rubrics in his other works.

The third area Herbert supervised was illustrating the text. This served to enhance the two previous areas (authorities and organizational framework).

74 "Nichil tamen in illustris doctoris illius preiudicium qui horum fuit glosator, et meus in hac doctrina institutor precipuus, asseritur … . Qui tamen, si quid forte non ita ad unguem resecatum in suis operibus reliquerit, non arguendus ob id, sed excusandus omnino. Nam cum hec opera scriberet, nequaquam, sicut ipsomet referente didici, ipsi venit in mentem, quod in scolis publicis legerentur; solum ob id facta, ut antiquioris glossatoris, magistri videlicet Anselmi Laudunensis, brevitatem elucidarent obscuram." Herbert of Bosham, *Praefatio*, ed. Glunz, 343.

75 Theresa Gross-Diaz, *The Psalms Commentary of Gilbert of Poitiers: From 'Lectio Divina' to the Lecture Room* (Leiden, 1996), 56–64.

76 "Psalmus iste agit de primo adventu christi." B.5.4, fol. 52

77 Ibid. This kind of marginal list can be seen in the picture below [figure 8.1].

78 The contents to all psalms begins on fol. 7v of vol 1 (B. 5. 4). A table of contents for psalms 74–100 is on fol. 1 of vol. 2 (Auct. E. inf. 6), and for psalms 101–150, on fol. 54v.

When it comes to the illustrations, some distinctions must be made. First there are the letters themselves. The beginning of each psalm is marked by a heavily ornamented initial. The beginning of each verse is also marked by a distinctive, although not as elaborate, initial letter. These features are common to the whole work, and mark it out as a deluxe manuscript. Secondly, the disagreement of authorities is visually represented. In a number of folios, Cassiodorus or Augustine appears in the margin pointing at the text with a big stick. The words "I do not approve" are inscribed above their heads.[79] Thirdly, there are marginal illustrations that are placed at the beginning of psalms and represent the subject matter. The same illustration is used each time the subject appears, so they are used partly as finding aids, just like the marginal lists mentioned above.[80] A heading is provided for each of the illustrations. The psalms of lamentation are accompanied by an image headed *propheta lamentans*, a prophet lamenting.[81] The psalms dealing with the first advent show the Virgin Mary cradling the baby Jesus, and this is titled *incarnatum verbum*, the incarnate word.[82] The moral psalms have a figure struggling with a dove and serpent, labelled *ethica*.[83] This technique of signposting the psalms of a particular subject group had been used previously by Gilbert of Poitiers. In the case of the manuscripts of his psalms commentary, however, symbols based on Greek letters were used rather than interpretative illustrations.[84]

79 B. 5. 4, fol. 10v; Cahn, *Romanesque Manuscripts: The Twelfth Century*, 1: pl. 212.

80 Panayotova, "Tutorial in Images for Thomas Becket," 79–83, provides the first thorough discussion of the subject illustrations.

81 This survives in B.5.4, fol. 180, illustrating Psalm 73. The other psalms of lamentation, 78 and 136, in Auct. E. inf. 6, fols. 14v and 124 respectively, have lost images that were presumably the same.

82 B.5.4, fol. 52 (Ps. 18). The images for the other psalms on the subject, 79, 84, 96, and 117, are lost, but the heading "verbum incarnatum" survives for Psalm 79, on fol. 16v. of Auct. E. inf. 6.

83 This appears on B.5.4, fol. 15 for Psalm 4. and fol. 35v for Psalm 11. Some of the other moral psalms, which have a figure cut out, would have had the same illustrations: 14 (B.5.4, fol. 39v), 36 (B.5.4, fol. 98v). See further Panayotova, "Tutorial in Images for Thomas Becket," 81, who comments that this "personification of *Ethica* is novel and probably unique in the medieval period."

84 Gross-Diaz, *The Psalms Commentary of Gilbert of Poitiers*, 55–59. See also the symbols in the appendix, 158–159. Gross-Diaz believes that "a limitation of Gilbert's indexing system is that it only operates in forward, not in reverse." Herbert solves this problem with his marginal cross-reference list.

Sadly, many of these illustrations have not survived. They were cut out of the manuscript by so-called collectors. Fortunately, there are sometimes clues to what the pictures were. For example, the words *martyr vulneratus* (a wounded martyr) can be seen above the area where the illustration for Psalm 115 was removed.[85] This was one of three psalms designated as referring to martyrs, and it would certainly have had resonance for Herbert. His instructions to the illuminators can also provide clues. Sometimes there is simply the direction *imago* (a picture), or at least that is all that is still visible.[86] But for one of the psalms that, according to Peter, "deals at length with the passion and resurrection of Christ," Herbert's instruction *imago crucis* (a picture of the cross) is still visible.[87] There is no indication, however, besides large cut-outs, of how the illuminators tackled challenging subjects like the second coming or the love of God.[88]

All of this – the tables of contents, the illustrations, and the lists of subjects – would make the text easier to navigate. The overall visual impact of Herbert's edition has attracted much comment, particularly the new departures in page layout he introduced.[89] The subject illustrations functioned as visual aids to memory[90] and as a way to root the visual imagination during study. This resulted partly from Herbert's experience. He had studied the Psalms with Becket at Pontigny as a devotional undertaking. It was considered beneficial to keep an image in the mind during prayer and devotion. This idea was long established by the late twelfth century.[91]

85 Auct. E. inf. 6, fol. 91v. We can then infer that Psalm 43, also on the martyrs with a figure cut out, would have had the same illustration.

86 Herbert's directions were not written in as durable an ink. For Herbert's handwritten instructions in the manuscript, see Panayotova, "Tutorial in Images for Thomas Becket," 79.

87 B. 5. 4, fol. 165v, Psalm 68.

88 The psalms on the second coming are 52 (B.5.4, fol. 135v) and 82 (Auct. E. inf. 6, fol. 22). Those on the love of God are 12 (not illustrated), 41 (B.5.4. fol. 112), 83 (Auct. E. inf. 6, fol. 23v), and 133 (Auct. E. inf. 6, fol. 119).

89 For Christopher de Hamel, it was a "revolutionary innovation" that the "continuous gloss was pushed to the side of the page, and the text of the Psalter or Epistles was re-instated in a new bold script written in alternate lines." *Glossed Books of the Bible*, 27. See his rough outlines, which show the change in page layout, reproduced also in Rosemann, *Peter Lombard*, 51–53.

90 For this, see Panayotova, "Tutorial in Images for Thomas Becket," 83, and Carruthers, *The Book of Memory*, 216.

91 See, for example, the discussion in chapter six, above, 138–139, of how Peter and Bernard of Clairvaux approached the passion of Christ.

The edition would certainly enhance Peter's reputation. By filling out the references, Herbert could show his master's fidelity to patristic authority. There are also specific references to the controversy. In his preface, Herbert talks about unknown critics "barking like dogs, tearing the work to pieces with their teeth and tongues, after such a brief passage of years."[92] He took this personally, and pointed out that this was not his work: "I seek not my own glory, but that of others."[93] Herbert leaves us in no doubt that Peter Lombard's work was suffering from attack and that even Herbert's work of revision was being criticized.

The commentary could also aid against the specific charges in the controversy. Peter's view of the Psalms, long established and here influenced by Gilbert of Poitiers,[94] was that they were all about Christ:

> Others prophesied about Christ in an obscure and enigmatic manner. David, on the other hand, discussed in the clearest manner the incarnation, the passion, the resurrection, and the life to come … . The subject-matter, therefore, of this book is the whole Christ, the bride and bridegroom. The premise, to make men, disfigured in Adam, new in the man Christ. And the manner of addressing is as follows. Sometimes it deals with Christ according to the head, sometimes according to the body, and sometimes according to both. According to the head in three ways concerning Christ: Sometimes according to his divinity, as in, "with you is the principality" (Ps. 109), sometimes according to his humanity, as in "I lay down and slept" (Ps. 3).[95]

92 "Igitur si solius veritatis indagine ducimur, ut absque lesione alterium in alieno opere non meam gloriam, sed aliorum queram profectum, quid adhuc scillei latrant me adversum me canes? Quid dentibus suis et linguis una et brevi hora annorum dilaniant opus?" Herbert of Bosham, *Praefatio*, ed. Glunz, 344.

93 "non meam gloriam, sed aliorum queram … ." Ibid.

94 Gross-Diaz, *The Psalms Commentary of Gilbert of Poitiers*, 79–80.

95 "Alii namque obscure, et quasi per aenigmata prophetarunt de Christo: Iste vero David, quod et de incarnatione et de passione, et de aeterna genitura, et de resurrectione, evidentissime disseruit … . Materia itaque hujus libri est totus Christus, scilicet sponsus et sponsa. Intentio, homines, in Adam deformatos, Christo novo homini conformare. Modus tractandi talis est. Quandoque agit de Christo secundum caput, aliquando secundum utrumque. De Christo autem agit secundum caput tribus modis. Quandoque secundum divinitatem ut, 'Tecum principium' (Ps. 109), aliquando secundum humanitatem, ut, 'Ego dormivi et somnum coepi' (Ps. 3)." Peter Lombard, *Commentaria in psalmos: Praefatio* (PL 191: 59).

In that sense, David, the supposed author of the Psalms, was more evangelist than prophet.[96] Herbert could thus show that the human Christ remained at the centre of Peter Lombard's intellectual world view.

This is also clear from Peter's subjects, which Herbert was at pains to draw attention to. There are psalms dealing with the passion and resurrection, the first advent, the second coming, and a group that we will soon examine in detail, the two natures in Christ. This Christological focus is also reinforced by the illustrations of the baby Jesus, Christ on the cross, and David kneeling before Christ. Most importantly, all of the psalms that refer to the two natures in Christ are illustrated by a picture of a man in flames. Above this, the scribe has written *homo in igne, deus in homine,* "man on fire, God in man." The picture cannot be a visual representation of the *habitus* theory.[97] It does not show humanity as a garment or cloak. Rather, it shows an intact human being bursting into flames. Furthermore, Herbert explicitly rejects the *habitus* theory in his *Liber melorum*.[98] On one folio we can still see Herbert's direction to the illustrator: *imago hominis igniti,* "a picture of a man on fire."[99] This means that Herbert specified the form this visual representation should take. It was not something that was left to the imagination of the illustrator, and it is certainly not a typical image.[100] It quite definitely draws attention to Christ's humanity, at a time when some were claiming that Peter had negated it. A reproduction of it is provided below (see figure 2). It is important to consider Peter's treatment of the eight psalms illuminated by this picture in detail. He specifies that all eight refer to the humanity *and* the divinity of Christ. The first is Psalm 2, "Why do the nations rage?" Peter does not indicate at the beginning that this is the subject matter, so Herbert adds this information in a superscript note[101]

96 "Ea quippe quae alii prophetae obscure et quasi per aenigmata dixerunt de passione et resurrectione Christi, et aeterna genitura et de caeteris mysteriis, David prophetarum excellentissimus ita evidentissime aperuit, ut magis videatur evangelizare quam prophetare." Ibid., 57.

97 This suggestion is made by Panayotova, "Tutorial in Images for Thomas Becket," 81: "Patricia Stirnemann has suggested (in private correspondence) that the caption *homo in igne, deus in homine* might be a simile: as man is clothed in fire so God is clothed in humanity."

98 Herbert of Bosham, *Liber melorum* (PL 190: 1294–1404, at 1378–1379). See below.

99 Auct. E. inf. 6, fol. 21v. This is to the left of the picture.

100 Panayotova, "Tutorial in Images for Thomas Becket," 81.

101 "et iste primus psalmus de duabis in christo naturis." B.5.4, fol. 11.

Figure 2: Herbert of Bosham's Edition of Peter Lombard's *Commentary on the Psalms*

The illustration, a detail from Oxford, Bodleian Library, MS Auct. E. inf. 6, fol. 21v, shows the opening of Psalm 81, *Deus stetit in synagoga deorum* (©Bodleian Library, Oxford; reproduced with permission of the Bodleian Libraries, University of Oxford).

The image shows several noteworthy features: (1) This is one of the three pictures of the man on fire that have not been cut out. Above the man we can see that the scribe has written *homo in igne, deus in homine* – "man on fire, God in man." (2) To the left of the drawing, Herbert's own writing can be glimpsed. This is part of his instruction to the illuminator, *imago hominis igniti* – "a picture of a man on fire." (3) In the main text Peter states that *Psalmus iste est de duabus naturis in Christo* – "this Psalm concerns the two natures in Christ." Above this we can see that Herbert has added: *de quibus iam quattuor pracecesserat* – "concerning this four had already preceded." (4) To the immediate left of the large illuminated *Deus*, the list of other psalms on the subject of the two natures, the cross-reference list, can be seen.

and directs the reader to a list of other psalms on the same subject in the margin. This, as we have already seen, is Herbert's standard organizational method, and the same pattern recurs in all the psalms that deal with two natures. Prefacing his reading of this psalm, Peter points out that it is in three parts, and in the second part, "we learn much about Christ's divinity and humanity."[102] In the first part, the raging *gentes* and the kings are the persecutors of Christ (Herod, Pilate, and the Roman soldiers), while the breaking of the yoke refers to Christ freeing people from the old law. In the second part, the verse that has the most significance is "The Lord has said to me: You are my son, this day I have begotten you." Peter points out that the *hodie* of this verse "can be taken to refer to the day when Christ was born in his humanity, but, because 'this day' also signifies the present, and that is eternity, which is always, it can thus be taken to refer to divinity, to the eternal begetting of the wisdom of God."[103]

The drawing of the man on fire recurs at the beginning of Psalm 8, "O Lord our Lord, how admirable is your name in the whole earth." Again, in the preface, Peter points out that the psalm refers to the two natures: "It concerns Christ exalted, according to both natures."[104] Once again it is a particular verse that is heavy with significance: "What is man that you are mindful of him? or the son of man that you visit him?" Peter comments on this passage by considering it as a distinction:

> This distinction hints at how "man" and the "son of man" are different. For every son of a man is a man, but not the opposite: Adam was a man, but not the son of man. Therefore "a man" can be taken as all who bear the earthly image, that is, all carnal sinners; the "son of man" can be taken as all who bear the heavenly image, namely Christ. And the new man is

102 "Secundo, inducit verba Christi agentis de omnipotentis regno, et inerrabili genitura sua ubi de divinitate et humanitate ejus multa discimus." Ibid., fol. 12. cf. PL 191: 69.

103 "Quod dicit, hodie genui, et si posset accipi de die illo quo Christus secundum hominem natus est, tamen hodie praesentiam significat, et quod aeternum est, semper est, de aeterna generatione sapientiae Dei divinitus accipitur." Ibid., fol. 13. cf. PL 191: 72 where there are slight differences.

104 "Et est sensus tituli, 'Psalmus' iste, 'David' prophetae tendens 'in finem,' id est in Christum, quia agit de exaltatione Christi, secundum duas naturas." Ibid., fol. 26. cf. PL 191: 123.

> rightly called the son of man, because he became new from a certain change to the old.[105]

Peter then brings in the authority of John 1:1, "the word was made flesh": "In this incarnation the heavenly doctor came to the infirm, and the Son of God was made son of man."[106]

Psalm 20, "In your strength O Lord," would also have been illustrated by a man on fire, but this was cut out.[107] In his introduction, Peter goes into more theological detail about the two natures: "This is the third psalm of those that deal with the two natures in Christ ... in all of them a single person of Christ is shown, subsisting in two natures, against the heretics who either divide the person or combine the natures through an unlawful mingling."[108] Herbert adds his own gloss above this, associating these positions with well-known exponents from the early church. Nestorius divided the two persons, while Eutyches "was claiming there to be one holy being from the two natures."[109] Herbert's gloss therefore does not make any reference to contemporary debates. However, it does draw attention to an occasion where Peter Lombard took a position rooted in orthodoxy, at a time when his work was being criticized and misrepresented.

The illustration for Psalm 71, the fourth psalm on the two natures, has also been removed.[110] Peter uses the verses dealing with judgement to illus-

105 "Disjunctio enim innuit distare inter hominem et filium hominis. Omnis enim filius hominis, homo est; sed non econverso: ut Adam qui fuit homo, sed non filius hominis. Homo ergo hic accipitur; omnis qui portat imaginem terreni, id est omnis peccator carnalis; filius hominis accipitur omnis qui portat imaginem coelestis, id est Christi. Et merito novus homo filius hominis dicitur, quia novus ex veteri quadam mutatione fit." Ibid., fol. 27. cf. PL 191: 126.

106 "quod fuit cum 'Verbum caro factum est.' In qua incarnatione medicus coelestis venit ad infirmos, et factus est Dei Filius, hominis filius, de quo propter carnis infirmitatem, subdit." Ibid.

107 B.5.4, fol. 56. Herbert's direction *imago* is still visible.

108 "Iste est tertius psalmus eorum qui de duabus in Christo naturis agunt, de qua praecesserunt duo, scilicet secundus et octavus, et sequuntur adhuc alii quidam de eodem, in quibus omnibus monstratur una persona Christi, subsistens in duabus naturis, contra haereticos qui ut personam dividunt: ut naturas nefanda conmixtione confundunt." Ibid. This is slightly different to the text in PL 191: 219.

109 "Euthices qui ex duabus naturis unam sanctam esse asserebat." B.5.4, fol. 56.

110 Ibid., fol. 174v.

trate Christ's divine nature. But he finds the sixth verse, "he will come down like rain upon the fleece, and as showers falling gently upon the earth," to have resonance for the human Christ:

> He will come down in the womb of the virgin, like rain upon the fleece ... he wanted to come down gently in the womb of the virgin, without any kind of noise, just like rain upon the fleece, so that he could show virtue all the more by showing restraint. For wool, when set against water, is not broken, but remains intact; so did the virgin's integrity, before birth, during birth, and after birth.[111]

It is not surprising to see Peter using a reference to descent in this manner. It is a frequent word in his sermons too.

The drawings continue in volume two of Herbert's edition, now in the Bodleian Library, Oxford. The third surviving illustration of a man in flames occurs next to the beginning of Psalm 81.[112] It is on this folio that Herbert's instruction to the illuminators (*imago hominis igniti*) can be seen. Above Peter's announcement that "this Psalm concerns the two natures in Christ,"[113] Herbert has added, "concerning this four had already preceded."[114] The intention, according to Peter, is "that Christ is understood as truly God and truly man,"[115] but his treatment of the theme is slightly different. Here, the visual image in the psalm text parallels Jesus standing in the synagogue. For Peter, this explains the human and divine natures:

> "God," made man, "stood in the synagogue of the gods," that is, among the Jewish people, where the son of God, as a man, stood ... it was not the

111 "Descendet in uterum Virginis, sicut pluvia in vellus. Christus enim quem nichil utique sustinere posset, si vellet manifesta potestate cognosci, voluit leniter in uterum Virginis sine aliquo strepitu, sicut pluvia in vellus descendere, ut magis ostenderet virtutem si eam temperasset. Et est congrua similitudo. Lana enim accipiendo aquam non rumpitur, sed integra manet; sic et in Virgine integritas ante partum, in partu, post partum." Ibid., fol. 175v. cf. PL 191: 661.

112 Auct. E. inf. 6, fol. 21v.

113 "Psalmus iste est de duabus naturis in Christo." Ibid., cf. PL 191: 775. Peter also says this about psalms 20, 107 and 109, described as the third, sixth and seventh respectively to deal with this issue.

114 "De quibus iam, quattuor pracecesserat." Auct. E. inf. 6, fol. 21v.

115 "Intentione: monet credere Christum verum Deum esse et verum hominem." Ibid.

father, nor the Holy Spirit that stood in the synagogue of the Jews, but the Son, corporeally. But why did he stand there? For behold, he "judges gods," as God. The man stands, God discerns.[116]

Psalms 107 and 109 also have illustrations cut out, but in the case of one, the heading *homo in igne deus in homine* partially survives.[117] For Psalm 109, *dixit dominus*, Peter provides his most thorough exposition of the two natures subject, so it is worth examining in detail.[118] In his view, the psalm falls into a three-part structure based on the two natures of Christ. In the first part (verses 1–3), the two natures are referenced together. Peter summarizes these verses as "the words of the father about the Son, where the divine and human nature of Christ is explained."[119] Christ's human nature appears in verse 1, "The Lord said to my Lord, sit at my right hand": "What did the father say to the Son? The word *sit* means take rest after labour, and reign as man."[120] This labour is the passion.[121] Peter is adamant that the third verse, "the Lord will send forth the sceptre of your power out of Sion, to rule in the midst of your enemies," refers to the divine nature of Christ: "the rod of power is the sceptre of royal power, by which the good are sustained and evildoers broken. And note that it adds *your* to *power*, because this is the power of Christ from his divinity."[122]

According to this three-part structure, Peter sees verse 4, "With you is the principality in the day of your strength," as the second part of the psalm. Here, "the father indicates the divine nature of Christ to the extent of our

116 "Ergo 'Deus' factus homo 'stetit in Synagoga deorum,' id est in populo Judaeorum, ubi Filius Dei, secundum quod homo stetit … . Non itaque Pater, non Spiritus sanctus, sed Filius corporaliter stetit in Synagoga Judaeorum. Sed cur ibi stetit? ecce 'deos dijudicat' secundum quod Deus; stat homo, discernit Deus." Ibid.

117 "Homo in igne, de[us in homine]." Auct. E. inf. 6, fol. 78v.

118 Ibid., fol. 83–87. In Migne, the text is PL 191: 997–1001

119 "Primo, refert propheta verba Patris de Filio, ubi natura deitatis et humanitas Christi exponitur." Auct. E. inf. 6, fol. 83.

120 "'Dixit Dominus Domino meo: sede a dextris meis': Quid dixit Pater filio? 'Sede,' id est post laborem quiesce, et conregna secundum quod homo." Ibid., cf. PL 191: 997.

121 "Sede, duo notat, scilicet eum post laborem passionis quiescere." Auct. E. inf. 6, fol. 83.

122 "'Virgam virtutis tuae emittet Dominus ex Sion' … . Virga ergo virtutis est, sceptrum regiae potestatis, qua sustenantur boni, et franguntur mali. Et nota quod ait, 'virtutis,' et addit, 'tuae,' quia haec potestas proprie est Christi ex deitate." Ibid., fol. 83v. cf. PL 191: 999.

capacity ... 'in the day of your strength' is when Christ, who was once seen in the form of a slave, will be seen in the form of God by the hearts of the world."[123] The remainder of the psalm, beginning at verse 5, "the Lord has sworn and he will not repent," is "the third part, where the prophet discusses the humanity of Christ. For 'the Lord has sworn' to you, i.e., firmly promised to you, insofar as he was a man. For the oath of God is the chief support of all promising, 'and he will not repent,' that is, he will not change."[124]

The last of the six psalms on the two natures, Psalm 138, was presumably illustrated in the same way, but it is one of five psalms in Herbert's edition where the pages have been lost. Peter took the view that in this psalm "the whole Christ" was speaking as "a single and complete man," *unus et integer vir*.[125] In the first verse, "Lord you have proved me and known me," "Christ, as a man, is speaking to the father," proved in the passion and known in the resurrection.[126] Peter also comments on the second line of the verse: "You have known 'my sitting down' in the humility of the passion, and 'my rising' in the glory of the resurrection."[127]

We can see why these passages were perfect for Herbert. The commentary explicitly rejects a nihilistic view of the human Christ, particularly when Peter uses the word *integer* (complete, entire, perfect) to describe Christ as a man. This is backed up by the illustrations of a man in flames, which underline the view that Christ, as a man, was indeed something. More generally, the discussion of the incarnation in the commentary is safely founded on patristic authority and accepted doctrine. Herbert would

123 "'Tecum principium in die virtutis tuae in splendoribus sanctorum; ex utero ante Luciferum genui' ... . Secunda pars, ubi indcat Pater naturam deitatis Christi aliquatenus pro nostra capacitate ... cum Christus, qui olim visus est in forma servi, videbitur a mundis cordibus in forma Dei." Auct. E. inf. 6, fol. 83.

124 "'Juravit Dominus, et non poenitabit eum' ... . Tertia pars, ubi Propheta agit de humanitate Christi ... . Nam 'Dominus juravit' tibi, id est firmiter promisit tibi, secundum quod tu es homo. Juratio enim Dei firmamentum est promissionis. 'Et non poenitabit eum' id est non mutabit." Ibid., fol. 84.

125 "Loquitur autem in hoc psalmo totus Christus, tanquam unus et integer vir." Peter Lombard, *Commentaria in psalmos* (PL 191: 1211).

126 "'Domine, probasti me et cognovisti me' ... . Hoc dicat Christus Patri secundum quod homo ... . Qui, secundum quod homo, ad Patrem ait: 'Domine, probasti me' experimentis ut in passione, 'et cognovisti me,' ut in resurrectione." Ibid., 1212.

127 "Quid cognovisti? 'sessionem meam,' id est humilitatem in passione, et 'resurrectionem meam,' id est glorificationem in resurrectione." Ibid.

clearly want to highlight the orthodox position on the two natures that Peter takes in his introduction to Psalm 20. This was not controversial. In his commentary Peter does not discuss the incarnation in the kind of extensive detail that he did in the *Sentences.* A discussion of the meaning of the neuter noun *aliquid* would hardly be appropriate in this work. This is not to say, however, that this work is all on the surface. The reading of Psalm 109, for example, as a three-part structure governed by an explanation of the two natures, is highly subtle.

Herbert's edition might also have been intended to play a role in any public debate over Peter Lombard's teachings. As the 1170s wore on, the controversy became more and more of a propaganda war. Walter of St Victor's pamphlet is the obvious example from the anti-Lombard side.[128] As we have seen, the pope asked William of the White Hands to assemble his clergy and publicly denounce Peter's supposed nihilism. At such an occasion, Herbert's book could be a vital weapon for Peter's defenders. At the Council of Rheims of 1148, the presentation of books was important.[129] Gilbert of Poitiers pointed to particular passages in his works to underline his orthodoxy and his dependence on the fathers. He "insisted on displaying his evidence in its authentic context."[130] His attackers countered by sending Geoffrey of Auxerre to the cathedral library to find books.[131] Geoffrey displayed them. There was also a strong element of performance about this. It would be difficult to gain a comprehensive understanding of a text from such a public display. A selective presentation would therefore be required. William of the White Hands could call on Herbert to display his book and point to the citing of the fathers, the images representing the two natures, or indeed any of the pictures portraying a human Christ. This might go some way toward persuading an assembly not to condemn Peter Lombard for nihilism. In the event, there is no record of any such gathering taking place.

128 See chapter nine, below, 246–250.

129 Nikolaus M. Häring, "Notes on the Council and Consistory of Rheims," *Mediaeval Studies* 28 (1966): 39–59, at 48–49.

130 Ibid., 48. See also Otto I, Bishop of Freising, *Gesta Friderici I Imperatoris* 1.58 (MGH SS 46: 82): "Ille ortodoxorum patrum, quas non in scedulis decisas, sed in corpore lirorum integras attulerat, legi faciens auctoritates, eandem se quam illi fidem tenere asserebat."

131 Häring, "Notes on the Council and Consistory of Rheims," 49. See, also, Geoffrey of Auxerre, *Epistola ad Albinum* (PL 185: 587–596, at 591).

Herbert also completed a two-volume edition of Peter's *Commentary on the Letters of Paul.*[132] It uses many of the same techniques in page layout: the text of each verse, in larger script, is set in the same column as the accompanying commentary; the margins include references to authorities and cross-references with other letters of Paul and with the Psalms; the initial letters are large and decorative. Most importantly, Herbert's aim was again to make his master's work accessible. The edition is as fine an achievement as the *Commentary on the Psalms,* but it has received less scholarly attention. It has certainly been mentioned in most treatments of Herbert's work on his master's commentaries, but the examples tend to come from the *Commentary on the Psalms.*[133] Furthermore, it has not been thought that this work can provide as many insights about Herbert as an editor. Unlike his work on the Psalms, Peter Lombard had revised and completed the *Commentary on the Letters of Paul.* Finally, and perhaps most importantly, the edition is somewhat less notable for illustration, so pages from the edition have rarely been reproduced or discussed.[134]

The fourteen Pauline letters, often extensive and wide ranging, cannot be easily divided into thematic subjects. There is consequently no system of subject illustrations in this edition. The marginal figures of the fathers do occasionally appear,[135] but the most arresting illustrations are the large initials that open each letter. All of the letters bar that to the Hebrews open with the word *Paulus,* and in this edition, the illuminator shows great invention in designing large initial *P*'s.[136] There are always two: one for the verse, with a long stem that extends to the length of a column, and a smaller one for the commentary. Often these initials show Paul within the round *o*-shaped body

132 The two volumes of the edition are now in the library of Trinity College, Cambridge, as B.5.6 and B.5.7. They are described in James, *The Western Manuscripts in the Library of Trinity College Cambridge,* 188–201. The prefaces can be found in Glunz, *History of the Vulgate in England,* 346–350. The volumes have recently been digitized as part of the Wren Digital Library project. They are available to view in full, along with B.5.4, through the website of Trinity College Library.

133 For example, de Hamel, *Glossed Books of the Bible,* 22–27, 42–44; Smalley, *Becket Conflict,* 82; Glunz, *History of the Vulgate in England,* 226.

134 There is a full-page reproduction of B.5.6, fol. 103 in Robinson, *Catalogue of Dated and Datable Manuscripts, c.737–1600 in Cambridge Libraries,* 2: pl. 83. A detail from B.5.6, fol. 8v is reproduced in de Hamel, *Glossed Books of the Bible,* pl. 18a.

135 See B.5.6, fol. 35, 72, 80, 189 and B.5.7, fol. 22v, 114v, 137v, 139v.

136 An example can be found in B. 5.6, fol. 8v, which is reproduced in de Hamel, *Glossed Books of the Bible,* pl. 18a.

of the letter, seated with a scroll, or engaged in blessing, or with angel wings. In such cases, the word *Paulus* appears at the edge of the page, written by the same hand that described the illustrations in the *Commentary on the Psalms*. Another human figure forms the long stem of the letter, holding up the body.[137]

Herbert's main concern is again to make his master's text accessible and easy to navigate. Each letter begins with a brief summary of its contents. These summaries, which Herbert refers to as hypotheses, are not the same as Peter Lombard's prefaces. They simply itemize each chapter, rather than discussing subject, intention, and structure. After this, Herbert highlights Peter's actual preface (or *accessus*) to each letter with a large, ornate opening initial, and (often) by inscribing *praefatio epistolae* in blue and red capitals. The commentary proper nearly always begins in a separate column from the preface.[138] This makes Herbert's edition considerably better organized than the first printed editions, which did not distinguish the preface, placing it instead after a large block of Paul's text.[139]

Herbert also assists the reader in handling the more complex sections of the commentary. In his treatment of Romans 1:3, "he was made" (*factus est*), Peter provides an extensive investigation of the incarnation, as we have seen in chapter four. Although he revised and shortened it for the second version of his commentary, it is still a thorough and systematic treatment of a theological topic. Aware of this, Herbert grasps that Peter's method here is to deal with the incarnation through questions. He draws attention to Peter's organizational method by adding headings in the margin. When Peter asks, "if, however, you should now ask how that incarnation was accomplished," Herbert adds "on the incarnation" in the margin with a mark pointing to the text.[140] Herbert also adds marginal headings for further questions arising from the text, these being "why the Apostle says 'made' and not 'born'" and "whether Christ can be described as a creature."[141] This method continues in

137 B.5.6, fol. 159 (2 Cor.), B.5.7, fol. 69 (Col.), fol. 92v (2 Thess.), fol. 98v (1 Tim.).

138 See, for example, B.5.6, fol. 95–95v (1 Cor.).

139 On the shortcomings of the printed edition incorporated in the *Patrologia Latina*, see Brady, Prolegomena 1: 72*.

140 "Si autem adhuc quaeris: ipsa incarnatio quomodo facta sit ... de incarnationis." B.5.6, fol. 10v.

141 "Quare factum non natum dicat Apostolus," and "an Christus sit dicendus creatura." Ibid.

the exposition of Romans 1:4, *qui predestinatus est filius dei in virtute*, "who was predestined the Son of God in power." Herbert highlights two further theological questions in the margin: "some are accustomed to ask whether, insofar as he is man, Christ is God or the Son of God" and "some are also accustomed to ask whether Christ, insofar as he is a man, is a person."[142] These questions are close to the centre of the debate over Peter's Christological teachings, and both are also addressed in distinction ten of book three of the *Sentences* (partially quoted above), "whether Christ, according to his being a man, is a person or anything."[143] Peter's treatment of "whether Christ is God or the Son of God" in the commentary is reproduced almost exactly in that part of the *Sentences.*[144] For the second question, however, Peter does not address the most controversial aspect – whether Christ, according to his being man, is anything (*aliquid*). Otherwise, his discussion of *persona* is similar, revolving around the sense in which *secundum* (according to) is understood.[145] He concludes his discussion by appealing to the authority of Augustine, a technique that is characteristic of the commentary.[146] On the whole, Herbert seems to have been confident that highlighting these passages, closely related to the *Sentences* rather than classroom *opinio*, would not harm his master's reputation. Also, as he had in the Psalms commentary, Herbert notes that Peter's Christology counters the best-known heretical treatments from late antiquity. Peter states a doctrine from St Hilary, which would also appear in the *Sentences*, "For he is the true and proper Son: by origin, not adoption; in truth, not title; by birth, not creation."[147] In the margin Herbert adds, "against Nestorius, against Sabellius, against Arius."[148]

142 "Quaeri solet a quibusdam, an secundum quod homo Christus sit Deus, vel Dei Filius." and "Quaeri etiam solet utrum Christus, secundum quod homo, sit persona." Ibid., fol. 11–11v.

143 *Sententiae* 3, dist. 10, ch. 1. ed. Brady, 2: 72–74. See above, 205–207.

144 Peter Lombard, *Glossa in epistolas* (PL 191: 1311–1312); *Sententiae* 3, dist. 10, ch. 1, ed. Brady, 2: 74.

145 PL 191: 1312. Compare *Sententiae* 3, dist. 10, ch. 1.2–3, ed. Brady 2: 72–73.

146 PL 191: 1312. Also on the appeal to the determining opinion in the commentary, see Rosemann, *Peter Lombard*, 48.

147 "Hic enim verus et proprius est Filius, origine, non adoptione; veritate, non nuncupatione; nativitate, non creatione." B.5.6, fol. 11. cf. PL 191: 1311. See also *Sententiae* 1, dist. 26, ch. 5, ed. Brady 1: 201, trans. Silano, 1: 44.

148 "Contra Nestorium, contra Sabellium, contra Arium." B.5.6, fol. 11.

In this section of the *Commentary on Romans*, Herbert's main goal was to increase understanding of the text and to facilitate the reader in following his master's theological method. There was also nothing unusual about using such marginal headings (or rubrics) to highlight the organization of a theological work in this period. It was a device Peter had used in the *Sentences*,[149] and other twelfth-century manuscripts of his *Commentary on the Letters of Paul* are notable for "excellent rubrics."[150] In the *Commentary on Philippians*, however, the approach is more unique (and eye-catching). In this case, Herbert seems particularly concerned that readers might misunderstand Peter Lombard's Christology. This can be seen in how he handled Philippians 2:7, "but he emptied himself, taking the form of a servant, being made in the likeness of men, and in habit found as a man" (*sed semetipsum exinanivit formam servi accipiens in similitudinem hominum factus, et habitu inventus ut homo*). Peter addressed the first section as follows, "How did he 'empty himself'? Not by voiding his substance, not by changing the form of his divinity, but by taking the form of a servant, and not losing the form of God. He took the form of a slave, but he did not leave aside the form of God ... 'made,' I say, in the likeness of man, that is mortal and capable of suffering as all men are."[151] Herbert brings in the additional authority of Augustine, who addressed this passage in a sermon on the apostle Paul. Augustine also states that by accepting the form of a slave, Christ did not lose the form of God, and he goes on to point out that in the form of a servant he was born, suffered, died, rose, and ascended into heaven: "in the first two he shows your condition to you, in the latter two he offers an example of your reward."[152] Brief marginal references to the fathers are a standard feature of Herbert's editions. In this case, however, an entire section of Augustine's sermon (in a smaller font) is incorpo-

149 Ignatius C. Brady, "The Rubrics of Peter Lombard's *Sentences*," *Pier Lombardo* 6 (1962): 5–25. See also Rosemann, *Peter Lombard*, 65. The use of rubrics in the sermon manuscripts has been noted in the previous chapter.

150 Brady, Prolegomena 1: 68*–69*.

151 "'Exinanivit semetipsum.' Quomodo? non substantiam evacuans, non formam deitatis mutans, sed formam servi accipiens, non formam Dei amittens. Forma servi accessit, non forma Dei discessit ... factus, inquam, in similitudinem hominis, id est mortalis et passibilis ut alii homines." B.5.7, fol. 60. cf. PL 192: 234.

152 "In duobus primis conditionem tuam tibi ostendit: in duobus novissimis mercedis exemplum praebuit." Augustine, *Sermo 279: De Paulo apostolo* (PL 38: 1275–1280, at 1279).

rated into the text of the commentary, rather than in the margin.[153] This means Herbert planned it in this way and instructed the scribe to reserve space for it within the column of text.

Such a technique also occurs in the discussion of "in habit found as man" (*habitu inventus ut homo*). Peter's discussion of this passage is completely dependent on Augustine's *De diversis quaestionibus octoginta tribus.*[154] Rather than simply place a marginal reference to this, Herbert incorporates a further section of Augustine's work directly into the text (again in a smaller font).[155] Peter had not made use of Augustine's discussion of the Greek equivalent of *habitus,* and its sense. It is characteristic of Herbert, with his scholarly interest in language, to include this section. Furthermore, to ensure that the Augustine passage would be widely understood, when the Greek terms *hexis* and *skhēma* are quoted in the Greek alphabet, the Latin version is also provided just above.[156]

Herbert added one further lengthy extract from the fathers to the exposition of Philippians 2:7. This was Ambrose's treatment of 'the form of a servant" from his *De Fide.*[157] This seems to have been done in haste, possibly as an afterthought. It was not planned out as the Augustine passages were. The Ambrose section is quoted in Herbert's own heavily abbreviated hand, the same hand that provides the instructions for the scribe and illuminator.[158] Herbert uses the foot of the page for this, and it is rare in the edition for anything besides scribal doodling to appear there.[159]

Why should Herbert have taken such care over this particular verse? Philippians 2:7 can be a somewhat thorny passage to interpret, given that it provides the starting point for the *habitus* theory of the incarnation.[160] Colish suggests that Peter's treatment of this verse may have led his critics to sup-

153 B.5.7, fol. 60v. Augustine's text from the *Sermo de Paulo apostolo,* ch. 8 (PL 38: 1279), is quoted in its entirety from "semetipsum exinanivit" to the end of the chapter.

154 PL 192: 235. Augustine, *De diversis quaestionibus* 73 (PL 40: 11–100, at 85). An English translation can be found in Augustine, *Eighty Three Different Questions,* trans. David L. Mosher (Washington, DC, 2005), 189.

155 B.5.7, fol. 60v. The section is in the second chapter of Augustine, *De diversis quaestionibus,* 73, beginning with "sed illum habitum" (PL 40: 85).

156 B.5.7, fol. 60v.

157 The section quoted by Herbert can be found in PL 16: 671.

158 B.5.7, fol. 60.

159 An example of heavy doodling can be seen at the foot of B.5.6, fol. 162.

160 For the *habitus* theory, see above, 207.

pose that he advocated the *habitus* theory.[161] This would be potentially worrying for Herbert and Peter's other defenders. As Luscombe points out, "from the *habitus* theory to nihilism is only a short step. If it is conceded that Christ 'wore' manhood like a garment, this manhood is difficult to qualify."[162] Peter's treatment of Philippians 2:7, when read as a whole, cannot be suspected of nihilism, since it emphasizes the fullness of Christ's humanity. The problem was that passages were not always carefully read, or were selected out of context, or were reported by word of mouth. Again, therefore, we can see Herbert, with an eye on the Christological controversy, drawing attention to his master's dependence on patristic authority.

Herbert's technique of incorporating portions of the fathers' texts was not always prompted by controversial or difficult passages. On other occasions, they flesh out the commentary if Peter's treatment is overly brief. This is certainly true of the Letter to Titus. Herbert here includes Jerome's gloss, which is generally more thorough, in its entirety.[163] In the commentaries on Galatians and Philemon, extracts from the glosses of Haymo and Jerome also appear within the text. Just as in the case of the Augustine passages, they are incorporated within the columns of the main text.[164] Their inclusion suggests that Herbert wanted the edition to be as definitive as he could make it.

Although there are no subject illustrations, Herbert does note when this commentary covers similar ground to the *Commentary on the Psalms.* The outer margin is generally reserved for references to the Psalms (and occasionally to other scriptural passages). Herbert intended the two editions to form a set that could be used together. In the *Commentary on Hebrews,* in 1:2 ("his son, whom he has appointed heir of all things"), Peter notes that "here he commends him according to his human nature,"[165] and in 1:3 ("who, being the brightness of his glory"), Peter notes that "here he commends the divine

161 Colish, *Peter Lombard,* 223; Colish, "Christological Nihilianism in the Second Half of the Twelfth Century," 147–148.

162 Luscombe, *The School of Peter Abelard,* 272.

163 B.5.7, fol. 124–129. Jerome's *Commentaria in Epistolam ad Titum* can be found in PL 26: 555–600.

164 B.5.7, fol. 2v. The prefaces of Jerome (PL 26: 353–354) and Haymo (PL 117: 66) appear on either side of Peter's preface on Galatians, in smaller writing. The prefaces of Jerome (PL 26: 599) and Haymo (PL 117: 813) are also included next to Peter's preface on Philemon, fol. 129.

165 "Hic commendat eum secundum humanam naturam." (PL 192: 402).

nature of Christ by showing him co-eternal and co-equal with the father."[166] In the long section that follows, Herbert adds a list of five related psalms, all of which belong to the two natures group, and which are illustrated by the man on fire.[167]

Herbert's work on the *Commentary on the Letters of Paul* is not as immediately striking as his other edition. It is nevertheless the product of considerable labour, on his part and on that of his team of scribes and illuminators. He intended that it would be the definitive edition of his master's commentary and that it would serve as a tool for those teaching or studying the text. There can be little doubt that the controversy over Peter's teachings formed the background to this work. As with the edition of the *Commentary on the Psalms,* Herbert highlights his master's orthodoxy and dependence on the fathers.

In the mid-1170s, Herbert attempted to set up his own school of theology. He managed to enlist the support of Pope Alexander III for this. Alexander knew him as Becket's associate, and he had sent him a letter of sympathy after the archbishop's murder.[168] Now he wrote to Becket's successor, Richard, asking that Herbert, *dilectus noster magister,* "our beloved master," be allotted money from his property in England so that he could teach theology.[169] Smalley points out that if Herbert's property was still confiscated (it had been so since the Becket affair), it would have been difficult for the archbishop to send the money.[170] It is interesting that the pope supported this endeavour. Clearly, Alexander did not have a personal vendetta against Peter Lombard, or he would not have gone out of his way to allow one of his students to teach. Again, we are left with the conclusion that what bothered Alexander was masters teaching nihilism and citing Peter Lombard as their source. We do not know, however, whether Herbert was successful in attracting pupils, or how long he was able to keep his school open.

166 "Hic secundum divinam naturam commendat Christum ostendens eum coaeternum et coaequalem Patri." Ibid., 403.

167 B.5.7, fol. 132–133v. Hebrews 1:2 corresponds with psalms 2 and 8, 1:3 with psalms 71, 81, and 109.

168 Alexander III, *Epistola ad Herbertum* (PL 200: 731).

169 *Epistolae Pontificum Romanorum Ineditae,* ed. Samuel Lowenfeld (Leipzig, 1885), 207.

170 Smalley, *Becket Conflict,* 71.

Herbert's two major works about Becket, the *Life* and the *Liber melorum*, both contain substantial theological sections, suggesting that the experience of teaching was still fresh when he came to write them in the 1180s. In this sense, they are memorials both to Becket and to Herbert's years of study under his *magister*, Peter Lombard. The *Life* is filled with what appear to be digressions, and scholars used to criticize Herbert for this. Frank Barlow found the work "garrulous, sometimes tedious, the searchings of a disappointed old man ... blundering."[171] More recent assessments have been kinder. Michael Staunton points out that Herbert's intellectual formation was in theology: "he applied these skills to the story of Thomas's life and death, which he approached in the manner of an exegete ... many have found his theological digressions tedious and irrelevant, but clear inspection shows them to be an integral part of his work."[172] Probably the best account of how necessary theology is to the *Life* is that by Jessica Weiss, in her thesis on Herbert's *Liber melorum.*[173] For her, "Herbert sees theology as his way of explaining the cause of the deeds and the mind of the doer."[174] There are echoes of the theology school throughout the *Life*. Take, for example, Herbert's treatment of how the young Thomas found favour socially. He explains the difference between two kinds of grace at length: "there is ... a grace that is civil, urbane, kind, sweet, social and invites people to love, and by it a man is made more pleasing to the world but less to God,"[175] whereas another grace is "more sad,

171 Barlow, *Thomas Becket*, 3. Barlow is similarly harsh in "Herbert of Bosham," in *Oxford Dictionary of National Biography*, ed. Henry C.G. Matthew and Brian Harrison (Oxford, 2004), 6: 711–713: "his life of the archbishop, written after most of the other *vitae*, is rambling and verbose ... His commentary on the Hebrew psalter and his edition of Peter Lombard's 'great gloss' on the Psalms and St Paul's epistles, which he dedicated to Archbishop William of Sens (r. 1169–1176), are, however, scholasticism pure and simple, and have had their day." This seems like a very shortsighted statement for a historian to make.

172 Michael Staunton, *The Lives of Thomas Becket* (Manchester, 2001), 10. See also his book *Thomas Becket and His Biographers* (Woodbridge, 2006), 63–75.

173 Weiss, "Herbert of Bosham's *Liber melorum*," ch. 2: "Theological and Biblical Rhetoric in the *Historia Thomae*," 46–78.

174 Ibid., 52.

175 "Duplex enim est in hominibus gratia; est quippe civilis quaedam gratia, urbana, benigna, dulcis, socialis, et ad sui dilectionem invitans qua homo plus placet saeculo sed Deo minus." Herbert of Bosham, *Vita Sancti Thomae archiepiscopi et martyris* 3.5, ed. Robertson, 3: 163.

grave, severe ... only pleasing to God."[176] This is the kind of distinction-based writing that would have been second nature to anyone who had been in the schools as long as Herbert.

Herbert's theological training is even more apparent in the *Liber melorum* ("Book of Songs"), an extended work in praise of Becket.[177] He breaks off at one point to prove the existence of God and follows this with a section on the nature of Christ. This probably recalls the 1170s, when Herbert taught theology. When he wrote this work in the 1180s, the debate over Peter Lombard's Christology had subsided, at least below a critical level. But Herbert's thoughts on the incarnation should be more widely known. The *Liber melorum* has not been included in any of the treatments of the Christological controversy, because it is not an explicitly theological work. Lauge-Olaf Nielsen did not consider Herbert in his long discussion of Peter Lombard's school.[178] But future studies of the debate should not ignore his contribution (or indeed Peter Comestor's brief remarks in the *Historia Scholastica*).[179] Herbert's treatment of the issue, which must mirror how he taught it, is abbreviated in comparison with that of Peter Lombard in the *Sentences*.[180] Like his master, he recounts the main theories of the hypostatic union. He rejects the *habitus* theory, associating it with "many people of our own day,"[181] and questions them

176 "Gratia etenim haec tristior, districtior, severior, non ut prior omnibus omnia, sed sibi soli et Deo." Ibid., 164.

177 Herbert of Bosham, *Liber melorum* (PL 190). Before Weiss, only Smalley really discussed it, in *Becket Conflict*, 79–81.

178 Nielsen, *Theology and Philosophy in the Twelfth Century*, 279–362.

179 After recounting the story of Mary and the angel Gabriel, from Luke 1, Comestor adds "et statim conceptus est Christus de Virgine, plenus homo in anima, et carne." Peter Comestor, *Historia Scholastica* (PL 198: 1537). This is a good example of Comestor adding theological explanation to the scriptural narrative.

180 Herbert of Bosham, *Liber melorum* (PL 190: 1378–1381). Weiss, "Herbert of Bosham's *Liber melorum*," 195–196, points out that "Herbert's approach echoes that of his master Peter Lombard who, in his *Sentences*, recounted some contemporary opinions on the matter," but also that "Herbert's argument is not elaborate enough to add something to such a complex debate."

181 "Plerique tamen nostri temporis hujus mentem tantae unitatis inter Deum assumptum et assumentem hominem tam humile et eo magis gratuitum vinculum, velut de morticinio nostro calciatae divinitatis cortigiam conantes solvere, sola illius habitus ratione, Deum hominem praedicant." Herbert of Bosham, *Liber melorum* (PL 190: 1378).

for believing something the fathers rejected.[182] This adds weight to his implied rejection of the *habitus* theory in the drawings of a man in flames. Unlike Peter, he did not continue with a discussion of nihilism. Smalley suggests that the structure of the *Liber melorum* in these sections resembles "the torso of a *Summa*,"[183] and it is to be regretted that Herbert never wrote a comprehensive theological work.

Herbert's decision to enter state service after graduating from Peter's school placed him outside the enterprise of the theologians. But he was not as distanced from them as William of Tyre. He returned to the intellectual world at intervals, and theology was central to his employment under Becket. The editions of the two commentaries were Herbert's payment of a debt to his teacher in theology. He was not beyond criticizing his master for making a mistake,[184] but he clearly felt Peter's absence. While the editions may have come from the same motivation as the work on the *Sentences* done by Peter Comestor and the *chorus*, they were far more lovingly prepared. However, preparing them was more than an act of piety. Rumours about Peter's oral teachings were damaging his reputation. Herbert, with his edition of the commentary, endeavoured to place attention again on Peter's *written* word. The illustrations, the tables of contents, and the marginal notes allow readers to navigate the texts with ease.

182 "Item detestantur hi aliquid recens; fateri Deum, et in aliquid credere statu novae legis, in quod non crediderunt patres veteris, nec ipse Abraham, qui omnium est credentium pater." Ibid., 1378–1379.

183 Smalley, *Becket Conflict*, 81.

184 Herbert of Bosham, *Epistola ad Henricum comitem Tricensem* (PL 190: 1418–1419). Smalley, "A Commentary on the *Hebraica*," 37–41.

CHAPTER NINE

Adam of Wales and John of Cornwall

Adam of Wales (c.1120–1181)

The students we have dealt with so far were men of affairs, but they also found time to carve out reputations as writers. Adam of Wales was certainly capable of intellectual work. He spent a large part of his life in the schools, as a student, *praepositus*, and *magister*. Yet there is no trace of any work bearing his name. Despite this, he played an important role in ensuring that his master's work survived. While his teaching would certainly have been influenced by Peter, his main contribution was to defend his master before the pope at a critical time.

The other students are also familiar – if only as names – to those acquainted with the twelfth century. The same cannot be said for Adam. His name rarely features, and, aside from two useful notices in dictionaries, nothing has been written about him.[1] Furthermore, until 1954, he was erroneously identified with another Adam, Adam of the Petit Pont, one of John of Salisbury's teachers.[2] Adam's story illustrates the varied careers students of Peter

1 John Edward Lloyd, "Adam, Bishop of St Asaph," in *Dictionary of Welsh Biography down to 1940*, ed. John E. Lloyd and Robert T. Jenkins (London, 1959), 1–2; Raymond Klibansky, "Adam, c.1130–1181," in *Oxford Dictionary of National Biography*, ed. Henry C.G. Matthew and Brian Harrison (Oxford, 2004), 1: 191–192. Klibansky's article relies heavily on Gerald of Wales. He is of the opinion that Adam's defence of Peter Lombard took place at the Third Lateran Council.

2 See, for example, James Conway Davies, *Episcopal Acts and Cognate Documents Relating to Welsh Dioceses, 1066–1272* (Cardiff, 1948), 2: 548–550. In an article published that year, Minio-Paluello demonstrates conclusively that such an identification was erroneous, and he also provides a valuable list of documentary references to Adam. Lorenzo Minio-Paluello, "The *Ars Disserendi* of Adam of Balsham, 'Parvipotanus,'" *Mediaeval and Renaissance Studies* 3 (1954): 116–169, at 165–166. Lloyd, "Adam, Bishop of St Asaph," also argues against the identification. Lloyd, in his earlier *History of Wales from the Earliest Times to the Edwardian Conquest* (London, 1911), 558 n119, considered the two Adams to be the same.

Lombard (and of theology schools generally) could have. It also shows, again, that a lengthy theological training did not guarantee a clerical position. Adam, like his master, ended his life as a bishop, but his security had been hard won.

Adam was born in Wales, although we can only conjecture whether his family was native Welsh or Marcher-Norman. The issue of his background is relevant to the reasons for his appointment to the see of St Asaph, and will be discussed below. He was of the same generation as William of Tyre, but he was probably a few years older. Like William, he would have spent several preparatory years in the arts before enrolling in Peter Lombard's school of theology. It therefore seems safe to place his birth at around 1120 and his studies under Peter Lombard between 1150 and 1159. He remained with Peter long enough to be appointed *praepositus*.[3] *Praepositus* is something of a catch-all term, reflecting the elastic nature of duties in twelfth-century cathedral schools. It is not found in the universities of the thirteenth century.[4] It simply means one placed in charge, and it is found in classical authors, usually in a military context.[5] In the Middle Ages, *praepositus* could signify a secular or ecclesiastical office.[6] The French and English words *prévost* and *provost* were being used in the twelfth century to refer to salaried positions involving administrative duties.[7] In the twelfth-century schools, however, any money the *praepositus* received probably came out of the fees paid to the master.[8] In

3 "Episcopus Adam Wallensis exivit dicens: 'Domine Papa, ego et clericus et praepositus olim scholarum eius defendam sententias magistri.'" Walter of St Victor, *Contra quatuor labyrinthos Franciae*, ed. Paul Glorieux, "Le 'Contra quatuor labyrinthos Franciae' de Gauthier de Saint-Victor," *Archives d'histoire doctrinale et littéraire du moyen âge* 19 (1952): 187–335, at 201. This source is discussed below.

4 Olga Weijers, *Terminologie des universités au XIIIe siècle* (Rome, 1987), does not deal with it in her exhaustive treatment of university offices and terms. Neither does Mariken Teeuwen, *The Vocabulary of Intellectual Life in the Middle Ages* (Turnhout, 2003). This is surprising, since, unlike Weijers's study, it is meant to include twelfth-century terms.

5 *Oxford Latin Dictionary* (Oxford, 1982), 1437, lists occurrences in Fronto, Suetonius, and Tacitus.

6 For examples of some of these offices, see *Lexicon Latinitatis Nederlandicae Medii Aevi*, ed. Johanne W. Fuchs, Olga Weijers, and Marijke Gumbert-Hepp (Leiden, 1977–2005), 6: 821–825.

7 *Oxford English Dictionary* (Oxford, 1989), 12: 722–723. We have already encountered some examples in this book: Gerhoh was *praepositus* of Reichersberg. William of the White Hands held a similar position at Troyes, which Herbert of Bosham later applied for.

8 We have seen in chapter three that Odo of Soissons supported his *praepositus* financially.

the context of the schools, "assistant" is probably the best translation. Powicke suggests that compiling the official *reportatio* would be one of the possible duties of the *praepositus*,[9] although, as we have seen in chapter two, this does not seem to have been the case in Peter Lombard's school. Other duties, like deputizing for the master or seeing to fees and attendance, might have fallen within Adam's remit. On a social level, particularly for the newer pupils, the assistant would have been something of a go-between for those too intimidated to approach their master directly.

Adam seems to have remained in Paris for sixteen years after Peter Lombard left the schools to become bishop in 1159. In 1173–1174, *Magister Adam Walensis* appears as a witness in one of Maurice of Sully's episcopal documents.[10] Adam would have been given his *licentia docendi* by either Peter Comestor or Odo of Soissons. As the former *praepositus* of Peter Lombard's school, Adam would have been in a good position to attract students. It is unlikely that he taught theology, since there are no works bearing his name, and he does not even appear in *quaestiones*.[11] A *praepositus* sometimes succeeded his master. This happened in the case of Peter of Poitiers when his master, Peter Comestor, gave up teaching.[12] But, as we have seen in chapter seven, it seems that Peter Comestor took over the theology chair vacated by Peter Lombard in 1159. It is not inconceivable that Adam could have been one of the *chorus*, working on commentaries of the *Sentences* in the 1160s and early 1170s. We would then have to assume that he spent some time studying with Peter Comestor before beginning to teach.

The more lucrative clerical positions eluded Adam. When Gerald of Wales met him, between 1165 and 1172, he was still "in a private station,"[13] meaning he had no prebend in a church. However, the chronicler Ralph Diceto, reporting his election to the bishopric of St Asaph, describes him

9 Hastings Rashdall, *Universities of Europe in the Middle Ages*, ed. Frederick M. Powicke and Alfred B. Emden (Oxford, 1936), 1: 450. The note dealing with this was the work of Powicke, not Rashdall.

10 *Recueil des chartres et documents de Saint Martin des Champs*, ed. Joseph Depoin (Paris, 1912–1921), 2: 328.

11 Brady, "Peter Manducator," 481, points out that "no theological work or, much less, any theological opinion is even credited to him." If Adam had taught theology, one would expect him to at least feature somewhere in *quaestiones*.

12 For Peter of Poitiers in Comestor's school, see chapter seven, above, 167.

13 Gerald of Wales, *De rebus a se gestis* 6, in *Giraldi Cambrensis opera*, ed. John S. Brewer (London, 1861–1891), 1: 1–122, at 38.

incorrectly as a canon of Paris.[14] The only person named Adam in the twelfth-century church of Paris was a cantor who held his post from 1108 until around 1140.[15] Ralph Diceto, who was busy in the 1160s and 1170s as archdeacon of Middlesex,[16] was probably misinformed.

At some point between 1165 and 1172, Adam befriended the young Gerald of Wales, who had come to Paris to further his education.[17] We know this from Gerald's autobiography. Gerald passes over his student years very quickly, but he refers to Adam later in the work. When Adam was bishop of St Asaph, and Gerald archdeacon of St David's, the two clashed over the right to consecrate a church. Gerald spends some time on this incident, and in so doing, he provides valuable details about his association with Adam. For Gerald, they had been equals – two impoverished Welsh students and firm friends: "I put it to him that, since we had been good friends in Paris, when we were much poorer and had no position, we should be good friends and neighbours, now that we have come into some power."[18]

But Adam was much older, and, as a master, he would have had more money than Gerald. A friendship it undoubtedly was, but perhaps it was more a case of the older man taking someone from his homeland under his wing. Adam could even have taught Gerald. It is certainly interesting that Gerald, who had such a volatile relationship with his native land, should identify with it when abroad and gravitate toward his countrymen.[19]

14 "Adam canonicus Parisiensis electus in episcopatum Sancti Assavi, consecratus est a Ricardo Cantuariensi archiepiscopo apud Westmonasterium." Ralph Diceto, *Ymagines Historiarum*, ed. William Stubbs as *The Historical Works of Ralph de Diceto* (London, 1876), 1: 402. Brady points out that this was incorrect in "Peter Manducator," 48.

15 *Cartulaire*, ed. de Lasteyrie, no. 149, p. 168 through no. 253, p. 253.

16 John F.A. Mason, "Ralph de Diceto," in *Oxford Dictionary of National Biography*, 16: 40–42.

17 The study years of Gerald were 1165–1172 and 1176–1179. Robert Bartlett, *Gerald of Wales, 1146–1223* (Oxford, 1982), 29. Since Adam left Paris to become a bishop in 1175, it would have to be in the earlier period.

18 "Rogavit etiam, quod sicut olim in Francia socii fuerant boni, quando pauperiores erant et privati, sic et nunc vicini boni et amici forent in potestate constituti" Gerald of Wales, *De rebus a se gestis* 6, ed. Brewer, 38.

19 Gerald's modern biographers, Michael Richter and Robert Bartlett, discuss the issue of Gerald and Wales. See Bartlett, *Gerald of Wales*, ch. 1: "Gerald of Wales or Gerald the Welshman?" 9–27, and Michael Richter, *Giraldus Cambrensis: The Growth of the Welsh Nation* (Aberystwyth, 1976). See the sections entitled "Wales and the Welsh as seen by Giraldus," 66–78, and "Giraldus' development into a Cambrensis," 84–94.

Adam was bishop of St Asaph from 1175 to 1181. This appointment finally brought him a secure income. St Asaph was the most turbulent of the four Welsh dioceses set up in the aftermath of the Norman conquest. The territory it covered in North East Wales was nominally under the Angevin king, but in reality, since the Welsh revival of 1135, a variety of native princes held sway there. Part of the lower end of the diocese extended into the territory of the Prince of Powys, at that time divided into North and South Powys.[20] The weak position of Powys meant that the Prince of Gwynedd was the most powerful local figure in the diocese.[21] Godfrey, Adam's predecessor, was not Welsh and had avoided the diocese. He simply used the privileges brought by episcopal rank to his own advancement.[22] In any case, the revolt of Owain Gywnedd rendered much of his diocese inaccessible. In the end, it was complaints brought by his own clergy in St Asaph that forced his resignation. Why would Adam desert a twenty-year career in Paris to take up such a remote post?

He must have been a compromise candidate. The year of his elevation, 1175, is isolated by Lewis Warren as ushering in a new era in the Welsh policy of Henry II.[23] He had begun to favour accommodation over confrontation. Owain Gwynedd died in 1170, and by 1173 his son Daffyd had emerged as a successor more amenable to Henry's plans.[24] Warren points to a council devoted to Welsh affairs held by the king at Gloucester in June 1175.[25] A large number of native Welsh princes and members of the Marcher aristocracy were in attendance. The meeting "seems to have concluded with a solemnly sworn mutual assistance pact for the preservation of peace and order in Wales."[26] R.R. Davies looks at the policy somewhat differently. For him, "the councils of 1175 and 1177 and the oaths extracted at them mark an important

20 A map of the medieval Welsh dioceses can be found in Roger Turvey, *The Welsh Princes: The Native Rulers of Wales, 1063–1283* (London, 2002), xxx.

21 David Walker, *Medieval Wales* (Cambridge, 1990), 74. See also Glanmor Williams, *The Welsh Church from Conquest to Reformation* (Cardiff, 1976).

22 Davies, *Episcopal Acts and Cognate Documents Relating to Welsh Dioceses*, 437–442.

23 Wilfred Lewis Warren, *Henry II* (London, 1973), 161–169.

24 Seán Duffy, "Henry II and England's Insular Neighbours," in *Henry II: New Interpretations*, ed. Christopher Harper-Bill and Nicholas Vincent (Woodbridge, 2007), 129–153, at 144–145.

25 Warren, *Henry II*, 167. The council is described in *Gesta Regis Henrici Secundi Benedicti abbatis*, ed. William Stubbs (London, 1867), 1: 92.

26 Warren, *Henry II*, 167.

stage in the intensification and definition of Royal overlordship in Wales. Henry II was intent on reconstructing and reasserting his authority in the wake of the revolt of 1173–4."[27] Certainly the threat of force was always in the background as Seán Duffy points out.[28] The appointment of Adam of Wales, however, does suggest accommodation. Adam's elevation to the bishopric of St Asaph took place just over a month before the Gloucester council, on 18 May.[29] This is surely no coincidence. The forced resignation of Godfrey and the elevation of Adam were part of the new Welsh policy. Henry II and Richard, archbishop of Canterbury, had to show themselves sensitive to the concerns of the Welsh. The new bishop had to be acceptable to his clergy and to the prince of Gwynedd. Adam of Wales was the man for the job.

Adam spent considerably more time in his diocese than his predecessor. Matthew Pearson speculates that he may have begun the process of forming a St Asaph cathedral chapter: "His dynamic character ... makes him a likely reforming bishop, but there is no evidence either way."[30] He also quickly set about asserting the rights of his diocese. Documents are scarce. No episcopal register of any kind was kept in Wales until 1293,[31] and other sources that shed light on the diocese of St Asaph also do not begin until well into the thirteenth century.[32] The best documented event in Adam's episcopate is a dispute with the diocese of St David's over the right to consecrate a church.[33] While this event sheds much light on the legal process in the church, it also

27 Robert R. Davies, *The Age of Conquest: Wales, 1063–1415* (Oxford, 1991), 290–291.

28 Duffy, "Henry II and England's Insular Neighbours," 149–150, 152–153.

29 *Gesta Regis Henrici Secundi*, ed. Stubbs (London, 1867), 1: 91.

30 Matthew J. Pearson, "The Creation and Development of the St Asaph Cathedral Chapter, 1141–1293," *Cambrian Medieval Celtic Studies* 40 (2000): 35–56, at 40–41.

31 David M. Smith, *Guide to Bishop's Registers of England and Wales* (London, 1981).

32 For example, the *Llfyr Coch Asaph*, or "Red Book of St Asaph," is a fourteenth-century text. See Pearson, "The Creation and Development of the St Asaph Cathedral Chapter," 36. Also, for the scarcity of sources, see Davies, *Episcopal Acts and Cognate Documents Relating to Welsh Dioceses*, 1: 34. Davies's publication of episcopal *Acta* for the four Welsh dioceses never progressed beyond volume two. Volume three, which was to include St Asaph, reached the typescript stage. Matthew J. Pearson consulted it for *Fasti Ecclesiae Anglicanae, 1066–1300*: Volume 9: *The Welsh Cathedrals* (London, 2003), 34.

33 For the dispute, see Lloyd, *History of Wales*, 558–559, which is the best account for situating the dispute in the context of Welsh politics. While Lloyd is favourable to Gerald, Richter, *Giraldus Cambrensis*, 4, and Klibansky, "Adam, c.1130–1181," are both critical of him.

explains why Adam was at the papal curia when he defended Peter Lombard. The church was St Michael's in Ceri, which lay on the border between St David's and St Asaph. David, bishop of St David's, died in May 1176, and the diocese remained vacant until November. Adam took advantage of the vacancy and attempted to consecrate the church, but he was prevented by the archdeacon of St David's, Gerald of Wales. Our main source for this is Gerald's autobiography, written thirty years later.[34] Richter suggests that Gerald – keen to paint himself as the champion of St David's – obscures the issue by giving the impression that he had the right to consecrate the church.[35] Gerald writes as if he and Adam were equals, just as he claims they were in their student days, but Adam probably did not see it this way. Gerald also seems keen not to criticize Adam too harshly. He claims Adam was unwilling to excommunicate him, on account of their former friendship.[36] Later, when Adam was on his way to meet with a local prince over the issue,[37] Gerald sent the bishop some choice things for supper. The bishop, ignoring the advice of his retinue, invited Gerald in to dine.[38] But despite their show of good feeling, neither man was giving an inch. Gerald protested to Henry II,[39] who he claims took his side.

Gerald's account ends there. What happened next must be pieced together from papal documents. It appears that when the new bishop of St David's, Peter de Leia, was appointed in November, he lost no time in consecrating St Michael's. Adam appealed to the pope, who in turn delegated Bartholomew, bishop of Exeter, and Roger, bishop of Worcester, as judges in the matter.[40] This procedure was quite popular among bishops in England

34 Gerald of Wales, *De rebus a se gestis* 6, ed. Brewer, 32–38.

35 "Despite the impression which is given to the reader, Giraldus as archdeacon could not consecrate a church, although he could, and did, prevent the bishop of St Asaph from doing so." Richter, *Giraldus Cambrensis*, 5.

36 "Alioquin ipsum, licet invitus, quia Parisius olim socii fuerant et conscolares, excommunicaret." Gerald of Wales, *De rebus a se gestis* 6, ed. Brewer, 34. Also, 36: "Episcopus autem, hoc audiens ait: 'Propter amicitiam quae inter nos olim fuerat et scolasticam societatem, parcemus nunc personae vestrae et his qui vobiscum sunt.'"

37 This was Cadwallon of Maeliennydd, whose territory bordered Ceri to the south.

38 "Episcopus autem licet dissuadentibus suis propter dedecus ei factum perpessamque repulsam quod non susciperet, tamen saniori consilio cum gratiarum actione suscepit." Gerald of Wales, *De rebus a se gestis* 6, ed. Brewer, 38.

39 Ibid., 39–40. See also Klibansky, "Adam, c.1130–1181."

40 Alexander III's decretal is printed in Adrian Morey, *Bartholomew of Exeter: Bishop and Canonist* (Cambridge, 1937), 129–130. It is analyzed in Mary G. Cheney, *Roger, Bishop of Worcester, 1164–1179* (Oxford, 1980), 328.

as "a short cut to a final decision."[41] Sometimes the request for the appointment of judges was made by letter, sometimes in person. Bartholomew and Roger certainly handled their fair share of such cases, although "almost every bishop in England acted sometimes as a judge delegate of Pope Alexander."[42] A statement by Gerald of Wales that these two bishops handled almost all cases is now seen as an exaggeration.[43]

According to Alexander's decretal to the two bishops, "our venerable brother Adam" went in person to Rome and complained that the bishop of St David's had consecrated the church, despite the fact that Adam and a number of his clergy had appealed to him to stop in the name of the pope.[44] This is virtually the same as Gerald's account, albeit with the roles reversed: an aggressor, determined to proceed despite appeals.[45] Alexander asked his judges to look carefully into the matter and to let him know if indeed the church had been consecrated in spite of an appeal in his name.[46] It is clear from the decretal that Adam had gone in person to Rome,[47] but Peter of St

41 Morey, *Bartholomew of Exeter*, 47. Charles Duggan and Jane Sayers are the current authorities on this legal process. See, for example, Jane Sayers, *Papal Judges Delegate in the Province of Canterbury, 1198–1254: A Study in Ecclesiastical Jurisdiction and Administration* (Oxford, 1971), and Charles Duggan, "Decretals of Alexander III to England," in *Miscellanea Rolando Bandinelli*, ed. Filippo Liotta (Siena, 1986), 87–151, reprinted in *Decretals and the Creation of "New Law" in the Twelfth Century* (Aldershot, 1998).

42 Cheney, *Roger, Bishop of Worcester*, 126.

43 Ibid., and Duggan, "Decretals of Alexander III to England," 96.

44 "Conquestus est nobis uenerabilis frater noster Adam episcopus Sancti Asaph, quod, cum ecclesia sancti Michaelis de Ken ad ecclesiam suam iure parochiali pertineat, Meneuensis episcopus ad eam dedicandam accessit. Cum autem id ad notitiam predicti episcopi sancti Asaph peruenisset, quendam capellanum suum cum quibusdam aliis clericis ad memoratum Meneuensem destinauit, qui ei ex nostra parte inhibuerunt, ne ecclesiam ipsam presumeret aliquatenus dedicare, et ad nostram exinde presentiam appellarunt. Sed ipse nec appellationi nec inhibitioni ex nostra parte deferens ecclesiam ipsam dedicauit." In Morey, *Bartholomew of Exeter*, 129–130.

45 Gerald of Wales, *De rebus a se gestis* 6, ed. Brewer, 34.

46 "Inde est, quod fraternitati uestre per apostolica scripta precipendo mandamus, quatenus rei ueritate diligenter inquisita et cognita, si uobis consisterit, quod prescripta ecclesia ad episcopatum sancti Asaph iure parochiali pertineat et quod memoratus Meneuensis contra inhibitionem ex parte nostra sibi factam eam presumpserit dedicare, in ipsa diuina prohibeatis officia celebrari nisi sicut in ecclesia nondum consecrationis munere decorata." In Morey, *Bartholomew of Exeter*, 130.

47 "Unde memoratus episcopus ad eum in propria persona accedens ipsum ad nostram audientiam appellauit." Ibid.

David's had yet to give his side of the matter. When did this happen? We know that Adam attended the Third Lateran Council in 1179, but Peter of St David's was there too.[48] As we are about to see, Walter of St Victor described a gathering in Rome in early 1177, which Adam attended.[49] So Adam must have gone to Rome in November or December 1176. He had returned by 13 March 1177, when he attended a council in London.[50] Given how long travel could take in this period, Adam clearly made good time.[51] Another member of Adam's party stayed longer. Alexander issued another decretal on behalf of the archdeacon of Chester, who had apparently been traveling with Adam, and who had remained in the curia "from necessity, not from malice."[52]

There is no evidence that the judges' delegate made a decision about the case.[53] However, they were also in London that March. Henry II was acting as arbiter in a territorial dispute between the kings of Castile and Navarre. An important council was held at Westminster, and a large number of dignitaries were in attendance. We can see why Adam would have hurried back from Rome to attend.[54] Peter of St David's was there too,[55] and the judges' delegate probably heard the territorial dispute between the two dioceses, or at least took preliminary soundings. Since Adam went in person to Rome, he would have brought the papal decretal on the St Michael's dispute back with him.

48 Giovanni D. Mansi, *Sacrorum Conciliorum Nova et Amplissima Collectio* (Florence and Venice, 1759-1798), 21: 217, and 467 lists "Adam de Sancto Asaph" and Peter of St David's as two of the prelates that attended Lateran III.

49 Walter of St Victor, *Contra quatuor labyrinthos Franciae*, ed. Glorieux, 201.

50 *Gesta Regis Henrici Secundi* 1, ed. Stubbs, 154.

51 For the speed and nature of medieval travel, see Norbert Ohler, *The Medieval Traveller*, trans. Caroline Hiller (Woodbridge, 1989).

52 Duggan, "Decretals of Alexander III to England," no. 231, p. 122. Chester was close to St Asaph, and Norman penetration into North Wales had come from there. See the maps in Turvey, *The Welsh Princes*, xx–xxxi. On the relationship of the bishopric of Chester-Lichfield with North Wales, see Davies, *The Age of Conquest*, 183.

53 Cheney, *Roger, Bishop of Worcester*, 328.

54 For the council and a list of attendees, see *Gesta Regis Henrici Secundi* 1, ed. Stubbs, 144–154, and Roger of Hoveden, *Chronica*, ed. William Stubbs (London, 1870), 121–131.

55 According to *Gesta Regis Henrici Secundi* 1, ed. Stubbs, 154–155, Peter de Leia made his formal profession of obedience to Richard, archbishop of Canterbury, after the council.

The judges cannot have been able to arrive at a decision because both Adam and Peter went to the Lateran council. Their attendance is partially explained by the dispute.[56] However, other things could bring bishops to Rome. In the case of Adam and Peter de Leia, there was probably a question of prestige involved. The diocese of St Asaph had not had an active bishop before, so Adam was asserting his position, and the legitimacy of his diocese, by attending. At the council, according to Gerald of Wales, Adam won his case. The matter did not end there, however. Gerald later managed to reverse the decision, "not without great difficulty, thanks to the grace of God and my own hard work."[57] This was probably after Adam's death in 1181.[58] Ceri would remain part of St David's until 1849.[59]

The trouble both men went to indicates that the dispute clearly was about a lot more than a single church. The surrounding land was also at issue. As we have seen, most of Adam's diocese was in the province of Powys, which had been a larger kingdom before the ninth century.[60] R.R. Davies suggests that when the diocese was created in the mid–twelfth century, "St David's may have been required to surrender Powys."[61] Since 1160, the kingdom had been divided, and the ruling princes lacked power.[62] St Michael's church was in the commote of Ceri, a small area that had various overlords in the twelfth and thirteenth centuries.[63] Immediately south were the provinces of Maeliennydd

56 Only a small number of English bishops attended. Roger of Hoveden, *Chronica*, ed. Stubbs, 171.

57 "Sed in concilio Lateranensi ubi ipse interfuit [Peter], his intersignis quod ibi Keri amisit, quam tamen postea per Dei gratiam et industriam nostram non absque difficultate recuperavimus." Gerald of Wales, *Symbolum electorum*, in *Giraldi Cambrensis opera*, ed. Brewer, 1: 323. This comes from a letter critical of Bishop Peter. It is found in *Symbolum electorum*, a collection of letters and other writings that Gerald produced around 1199. See Bartlett, *Gerald of Wales*, 218–219.

58 After Adam died in 1181, there was no bishop again until 1183. It was not until 1186, when Reiner began his long episcopate, that St Asaph again had an interested bishop. See Pearson, "The Creation and Development of the St Asaph Cathedral Chapter," 40.

59 Lloyd, *History of Wales*, 559.

60 For early Powys, see Lloyd, *History of Wales*, 252–253.

61 Davies, *The Age of Conquest*, 183.

62 For twelfth-century Powys, see Turvey, *The Welsh Princes*, 22–23, and Davies, *The Age of Conquest*, 227–236. It is essential to also consult the maps in these books.

63 Lloyd, *History of Wales*, 559; Davies, *The Age of Conquest*, 312, 337; William Rees, *An Historical Atlas of Wales: From Early to Modern Times*, 3rd ed. (London, 1972), pl. 22.

and Elfael, and, according to Gerald, Adam had his eye on these and wanted to incorporate them into his diocese.[64] Moreover, he came with armed men from Powys and Cydewain.[65] Gerald also claimed that Adam produced an ancient book to back up his claim that Ceri belonged to him *iure parochiali*.[66] Presumably, Adam used some sort of similar argument in Rome, where he also pressed his claim *iure parochiali*.[67] However, the St Asaph diocese had only existed since 1143.[68] Lloyd supposed that he was referring to the early-medieval heyday of Powys. There is some indication that at that time, the kingdom controlled Maeliennydd and Elfael.[69] This would make Adam's policy very interesting indeed. He was styling himself bishop of the ancient territory of Powys, not bishop of the Norman diocese of St Asaph. It would also have extended his diocese beyond its native Welsh heartland in Powys and Gwynedd. Maeliennydd and Elfael were subject to Marcher-Norman incursions.[70] As an administrator and potential mediator, this would have made Adam more influential. Alternately, Gerald could have been portraying Adam as more of an aggressor than he actually was.

Although he went to Rome on domestic business, Adam showed that he had not forgotten his teacher Peter Lombard. It must have been while dealing with the consecration dispute that he found himself involved in the debate over Peter Lombard's Christological teachings. Adam appears as a defender of Peter Lombard in Walter of St Victor's *Contra quatuor labyrinthos Franciae* ("Against the Four Labyrinths of France"). This reinforces the idea that Adam went to Rome on an occasion prior to the Lateran council. To understand the part he played we must consider how the Christological contro-

64 Gerald of Wales, *De rebus a se gestis* 6, ed. Brewer, 32–33: "Asseverabant etiam, quod si provinciam illam occupare permissus fuerit, totam quoque terram usque Vagam, scilicet Meilenith et Elevein tanquam ad ecclesiam suam de S. Asaph pertinentem firmiter occupare proposuit."

65 Gerald requested men with horses and arms, since Adam came with "a strong force" from Powys and Cydewain. Ibid., 33.

66 Ibid., 35.

67 "ad ecclesiam suam iure parochiali pertineat." In Morey, *Bartholomew of Exeter*, 129–130.

68 Walker, *Medieval Wales*, 74.

69 Lloyd, *History of Wales*, 252–253, 559.

70 See the map in Turvey, *The Welsh Princes*, xxvi. To take an example of such border tensions, Cadwallon, the prince of Maeliennydd, was murdered by associates of Roger Mortimer in 1179. See Lloyd, *History of Wales*, 567.

versy was developing in the second half of the 1170s. Walter of St Victor's pamphlet is one of the key sources. It is the most hostile anti-Lombard tract of all. Walter was not just an opponent of Peter, as his introduction reveals:

> Anyone who reads this work will not doubt that there are four labyrinths of France, Abelard, the Lombard, Peter of Poitiers, and Gilbert of Poitiers, who, inflated with one Aristotelian mindset, deal lightly with the ineffable mysteries of the Holy Trinity, and the incarnation, so that they can spit out many heresies and spread errors.[71]

By attacking some of the major figures in Parisian theology at the start of his work, Walter shows a blatant lack of sympathy for what was happening in the cathedral schools. His theological views were probably shaped by Achard of St Victor and Robert of Melun, who both taught at St Victor in the 1150s.[72] Robert certainly harboured reservations about Peter Lombard's Christology, while Achard criticized the nihilist position.[73] The *Contra labyrinthos* has received almost universal condemnation from modern scholars. Glorieux, who edited it, sums it up as "mauvaise action, mauvais travail."[74] But one

71 "Quisquis hec legerit non dubitabit quatuor labirinthos Francie, id est Abeilardum et alium Lumbardum, Petrum Pictaviensem episcopum et Gislebertum Porretam uno aristotilico spiritu afflatos dum ineffabilia sancte Trinitatis et incarnationis scolastica leuitate tractarent, multas hereses olim vomuisse et adhuc errores pullulare." Walter of St Victor, *Contra quatuor labyrinthos Franciae*, ed. Glorieux, 201.

72 For Robert teaching at St Victor in the 1150s, see Dale M. Coulter, *Per Visibilia ad Invisibilia: Theological Method in Richard of St Victor* (Turnhout, 2006), 244–246. For the esteem in which he was held there, see Constant Mews, "Between the Schools of Abelard and Saint-Victor in the Mid-Twelfth Century: The Witness of Robert of Melun," in *L'école de Saint-Victor de Paris: Influence et rayonnement du Moyen Âge à l'epoque moderne*, ed. Dominique Poirel (Turnhout, 2010), 137. For Achard, see chapter eight, above, 204.

73 Nikolaus M. Häring, "The *Eulogium ad Alexandrum Papam Tertium* of John of Cornwall," *Mediaeval Studies* 13 (1951): 253–300, at 268. This text is discussed below. For Robert's criticisms of Peter, see also Mews, "Between the Schools of Abelard and Saint-Victor," 125, 136–138. For Achard's criticisms, see chapter eight, above, 204.

74 Palémon Glorieux, "Mauvaise action et mauvais travail: Le *Contra Quatuor Labyrinthos Franciae*," *RTAM* 21 (1954): 179–193. See also his introduction to Walter of St Victor, *Contra quatuor labyrinthos Franciae*, ed. Glorieux, 193. Colish, *Peter Lombard*, 432, describes it as a "garbled, intemperate, misinformed and largely plagiarized work." Only Fourrier Bonnard, *Histoire de l'abbaye royale et de l'ordre des chanoines réguliers de St. Victor de Paris* (Paris, 1904–1908), 1: 121, provides a rela-

should not expect it to conform to the standards of other late–twelfth century theological works. The *Contra labyrinthos* must be understood as polemical literature. Walter was capable of other work. We know that his sermons were highly regarded at St Victor, where he formed part of a long preaching tradition.[75]

One reason for the intensity of his invective may be that, by the time he wrote, the tide was already turning in Peter Lombard's favour, and Walter could see this. In February 1177, Alexander III wrote another letter to William of the White Hands, now archbishop of Rheims, urging that masters should avoid Christological nihilism, particularly the words *Christus non est aliquid secundum homo*:

> Since Christ is perfect man and perfect God, it is amazing that anyone would have the temerity to dare to say that Christ, as a man, is not something. So that this abuse may not be associated with the church of God or this error introduced, we command you through this letter to assemble masters of Paris, Rheims and other surrounding towns, and, with our authority, to condemn, under pain of excommunication, anyone who would dare to say that Christ as a man is not something, because he was truly God and truly man, subsisting from a rational soul and human flesh.[76]

---

tively positive assessment of the work. Recently, Rossi has slightly modified the negative judgement: Pietro Rossi, "Contra Lombardum: Reazioni alla Cristologia di Pietro Lombardo," in *Pietro Lombardo: Atti del XLIII Convegno storico internazionale* (Spoleto, 2007), 128–144. His view is that Walter's work had not reached definitive form.

75 Walter's sermons, although not overly rigorous, do show a grasp of distinction-based writing and of relating the opening text to the feast day. See his *Sermo de purificatione*, in *Galteri a Sancto Victore et quorumdam aliorum: Sermones ineditos*, ed. Jean Châtillon (CCCM 30: 47–56). His fidelity to his Victorine masters is clearly observable in the *Sermo in Epiphania*, ibid., 57–62, where the opinion of "magister Hugo" is cited. For assessments of Walter as a preacher, see Châtillon, introduction to ibid., 10, and also Jean Longère, "La fonction pastorale de Saint-Victor à la fin du XIIe et au début du XIIIe siècle," in *L'Abbaye parisienne de Saint-Victor au moyen-âge*, ed. Jean Longère (Paris, 1991), 291–313, at 299.

76 "Cum Christus perfectus Deus perfectus sit homo, mirum est qua temeritate quisquam audet dicere quod Christus non sit aliquid secundum quod homo. Ne autem tanta possit in ecclesia Dei abusio suboriri vel error induci, fraternitati tue per apostolica scripta mandamus quatinus convocatis magistris scolarum parisen-

Like the letter of 28 May 1170, Alexander called for an assembly of scholars. William, addressed as a papal legate, had the power to do this. But in this letter, Peter Lombard is not named or associated with the doctrine. We have seen how Herbert of Bosham and William of the White Hands worked to disassociate Peter from it. This letter also has a more urgent quality. It is directed at masters who were active in the schools, and who were apparently teaching nihilism. The pope had not threatened excommunication in the earlier letter.[77] Walter of St Victor was aware of the 1177 letter and quoted it in his prologue. Hence, scholars have argued that he wrote his work in 1178, in an attempt to influence the outcome of the Lateran council.[78] The *Contra labyrinthos* then was very much a pamphlet written with a specific purpose – to ensure that any condemnation of nihilism included condemnation of Peter Lombard.

Walter refers to an occasion when the pope, assembled cardinals, and, curiously, Adam of Wales, debated the issue of Peter Lombard's teachings. It occurs in the prologue, midway between a general introductory paragraph about the heresies of Lombard and his other targets and a copy of the 1177 letter. He begins,

> It should also be known that recently, at a council in Rome, Pope Alexander had prepared to condemn Lombard's opinions by name, through the argument that the diabolical error of Arius, Sabellius and more recent heretics had raised its ugly head again, i.e., that Christ, as a man, is nothing. Now some of the cardinals, disregarding the cause of God and the Christian faith by which we live and by which we stand for other

---

sium et remensium et aliarum circumpositarum civitatum, auctoritate nostra sub anathemate interdicas ne quis de cetero dicere audeat Christum non esse aliquid secundum quod homo, quia sicut verus Deus ita verus est homo ex anima rationali et humana carne subsistens." The text can be found in *Chartularium universitatis parisiensis,* ed. Heinrich Denifle (Paris, 1889–1897), 1: 8–9.

77 See the discussion of the first letter in chapter eight, above, 210.

78 Glorieux challenged the idea that Walter was talking about the Lateran Council of 1179 by pointing to the use of the 1177 letter. Walter of St Victor, *Contra quatuor labyrinthos Franciae,* ed. Glorieux, 195. Glorieux's thesis was largely accepted, although Châtillon, "Latran III et l'enseignement christologique de Pierre Lombard," 87–88, had some reservations. One of them was how to explain the presence of Adam in Rome, if it was not for the Lateran council. The dispute with St David's solves that problem.

> business, said to the venerable pope, "Lord Pope, we think we should deal with other important matters." In response, the pope said, "First and foremost then we must deal with the issues of faith and heresy." Hearing that, those cardinals left the consistory. Even a bishop who was there, Adam of Wales, stood up and walked out, saying as he did so, "Lord Pope, I was once a student and *praepositus* of Peter Lombard's school, and I will defend the opinions of my master." What was the result of all this? With the apostolic see resounding and stating definitively from Rome in this way, the putrid croaking of frogs ceased [the letter of 1177 follows].[79]

Since Walter claims that this gathering occasioned the letter of 18 February 1177, he cannot be referring to the Lateran council of 1179. He is not entirely clear on what kind of gathering it was, however, since he uses the words council and consistory interchangeably.[80] This inconsistency has implications for Walter's reliability. His account is usually repeated without question, as if he were an eyewitness writing a chronicle. It should not be assumed that he was present. He could just as easily have received an account of the proceedings from someone in the curia. This is why it is too easy to point to Walter's bitterness as a reason why the challenge to Peter Lombard failed. Clearly, there were people much closer to Alexander III who were hostile to Peter, and who were probably behind the letters of 1170 and 1177. This makes Adam's intervention all the more important.

79 "Hoc etiam sciendum quod Alexander papa nuper in concilio romano parauerat nominatim illius sententias damnare quarum argumentis etiam Arrii et Sabellii et nouorum hereticorum error diabolicus recrudescit, scilicet quod Christus nichil sit secundum quod homo. Quidam uero cardinalium causam Dei et fidei Christianae religionis qua stamus et uiuimus, alienis negociis postponentes, non recte respondentes dixerunt uenerabili pape: Domine, alia maiora suscepimus tractanda. Tunc apostolicus: Immo primum et maximum de fide et hereticis agendum est. Quod illi audientes egressi sunt de consistorio. Quidam etiam episcopus, Adam Walensis exiuit cum illis dicens: Domine papa, ego et clericus et prepositus olim scolarum eius, defendam sententias magistri. Quid plura? Cessent iam putridie ranarum garrulitates, apostolica Sede de Roma ita intonante ac diffiniente." Walter of St Victor, *Contra quatuor labyrinthos Franciae*, ed. Glorieux, 201. It is notable here that Walter uses the word *nichil* (nothing), instead of *non aliquid* (not something).

80 Châtillon, "Latran III et l'enseignement christologique de Pierre Lombard," in *Le Troisième Concile de Latran (1179): Sa place dans l'histoire*, ed. Jean Longère (Paris, 1982), 75–90, at 86–89; Colish, *Peter Lombard*, 433–444.

Despite the efforts of the intervening years, the idea that Peter Lombard had taught nihilism was still current. It seems that Adam was the only person on hand capable of giving a competent explanation of what his master's position had been. The cardinals had merely tried to deflect the issue, and then walked out. Adam probably said more than Walter reports, either at the gathering or later. Something discouraged the pope from acting. Châtillon provides the fullest analysis of the probable motivations of the participants. For him, the primary motivation of Adam and the Cardinals was not to defend the teachings as much as Peter Lombard himself.[81] But the upright character of Peter Lombard, the orthodoxy of his opinions, and his overall authority as a *magister* would all have been bound closely together in the minds of the participants. An accusation of heresy was often coupled with accusations of bad character. The position of a master in the schools rested on his good character, and this, together with his firm grasp of his subject, was the source of his authority.[82] So Adam and the cardinals were defending Peter Lombard from any attempt to besmirch him. Adam in particular may have prevented the pope from making a firm decision. We will return to the pope's policy on this issue in our overall conclusion.

Leading the men of Powys across the hills that divided Cydewain from Ceri is a very long way from Peter Lombard's theology school. Yet it is also a powerful reminder of the broad reach of activity in medieval Europe, and the pull of traditional loyalties. In Adam, traditional loyalties co-existed with an international outlook and a strong sense of duty to Peter Lombard, his master in Paris. Adam's assertiveness about the church of St Michael's shows that he took being bishop of St Asaph seriously. He was the only one of St Asaph's

81 Châtillon, "Latran III et l'enseignement christologique de Pierre Lombard," 89: "L'indignation des défenseurs de Pierre Lombard s'explique mieux encore si on se souvient des calomnies que certains de ses adversaires n'hésitaient pas à inventer contre lui." Lauge-Olaf Nielsen, *Theology and Philosophy in the Twelfth Century: A Study of Gilbert Porreta's Thinking and the Theological Expositions of the Doctrine of the Incarnation during the Period 1130–1180* (Leiden, 1982), 361, is of the unusual opinion that Adam supported the *habitus* position and was defending Peter for adhering to it. But it does not make sense that Adam would defend a position that the pope was preparing to condemn as heretical.

82 On this issue, see Verger, "Teachers," in *A History of the University in Europe*: Volume 1: *Universities in the Middle Ages*. ed. Hilde de Ridder-Symoens (Cambridge, 1992), 161–164, and Astrik L. Gabriel, "The Ideal Master of the Medieval University," *Catholic Historical Review* 60 (1974): 1–40, at 39.

first four bishops to spend a significant amount of time in his diocese.[83] He was also politically astute. His appeal to both the authority of the archbishop of Canterbury and an "ancient Welsh book" shows awareness of political reality, the mingling of new authority and ancient tradition. His journey to Rome shows him fully conversant with the legal processes available to bishops. The appeal seems to have centered on the idea of the traditional territory of Powys. Adam's interest in extending boundaries on the strength of rightful tradition makes sense: he was an adolescent when the Welsh recovery began in the mid-1130s, and he left for his studies while this was gaining momentum. Returning to Wales to take up his episcopal post, he retained the spirit of the recovery, the desire to reclaim what had been lost.

John of Cornwall (c.1125–1198)

Another contribution to the debate, the *Eulogium* by John of Cornwall, appeared in the run up to the Lateran council. John reveals in this work that he had heard Peter teach. His purpose in writing was to persuade Alexander III to condemn the nihilist position of "Christ, insofar as he is a man, is not something." Historians have disagreed about whether he aimed to distance Peter from that position. Unlike the other pupils covered in this book, John only studied with Peter for a short period. Despite this, he was aware of the importance of the *Sentences*, and he made extensive use of it in preparing the *Eulogium*. He had certain reservations about aspects of Peter's teaching, but he did not deny his overall achievement. John's career was not as varied as Herbert of Bosham's or Adam of Wales's. After studying theology in Paris, he was able to embark on a lengthy career as a *magister* in England.

John was born some time between 1125 and 1130, and he studied the arts in the 1140s and early 1150s.[84] After completing his course in the arts, he worked for Robert Warelwast, bishop of Exeter.[85] This led to his first literary work, a translation of the *Prophecies of Merlin*, probably completed between

83 Pearson, "The Creation and Development of the St Asaph Cathedral Chapter," 40.
84 For John, see David Luscombe, "John of Cornwall," in *Oxford Dictionary of National Biography*, 13: 468–469, and Eleanor Rathbone, "John of Cornwall: A Brief Biography," *RTAM* 17 (1950): 46–60.
85 Rathbone, "John of Cornwall: A Brief Biography," 47–48.

1153 and 1155.[86] At some point in the mid-1150s, John left England to study theology in Paris. This again demonstrates the appeal of advanced study in theology. Although it did not guarantee material rewards, students were willing to desert existing careers for it. John enrolled with Peter Lombard and studied Christology with him "shortly before he became bishop of Paris."[87] This must have been in the 1157–1158 academic year because, as we have seen, Peter gave a course on the Psalms in 1158–1159. Peter's departure from the schools meant that John would have to continue his training with other masters. He would not be able to take the title *magister* and seek a chair in theology after only two or three years. He began to attend the school of Master Maurice of Sully in 1159–1160 and must have cursed his luck when, after he had spent only a year in this school, Maurice succeeded Peter as bishop of Paris. John then completed his studies with Robert of Melun. It was a somewhat disjointed training, since Robert and Peter did not have much in common. We know, partly from John's testimony, that Robert criticized Peter's positions.[88] The curse of episcopal appointment continued to follow John, however: Robert of Melun became bishop of Hereford in 1163.

With at least five or six years of training completed, John was now equipped to set himself up as a theology master, and he returned to England. He taught for almost forty years, probably at Oxford, although the location is not certain.[89] Two books of his gloss on Gratian's *Decretum*, which may reflect his classroom teaching, have survived.[90] He also may have written a work called "on the different ways of reading sacred scripture" since it makes reference to the teaching of both Peter Lombard and Robert of Melun.[91] His own students did not face the same problems as he had endured. Although he was twice recommended to Henry II for the bishopric of St David's, he was not appointed.

86 Michael J. Curley, "A New Edition of John of Cornwall's *Propheta Merlini*," *Speculum* 57 (1982): 217–249, at 217–218. The text is on 231–249.

87 "Praetera paulo ante quam electus esset in episcoporum Parisiensem, michi et omnibus auditoribus suis qui tunc aderant protestatus est, quod hoc non esset assertio sua sed opinio sola, quam a magistris acceperat." Häring, "The *Eulogium ad Alexandrum Papam Tertium* of John of Cornwall," 265.

88 Ibid., 268.

89 Luscombe, "John of Cornwall."

90 Ibid.

91 Ibid.

The work most associated with John, the *Eulogium*, appeared in the 1170s. *Eulogium* is used here in the sense of a speech or proposition, not a eulogy for the deceased, and the rest of the title is "to Pope Alexander III." The text provides unique insights into the relationship between theology masters and their students. We have seen that there was an obligation for students to defend their masters. Does John do this?

The *Eulogium* sets out to disprove that Christ's humanity was "not something" or was a garment (the *habitus* theory). John, in common with others at the time, seems to have been concerned about how some theologians were handling these issues: "There are certain men today who are more loquacious than perspicacious, and who are preaching things from rooftops that should not be heard even in private rooms."[92] John's theological approach has, until recently, come in for some heavy criticism. Colish calls his work a "spectacularly poor performance,"[93] while Häring refers to him as "a generally well informed scholar whose speculative abilities, however, hardly surpass the sterile formalism of grammatical logic."[94] As often, such harsh judgements provoked a reaction. Pietro Rossi prefers to characterize John as someone who "did not have a sharp mind ... but who moved over the theological ground with professionalism, if not originality."[95]

John's treatment of Peter Lombard is where things become complicated. In his second edition of the *Eulogium*, John includes Alexander III's letter of 1170, which specifies Peter Lombard as the source of the "vicious doctrine."[96] Scholars have been divided on the degree to which John was attacking Peter directly. Besides including the letter, John says that he had been "slowly converted" away from Peter's positions by Maurice of Sully and Robert of Melun:

92 " Postea vero per quosdam homines loquaces magis quam perspicaces que nec in cubiculis essent audienda usque hodie predicantur super tecta." Häring, "The *Eulogium ad Alexandrum Papam Tertium* of John of Cornwall," 265.

93 Colish, *Peter Lombard,* 431. Colish critiques John as a student of Peter "in the 1150s" and does not seem to take seriously his citation of Robert of Melun and Maurice of Sully: "Robert's works were not available to John and there is no evidence that Maurice wrote anything except ... sermons." Ibid., 430. This ignores the fact that, as a student of both, John was well placed to know their opinions.

94 Häring, "The *Eulogium ad Alexandrum Papam Tertium* of John of Cornwall," 254.

95 Rossi, "*Contra Lombardum,*" 158.

96 Häring, "The *Eulogium ad Alexandrum Papam Tertium* of John of Cornwall," 257–258.

"I was present at many of their lectures and disputations, in which they argued that Peter Lombard's teaching on the humanity of Christ (*de homine assumpto*) was false. They were not easily able to wean me off what I had held for so long."[97] But throughout his work it is clear that he is actually using the *Sentences* as his chief source.[98] This is what provoked the indignation of scholars like Colish and Häring. To attack Peter while using his work would seem to be disingenuous at best.

Rossi refers to John's work, albeit humorously, as "intellectual parricide"[99] but goes on to say that it represents a calculated attempt to discredit Peter in favour of Robert of Melun.[100] The second statement is certainly accurate, and in fact disproves the first. It was not parricide, because by saying that he had been converted to Robert's viewpoint, John was making it clear that he was *not* a son of Peter Lombard in the intellectual sense. Robert became his master. Thus John would not fit into Peter Comestor's criterion for "safe ears."[101] He had not completed the course with Peter. His theological training was not solely with him. The ties of loyalty and obligation were not the same. John is the exception that proves our rule.

And yet he still had some regard for Peter. It has been suggested that John's widespread use of the *Sentences* in his *Eulogium* was from a desire to "exonerate Peter Lombard the person ... he wanted to save as much of the *Sentences* as possible."[102] Furthermore, although John claims in his prologue that Peter propounded nihilist views, he almost defends him for it. Peter was stating "not his own position but only an opinion which he accepted from

97 "Multis eorum lectionibus et disputationibus interfui, in quibus et de homine assumpto et de aliis quibusdam magistri Petri Lumbardi doctrinam falsitatis arguebant, ne dicam erroris. Michi tamen non facile nec cito potuerunt auellere quod diu tenueram." Ibid., 268.

98 Ibid., 245–255: "he rifled [Lombard] without acknowledgement in his fast search for auctoritates."

99 Rossi, "*Contra Lombardum*," 126–127: "il parricidio non è infrequente nelle famiglie accademiche."

100 Ibid., 158.

101 See chapter five, above, 119.

102 Clare Monagle, "Christological Nihilism in the Twelfth Century: The Contested Reception of Peter Lombard's Sententiae," (PhD diss., Johns Hopkins University, 2007), 107–108. Monagle also discusses John in *Orthodoxy and Controversy in Twelfth-Century Religious Discourse: Peter Lombard's Sentences and the Development of Theology* (Turnhout, 2013), 104–107.

masters."[103] Peter had clarified this further for his students by saying, "God willing I may never take a position contrary to the Catholic faith."[104] For John, this contrasted favourably with contemporary masters who were "shouting things from rooftops."[105] What is significant is John's distinction between opinion and position, and his inclusion of the oath. It seems that he wanted the position, but not Peter Lombard, condemned. A condemnation could only be issued for a stated position, not for an opinion. Interestingly, however, John did not include the 1177 letter, where the pope had done precisely that. John may not have been aware of it at the time of writing the work.

103 "Praetera paulo ante quam electus esset in episcoporum Parisiensem, michi et omnibus auditoribus suis qui tunc aderant protestatus est, quod hoc non esset assertio sua sed opinio sola, quam a magistris acceperat." Häring, "The *Eulogium ad Alexandrum Papam Tertium* of John of Cornwall," 265.

104 "Hec etiam verba subiecit, 'nec umquam Deo volente erit assertio mea nisi que fuerit fides catholica.'" Ibid.

105 Ibid.

Conclusion

Peter Lombard's achievements in teaching and writing were assisted by an ability to take advantage of his surroundings and connections. In Italy he attracted the attention of two figures prominent in schism diplomacy, Uberto of Lucca and Bernard of Clairvaux. With their help, he was able to study theology in France. His abilities as a theologian were recognized in Paris and were the foundation of his prestige there. By basing himself in Paris, he ensured that his theological works would continue to be read. When he became a canon of Notre Dame, he was on equal terms with a group that was important not only in the diocese but in Capetian France as a whole. His fellow canons included four royal chancellors and (including himself) six future bishops. It is important now to draw the two parts of this book together by looking at Peter and his students in tandem, at what united them, and at the areas where they intersect.

The students (with the exception of John of Cornwall) all studied theology with Peter for at least six years. During that time, they came regularly to the rooms where he held his school, and they listened to him lecture, asked questions, and held discussions. This was very close proximity. Now and again, they also had the opportunity to hear him preach. Beyond that, we can assume that he spoke to them socially, and occasionally dined with and advised them. They knew him, and he knew them, very well. That is beyond doubt. It is hardly surprising that from so close a relationship a strong sense of loyalty would build up. In effect, the students were apprentices, and the craft was theology. This is the best way to explain the daily refining of skills that Peter's school involved. The students learned under the supervision of the master. Undoubtedly, there would have been time for private study, but attendance at the school was of the highest importance.

Alongside that loyalty developed a very clear sense of obligation. Having studied with him for such a long period, the students knew Peter Lombard's work better than anyone, and they had the essential ability to present it to those who asked. They saw it as their duty to ensure that his works were copied, read, commented on, and understood. We know from William of Tyre that this was happening in the 1170s, and Herbert of Bosham's edition is the most visually arresting example of the process. Herbert's distinctive pages, and William's reference to *reverentia*, indicate the devotion of close followers, but they also show that Peter's works were recognized to be innovative. There was much to say about them. They stimulated discussion, debate, commentary, condemnation, pictorial illustration, vicious invective, and passionate defence. Surely that is the best refutation of those modern scholars who have downplayed Peter's significance. It is often the most original and creative work that generates such a varied reaction.

Could Peter have anticipated this? He was successful in his own time, but he could not have foreseen how popular his *Sentences* would become. There was definitely a modesty about him. It stands out very plainly in the fact that he was a late developer, waiting until his last decade to write the *Sentences*. It is also there in his sermons. Peter just did not have the temperament to harangue his audience or to make any directly personal references while preaching. But he did know that his work would face challenges. Toward the end of his life, this was already happening.

What then was his debt to his students? What did he hope they would gain from their time in his school? The careers of just the few mentioned here illustrate the different directions students could go in after leaving a theology school. We can guess that Peter's other students had similarly diverse careers. Only some taught theology. None were as exclusively committed to it as their master. Peter believed in theology. He extolled it in his sermon on the epiphany, viewing the Magi as forebears. The example was not lost on his students. Peter Comestor placed theology above the other disciplines, as being something only a few could do. But all of these things – the employing of symbolism, the surrounding in bright colours, and the appropriating of tradition – were the trappings of something that was basic, practical, and necessary. Each of Peter's students went on to some kind of clerical career, and each of them used their theological training. This awareness of the practical application of theology was shared by all of the students. Two became bishops, while Herbert of Bosham was appointed "theological consultant" to a bishop who had not received that sort of training. William of Tyre put his training to use in his debates with King Amalric. Peter Comestor tried to make his master's findings accessible to those who could not afford to have the *Sentences* copied, or who lacked the time or training to make their way through it. The theology school gave the students the ability to deal with questions arising from doctrine and scriptural interpretation. There they received a grounding in traditional patristic responses in more recent authorities, and repeated practice in debate. Wherever they went they would retain this.

Some of the students also went on to have the care of souls. Peter's sermons show that he took this role very seriously. William and Adam, as bishops, would have preached sermons, although no copies survive. Herbert of Bosham was a sometime freelance sermon writer, sought out by an abbot in one letter.[1] Only Peter Comestor's sermons have survived, and they show the definite, but not dominating, influence of Peter Lombard. For the students who heard Peter preach, however, the debt was much more than that of apprentices learning the craft of composing sermons. The real significance of the sermons is the spiritual guidance Peter provided through them, and this must have stayed with the students.

Looking at the works the students later produced, we might say that Peter influenced their development as writers. More than anything, he seems to have instilled in them the sense of the great project. This was probably unconscious and was the result of the students being in close proximity to their master as he worked on the *Sentences*. Some of them were present when Peter taught it in his school. The writings of the students are great, ambitious projects, as the *Sentences* is. William of Tyre aimed to write the history of the Latin Kingdom and to show people in the West that it was worth fighting for. Herbert was able to produce a monumental life of Thomas Becket, tracing a journey from birth to martyrdom. And there is Peter Comestor's *Historia Scholastica,* as vast an undertaking as the *Sentences* itself.

As well as the idea of great themes, the ability to conceive such works and write them over a sustained period of time must have been nurtured by working under Lombard. But is it also significant that the three works just mentioned were all works of history? This is not the place to survey the students as historians, but it is worth asking whether they could have obtained a sense of history's importance, or even a theory of history, from Peter. It is difficult to say. Certainly the students would have learned from his coherent, methodical approach. As we have seen, the outline of universal history pervades the

1 Smalley, *Becket Conflict,* 65–66; PL 190: 1457–1459.

Sentences and recurs also in some of the sermons. Additionally, the *Sentences* presents a tradition of authorities, in a coherent, readable, and often broadly chronological manner. Finally, his approach to the Letters of Paul is sometimes governed by historical context.

Something else that unites the students is a vigorous assertion of their rights and privileges. Peter Comestor refused to back down on the *licentia docendi* issue when the papal legate, Peter Chrysogonus, tried to prevent him from charging his customary fees. Adam of Wales, unlike his predecessors in the St Asaph diocese, tried to make something of his bishopric by extending its boundaries. He was fully convinced that he was entitled to do this, on the strength of the once-unified early medieval kingdom of Powys. Most drastic was Herbert of Bosham's advice to Becket not to compromise. This is not to say that if Peter's episcopate had been longer it would have gone in a similar direction to Becket's. His career at Notre Dame shows a skillful ability to find favour with the court while retaining his intellectual independence. Peter's sense of clerical entitlement would undoubtedly have been shaped by his knowledge of canon law, particularly Gratian. We can assume that as archdeacon he would not have attempted to overreach his authority. He owed too much to bishop Theobald to do that, and his former master Hugh of St Victor had made clear that archdeacons should be *sub episcopo*. At the same time, he would certainly have insisted on his entitlement to a portion of the revenue of his archdeaconry, since this was standard practice and had been confirmed by the pope. Peter's rise in Notre Dame seems to suggest an active interest in furthering his career. He was dynamic and so were his students.

If they were driven in this way, it came partly from their backgrounds. The students, and Peter himself, all appear to have been self-made men from humble beginnings. They cannot be connected with illustrious families. No ecclesiastical career was guaranteed for them. Like Peter, they needed patronage to continue their studies. After that, some – William, Comestor, and, to a lesser extent, John of Cornwall – made a comfortable living. Adam and Herbert had to make do only with periods of security. For Adam, that security was hard won after years of teaching without prestige. Comestor was the only one who followed the example of his master in making a name for himself in Paris. He was able to navigate the royal and ecclesiastical connections in that city to gain position and security. Paris was not an easy place to succeed in, but the others also found the lure of home too strong to resist. We should not assume that intellectuals at this time lived in happy exile. Peter Lombard himself once talked to the canons of St Victor about how difficult it was to leave "the house of your father, your homeland, and your people, as the Lord had bid Abraham."[2]

Peter's debt to his students then was part intellectual, part practical, part literary, part political, and part spiritual. How did the students reciprocate? How did they externalize that sense of obligation? Their efforts can be divided into three categories: appreciative references, dissemination of works, and countering of opposition. The appreciation was sincerely meant. We have seen the glowing tributes in the works of the students. We have also seen that Herbert, Comestor, and the *chorus* diligently prepared new editions and versions of the works. Let us look then at the opposition.

Peter's years in Paris are a classic example of someone successfully climbing the twelfth-century ecclesiastical career ladder. He was a canon, deacon, and archdeacon at Notre Dame Cathedral, and this was unusual for an Italian of humble beginnings. The bishopric of Paris was his high point. Moreover, Peter's works were very successful. He was not the only theologian to complete a work called the *Sentences* at the time, but his was copied more rapidly and frequently than any others. His *Commentary on the Psalms* became more popular than the work that it was largely based on, the commentary by Gilbert of Poitiers. It is scarcely surprising that a backlash would set in after he died.

The Christological controversy of the 1160s and 1170s must be understood partly in the context of that backlash. We have seen that a number of critics found fault with elements of Peter's teaching. This was partly healthy debate. Practicing theologians could only expect this, but they preferred it to come from their own ranks. Robert of Melun and Maurice of Sully criticized the *Sentences* in their classrooms. Peter refused to debate Robert Cricklade, the prior of St Frideswide's. Gerhoh of Reichersberg's allegations were serious, rooted in Peter's works, but he had a long history of taking issue with theologians. Beyond his own circle his effectiveness was little.

2 Peter begins a sermon on the text "Egredere de terra tua, et de cognatione tua, et de domo patris tui" (Gen. 12:1) in this way: "Magnum quidem est difficile, ad quod nos Dominus hortatur sub figura Abrahae, sed utile observantibus et salubre." Peter Lombard, *Sermo in laetere Ierusalem* (PL 171: 853–864, at 853). For this sermon being preached at St Victor, see Barthélemy Hauréau, *Notices et extraits de quelques manuscrits latins de la Bibliothèque Nationale* (Paris, 1888–1891), 3: 65, and Brady, Prolegomena 1: 103*.

The most serious criticism revolved around the nihilist position referred to in three papal letters, summarized as "Christ, as a man, is not something." According to John of Cornwall, by the 1170s a climate existed of this position being taught. He fails to name names. For the opposition, and for the students, the crucial issue was whether Peter Lombard was to be associated with the nihilist position. The earliest work condemning the position, the *Objectiones* of the early 1160s, did not associate it with Peter, and, in fact, the author used the *Sentences* extensively in his search for authorities.[3] The pope also took action in the 1160s against "undisciplined questions in theology" but did not mention any names. Although allegations against Peter were undoubtedly passed by word of mouth in this period, they did not appear in writing. This changed in the 1170s. One of the three papal letters, that of 28 May 1170, associated the nihilist position with Peter. There it is described as a "vicious doctrine," and Peter is identified as the source. Walter of St Victor also associated it with Peter. The other author to mention the position was John of Cornwall, who urged the pope to condemn it. For him, Peter favoured the position only as an opinion, not a position.

The attitude of Alexander III was not one of pure hostility to Peter Lombard. He certainly did not have a vendetta against him, for he showed favour to Comestor, Herbert, and Adam. He was concerned, however, about what was happening in the schools of Paris. In May 1170, the pope seems to have been persuaded that Peter Lombard was responsible for theology teachers supporting nihilism. Later, in 1177 and at the Lateran Council, he softened that view. But he remained committed to rooting out the position. While the February 1177 letter removes Lombard from the equation, it also shows a hardening of attitude on Alexander's part. Anyone teaching that "Christ, as a man, is not something" now faced excommunication. This threat appeared to work. Omitting mention of Peter Lombard by name probably increased the letter's effectiveness. Alexander may well have realized that condemning him brought too much of a personal element into the process and allowed for both loyalty and antagonism to cloud the issue. By leaving him out, the focus would be on the position, not the person.

This focus on the position, not the person, also resulted from the work of Herbert of Bosham, William of the White Hands, Adam of Wales, and John

3 Nikolaus M. Häring, "The So-Called *Apologia de Verbo Incarnato,*" *Franciscan Studies* 16 (1956): 102–103.

of Cornwall, all of whom did not want to see Peter Lombard condemned. They worked to dissociate Peter from any suggestion of nihilism. They had to work against obstacles. It seems there was a curia-based opposition to Peter, with links to Paris. Their only record is Walter of St Victor's tract, which he was probably commissioned to write. It is important not to take Walter at his word. The pamphlet is not the work of a hysterical madman. Walter was not hysterical by nature. His sermons reveal that. This was a pamphlet, and there was pamphlet warfare in the twelfth century much as there would be in later ages.

The period between 1177 and 1179 was crucial, and it is probable that only a fraction of material produced at the time has actually come down to us about it. Alexander III mentions in the letter of May 1170 that he had already discussed with William of the White Hands condemning the position. Countless other verbal discussions must have taken place throughout the 1170s among church figures. However, contemporaries were not always aware of the finer points of the sequence of events. Walter of St Victor was well informed. His quotation of the 1177 letter, and account of the consistory that preceded it, shows that someone was keeping him up-to-date. But John of Cornwall quotes only the May 1170 letter in his work, showing that he was probably unaware of what had taken place in 1177.[4] Essentially, what John of Cornwall asked the pope to do at the Lateran Council – to condemn Christological heresies without specifying particular masters – had already happened.

At the Lateran council, no condemnation was made, and there is no record of a debate on the issue. The pope had apparently said all he wanted to say about it in his letters. They were directed at the cathedral schools of France, whereas the canons of the council were aimed at the whole church. The council certainly dealt with some of the practicalities of teaching in the schools, reasserting, for example, the ban on charging a fee for the *licentia docendi*. If anyone there attempted to raise a voice against Peter Lombard, they were probably forestalled by his former students (Adam of Wales and William of Tyre were there) and by William of the White Hands. It is also very possible that somebody brought a copy of the *Sentences* along.

4 Ibid., 108.

Why did the controversy die down? The pope's pronouncements on nihilism undoubtedly had some effect. If people ceased teaching that "Christ, as a man, is not something" for fear of ecclesiastical censure, then Peter Lombard was no longer invoked as their authority. The effort to dissociate him from that position also helped. But the main reason was the passage of years. Competitors left the scene, and rumours were no longer tinged with venom. As often happens, the younger generation is left wondering what all the fuss was about, when faced with the partisan squabbles of the older, built as they are on personality conflict, jealousy, questions of ego, and misunderstanding. Misunderstanding had perhaps been the biggest culprit. Peter had not been around to explain his positions or to check the spread of certain oral statements. With the passage of years also came a greater understanding of the *Sentences*, through commentary, lecturing, questions, and explanation. A tradition had begun. Peter's *written* word was now pre-eminent. Rumours surrounding what he had said in his classroom faded into obscurity.

Bibliography

Manuscripts

Cambridge, Trinity College Library, B.5.4
Herbert of Bosham's Edition of Peter Lombard's *Commentary on the Psalms*, vol. 1.

Cambridge, Trinity College Library, B.5.6
Herbert of Bosham's Edition of Peter Lombard's *Commentary on the Letters of Paul*, vol. 1.

Cambridge, Trinity College Library, B.5.7
Herbert of Bosham's Edition of Peter Lombard's *Commentary on the Letters of Paul*, vol. 2.

Oxford, Bodleian Library, Auct. E. inf. 6
Herbert of Bosham's Edition of Peter Lombard's *Commentary on the Psalms*, vol. 2.

Paris, Bibliothèque nationale de France, lat. 13374, fol. 1–49v
Sermons of Peter Lombard.

Paris, Bibliothèque nationale de France, lat. 14590
Peter Lombard's *Sermo Communis*, along with other contemporary sermons.

Primary and Early Historical Sources

Abelard, Peter. *Historia calamitatum*. Ed. Jacques Monfrin. Paris: J. Vrin, 1959.

—. *Opera Theologica III: Theologia "Summi Boni"; Theologia "Scholarium."* Ed. Eligius M. Buytaert and Constant J. Mews. CCCM 13. 1987.

Achard de St Victor. *Sermons inédits*. Ed. Jean Châtillon. Paris: J. Vrin, 1970. Translated by Hugh Feiss in *Achard of St Victor: Works*. Kalamazoo, MI: Cistercian Publications, 2001.

Acta pontificum Romanorum inedita 2. Ed. Julius von Pflugk-Harttung. Stuttgart: W. Kohlhammer, 1884.

Alberic of Trois Fontaines. *Chronicon*. Ed. Paul Scheffer-Boichorst. MGH SS 23. 1874.

Alexander III, pope. *Epistolae et privilegia.* PL 200.
Ambrose, saint, bishop of Milan. *De Fide.* PL 16: 523–702.
Annales Reicherspergenses. Ed. Wilhelm Wattenbach. MGH SS 17. 1861.
Anonymous. *Objectiones contra eos qui dicunt quod Christus non est aliquid secundum quod est homo.* Edited by Nikolaus M. Häring in "The So-Called *Apologia de Verbo Incarnato.*" *Franciscan Studies* 16 (1956): 102–143.
—. *Sermo ad populum.* PL 171: 921–924.
Archives de l'Hôtel-Dieu de Paris (1157–1300). Ed. Léon Brièle. Paris: Imprimerie nationale, 1894.
Aubert de La Chesnaye-Desbois, François-Alexandre. *Dictionnaire de la noblesse.* 15 vols. Paris: Badier, 1770–1786.
Augustine, saint, bishop of Hippo. *De diversis quaestionibus octoginta tribus.* PL 40: 11–100. Translated by David L. Mosher as *Eighty Three Different Questions.* Washington, DC: Catholic University of America Press, 2005.
—. *Sermo de Paulo apostolo.* PL 38: 1275–1280.
Bartholomew of Senlis. *Epistola ad Sugerium.* PL 186: 1408–1409.
Bernard of Clairvaux. *De Diligendo Dei.* In *Sancti Bernardi opera* 3, ed. Jean Leclercq, Charles H. Talbot, and Henri Rochais. 8 vols. Rome: Editiones Cistercienses, 1957–1977.
—. *Epistolae.* In *Sancti Bernardi opera* 7–8, ed. Jean Leclercq, Charles H. Talbot, and Henri Rochais. 8 vols. Rome: Editiones Cistercienses, 1957–1977. Translated by Bruno Scott James as *The Letters of St Bernard of Clairvaux.* London: Burns Oates, 1953.
—. *Sermones de diversis.* In *Sancti Bernardi opera* 6, ed. Jean Leclercq, Charles H. Talbot, and Henri Rochais. 8 vols. Rome: Editiones Cistercienses, 1957–1977.
—. *Sermones super canticum canticorum.* In *Sancti Bernardi opera* 1–2, ed. Jean Leclercq, Charles H. Talbot, and Henri Rochais. 8 vols. Rome: Editiones Cistercienses, 1957–1977. Translated by Kilian Walsh as *On the Song of Songs.* 4 vols. Spenser, MA: Cistercian Publications, 1971–1980.
[Bible.] *The Holy Bible: A Translation from the Latin Vulgate in the Light of the Hebrew and Greek Originals.* Trans. Ronald Knox. London: Burns & Oates, 1956.
Bibliotheca rerum Germanicarum 5. Ed. Philipp Jaffé. 6 vols. Berlin: Weidmann, 1864–1873.
Cartulaire de l'église Notre-Dame de Paris. Ed. Benjamin Guérard. 4 vols. Paris: Crapelet, 1850.
Cartulaire général de Paris. Ed. Robert de Lasteyrie. Paris: Imprimerie nationale, 1887.
Cartulaire de Notre-Dame de Chartres. Ed. Lucien Merlet and Eugène de Buchère de Lépinois. 3 vols. Chartres: Garnier, 1862–1865.
Cartulaire de Saint-Spire de Corbeil au diocèse de Paris. Ed. Emile Coüard-Luys. Rambouillet: A. Douchin, 1882.

[*Catonis disticha.*] *The Distichs of Cato: A Famous Medieval Textbook.* Ed. and trans. Wayland J. Chase. Madison: University of Wisconsin Press, 1922.

Chartularium universitatis parisiensis. Ed. Heinrich Denifle. 4 vols. Paris: Delalain, 1889–1897.

Chronicle of Morigny. PL 180: 131–176.

Dante Alighieri. *The Divine Comedy: Paradise.* Trans. Dorothy L. Sayers and Barbara Reynolds. Baltimore: Penguin, 1962.

Du Boulay, César Égasse. *Historia Universitatis Parisiensis.* 6 vols. Paris: F. Noel, 1665. Repr. Frankfurt: Minerva, 1966.

Dubois, Gérard. *Historia Ecclesiae Parisiensis.* 2 vols. Paris: F. Muguet, 1690–1710.

Eberhard of Bamberg. *Epistola ad Gerhohum.* PL 193: 552–564.

Epistolae pontificum Romanorum ineditae. Ed. Samuel Lowenfeld. Leipzig: Veit, 1885.

Eugenius III. *Epistola ad Henricum Belvacensem episcopum. RHF* 15: 469.

Gandulf of Bologna. *Sententiarum libri quatuor.* Ed. Joannes de Walter. Vienna: Aemilius Haim, 1924.

Geoffrey of Auxerre. *Epistola ad Albinum.* PL 185: 587–596.

Geoffrey Babion. *Sermo in coena Domini.* PL 171: 505–510.

Gerald of Wales. *De rebus a se gestis.* In *Giraldi Cambrensis opera,* ed. John S. Brewer, 1: 1–122. 8 vols. London: Longman, 1861–1891.

—. *Symbolum electorum.* In *Giraldi Cambrensis opera,* ed. John S. Brewer, 1: 197–396. 8 vols. London: Longman, 1861–1891.

Gerhoh of Reichersberg. *Epistolae.* PL 193: 489–618.

—. *Liber de gloria et honore filii hominis.* PL 194: 1074–1160.

—. *Opera inedita.* Ed. Damien Van den Eynde. 2 vols. Rome: Pontificium Athenaeum Antonianum, 1955–1956.

Gesta regis Henrici Secundi Benedicti abbatis. Ed. William Stubbs. 2 vols. London: Longman, 1867.

Gratian. *Decretum.* Ed. Emil Friedberg. *Corpus iuris canonici* 1. Leipzig: B. Tauchnitz, 1879.

Haymo of Halberstadt. *In Epistolas Pauli.* PL 117: 361–936.

Henry of France, archbishop of Rheims. *Epistolae. RHF* 16: 171–200.

Herbert of Bosham. *Epistola ad Henricum comitem Tricensem.* PL 190: 1416–1422.

—. *Liber melorum.* PL 190: 1294–1404.

—. *Praefatio.* Edited by Hans H. Glunz in *History of The Vulgate in England from Alcuin to Roger Bacon,* 342–346. Cambridge: Cambridge University Press, 1933.

—. *Vita Sancti Thomae archiepiscopi et martyris.* In *Materials for the History of Thomas Becket, Archbishop of Canterbury,* ed. James C. Robertson, 3: 155–534. 7 vols. London: Longman, 1875–1885.

Hugh of Champfleury. *Otium Hugonis ad Helwidem.* Ed. André Wilmart. In "Les 'loisirs' ou sentiments intimes d'un chancelier de France." *Revue Bénédictine* 51 (1939): 182–204.

Hugh of St Victor. *De arca Noe*. PL 176: 617–704.

—. *De institutione novitiorum*. PL 176: 925–952.

—. *De modo orandi*. PL 176: 977–988.

—. *De Sacramentis Christiane fidei*. Ed. Rainer Berndt. Münster: Aschendorff, 2008.

—. *Didascalicon*. Ed. Charles H. Buttimer. Washington, DC: Catholic University of America Press, 1939.

Hugh of Toucy, archbishop of Sens. *Epistola ad canonicos Parisiensis ecclesiae*. *RHF* 15: 711.

Jacobus Aquensis. *Chronicon imaginis mundi*. In *Historiae patriae monumenta*, ed. Gustavo Avogadro, 5.3 (*Scriptores*): 1357–1626. Turin: E regio typographeo, 1848.

Jerome. *Commentaria in Epistolam ad Titum*. PL 26: 555–600.

John of Cornwall. *Eulogium*. Ed. Nikolaus M. Häring. "The *Eulogium ad Alexandrum Papam tertium* of John of Cornwall." *Mediaeval Studies* 13 (1951): 253–300.

John Damascene. *De fide orthodoxa: Versions of Burgundio and Cerbanus*. Ed. Eligius M. Buytaert. New York: Franciscan Institute, 1955.

John of Salisbury. *Historia pontificalis; Memoirs of the Papal Court*. Ed. and trans. Marjorie Chibnall. London: Nelson, 1956.

—. *Metalogicon*. Ed. John B. Hall and Katharine S.B. Keats-Rohan. Trans. John B. Hall. CCCM 98. 1991.

Lambert of Waterlos. *Annales Cameracenses*. Ed. Georg H. Pertz. MGH SS 16. 1859.

Lawrence of Westminster. *Sententiae de divinitate*. Ed. Ambrosio M. Piazzoni. "Ugo di San Vittore, 'auctor' delle *Sententiae de Divinitate*." *Studi Medievali* 23 (1982): 861–955. Translated in *Trinity and Creation: A Selection of the Works of Hugh, Richard and Adam of St Victor*, ed. Boyd T. Coolman and Dale M. Coulter, 103–178. Turnhout: Brepols, 2010.

Liber ordinis Sancti Victoris Parisiensis. Ed. Lucas Jocqué and Ludovicus Milis. CCCM 61. 1984.

Memorie e documenti per servire all'istoria del Ducato di Lucca. Ed. Domenico Barsocchini and Domenico Bertini. 2 vols. Lucca: Academia Lucchese di scienze, lettere et arti, 1818–1844.

Obituaires de la Province de Sens. Ed. Auguste Longnon and Auguste Molinier. 4 vols. Paris: G. Klinksieck, 1902–1923.

Odo of Soissons. *Epistolae*. In *Analecta Novissima Spicilegii Solesmensis Altera Continuatio*, ed. Jean-Baptiste Pitra, 2: xxxix–xlii. 2 vols. Paris: Roger et Chernowitz, 1885–1888. Edited by Jean Leclercq in "Lettres d'Odon d'Ourscamp." *Analecta Monastica* 3 (1955): 145–157.

—. *Sermo*. In *Analecta Novissima Spicilegii Solesmensis Altera Continuatio*, ed. Jean-Baptiste Pitra, 2: xlii–xlvii. 2 vols. Paris: Roger et Chernowitz, 1885–1888.

Otto I, Bishop of Freising. *Gesta Frederici I imperatoris*. Ed. Georg Waitz and Bernhard von Simson. MGH SS 46. 1912. Translated by Christopher C. Mierow and Richard Emery as *The Deeds of Frederick Barbarossa*. New York: Columbia University Press, 1953.

Pandulphus of Pisa. *Vita Gelasii*. PL 163: 473–484.

Paulus Aemilius Veronensis. *De Rebus Gestis Francorum*. Paris: Vascosani, 1566.

Peter Chrysogonus. *Epistola ad Alexandrum papam*. PL 200: 1370–1372.

Peter Comestor. *De Sacramentis*. Ed. Raymond M. Martin. In *Maitre Simon et son groupe: De sacramentis*, ed. Henri Weisweiler, 3–105. Louvain: Spicilegium sacrum lovaniense bureaux, 1937.

—. *Historia Scholastica*. PL 198: 1045–1720.

—. *Materia super librum sententiarum*. Ed. Raymond M. Martin. "Notes sur l'oeuvre littéraire de Pierre le Mangeur." *RTAM* 3 (1931): 61–62.

—. *Scholastica historia: Liber Genesis*. Ed. Agneta Sylwan. CCCM 191. 2005.

—. *Sermo in annuntiatione B. Virginis*. PL 198: 1772–1775.

Peter Lombard. *Commentaria in psalmos*. PL 191: 55–1297.

—. *Glossa in epistolas*. PL 191: 1297–1696. PL 192: 9–520.

—. *Sententiae in IV libris distinctae*. Ed. Ignatius C. Brady. 2 vols. Grottaferrata: Editiones Collegii S. Bonaventurae ad Claras Aquas, 1971–1981. Translated by Giulio Silano as *The Sentences*. 4 vols. Toronto: Pontifical Institute of Mediaeval Studies, 2007–2010. Translated by Mark Ozilou as *Pierre Lombard: Les quatre livres des Sentences*. 4 vols. Paris: Cerf, 2012–2015.

—. *Sermones*:

De adventu. PL 171: 370–376.

De adventu (sermo secundus). PL 171: 376–381.

De annuntiatione. PL 171: 605–610.

De parasceve. PL 171: 685–695.

De paschali tempore. PL 171: 871–873. The remainder edited by Barthélemy Hauréau in "Notice sur les sermons attribués à Hildebert de Lavardin." *Notices et extraits des manuscrits de la Bibliothèque nationale* 32 (1888): 107–166, at 152–158.

De purificatione. PL 171: 615–623.

De purificatione (sermo secundus). PL 171: 623–627.

De Sancto Joanne evangelistae. PL 171: 723–727.

De Sancto Stephano. PL 171: 715–720.

De septuagesima. PL 171: 845–853.

De trinitate et de pascha partim. PL 171: 432–439. The remainder edited by Barthélemy Hauréau in "Notice sur les sermons attribués à Hildebert de Lavardin." *Notices et extraits des manuscrits de la Bibliothèque nationale* 32 (1888): 107–166, at 121–124.

In ascensione and *De adventu Domini.* Edited by Damien Van den Eynde in "Deux sermons inédits de Pierre Lombard." In *Miscellanea Lombardiana,* 75–87. Novara: Istituto geografico de Agostini, 1957.

In circumcisione Domini. PL 171: 394–401.

In coena Domini. PL 171: 510–524.

In die cineris. PL 171: 451–456.

In die paschae. PL 171: 352–363.

In die paschae (sermo secundus). PL 171: 556–564.

In dominica ante palmas. PL 171: 456–463.

In epiphania. PL 171: 401–409.

In laetare Ierusalem. PL 171: 853–864.

In letaniis. PL 171: 567–572.

In natali. PL 171: 381–388.

In parasceve. PL 171: 796–806.

In prima dominica quadragesimae. PL 171: 443–451.

In ramis palmarum. PL 171: 491–502.

In receptione poenitentium. PL. 171: 524–530.

Sermo communis. In *Notices et extraits de quelques manuscrits latins de la Bibliothèque nationale,* ed. Barthélemy Hauréau, 3: 44–49. 6 vols. Paris: C. Klincksieck, 1890–1893.

Sine rubrica. Edited by Henri M. Rochais in "Une collection de textes de S. Bernard dans le manuscrit Tours 343." *RTAM* 29 (1962): 106–111.

Sine titulo. PL 171: 942–944.

Peter the Venerable. *Epistolae.* Edited by Giles Constable as *The Letters of Peter the Venerable.* 2 vols. Cambridge, MA: Harvard University Press, 1967.

Pseudo-Peter of Poitiers. *Glossae super Sententias: Prologus.* Ed. Raymond M. Martin. "Notes sur l'oeuvre littéraire de Pierre le Mangeur." *RTAM* 3 (1931): 64–65.

Ralph de Diceto. *Ymagines Historiarum.* Edited by William Stubbs as *The Historical Works of Ralph de Diceto.* 2 vols. London: Longman, 1876.

Recueil des actes de Louis VI: Roi de France (1108–1137). Ed. Robert Henri-Bautier and Jean Dufour. 4 vols. Paris: Académie des inscriptions et belles-lettres, 1992–1994.

Recueil des chartes et documents de Saint Martin des Champs. Ed. Joseph Depoin. 5 vols. Paris: Jouve, 1912–1921.

Recueil des historiens des croisades. Volume 1: *Historiens occidentaux.* 5 vols. Paris: Imprimerie royale, 1844–1895.

Robert of Auxerre. *Chronicon.* Ed. Oswald Holder-Egger. MGH SS 26. 1882.

Robert Cricklade. *Speculum Fidei* 3.5. Ed. Richard W. Hunt. In "English Learning in the Late Twelfth Century." *Transactions of the Royal Historical Society* 19 (1936): 37–38.

Robert of Torigny. *Chronicon*. Ed. Ludwig Conrad Bethmann. MGH SS 6. 1844. Edited by Richard Howlett in *Chronicles of the Reigns of Stephen, Henry II, and Richard I*, 4: 3–316. 4 vols. London: Longman, 1884–1889. Edited by Léopold Delisle as *Chronique de Robert de Torigni, abbé de Mont Saint-Michel*. 2 vols. Rouen: A. Le Brument, 1872–1873.

Roger of Hoveden. *Chronica*. Ed. William Stubbs. London: Longman, 1870.

Servius. *Commentary on Book Four of Virgil's Aeneid*. Ed. and trans. Christopher McDonough, Richard E. Prior, and Mark Stansbury. Wauconda, IL: Bolchazy-Carducci Publishers, 2004.

Stephen of Bourbon. *Tractatus de diversis Materiis Praedicabilibus*. Edited by Albert Lecoy de la Marche as *Anecdotes historiques, légendes et apologues tirés du recueil inédit d'Etienne de Bourbon, Dominicain du XIIIe siècle*. Paris: Renouard, 1877.

Stephen of Senlis. *Epistola ad Henricum Senonensem archiepiscopum, RHF* 15: 329–330.

Suger, Abbot of St Denis. *Epistola ad Eugenium Papam*. PL 186: 1380–1382.

Uberto of Lucca. *Epistola ad Norbertum*. In *Pontificum Romanorum Vitae*, ed. Johann M. Watterich, 2: 179–185. 2 vols. Leipzig: Engelmann, 1826–1904.

Veterum scriptorum et monumentorum historicorum, dogmaticorum, moralium, amplissima collectio. Ed. Edmund Martène and Ursini Durand. 9 vols. Paris: apud Montalant, 1724–1733.

Virgil. *The Aeneid of Virgil*. Ed. Robert Deryck Williams. 2 vols. London: Macmillan, 1972–1973.

Vita Tertia Innocentii Papae II Auctore Cardinali Aragonio. PL 179: 31–36.

Walter of St Victor. *Contra quatuor labyrinthos Franciae*. Ed. Palémon Glorieux. "Le 'Contra quatuor labyrinthos Franciae' de Gauthier de Saint-Victor." *Archives d'histoire doctrinale et littéraire du moyen âge* 19 (1952): 187–335.

—. *Galteri a Sancto Victore et quorumdam aliorum: Sermones ineditos*. Ed. Jean Châtillon. CCCM 30. 1975.

William of Lucca. *Commentum in tertiam ierarchiam Dionisii que est de divinis nominibus*. Ed. Ferruccio Gastaldelli. Florence: Leo S. Olschki, 1983.

William of Saint Thierry, Arnold of Bonnevaux, and Geoffey of Auxerre. *Vita Prima Sancti Bernardi*. PL 185: 223–642.

William of Tyre. *Chronicon*. Ed. Robert B.C. Huygens, Hans Eberhard Mayer, and Gerhard Rösch. 2 vols. CCCM 63, 63A. 1986. Translated by Emily A. Babcock and August C. Krey as *A History of Deeds Done Beyond the Sea*. 2 vols. New York: Columbia University Press, 1943.

Secondary Sources

Amanieu, A. "Archdiacre." In *Dictionnaire de droit canonique,* 1: 948–1004. 7 vols. Paris: Letouzey et Ané, 1935–1965.

Andenna, Giancarlo. "La Chiesa Novarese sotto l'Impero dei Sassoni e dei Salici." In *Diocesi di Novara,* ed. Luciano Vaccaro and Dorino Tuniz, 83–110. Brescia: Editrice La Scuola, 2007.

Angotti, Claire. "Le rayonnement du Livre des Sentences de maître Pierre Lombard, évêque de Paris." In *Notre-Dame de Paris 1163–2013,* ed. Cédric Giraud, 79–95. Turnhout: Brepols, 2013.

—. "Sur les traces de la *lectio* des *Sentences* de Pierre le Mangeur." In *Pierre le Mangeur ou Pierre de Troyes: Maître du XIIe siècle,* ed. Gilbert Dahan, 149–189. Turnhout: Brepols, 2013.

Baldwin, John W. *The Government of Philip Augustus: Foundations of French Royal Power in the Middle Ages.* Berkeley: University of California Press, 1986.

—. "Masters at Paris from 1179 to 1215: A Social Perspective." In *Renaissance and Renewal in the Twelfth Century,* ed. Robert L. Benson and Giles Constable, 138–172. Cambridge, MA: Harvard University Press, 1982.

—. *Masters, Princes, and Merchants: The Social Views of Peter the Chanter and His Circle.* 2 vols. Princeton: Princeton University Press, 1970.

Barlow, Frank. "Bosham, Herbert of." In *Oxford Dictionary of National Biography,* ed. Henry C.G. Matthew and Brian Harrison, 6: 711–713. 60 vols. Oxford: Oxford University Press, 2004.

—. "The English, Norman, and French Councils Called to Deal with the Papal Schism of 1159." *English Historical Review* 51 (1936): 264–268.

—. *Thomas Becket.* Berkeley: University of California Press, 1986.

Baron, Roger. "Note sur l'énigmatique *Summa Sententiarum.*" *RTAM* 25 (1958): 26–42.

Barsocchini, Domenico. "Dissertazione IX: I Vescovi di Lucca, Saecolo XII: Otto." *Memorie e documenti per servire all'istoria del Ducato di Lucca* 5.1 (1844): 453–462.

—. "Dissertazione IX: I Vescovi di Lucca, Saecolo XII: Uberto." *Memorie e documenti per servire all'istoria del Ducato di Lucca* 5.1 (1844): 435–446.

Bartlett, Robert. *Gerald of Wales, 1146–1223.* Oxford: Clarendon Press, 1982.

Bataillon, Louis Jacques. "Approaches to the Study of Medieval Sermons." *Leeds Studies in English* 11 (1980): 19–35. Repr. in *La prédication au XIIIe siècle en France et Italie,* chapter 1. Aldershot: Ashgate, 1993.

Bautier, Robert Henri. "Paris au temps d'Abélard." In *Abélard en son temps,* ed. Jean Jolivet, 21–77. Paris: Belles Lettres, 1981.

Benton, John F. "The Court of Champagne as a Literary Centre." *Speculum* 36 (1961): 551–591.

—. "Suger's Life and Personality." In *Abbot Suger and Saint-Denis: A Symposium*, ed. Paula L. Gerson, 3–15. New York: Metropolitan Museum of Art, 1986.

Bériou, Nicole. *L'avènement des maîtres de la parole: La prédication à Paris au XIIIe siècle*. 2 vols. Collection des Études Augustiniennes: Série Moyen-Âge et Temps Modernes, 31–32. Paris: Institut d'études augustiniennes, 1998.

—. "Maurice et Eudes de Sully et la cathédrale de Paris." In *Notre-Dame de Paris 1163–2013*, ed. Cédric Giraud, 19–28. Turnhout: Brepols, 2013.

Bertola, Ermenegildo. "Pietro Lombardo nella storiografia filosofica medioevale." *Pier Lombardo* 4 (1960): 95–113.

Binski, Paul, and Stella Panayotova, eds. *The Cambridge Illuminations: Ten Centuries of Book Production in the Medieval West*. London: Harvey Miller, 2005.

Birkner, Günther. "Notre Dame Cantoren und Succentoren vom Ende des 10. bis zum Beginn des 14. Jahrhunderts." In *In Memoriam Jacques Handschin*, ed. Higini Anglès, 107–126. Strasbourg: P.H. Heitz, 1962.

Bischoff, Bernhard. "Aus der Schule Hugos von St. Viktor." In *Mittelalterliche Studien: Ausgewählte Aufsätze zur Schriftkunde und Literaturgeschichte*, ed. Bernhard Bischoff, 2: 182–187. 3 vols. Stuttgart: Hiersemann, 1966–1981.

Black, Robert. *Humanism and Education in Medieval and Renaissance Italy: Tradition and Innovation in Latin Schools from the Twelfth to the Fifteenth Century*. Cambridge: Cambridge University Press, 2001.

Black, Winston. "The Medieval Archdeacon in Canon Law with a Case Study of the Diocese of Lincoln." PhD diss., University of Toronto, 2008.

Boase, Thomas Sherrer Ross. *English Art, 1100–1216*. Oxford: Clarendon Press, 1953.

Bonnard, Fourrier. *Histoire de l'abbaye royale et de l'ordre des chanoines réguliers de St. Victor de Paris*. 2 vols. Paris: A. Savaète, 1904–1908.

Bonner, Stanley. *Education in Ancient Rome: From the Elder Cato to the Younger Pliny*. London: Methuen, 1977.

Bonnes, Jean-Paul. "Un des plus grands prédicateurs du XIIe siècle: Geoffroy du Loroux, dit Geoffroy Babion." *Revue Bénédictine* 56 (1945–1946): 174–215.

Bourgain, Louis. *La chaire française au XIIe siècle d'après les manuscrits*. Paris: Société générale de librairie catholique, 1879.

Bournazel, Eric. *Le gouvernement capétien au XIIe siècle, 1108–1180*. Paris: Presses universitaires de France, 1975.

Boussard, Jacques. *Nouvelle histoire de Paris*. Volume 1: *De la fin du siège de 885–886 à la mort de Philippe Auguste*. 18 vols. Paris: Diffusion Hachette, 1970–2001.

Bradbury, Jim. *The Capetians: Kings of France, 987–1328*. London: Hambledon Press, 2007.

Brady, Ignatius C. "The Distinctions of Lombard's *Book of Sentences* and Alexander of Hales." *Franciscan Studies* 25 (1965): 90–116.
—. "Peter Lombard: Canon of Notre Dame." *RTAM* 32 (1965): 277–295.
—. "Peter Manducator and the Oral Teachings of Peter Lombard." *Antonianum* 41 (1966): 454–490.
—. "The Rubrics of Peter Lombard's *Sentences*." *Pier Lombardo* 6 (1962): 5–25.
—. "The Three Editions of the *Liber Sententiarum* of Master Peter Lombard (1882–1977)." *Archivum Franciscanum Historicum* 70 (1977): 400–411.
Bredero, Adriaan H. *Bernard of Clairvaux: Between Cult and History*. Edinburgh: T&T Clark, 1996.
Brentano, Robert. *Two Churches: England and Italy in the Thirteenth Century*. Princeton: Princeton University Press, 1968.
Brooke, Christopher. "The Archdeacon and the Norman Conquest." In *Tradition and Change: Essays in Honour of Marjorie Chibnall*, ed. Diana Greenway, Christopher Holdsworth, and Jane Sayers, 1–19. Cambridge: Cambridge University Press, 1985.
—. *Churches and Churchmen in Medieval Europe*. London: Hambledon Press, 1999.
—. *Europe in the Central Middle Ages, 962–1154*. London: Longman, 2000.
Bynum, Caroline W. *Docere verbo et exemplo: An Aspect of Twelfth-Century Spirituality*. Missoula: Scholars Press, 1979.
—. "The Spirituality of Regular Canons in the Twelfth Century: A New Approach." *Medievalia et Humanistica* 4 (1993): 3–24
Cahn, Walter. *Romanesque Manuscripts: The Twelfth Century*. 2 vols. London: H. Miller, 1996.
Camargo, Martin. "Rhetoric." In *The Seven Liberal Arts in the Middle Ages*, ed. David L. Wagner, 96–124. Bloomington: Indiana University Press, 1983.
Caplan, Harry. "Classical Rhetoric and the Mediaeval Theory of Preaching." *Classical Philology* 28 (1933): 73–96.
Carruthers, Mary. *The Book of Memory: A Study of Memory in Medieval Culture*. Cambridge: Cambridge University Press, 1990.
Casey, Michael. "Towards a Methodology for the *Vita Prima*: Translating the First Life into Biography." In *Bernardus Magister: Papers Presented at the Nonacentenary Celebration of the Birth of Saint Bernard of Clairvaux, Kalamazoo, Michigan, Sponsored by the Institute of Cistercian Studies, Western Michigan University, 10–13 May 1990*, ed. John R. Sommerfeldt, 55–70. Cistercian Studies Series 135. Cîteaux: Cistercian Publications, 1992.
Châtillon, Jean. "L'influence de S. Bernard sur la pensée scolastique au XIIe et au XIIIe siècle." In *Saint Bernard théologien: Actes du Congrès de Dijon, 15–19 septembre, 1953*. Analecta sacri ordinis Cisterciensis 3–4. Rome: Editiones Cister-

cienses, 1953. Repr. in *D'Isidore de Séville à Saint Thomas d'Aquin*, ed. Jean Châtillon, 268–288. London: Variorum Reprints, 1985.

—. "Latran III et l'enseignement christologique de Pierre Lombard." In *Le Troisième Concile de Latran (1179): Sa place dans l'histoire*, ed. Jean Longère, 75–90. Paris: Études augustiniennes, 1982.

—. "Sermons et prédicateurs victorins de la seconde moitié du XIIe siècle." *Archives d'histoire doctrinale et littéraire du moyen âge* 32 (1965): 7–60.

—. *Théologie, spiritualité, et métaphysique dans l'oeuvre oratoire d'Achard de Saint-Victor: Études d'histoire doctrinale précédées d'un essai sur la vie et l'oeuvre d'Achard.* Paris: J. Vrin, 1969.

Cheney, Mary G. "The Recognition of Pope Alexander III: Some Neglected Evidence." *English Historical Review* 84.332 (1969): 474–497.

—. *Roger, Bishop of Worcester, 1164–1179*. Oxford: Clarendon Press, 1980.

Clanchy, Michael. *Abelard: A Medieval Life*. Oxford: Blackwell, 1997.

Clark, Mark J. "The Biblical *Gloss*, the Search for the Lombard's Glossed Bible, and the School of Paris," *Mediaeval Studies* 76 (2014): 57–113.

—. *The Making of the* Historia scholastica, *1150–1200*. Toronto: Pontifical Institute of Mediaeval Studies, 2015.

—. "Peter Comestor and Peter Lombard: Brothers in Deed." *Traditio* 60 (2005): 85–142.

—. "Stephen Langton and Hugh of St Cher on Peter Comestor's *Historia scholastica*: The Lombard's *Sentences* and the Problem of Sources Used by Comestor and His Commentators." *Recherches de théologie et philosophie médiévales* 74 (2007): 63–117.

Classen, Peter. *Gerhoch von Reichersberg: Eine Biographie mit einem Anhang über die Quellen, ihre handschriftliche Überlieferung und ihre Chronologie.* Wiesbaden: F. Steiner, 1960.

Clerval, André. *Les écoles de Chartres au moyen âge.* Paris: A. Picard, 1895. Repr. Frankfurt: Minerva, 1965.

Colish, Marcia L. "Christological Nihilianism in the Second Half of the Twelfth Century." *RTAM* 63 (1996): 146–155.

—. "The Development of Lombardian Theology, 1160–1215." In *Centres of Learning: Learning and Location in Pre-Modern Europe and the Near East*, ed. Jan Willem Drijvers and Alasdair A. MacDonald, 207–216. Leiden: E.J. Brill, 1995. Repr. in *Studies in Scholasticism*, ed. Marcia L. Colish, 1–9. Aldershot: Ashgate, 2006.

—. "From the Sentence Collection to the Sentence Commentary and the *Summa:* Parisian Scholastic Theology, 1130–1215." In *Manuels, programmes de cours et techniques d'enseignement dans les universités médiévales*, ed. Jacqueline Hamesse,

9–29. Louvain-la-Neuve: Institut d'Études Médiévales de l'Université Catholique de Louvain, 1994.

—. *Peter Lombard.* 2 vols. Leiden: E.J. Brill, 1994.

—. "Peter Lombard as an Exegete of St Paul." In *Ad Litteram: Authoritative Texts and Their Medieval Readers,* ed. Mark D. Jordan and Kent Emery, 71–92. Notre Dame, IN: University of Notre Dame Press, 1992.

—. "The Pseudo-Peter of Poitiers Gloss." In *Mediaeval Commentaries on the Sentences of Peter Lombard,* ed. Philipp Rosemann, 2: 1–33. 3 vols. Leiden: E.J. Brill, 2002–2015.

Constable, Giles. "The Language of Preaching in the Twelfth Century." *Viator* 25 (1994): 131–152.

—. *The Reformation of the Twelfth Century.* Cambridge: Cambridge University Press, 1996.

Coulter, Dale M. *Per Visibilia ad Invisibilia: Theological Method in Richard of St. Victor (d. 1173).* Turnhout: Brepols, 2006.

Courcelle, Pierre. "Tradition néo-platonicienne et traditions chrétiennes de la 'région de dissemblance.'" *Archives d'histoire doctrinale et littéraire du moyen âge* 25 (1958): 5–33.

Courtenay, William J. "SIEPM Project: Report on the Repertory of Commentaries on Peter Lombard's *Sentences.*" *Bulletin de Philosophie Médiévale* 54 (2013): 55–57.

Courtney, Francis. *Cardinal Robert Pullen: An English Theologian of the Twelfth Century.* Rome: Gregorian University Press, 1954.

Cowdrey, Herbert E.J. "The Structure of the Church, 1024–1073." In *New Cambridge Medieval History,* ed. David Luscombe and Jonathan Riley-Smith, 4.1: 229–267. 8 vols in 7. Cambridge: Cambridge University Press, 1995–2005.

Croydon, F.E. "Abbot Lawrence of Westminster and Hugh of St. Victor." *Medieval and Renaissance Studies* 2 (1950): 169–171.

Curley, Michael J. "A New Edition of John of Cornwall's *Propheta Merlini.*" *Speculum* 57 (1982): 217–249.

Daly, Saralyn R. "Peter Comestor: Master of Histories." *Speculum* 32 (1957): 62–73.

Davies, James Conway. *Episcopal Acts and Cognate Documents Relating to Welsh Dioceses, 1066–1272.* Cardiff: Historical Society of the Church in Wales, 1948.

Davies, Robert R. *The Age of Conquest: Wales, 1063–1415.* Oxford: Oxford University Press, 1991.

Davis, Ralph Henry Carless. "William of Tyre." In *Relations Between East and West in the Middle Ages,* ed. Derek Baker, 64–76. Edinburgh: Edinburgh University Press, 1973.

De Hamel, Christopher. "A Contemporary Miniature of Thomas Becket." In *Intellectual Life in the Middle Ages: Essays Presented to Margaret Gibson*, ed. Lesley Smith and Benedicta Ward, 179–184. London: Hambledon Press, 1992.

—. *Glossed Books of the Bible and the Origins of the Paris Booktrade*. Woodbridge: Brewer, 1984.

—. "Manuscripts of Herbert of Bosham." In *Manuscripts at Oxford: An Exhibition in Memory of Richard William Hunt (1908–1979), Keeper of Western Manuscripts at the Bodleian Library, Oxford, 1945–1975*, ed. Albina C. de la Mare and B.C. Barker-Benfield, 38–41. Oxford: Bodleian Library, 1980.

Delhaye, Philippe. "L'organisation scolaire au XIIe siècle." *Traditio* 5 (1947): 211–268.

—. *Pierre Lombard: Sa vie, son oeuvre, sa morale*. Montreal: Institut d'Études Médiévales, 1961.

Devoto, Giacomo. *The Languages of Italy*. Trans. V. Louise Katainen. Chicago: University of Chicago Press, 1978.

Dodwell, Charles Reginald. *The Canterbury School of Illumination, 1066–1200*. Cambridge: Cambridge University Press, 1954.

Doyle, Matthew A. *Bernard of Clairvaux and the Schools: The Formation of an Intellectual Milieu in the First Half of the Twelfth Century*. Studi 11. Spoleto: Fondazione Centro italiano di studi sull'alto Medioevo, 2005.

—. "The Career and Students of Peter Lombard." PhD diss., University of Toronto, 2006.

Du Cange, Charles du Fresne. *Les Familles d'Outre Mer*. Ed. Emmanuel Guillaume Rey and Nicolas Rodolphe Taranne. Paris: Imprimerie impériale, 1869.

—. *Glossarium mediae et infimae Latinitatis*. Ed. Léopold Favre. 10 vols. Niort: L. Fabre, 1883–1887.

Duffy, Seán. "Henry II and England's Insular Neighbours." In *Henry II: New Interpretations*, ed. Christopher Harper-Bill and Nicholas Vincent, 129–153. Woodbridge: Boydell, 2007.

Dunford, David. "Dean." In *The Catholic Encyclopedia: An International Work of Reference on the Constitution, Doctrine, Discipline, and History of the Catholic Church*, ed. Charles G. Herbermann, 4: 659–660. 15 vols. New York: Robert Appleton, 1907–1914.

Duggan, Anne J. "Cricklade, Robert of." In *Oxford Dictionary of National Biography*, ed. Henry C.G. Matthew and Brian Harrison, 14: 191–192. 60 vols. Oxford: Oxford University Press, 2004.

Duggan, Charles. "Decretals of Alexander III to England." In *Miscellanea Rolando Bandinelli*, ed. Filippo Liotta, 85–151. Siena: Accademia senese degli intronati,

1986. Repr. in *Decretals and the Creation of "New Law" in the Twelfth Century*, 87–151. Aldershot: Ashgate, 1998.

Dumeige, Gervais. "Dissemblance (*regio dissimilitudinis*)." In *Dictionnaire de spiritualité ascétique et mystique: doctrine et histoire*, 3: 1130–1346. 17 vols. Paris: Beauchesne, 1932–1995.

Edbury, Peter, and Gordon John Rowe. *William of Tyre: Historian of the Latin East.* Cambridge: Cambridge University Press, 1988.

Edwards, Kathleen. *The English Secular Cathedrals in the Middle Ages.* Manchester: Manchester University Press, 1949.

Emden, Alfred Brotherston. *A Biographical Register of the University of Oxford.* 3 vols. Oxford: Clarendon Press, 1957–1959.

Espenberger, Johannes N. *Die Philosophie des Petrus Lombardus und ihre Stellung im zwölften Jahrhundert.* Münster: Aschendorff, 1901.

Evans, Gillian R. *Bernard of Clairvaux.* New York: Oxford University Press, 2000.

Evergates, Theodore. "Louis VII and the Counts of Champagne." In *The Second Crusade and the Cistercians*, ed. Michael Gervers, 109–117. New York: St Martin's Press, 1992.

Falkenstein, Ludwig. "Alexandre III et Henri de France: Conformités et conflits." In *L'église de France et la papauté (Xe–XIIe siècle): Actes du XXVIe colloque historique Franco-Allemand*, ed. Rolf Grosse, 103–176. Bonn: Bouvier Verlag, 1993.

—. "Guillaume aux Blanches Mains, archevêque de Reims et légat du siège apostolique (1176–1202)." *Revue d'histoire de l'église de France* 91 (2005): 5–25.

—. "Wilhelm von Champagne, elekt von Chartres (1164–1168), Erzbischof von Sens (1168/9–1176), Erzbishof von Reims (1176–1202), Legat des apostolischen Stuhles, im Spiegl päpstlicher Schreiben und Privilegien." *Zeitschrift der Savigny-Stiftung für Rechtsgeschichte, Kanonistische Abteilung* 89 (2003): 107–284.

Fanning, William. "Subdeacon." In *The Catholic Encyclopedia: An International Work of Reference on the Constitution, Doctrine, Discipline, and History of the Catholic Church*, ed. Charles G. Herbermann, 14: 320–321. 15 vols. New York: Robert Appleton, 1907–1914.

Fantini, Lorenzo. "I Discorsi di Pier Lombardo." *Pier Lombardo* 5 (1961): 69–80.

Fassler, Margot. "Who Was Adam of St Victor? The Evidence of the Sequence Manuscripts." *Journal of the American Musicological Society* 37 (1984): 233–269.

Favier, Jean. *Les Archives Nationales: État général des fonds* I. Paris: Archives nationales, 1978.

Feiss, Hugh. "Bernardus Scholasticus: The Correspondence of Bernard of Clairvaux and Hugh of Saint Victor on Baptism." In *Bernardus Magister: Papers Presented at the Nonacentenary Celebration of the Birth of Saint Bernard of Clairvaux, Kala-*

mazoo, Michigan, sponsored by the Institute of Cistercian Studies, Western Michigan University, 10–13 May 1990, ed. John R. Sommerfeldt, 360–377. Cistercian Studies Series 135. Cîteaux: Cistercian Publications, 1992.

Ferruolo, Stephen C. *The Origins of the University: The Schools of Paris and their Critics, 1100–1215*. Stanford: Stanford University Press, 1985.

Fliche, Augustin, Raymonde Foreville, and Jean Rousset de Pina. *Du Premier Concile du Latran à l'avènement d'Innocent III.* Histoire de l'église 9. Paris: Bloud & Gay, 1944–1953.

Flint, Valerie I.J. "The 'School of Laon': A Reconsideration." *RTAM* 43 (1976): 89–110.

Forster, Grace. "Three Short Sermons on the Ascension by St Bernard of Clairvaux." *Cistercian Studies* 25 (1990): 3–8.

Friedmann, Adrien. "Notre-Dame et les paroisses de Paris aux XIIIe siècle." *Revue d'histoire de l'église de France* 50 (1964): 27–33.

Gabriel, Astrik L. "The Cathedral Schools of Notre-Dame and the Beginning of the University of Paris." In *Garlandia: Studies in the History of the Medieval University*, ed. Astrik L. Gabriel, 39–64. Notre Dame, IN: The Medieval Institute, 1969.

—. "The Ideal Master of the Medieval University." *Catholic Historical Review* 60 (1974): 1–40.

Gams, Pius Bonifatius. *Series Episcoporum Ecclesiae Catholicae*. 2nd ed. Leipzig: K.W. Hiersemann, 1931.

Gandil, Pierre. "Pierre le Mangeur, doyen du chapitre cathédral de Troyes." In *Pierre le Mangeur ou Pierre de Troyes: Maître du XIIe siècle*, ed. Gilbert Dahan, 17–25.

Gane, Robert and Claudine Billot. *Le chapitre de Notre-Dame de Paris au XIVe siècle: Étude sociale d'un groupe canonial.* Saint-Etienne: Université de Saint-Etienne, 1999.

Gastaldelli, Ferruccio. "La *Summa Sententiarum* di Ottone di Lucca: Conclusione di un dibattito secolare." *Salesianum* 42 (1980): 537–546.

—. "Le tre ultime lettere dell'epistolario di San Bernardo." *Analecta Cisterciensia* 50 (1994): 251–292

Gaudemet, Jean. "Les institutions ecclésiastiques en France du milieu du XIIe siècle au début du XIVe siècle." In *Histoire des institutions Françaises au moyen âge III: Institutions ecclésiastiques*, ed. Robert Fawtier and Ferdinand Lot, 143–335. Paris: Presses universitaires de France, 1962.

Ghellinck, Joseph de. *L'essor de la littérature latine au XIIe siècle.* 2 vols. Brussels: L'Édition universale, 1946.

—. "La carrière de Pierre Lombard: Nouvelles précisions chronologique." *Revue d'histoire ecclésiastique* 30 (1934): 95–100.

—. "La carrière de Pierre Lombard: Quelques précisions chronologiques." *Revue d'histoire ecclésiastique* 27 (1931): 792–830.

—. *Le mouvement théologique au XIIe siècle.* 2nd ed. Bruges: Éditions de Tempel, 1948.

—. "Les opera dubia vel spuria attribués a Pierre Lombard." *Revue d'histoire ecclésiastique* 28 (1932): 829–845.

—. "Pierre Lombard." In *Dictionnaire de théologie catholique,* ed. Alfred Vacant, 12: 1941–2019. 15 vols. Paris: Letouzey et Ané, 1930–1950.

Giordano, Alessandro. "La Chiesa Novarese dal primo dopoguerra al Vaticano II." In *Diocesi di Novara,* ed. Luciano Vaccaro and Dorino Tuniz, 369–383. Varese: Editrice La Scuola, 2007.

Glorieux, Palémon. "Autour d'une lettre." *RTAM* 21 (1954): 137–144.

—. "L'enseignement au moyen âge. Techniques et méthodes en usage à la faculté de théologie de Paris, au XIIIe siècle." *Archives d'histoire doctrinale et littéraire du moyen âge* 35 (1968): 65–186.

—. "Mauvaise action et mauvais travail: Le *Contra Quatuor Labyrinthos Franciae.*" *RTAM* 21 (1954): 179–193.

Glunz, Hans H. *History of the Vulgate in England from Alcuin to Roger Bacon.* Cambridge: Cambridge University Press, 1933.

Goodwin, Deborah L. "Herbert of Bosham and the Horizons of Twelfth-Century Exegesis." *Traditio* 58 (2003): 133–173.

—. "A Study of Herbert of Bosham's Psalms Commentary (c.1190)." PhD diss., University of Notre Dame, 2001.

—. *"Take Hold of the Robe of a Jew": Herbert of Bosham's Christian Hebraism.* Leiden: E.J. Brill, 2006.

Grabmann, Martin. "Le breviloquium sententiarum artis theologiae du chanoine Odalric de Verdun." *RTAM* 8 (1936): 296–299.

—. *Die Geschichte der scholastischen Methode.* 2 vols. Freiburg im Breisgau: Herdersche Verlagshandlung, 1909–1911.

Graboïs, Ayreh. "Le schisme de 1130 et la France." *Revue d'histoire ecclésiastique* 76 (1981): 593–612.

Grant, Lindy. *Abbot Suger of St. Denis: Church and State in Early Twelfth Century France.* London: Longman, 1998.

—. "Geoffrey of Lèves, Bishop of Chartres: Famous Wheeler and Dealer in Secular Business." In *Suger en question,* ed. Rolf Grosse, 45–56. Munich: Oldenbourg, 2004.

Grauwen, Wilfried Marcel. *Norbertus: Aartsbisschop van Maagdenburg (1126–1134).* Brussels: Paleis der Academiën, 1978.

Gross-Diaz, Theresa. *The Psalms Commentary of Gilbert of Poitiers: From 'Lectio Divina' to the Lecture Room.* Leiden: E.J. Brill, 1996.

Grosse, Rolf. "Entre cour et cloître: Saint-Victor et les Capétiens au XIIe siècle." In

L'école de Saint-Victor de Paris: Influence et rayonnement du Moyen Âge à l'époque moderne, ed. Dominique Poirel, 79–100. Turnhout: Brepols, 2010.

Häring, Nikolaus M. "The Case of Gilbert de la Porrée, Bishop of Poitiers (1142–1154)." *Mediaeval Studies* 13 (1951): 1–40.

—. "Chartres and Paris Revisited." In *Essays in Honour of Anton Charles Pegis*, ed. J. Reginald O'Donnell, 268–329. Toronto: Pontifical Institute of Mediaeval Studies, 1974.

—. "The Cistercian Everard of Ypres and His Appraisal of the Conflict between St. Bernard and Gilbert of Poitiers." *Mediaeval Studies* 17 (1955): 143–172.

—. "The *Eulogium ad Alexandrum Papam Tertium* of John of Cornwall." *Mediaeval Studies* 13 (1951): 253–300.

—. *Gerhoh of Reichersberg: Letter to Pope Hadrian about the Novelties of the Day.* Toronto: Pontifical Institute of Mediaeval Studies, 1974.

—. "A Latin Dialogue on the Doctrine of Gilbert of Poitiers." *Mediaeval Studies* 15 (1953): 243–289.

—. "Notes on the Council and Consistory of Rheims." *Mediaeval Studies* 28 (1966): 39–59.

—. "Das Pariser Konsistorium Eugens III vom April 1147." *Studiana Gratiana* 11 (1967): 91–117.

—. "Saint Bernard and the Litterati of His Day." *Cîteaux* 25 (1974): 199–222.

Harkins, Franklin T. "Filiae Magistri: Peter Lombard's *Sentences* and Medieval Theological Education 'On the Ground.'" In *Mediaeval Commentaries on the Sentences of Peter Lombard*, ed. Philipp W. Rosemann, 3: 26–78. 3 vols. Leiden: E.J. Brill, 2002–2015.

—. *Reading and the Work of Restoration: History and Scripture in the Theology of Hugh of St Victor.* Toronto: Pontifical Institute of Mediaeval Studies, 2009.

Haseldine, Julian P. "Friendship and Rivalry: The Role of *Amicitia* in Twelfth-Century Monastic Relations." *Journal of Ecclesiastical History* 44 (1993): 390–414.

—. "Thomas Becket: Martyr, Saint—and Friend?" In *Belief and Culture in the Middle Ages: Studies Presented to Henry Mayr-Harting*, ed. Richard Gameson and Henrietta Leyser, 305–317. Oxford: Oxford University Press, 2001.

—, ed. *Friendship in Medieval Europe.* Stroud: Sutton, 1999.

Haskins, Charles Homer. *The Renaissance of the Twelfth Century.* Cambridge, MA: Harvard University Press, 1927.

—. *The Rise of Universities.* New York: H. Holt, 1923.

—. *Studies in the History of Mediaeval Science.* Cambridge, MA: Harvard University Press, 1924.

Hauréau, Barthélemy. *Histoire de la philosophie scolastique.* 2 vols. Paris: Durand et Pedone-Lauriel 1872–1880.

—. "Notice sur les sermons attribués à Hildebert de Lavardin." *Notices et extraits des manuscrits de la Bibliothèque nationale* 32 (1888): 107–166.

—. *Notices et extraits de quelques manuscrits latins de la Bibliothèque nationale.* 6 vols. Paris: C. Klincksieck, 1890–1893.

Hiestand, Rudolf. "Zum Leben und zur Laufbaun Wilhelms von Tyrus." *Deutsche Archiv für Erforschung des Mittelalters* 34 (1978): 345–380.

Hödl, Ludwig. *Die Geschichte der scholastischen Literatur und der Theologie der Schlüsselgewalt.* Münster: Aschendorff, 1960.

—. "Die Sentenzen des Petrus Lombardus in der Diskussion seiner Schule." In *Mediaeval Commentaries on the Sentences of Peter Lombard: Current Research,* ed. Gillian R. Evans, 1: 25–41. 3 vols. Leiden: E.J. Brill, 2002–2015.

—. "Die theologische Auseinandersetzung zwischen Petrus Lombardus und Odo von Ourscamp nach dem Zeugnis der frühen Quästionen und Glossenliteratur." *Scholastik* 33 (1958): 62–80.

Holweck, Frederick G. "The Nativity of the Blessed Virgin Mary, Feast of." In *The Catholic Encyclopedia: An International Work of Reference on the Constitution, Doctrine, Discipline, and History of the Catholic Church,* ed. Charles G. Herbermann, 10: 712–713. 15 vols. New York: Robert Appleton, 1907–1914.

Hunt, Richard W. "English Learning in the Late Twelfth Century." *Transactions of the Royal Historical Society* 19 (1936): 19–42.

Huygens, Robert B.C. "Guillaume de Tyr étudiant: Un chapitre de son 'Histoire' retrouvé." *Latomus* 21 (1962): 811–829.

Jaeger, C. Stephen. *The Envy of Angels: Cathedral Schools and Social Ideas in Medieval Europe, 950–1200.* Philadelphia: University of Pennsylvania Press, 1994.

—. "Humanism and Ethics at the School of St. Victor in the Early Twelfth Century." *Mediaeval Studies* 55 (1993): 51–79

James, Montague Rhodes. *The Western Manuscripts in the Library of Trinity College Cambridge: A Descriptive Catalogue.* 4 vols. Cambridge: Cambridge University Press, 1900–1904.

Kaufmann, C. Michael. "Manuscripts." In *English Romanesque Art, 1066–1200,* ed. George Zarnecki, Janet Holt, and Tristram Holland. London: Weidenfeld and Nicolson, 1984.

Keen, Maurice. *A History of Medieval Europe.* London: Routledge & Keegan Paul, 1967.

Klibansky, Raymond. "Adam, c.1130–1181." In *Oxford Dictionary of National Biography,* ed. Henry C.G. Matthew and Brian Harrison, 1: 191–192. 60 vols. Oxford: Oxford University Press, 2004.

—. "Balsham, Adam of." In *Oxford Dictionary of National Biography,* ed. Henry C.G. Matthew and Brian Harrison, 3: 615–616. 60 vols. Oxford: Oxford University Press, 2004.

Krey, August Charles. "William of Tyre: The Making of an Historian in the Middle Ages." *Speculum* 16 (1941): 149–166.

Landgraf, Artur Michael. "Drei Zweige der Pseudo-Poitiers Glose zu den Sentenzen des Lombarden." *RTAM* 9 (1937): 167–204.

—. *Einführung in die Geschichte der theologischen Literatur der Früscholastik*. Regensburg: Gregorius-Verlag, 1948.

—. "The First Sentence Commentary of Early Scholasticism." *New Scholasticism* 13 (1939): 101–132.

—. "Notes de critique textuelle sur les Sentences de Pierre Lombard." *RTAM* 2 (1930): 80–99.

—. "Problèmes relatifs aux premières gloses des Sentences." *RTAM* 3 (1931): 140–157.

—. "Recherches sur les écrits de Pierre le Mangeur." *RTAM* 3 (1931): 292–306, 341–372.

—. "Some Unknown Writings of the Early Scholastic Period." *New Scholasticism* 4 (1930): 1–22.

—. "Udo und Magister Martinus." *RTAM* 11 (1939): 62–64.

Lebreton, Marie-Madeleine. "Recherches sur les manuscrits contenant des sermons de Pierre le Mangeur." *Bulletin d'information de l'Institut de Recherche et d'Histoire des Textes* 2 (1953): 25–44; 4 (1955): 35–36.

Leclercq, Jean. "Les deux rédactions du prologue de Pierre Lombard sur les épîtres de S. Paul." In *Miscellanea Lombardiana*, 109–112. Novara: Istituto geografico de Agostini, 1957.

—. "Lettres d'Odon d'Ourscamp." *Analecta Monastica* 3 (1955): 145–157.

—. "Lettres de S. Bernard: Histoire ou littérature." *Studi Medievali* 12 (1971): 1–71.

—. "The Mystery of the Ascension in the Sermons of Saint Bernard." *Cistercian Studies* 25 (1990): 9–16.

—. "The Renewal of Theology." In *Renaissance and Renewal in the Twelfth Century*, ed. Robert L. Benson and Giles Constable, 68–87. Cambridge, MA: Harvard University Press, 1982.

Lecoy de la Marche, Albert. *La chaire française au moyen âge: Spécialement au XIIIe siècle, d'apres les manuscrits contemporains*. 2nd ed. Paris: Renouard, 1886.

Lemarignier, Jean F. "Les institutions ecclésiastiques en France de la fin du Xe au milieu du XIIe siècle." In *Histoire des institutions françaises au moyen âge III: Institutions ecclésiastiques*, ed. Robert Fawtier and Ferdinand Lot, 1–139. Paris: Presses universitaires de France, 1962.

Leyser, Karl. "Frederick Barbarossa, Henry II and the Hand of St James." *The English Historical Review* 90 (1975): 481–506.

Lexicon Latinitatis Nederlandicae Medii Aevi. Ed. Johanne W. Fuchs, Olga Weijers, and Marijke Gumbert-Hepp. 8 vols. Leiden: E.J. Brill, 1977–2005.

Lloyd, John Edward. "Adam, Bishop of St Asaph." In *Dictionary of Welsh Biography down to 1940*, ed. John E. Lloyd and Robert T. Jenkins, 1–2. London: Honourable Society of Cymmrodorion, 1959.

—. *A History of Wales from the Earliest Times to the Edwardian Conquest*. London: Longman, 1911.

Lobrichon, Guy. "Chronologie des oeuvres de Saint Bernard de Clairvaux." In *Bernard de Clairvaux: Histoire, mentalités, spiritualité*, 32–41. Paris: Editions du Cerf, 1992.

Loewe, Raphael. "Herbert of Bosham's Commentary on Jerome's Hebrew Psalter." *Biblica* 34 (1953): 44–77, 159–192, 275–298.

Longère, Jean. "La fonction pastorale de Saint-Victor à la fin du XIIe et au début du XIIIe siècle." In *L'Abbaye parisienne de Saint-Victor au moyen âge*, ed. Jean Longère, 291–313. Paris: Brepols, 1991.

—. *Oeuvres oratoires de maîtres parisiens au XIIe siècle: Étude historique et doctrinale*. 2 vols. Paris: Études augustiniennes, 1975.

—. *La prédication médiévale*. Paris: Études augustiniennes, 1983.

—. *Les sermons latins de Maurice de Sully, évêque de Paris (1196): Contribution à l'histoire de la tradition manuscrite*. Dordrecht: Kluwer Academic Publishers, 1988.

Longnon, Auguste. "L'ancien diocèse de Paris et ses subdivsions." *Bulletin du comité d'histoire et d'archéologie du diocèse de Paris* 1 (1883): 10–19.

Lottin, Odon. "Le premier commentaire connu des *Sentences* de Pierre Lombard." *Recherches de théologie ancienne et médievale* 11 (1939): 64–71.

—. "Le prologue des Gloses sur les Sentences attribuées à Pierre de Poitiers." *RTAM* 7 (1935): 70–73.

—. "A propos des sources de la *Summa Sententiarum*." *RTAM* 25 (1958): 42–58.

—. *Psychologie et morale aux XIIe et XIIIe siècles*. Volume 1: *Problèmes d'histoire littéraire de 1160 à 1300*. Louvain: Abbaye du Mont César, 1942.

Lucchesini, Cesare. "Storia Letteraria del Ducato Lucchese." *Memorie e Documenti per servire all'istoria del Ducato di Lucca* 9 (1825): 18–80.

Luchaire, Achille. *Études sur les actes de Louis VII*. Paris: A. Picard, 1885.

—. *Histoire des institutions monarchiques de la France sous les premiers Capétiens (987–1180)*. 2 vols. Paris: A. Picard, 1883.

—. *Remarques sur la succession des grands officiers de la couronne qui ont souscrit les diplomes de Louis VI et de Louis VII (1108–1180)*. Paris: A. Picard, 1881.

Luscombe, David E. "Cornwall, John of." In *Oxford Dictionary of National Biography*, ed. Henry C.G. Matthew and Brian Harrison, 13: 468–469. 60 vols. Oxford: Oxford University Press, 2004.

—. "Peter Comestor." In *The Bible in the Medieval World: Essays in Memory of Beryl Smalley*, ed. Katherine Walsh and Diana Wood, 109–129. Oxford: Blackwell, 1985.

—. "The Place of Peter Comestor in the History of Medieval Theology." In *Pierre le Mangeur ou Pierre de Troyes: Maître du XIIe siècle*, ed. Gilbert Dahan, 27–48.

—. *The School of Peter Abelard: The Influence of Abelard's Thought in the Early Scholastic Period*. Cambridge: Cambridge University Press, 1969.

—. "Thought and Learning." In *New Cambridge Medieval History*, ed. David Luscombe and Jonathan Riley-Smith, 4.1: 461–498. 8 vols in 7. Cambridge: Cambridge University Press, 1995–2005.

—. "Tournai, Simon of." In *Oxford Dictionary of National Biography*, ed. Henry C.G. Matthew and Brian Harrison, 55: 84–85. 60 vols. Oxford: Oxford University Press, 2004.

Mansi, Giovanni Domenico. *Sacrorum Conciliorum Nova et Amplissima Collectio*. 31 vols. Florence and Venice: Expensis Antonii Zatta, 1759–1798.

Marenbon, John. *The Philosophy of Peter Abelard*. Cambridge: Cambridge University Press, 1997.

Martin, Raymond M. "Notes sur l'oeuvre littéraire de Pierre le Mangeur." *RTAM* 3 (1931): 54–66.

Mason, John F.A. "de Diceto, Ralph." In *Oxford Dictionary of National Biography*, ed. Henry C.G. Matthew and Brian Harrison, 16: 40–42. 60 vols. Oxford: Oxford University Press, 2004.

Massara, Antonio. "La Leggenda di Pier Lombardo." In *Miscellanea Storica Novarese*, ed. Raffaele Terella, 118–120. Novara: G. Parzini, 1906.

Mathorez, Jules. *Guillaume aux Blanches Mains, évêque de Chartres*. Chartres: Archives historiques du diocèse de Chartres, 1911.

Mayer, Hans Eberhard. "Zum Tode Wilhelms von Tyrus." *Archiv für Diplomatik* 5/6 (1959–1960): 182–201.

McDonough, Christopher J. "Hugh Primas and the Bishop of Beauvais." *Mediaeval Studies* 45 (1983): 399–409.

Mews, Constant J. "Between the Schools of Abelard and Saint-Victor in the Mid-Twelfth Century: The Witness of Robert of Melun." In *L'école de Saint-Victor de Paris: Influence et rayonnement du Moyen Âge à l'epoque moderne*, ed. Dominique Poirel, 121–138. Turnhout: Brepols, 2010.

—. "The Council of Sens (1141): Abelard, Bernard, and the Fear of Social Upheaval." *Speculum* 77 (2002): 342–382.

Meyer von Knonau, Gerold. *Jahrbücher des deutschen Reiches unter Heinrich IV und Heinrich V*. 7 vols. Leipzig: Duncker & Humblot, 1890–1909. Repr. Berlin: Duncker & Humblot, 1964–1965.

Minio-Paluello, Lorenzo. "The *Ars Disserendi* of Adam of Balsham, *Parvipotanus*." *Mediaeval and Renaissance Studies* 3 (1954): 116–169.

Monagle, Clare. "Christological Nihilism in the Twelfth Century: The Contested Reception of Peter Lombard's *Sententiae*." PhD diss., Johns Hopkins University, 2007.

—. *Orthodoxy and Controversy in Twelfth-Century Religious Discourse: Peter Lombard's* Sentences *and the Development of Theology*. Turnhout: Brepols, 2013.

Montaubin, Pascal. "Les chanoines de Notre-Dame de Paris à la mort de l'évêque Guillaume d'Auvergne (1249)." In *Notre-Dame de Paris 1163–2013*, ed. Cédric Giraud, 195–216. Turnhout: Brepols, 2013.

Moore, Philip S. *The Works of Peter of Poitiers: Master in Theology and Chancellor of Paris (1193–1205)*. Notre Dame, IN: University of Notre Dame Press, 1936.

Morenzoni, Franco. "L'*Ars praedicandi* de Pierre le Mangeur." In *Pierre le Mangeur ou Pierre de Troyes: Maître du XIIe siècle*, ed. Gilbert Dahan, 225–240. Turnhout: Brepols, 2013.

Morey, Adrian. *Bartholomew of Exeter: Bishop and Canonist*. Cambridge: Cambridge University Press, 1937.

Morey, James H. "Peter Comestor, Biblical Paraphrase, and the Medieval Popular Bible." *Speculum* 68 (1993): 6–35.

Morris, Colin. *The Discovery of the Individual: 1050–1200*. New York: Harper & Row, 1972. Repr. Toronto: University of Toronto Press, 1987.

Mortet, Victor. "Maurice de Sully, évêque de Paris (1160–1196): Étude sur l'administration épiscopale pendant la seconde moitié du XIIe siècle." *Mémoires de la Société de l'histoire de Paris et de l'Île-de-France* 16 (1890): 105–317.

Muessig, Carolyn. "Sermon, Preacher and Society in the Middle Ages." *Journal of Medieval History* 28 (2002): 73–91.

Mühlbacher, Emil. *Die streitige Papstwahl des jahres 1130*. Innsbruck: Wagner, 1876.

Nielsen, Lauge-Olaf. *Theology and Philosophy in the Twelfth Century: A Study of Gilbert Porreta's Thinking and the Theological Expositions of the Doctrine of the Incarnation during the Period 1130–1180*. Leiden: E.J. Brill, 1982.

Niermeyer, Jan Frederik, and C. van de Kieft. *Mediae Latinitatis lexicon minus*. Revised edition. Ed. Johannes W.J. Burgers. 2 vols. Leiden: E.J. Brill, 2002.

Ohler, Norbert. *The Medieval Traveller*. Trans. Caroline Hiller. Woodbridge: Boydell, 1989.

Orme, M.A. "A Reconstruction of Robert of Cricklade's *Vita et Miracula S. Thomae Cantuariensis*." *Analecta Bollandiana* 84 (1966): 379–398.

Osheim, Duane J. "The Episcopal Archive of Lucca in the Middle Ages." *Manuscripta* 17 (1973): 131–146.

—. *An Italian Lordship: The Bishopric of Lucca in the Late Middle Ages*. Berkeley: University of California Press, 1977.

Ott, Ludwig. "Pietro Lombardo: Personalita e opera." In *Miscellanea Lombardiana,* 11–23. Novara: Istituto geografico de Agostini, 1957.

Oury, Guy-Marie. "Les sermons de Geoffroi Babion et la chrétienté Bordelaise." *Cahiers de civilisation médiévale* 22 (1979): 285–297.

Oxford English Dictionary. 2nd ed. Ed. John A. Simpson and Edmund S.C. Weiner. 20 vols. Oxford: Clarendon Press, 1989.

Oxford Latin Dictionary. Ed. P.G.W. Glare. 2 vols. Oxford: Clarendon Press, 1968–1982.

Pacaut, Marcel. *Alexandre III: Étude sur la conception du pouvoir pontifical dans sa pensée et son oeuvre.* Paris, J. Vrin: 1956.

—. "Les légats d'Alexandre III, 1159–1181." *Revue d'histoire ecclésiastique* 50 (1955): 821–838.

—. "Louis VII et Alexandre III, 1159–1180." *Revue d'histoire de l'église de France* 39 (1953): 5–45.

—. *Louis VII et les élections épiscopales dans le royaume de France.* Paris: J. Vrin, 1957.

—. *Louis VII et son royaume.* Paris, S.E.V.P.E.N. 1964.

Pächt, Otto, and Jonathan J.G. Alexander. *Illuminated Manuscripts in the Bodleian Library Oxford 3: British, Irish and Icelandic Schools.* Oxford: Clarendon Press, 1973.

Palumbo, Pier Fausto. "Nuovi Studi (1942–1962) sullo scismo di Anacleto II." *Bolletino dell'Istituto storico italiano per il medio evo e Archivio Muratoriano* 75 (1963): 71–103.

—. *Lo scisma del MCXXX.* Rome: Presso la R. Deputazione alla Biblioteca Vallicelliana, 1942.

Panayotova, Stella. "Tutorial in Images for Thomas Becket." In *The Cambridge Illuminations: The Conference Papers,* ed. Stella Panayotova, 77–86. London: Harvey Miller, 2007.

[Paris, Bibliothèque nationale de France.] *Bibliothèque nationale: Catalogue général des manuscrits latins.* Ed. Philippe Lauer. 7 vols. Paris: Bibliothèque nationale, 1939–1988.

Pearson, Matthew J. "The Creation and Development of the St Asaph Cathedral Chapter, 1141–1293." *Cambrian Medieval Celtic Studies* 40 (2000): 35–56.

—. *Fasti Ecclesiae Anglicanae, 1066–1300.* Volume 9: *The Welsh Cathedrals.* London: Institute of Historical Research, 2003.

Peltzer, Jörg. *Canon Law, Careers and Conquest: Episcopal Elections in Normandy and Greater Anjou, c.1140–c.1230.* Cambridge: Cambridge University Press, 2008.

Peyrafort-Huin, Monique. *La bibliothèque médiéval de l'abbaye de Pontigny, XIIe–XIXe siècles: Histoire, inventaires anciens, manuscrits.* Paris: CNRS, 2001.

Phillips, Jonathan. *The Second Crusade: Extending the Frontiers of Christendom.* New Haven: Yale University Press, 2007.

Plongeron, Bernard, Jean Longère, Françoise Autrand, Luce Pietri, and Madeleine Foisil. *Le diocese de Paris.* Volume 1: *Des origines à la révolution.* Histoire des diocèses de France 20. Paris: Beauchesne, 1987.

Poirel, Dominique. *Hugues de Saint-Victor.* Paris: Éditions du Cerf, 1998.

Poole, Reginald Lane. *Illustrations of the History of Medieval Thought and Learning.* London: Williams and Norgate, 1884.

Post, Gaines. "Alexander III, the *Licentia docendi* and the Rise of the Universities." In *Anniversary Essays in Mediaeval History by Students of Charles Homer Haskins,* ed. Charles H. Taylor and John L. LaMonte, 255–277. Boston: Houghton Mifflin, 1929.

Protois, Félix. *Pierre Lombard: Évêque de Paris dit le maître des Sentences: Son époque, sa vie, ses écrits, son influence.* Paris: Sociéte générale de librairié Catholique, 1881.

Prutz, Hans. "Studien über Wilhelm von Tyrus." *Neues Archiv der Gesselschaft für ältere Deutsche Geschichtskunde* 8 (1883): 93–132.

Rampolla, Mary Lynn. "Melun, Robert de." In *Oxford Dictionary of National Biography,* ed. Henry C.G. Matthew and Brian Harrison, 37: 763–764. 60 vols. Oxford: Oxford University Press, 2004.

Rashdall, Hastings. *The Universities of Europe in the Middle Ages.* Ed. Frederick M. Powicke and Alfred B. Emden. Oxford: Clarendon Press, 1936.

Rathbone, Eleanor. "John of Cornwall: A Brief Biography." *RTAM* 17 (1950): 46–60.

Rees, William. *An Historical Atlas of Wales: From Early to Modern Times.* 3rd ed. London: Faber & Faber, 1972.

Reuter, Timothy A. "Zur Anerkennung Papst Innocenz II: Eine neue Quelle." *Deutsches Archiv für Erforschung des Mittelalters* 39 (1983): 395–416.

Reynolds, Roger. "The Subdiaconate as a Sacred and Superior Order." In *Clerics in the Early Middle Ages: Hierarchy and Image,* ed. Roger Reynolds, chapter IV. Aldershot: Ashgate, 1999.

Richter, Michael. *Giraldus Cambrensis: The Growth of the Welsh Nation.* 2nd ed. Aberystwyth: National Library of Wales, 1976.

Riley-Smith, Jonathan. *The Crusades: A Short History.* London: The Athlone Press, 1987.

Robins, Robert H. *The Byzantine Grammarians: Their Place in History.* Berlin: Mouton de Gruyter, 1993.

Robinson, Ian Stuart. *The Papacy, 1073–1198: Continuity and Innovation.* Cambridge: Cambridge University Press, 1990.

Robinson, Pamela R. *Catalogue of Dated and Datable Manuscripts c.737–1600 in Cambridge Libraries.* Cambridge: D.S. Brewer, 1988.

Robson, Charles A. *Maurice of Sully and the Medieval Vernacular Homily.* Oxford: Blackwell, 1952.

Roghi, Vanessa. "Gremigni, Gilla Vincenzo." In *Dizionario Biografico Degli Italiani*, ed. Alberto Maria Ghisalberti, 59: 310–312. 82 vols. Rome: Istituto della Enciclopedia italiana, 1960–2015.

Rorem, Paul. *Hugh of Saint Victor*. Oxford: Oxford University Press, 2009.

Rosemann, Philipp W. "Introduction: Three Avenues for studying the tradition of the *Sentences*." In *Mediaeval Commentaries on the Sentences of Peter Lombard*, ed. Philipp W. Rosemann, 3: 1–25. 3 vols. Leiden: E.J. Brill, 2002–2015.

—. *Peter Lombard*. Oxford: Oxford University Press, 2004.

—. The Story of a Great Medieval Book: Peter Lombard's Sentences. Peterborough, ON: Broadview Press, 2007.

Rossi, Pietro B. "*Contra Lombardum*: Reazioni alla Cristologia di Pietro Lombardo." In *Pietro Lombardo: Atti del XLIII Convegno storico internazionale*, 123–191. Spoleto: Fondazione Centro Italiano di studi sull'alto medioevo, 2007.

Rouse, Richard H., and Mary A. Rouse. *Preachers, Florilegia and Sermons: Studies on the Manipulus Florum of Thomas of Ireland*. Toronto: Pontifical Institute of Mediaeval Studies, 1979.

Saccenti, Ricardo. "The *Materia Super Liber Sententiarum* Attributed to Peter Comestor: Study of the Text and Critical Edition." *Bulletin de Philosophie Médiévale* 54 (2012): 155–215.

Sainte-Marthe, Scévole de, and Louis de Sainte-Marthe. *Gallia Christiana in provincias ecclesiasticas distributa*. 1715–1865. Ed. Paul Piolin. 16 vols. Paris, Apud V. Palmé, 1865–1870.

Sassier, Yves. *Louis VII*. Paris: Fayard, 1991.

Savigni, Raffaele. *Episcopato e società cittadina a Lucca da Anselmo II a Roberto*. Lucca: Edizioni S. Marco, 1996.

Sayers, Jane. *Papal Judges Delegate in the Province of Canterbury, 1198–1254: A Study in Ecclesiastical Jurisdiction and Administration*. Oxford: Oxford University Press, 1971.

Scheibelreiter, Georg. "Church Structure and Organization." In *New Cambridge Medieval History*, ed. Paul Fouracre, 1: 675–709. 8 vols in 7. Cambridge: Cambridge University Press, 1995–2005.

Schmale, Franz-Josef. *Studien zum Schisma des Jahres 1130*. Köln: Böhlau, 1961.

Schneyer, Johannes B. *Repertorium der lateinischen Sermones des Mittelalters: Für die Zeit von 1150–1350*. 11 vols. Münster: Aschendorff, 1969–1990.

Schwinges, Rainer Christoph. *Kreuzzugsideologie und Toleranz: Studien zu Wilhelm von Tyrus*. Stuttgart: Hiersemann, 1977.

Sicard, Patrice. *Diagrammes médiévaux et exégèse visuelle: Le Libellus de formatione arche de Hugues de Saint-Victor*. Turnhout: Brepols, 1993.

—. *Hugues de Saint-Victor et son école*. Turnhout: Brepols, 1991.

Smalley, Beryl. *The Becket Conflict and the Schools: A Study of Intellectuals in Politics.* Oxford: Blackwell, 1973.

—. "A Commentary on the *Hebraica* by Herbert of Bosham." *RTAM* 18 (1951): 29–65.

—. "Master Ivo of Chartres." *English Historical Review* 50 (1935): 680–686.

—. "Peter Comestor on the Gospels and His Sources." *RTAM* 46 (1979): 84–129.

—. "Some Gospel Commentaries of the Early Twelfth Century." *RTAM* 45 (1978): 147–180.

—. *The Study of the Bible in the Middle Ages.* 3rd ed. Oxford: Blackwell, 1983.

Smalley, Beryl and Georges Lacombe. "The Lombard's Commentary on Isaias and Other Fragments" *New Scholasticism* 5 (1931): 123–162.

Smith, David M. *Guide to Bishop's Registers of England and Wales: A Survey from the Middle Ages to the Abolition of Episcopacy in 1646.* London: Offices of the Royal Historical Society, 1981.

Smith, Lesley. *Masters of the Sacred Page: Manuscripts of Theology in the Latin West to 1274.* Notre Dame, IN: University of Notre Dame Press, 2001.

Somerville, Robert. *Pope Alexander III and the Council of Tours (1163): A Study of Ecclesiastical Politics and Institutions in the Twelfth Century.* Berkeley: University of California Press, 1977.

Southern, Richard William. "Aspects of the European Tradition of Historical Writing 2: Hugh of St Victor and the Idea of Historical Development." *Transactions of the Royal Historical Society* 21 (1971): 159–179. Repr. in *History and Historians: Selected Papers of R.W. Southern,* ed. Robert J. Bartlett, 30–48. Oxford: Wiley, 2004.

—. *The Making of the Middle Ages.* London: Hutchinson, 1953.

—. *Medieval Humanism and Other Studies.* Oxford: Blackwell, 1970.

—. *Platonism, Scholastic Method and the School of Chartres.* Reading: The University of Reading, 1979.

—. *Scholastic Humanism and the Unification of Europe I: Foundations.* Oxford: Wiley, 1995.

—. *Scholastic Humanism and the Unification of Europe II: The Heroic Age.* Oxford: Wiley, 2001.

—. "The Schools of Paris and the School of Chartres." In *Renaissance and Renewal in the Twelfth Century,* ed. Robert L. Benson and Giles Constable, 113–137. Cambridge, MA: Harvard University Press, 1982.

Spatz, Nancy. "Approaches and Attitudes to a New Theology Textbook: The *Sentences* of Peter Lombard." In *The Intellectual Climate of the Early University: Essays in Honor of Otto Gründler,* ed. Nancy Van Deusen, 27–52. Studies in Medieval Culture 39. Kalamazoo, MI: Medieval Institute Publications, 1997.

Spear, David S. "Torigni, Robert de." In *Oxford Dictionary of National Biography,* ed. Henry C.G. Matthew and Brian Harrison, 55: 46–47. 60 vols. Oxford: Oxford University Press, 2004.

Staunton, Michael. *The Lives of Thomas Becket.* Manchester: Manchester University Press, 2001.

—. *Thomas Becket and His Biographers.* Woodbridge: Boydell, 2006.

Stegmüller, Friedrich. *Repertorium commentariorum in Sententias Petri Lombardi.* 2 vols. Würzburg: F. Schöning, 1947.

Stirnemann, Patricia. "Histoire tripartite: Un inventaire des livres de Pierre Lombard, un exemplaire de ses *Sentences* et le destinataire du Psautier de Copenhague." In *Du copiste au collectionneur: Mélanges d'histoire des textes et des bibliothèques en l'honneur d'André Vernet,* ed. Donatella Nebbiai-Dalla Guarda and Jean-François Genest, 301–318. Turnhout: Brepols, 1998.

Stock, Brian. *The Implications of Literacy: Written Language and Models of Interpretation in the Eleventh and Twelfth Centuries.* Princeton: Princeton University Press, 1983.

Stoppacci, Patrizia. "Le *Glossae Continuae in Psalmos* di Pietro Lombardo: *Status quaestionis,* studi pregressi e prospettive di ricerca." In *Pietro Lombardo: Atti del XLIII Convegno storico internazionale,* 289–331. Spoleto: Fondazione Centro Italiano di studi sull'alto medioevo, 2007.

Stroll, Mary. *The Jewish Pope: Ideology and Politics in the Papal Schism of 1130.* Leiden: E.J. Brill, 1987.

Stump, Eleanor. "Dialectic." In *The Seven Liberal Arts in the Middle Ages,* ed. David L. Wagner, 125–146. Bloomington: Indiana University Press, 1983.

Sylwan, Agneta. "Petrus Comestor: *Historia Scholastica,* une nouvelle édition." *Sacris Erudiri* 39 (2000): 345–382.

Tabacco, Giovanni. "Northern and Central Italy in the Eleventh Century." In *The New Cambridge Medieval History,* ed. David Luscombe and Jonathan Riley-Smith, 4.2: 72–93. 8 vols in 7. Cambridge: Cambridge University Press, 1995–2005.

Teeuwen, Mariken. *The Vocabulary of Intellectual Life in the Middle Ages.* Turnhout: Brepols, 2003.

Teske, Gunnar. *Die Briefsammlungen des 12. Jahrhunderts in St. Viktor, Paris: Entstehung, Überlieferung und Bedeutung für die Geschichte der Abtei.* Bonn: Bouvier, 1993.

Thompson, Augustine. "From Texts to Preaching: Retrieving the Medieval Sermon as an Event." In *Preacher, Sermon and Audience in the Middle Ages,* ed. Carolyn Muessig, 13–37. Leiden: E.J. Brill, 2002.

Thorndike, Lynn. "Elementary and Secondary Education in the Middle Ages." *Speculum* 15 (1940): 400–408.
Thurston, Herbert. "Deacons." In *The Catholic Encyclopedia: An International Work of Reference on the Constitution, Doctrine, Discipline, and History of the Catholic Church*, ed. Charles G. Herbermann, 4: 647–653. 15 vols. New York: Robert Appleton, 1907–1914.
Tibber, Peter Harris. "The Origins of the Scholastic Sermon, c.1130–c.1210." DPhil diss., Unversity of Oxford, 1983.
Turvey, Roger. *The Welsh Princes: The Native Rulers of Wales, 1063–1283*. London: Longman, 2002.
Tyerman, Christopher. *God's War: A New History of the Crusades*. London: Penguin, 2007.
Ughelli, Ferdinando. *Italia sacra*. Ed. Nicola Coleti. 10 vols. Venice: S. Coleti, 1715–1722. Repr. Bologna: A. Forni, 1973–1987.
Vacandard, Elphège. *Vie de Saint Bernard*. 3rd ed. 2 vols. Paris: V. Lecoffre, 1902.
Van den Eynde, Damien. "Essai chronologique sur l'oeuvre littéraire de Pierre Lombard." In *Miscellanea Lombardiana*, 45–63. Novara: Istituto geografico de Agostini, 1957.
—. *L'oeuvre littéraire de Géroch de Reichersberg*. Rome: Pontificium Athenaeum Antonianum, 1957.
Verger, Jacques. "Teachers." In *A History of the University in Europe*. Volume 1: *Universities in the Middle Ages*, ed. Hilde de Ridder-Symoens, 144–168. Cambridge: Cambridge University Press, 1992.
Vessey, David W.T.C. "William of Tyre and the Art of Historiography." *Mediaeval Studies* 35 (1973): 433–455.
Visscher, Eva De. *Reading the Rabbis: Christian Hebraism in the Works of Herbert of Bosham*. Leiden: E.J. Brill, 2014.
Von Hefele, Karl Joseph. *Histoire des conciles d'après les documents originaux*. Trans. Henri Leclercq. 20 vols. Paris: Letouzey et Ané, 1907–1952.
Walker, David. *Medieval Wales*. Cambridge: Cambridge University Press, 1990.
Warichez, Joseph. *Les Disputationes de Simon de Tournai*. Louvain: Spicilegium sacrum lovaniense, 1932.
Warren, Wilfred Lewis. *Henry II*. London: Methuen, 1973.
Watson, Andrew G. *Catalogue of Dated and Datable Manuscripts, c.435–1600 in Oxford Libraries*. 2 vols. Oxford: Clarendon Press, 1984.
Webb, Clement C.J. *John of Salisbury*. London: Methuen, 1932.
Weijers, Olga. *Terminologie des universités au XIIIe siècle*. Rome: Edizioni dell'Ateneo, 1987.
Weiss, Jessica Lynn. "Herbert of Bosham's *Liber melorum*: Literature and Sacred Sciences in the Twelfth Century." PhD diss., Harvard University, 2003.

Weisweiler, Heinrich. "Eine Neue frühe Glosse zum Vierten Buch der Sentenzen des Petrus Lombardus." In *Aus der Geisteswelt des Mittelalters: Studien und Texte,* ed. Albert Lang, 360–400. Münster: Aschendorff, 1935.

—. "La *Summa Sententiarum:* Source de Pierre Lombard." *RTAM* 6 (1934): 143–183.

Wickham, Chris. *Community and Clientele in Twelfth-Century Tuscany*. Oxford: Clarendon Press, 1988.

Williams, Glanmor. *The Welsh Church from Conquest to Reformation*. 2nd ed. Cardiff: University of Wales Press, 1976.

Williams, John R. "The Cathedral School of Reims in the Time of Master Alberic, 1118–1136." *Traditio* 20 (1964): 93–114.

—. "William of the White Hands and Men of Letters." In *Anniversary Essays in Mediaeval History by Students of Charles Homer Haskins,* ed. Charles H. Taylor and John L. LaMonte, 365–387. Boston: Houghton Mifflin, 1929.

Wilmart, André. *Codices Reginenses Latini*. 2 vols. Rome: Bibliotheca Vaticana, 1937–1945.

—. "Les 'loisirs' ou sentiments intimes d'un chancelier de France." *Revue Bénédictine* 51 (1939): 182–204.

Winling, Raymond. "Théologie." In *Dictionnaire de spiritualité ascétique et mystique: doctrine et histoire,* 15: 463–500. 17 vols. Paris: Beauchesne, 1932–1995.

Wright, Craig M. *Music and Ceremony at Notre Dame of Paris, 500–1500*. Cambridge: Cambridge University Press, 1989.

Zerbi, Piero. "I rapporti di S. Bernardo di Chiaravalle con i vescovi e le diocesi d'Italia." In *Vescovi e diocesi in Italia nel medioevo (Sec. IX–XIII),* 219–313. Padua: Ed. Antenore, 1961.

Zier, Mark. "Peter Lombard and the *Glossa Ordinaria*: A Missing Link?" In *Pietro Lombardo: Atti del XLIII Convegno storico internazionale,* 361–409. Spoleto: Fondazione Centro Italiano di studi sull'alto medioevo, 2007.

—. "Preaching by Distinction: Peter Comestor and the Communication of the Gospel." *Ephemerides Liturgicae* 105 (1991): 301–329.

—. "Sermons of the Twelfth Century Schoolmasters and Canons." In *The Sermon,* ed. Beverly M. Kienzle, 325–362. Turnhout: Brepols 2000.

Index